LEGAL LARCENY

LEGAL LARCENY

A Novel

Dr. Jill B. Vosler

iUniverse, Inc.
New York Lincoln Shanghai

Legal Larceny

Copyright © 2006 by Jill B. Vosler

iUniverse books may be ordered through booksellers or by contacting:

iUniverse
2021 Pine Lake Road, Suite 100
Lincoln, NE 68512
www.iuniverse.com
1-800-Authors (1-800-288-4677)

This is a work of fiction. All of the characters, names, incidents, organizations, and dialogue in this novel are either the products of the author's imagination or are used fictitiously.

Illustration on front cover by Jackie McCafferty

ISBN-13: 978-0-595-39304-6 (pbk)
ISBN-13: 978-0-595-67691-0 (cloth)
ISBN-13: 978-0-595-83697-0 (ebk)
ISBN-10: 0-595-39304-7 (pbk)
ISBN-10: 0-595-67691-X (cloth)
ISBN-10: 0-595-83697-6 (ebk)

Printed in the United States of America

This book is dedicated to doctors everywhere who are fighting the good fight.

I would like to thank the following individuals for their help in this effort:

My husband, John, for his encouragement and support;

My son Joey for his enthusiasm;

My daughter Jackie for her cover design;

My mom and dad for their editorial assistance;

My brothers, Mark, Kent, and Scott, for their unwavering support and I inspiration;

Katrina, for being my sounding board;

Suzanne, for her helpful critique;

"Grandma Annie," for her wonderful room in which to write;

Bobbie and his staff, for their invaluable I.T. assistance;

Finally, to my dear friend, and to doctors everywhere, whose medical malpractice travails have inspired this effort.

To all of you who read this book-I hope only that you gain appreciation and understanding of how things are, and how they should be.

"A lawyer with a briefcase can steal more than a thousand men with guns."

—Mario Puzo, author of "The Godfather"

CHAPTER I

Irene Morrison was at one time a beautiful and charming lady. She was the kind of woman that people would admire from a distance, much like a well-kept automobile from a different era, or a piece of antique furniture more beautiful than any current item available. She'd grown up in a time when people held their heads high, no matter what difficulty they encountered. Her life's story was one of dignity and decency. She dressed and acted in a way that inspired respect and admiration.

That is what made her Alzheimer's disease so difficult to accept. It was amazing how quickly she became no longer elegant and inspiring, but dependent and depressed. This was terribly difficult for those who knew and loved her. Particularly her family. They watched as this remarkable woman that they loved became transformed before their very eyes into an angry and unpredictable individual. Rapidly she progressed into combativeness and, with very little fanfare, she was placed in the Noble Manor Nursing Home to live out her days under the care of people who'd never known her beauty and grace. Irene Morrison had essentially disappeared.

Hank Clarkson hadn't intended to become a physician. His real interest was in art, but he'd successfully been convinced by his father that art was not going to be able to provide him a living. Not a wealthy one anyway. And Hank's father was convinced that wealth was the cornerstone of happiness.

His father, Gerald Clarkson, was a man whose fate was forged in the era of the Great Depression. He watched as his family slowly lost the majority of their wealth while the world looked on, everyone caught in the same spiraling maelstrom of financial ruin. Gerald swore he would never allow that to happen to him, and—at the tender age of seventeen—he set out to make—and keep—his fortune.

This he did, as a very successful banker in Cleveland, Ohio, rising to the level of president in only a few short years. He managed his finances well, and tried to raise his two sons to think and act in the same manner.

Gerald Clarkson placed a very clear emphasis on the acquisition and importance of wealth, and—although Hank and his brother resented what they saw as a mercenary preoccupation, they nonetheless knew that their future and fortunes depended on their father's approval.

In spite of this, Hank had chosen art history—a less-than money-making pursuit—as his major in college and actually went through a year and a half thinking he would prove his father wrong and find a way to succeed in his area of interest.

Halfway through his sophomore year, however, he began to appreciate how limited his options really were. Other than teaching there weren't a lot of career choices for Hank to pursue with an Art History degree. His best friend in college was pursuing a premed degree, so Hank decided to look into medicine. He liked what he saw. More importantly, so did his father. A physician in the family was something Hank's dad could be proud of. And he let Hank know that he was proud of his decision. He began to support him in a way he had not done before.

Suddenly, Gerald Clarkson was calling Hank to ask how his studies were doing. Did he need any money? Maybe when he came home the two of them could go fishing on Lake Erie.

Hank enjoyed the attention, and began to re-establish a relationship with his dad that had—up until that point—been somewhat strained.

Hank poured himself into his pre-med courses, and managed to graduate with a 3.9 grade point average. This was good enough to get him into Ohio State's medical school, and from the minute Hank stepped into his first class, he knew he had found his calling.

It all came fairly easily to him, and he managed to graduate from medical school near the top of his class. He then applied for a family practice residency in a Columbus Hospital, and—three years later—was prepared to "open shop" and pursue his career back in Strongsville, Ohio.

Hank loved family medicine. It gave him so many options and opportunities. From babies all the way up to the elderly, Dr. Henry "Hank" Clarkson was able to help them all.

His nursing home practice was a natural progression of this and Hank pursued it with the same eagerness and enthusiasm that he placed into other aspects of his practice life. Taking care of the elderly was initially difficult for Hank. The sights and smells of a nursing home can be emotionally draining, and the problems these individuals faced were often complex and overwhelming.

Hank started with only two patients, but gradually, as his practice size enlarged so did his patient population in the Nursing Home. Soon he was visiting the facility weekly for several hours at a time. He eventually began to enjoy his time there—it was different from his office; the pace was slower and the people were usually more relaxed. Hank would walk in very early on Wednesday mornings, greet the nurses, grab a cup of coffee from the nursing station, and allow the charge nurse to fill him in on the important concerns of his varied case load. Although their many medical needs were discussed, the humorous anecdotes of the residents were discussed as well and Hank was delighted to hear it all. This was where they lived, and Hank imagined that his visits to the nursing facility were probably something like a house call; or at least as close as he was ever going to get to that bygone era of medicine, when time wasn't so limited and the connection between a doctor and his patient could become something more akin to a friendship.

Hank began taking care of Irene Morrison when she entered Noble Manor. He hadn't known her before; he'd not known her elegance or kindness. But he imagined that she had been quite a lady. She still possessed a smile that made other people smile, and Hank was taken by that smile from the minute he met Irene. She still carried herself with a straight and proud countenance, as though she'd at one time been quite a fine lady.

Her head was held high and her gaze was steady and sure. She acknowledged everyone around her, and was careful to not interrupt an ongoing conversation. She was comfortable, yet regal, all at the same time.

Her family physician didn't see nursing home patients. Like many physicians, he'd decided that all the phone calls and all the family concerns weren't worth the money that Medicare begrudgingly paid, or the many hours that were required. So Hank became Irene's physician, and Irene couldn't have cared less.

He cared for her for many months before the Alzheimer's Disease began to take hold and cause rapidly progressive decline in function. Irene's mood declined as well and soon her smile was nowhere to be found. She no longer looked anyone in the eye, and her remarkable thoughtfulness had all but disappeared.

She started to fall often and the nursing home tried it's best to keep the falls from recurring. The family became concerned about the repeat falls, and wondered why the nursing home wouldn't do something about it.

One fall occurred in the early morning hours, and Irene's daughter—who was the one most responsible for any concerns regarding Irene—was contacted immediately. It took her many rings to answer her phone, and when she finally did it was clear that she was irritated by the interruption to her sleep. She more or less snapped into the phone line. "Who is it?"

"I'm so sorry to bother you ma'am, but Irene has fallen and we are obligated to let you know this."

"Again?" Irene's daughter was clearly quite perturbed.

The nursing home nurse reluctantly continued. "I'm sorry, ma'am. We're doing all we can. She just keeps stumbling."

There was a pause on the other end of the line as Irene's daughter was digesting this response. She then spit back into the phone. "Can't you strap her down?"

Although the nurse had prepared herself for this question, the brutal nature of the request shocked her nonetheless. She had to hold back her emerging anger. She replied to Irene's daughter's comment with a slow and steady voice. "Ma'am, as we've told you before, it is illegal for us to do that. We are not allowed to use restraints of any kind."

This aspect of nursing home care was very difficult for the family to understand. Basically, restraints weren't allowed for any reason, even to protect a patient from falling and hurting themselves. Side rails on the beds were considered hazards as well, so if your loved one had a problem with falling out of bed the nursing homes were forced to place the resident's mattress low to the ground with another mattress on the floor in anticipation of the fall.

Physicians also felt frustration with these limitations as they saw their patients recurrently injuring themselves one way or another. Hank had repeatedly inquired about these laws and was always told the same thing: "The State has said we can't use restraints of any kind." Hank felt quite sure that it was only a matter of time before one of Irene's falls would injure her seriously.

That very fall occurred in June of the following year. As close as the nursing home could tell, the following events must have occurred. Irene was asleep in her bed. She somehow was awakened and must have tried to get out of bed. She likely slipped on the mattress laying beneath and in front of her bed—a precaution taken as a result of a prior fall. She apparently fell backwards, hitting the bed post as she fell, landing on her right side, sustaining fractures to both her right hip and her pelvis.

An ambulance was immediately called, and Irene was carefully placed on a stretcher. Her right leg was pitched at a dreadfully awkward angle, and she was writhing in pain. Her gown was disheveled and pulled down around her shoulder from the impact of the fall. No longer beautiful or elegant, Irene was placed in the ambulance, crying in pain as they closed the doors, and taken quickly to the nearest hospital, fourteen miles away.

Once there, Irene was given a morphine drip to control her pain, while the emergency doctors proceeded to determine the extent of her injuries. The family had been notified, and soon the two daughters and a grandson were stomping through the emergency room, once again angry at the interruption to their lives

The physicians soon determined that Irene's fractures were so severe and she was so fragile, they felt she could not endure the challenge of surgery. They sent her back to the nursing home essentially to die.

She was brought back the following day and returned her to her prior room. She didn't smile, she didn't even open her eyes. Irene just laid there, occasionally moaning in pain, her life nothing more than the pain of her injuries and the absence of her mind. Five days later, with no one other than a nursing assistant by her side, she died.

Irene's family never imagined themselves as the sorts of individuals that would sue anyone, regardless of what affront they might experience. They saw themselves as levelheaded people with only kindness and good will for others. It was frustrating however that the nursing home would let their beloved mother die such a senseless death. Even though the family had been involved in numerous discussions with the nursing home administration concerning her decline and her increased falls, they still couldn't help but think that something should've been done to prevent her death. After all, they loved her so much.

Although Noble Manor had gone to great lengths to inform the family of the laws governing such things, Irene's children were convinced that the nursing home and Dr. Clarkson could have done something more to prevent this tragedy. After all, it was the responsibility of Noble Manor, as well as Dr. Clarkson, to keep Irene safe twenty four hours a day. They clearly hadn't done this, both had failed Irene. And wasn't it important and justifiable that they make Noble Manor and Dr. Clarkson pay—a lot—so that these kinds of things wouldn't keep happening? As a matter of fact, wasn't it their obligation to do this? And certainly not for the money—for the principle. And it would have to be a lot of money to get their attention—so that things would really change.

Six months after they buried Irene, they hired an attorney … in order to improve the world of nursing home care.

The current trend in medical schools these days was to provide the following caveat for optimistic, hopeful future physicians: there are only two kinds of doctors—those who've been sued, and those who will be. Hank had been in practice for 20 years and had somehow avoided a lawsuit. He knew it was probably just luck, but he liked to think it was because of his approach to patients and his genuine concern for their wellbeing. But, ultimately, it was much more likely that he'd just been lucky.

Hank received his certified letter on a Saturday during his morning office hours. He read it quickly once through in disbelief, and then read it more slowly. He read through their summary of events. He read through their perceptions of the negligence; by the facility and the doctor. He read their accusation that he—her physician—was responsible for the clients' mother's safety at all times. He slowly returned the certified letter to its envelope and called his best friend from Med school, who'd already gone through this process, to ask what next to do. After 20 years of practice, Hank had finally been sued.

CHAPTER II

Henry Clarkson was born on June 6, 1958 into a loving, and somewhat wealthy family in Strongsville, Ohio. He was one of the few people he knew that actually spoke of their childhood with fondness. It was clear to him how fortunate he was and how differently he was growing up, compared to others his age.

His father loved boating so the family spent many days on Lake Erie and many summers on Put-in-Bay and Kelly's Island. Hank's favorite was Kelly's Island because of its tranquil pace that seemed to act like a contagion and spread its tranquility to all who landed there.

And there were the most incredible places to explore. He was sure that some sort of treasure had been left there as a result of one of the great, shipwrecked boats that used to travel through the Islands with frequency.

Hank knew all about the shipwrecks. He read everything he could find about each one of them. There was the Comet, the Bannockburn and the A.A. Parker—all shipwrecked in one of the Great Lakes. And each one had some mystery surrounding it. His favorite was the Indiana, which was lost in Lake Erie exactly 100 years to the day before Hank was born. He felt connected to the ship and its crew, and he often imagined what it all would have been like to have been a crew member on such a large boat, living with danger and excitement on every run. Hank imagined himself some day running one of the many ferries that ran between the Islands and the mainland. He felt it would be quite like the days when those large ships carried their cargo from port to port.

His time on Kelly's was wonderful, and it seemed as if one day led only to the next in an incredible parade of excitement and contentment. This was life as he remembered for a very long time.

It's strange how death can change things. And people. Hank's brother Michael was older than Hank and he so admired him, the way younger brothers do. They played basketball any chance they got—his brother was quite an athlete. His brother loved basketball and went to any camp he could find. There was an annual camp in Columbus, Ohio that Michael would always attend—every summer. Hank missed him terribly when he was gone and was so excited when the day finally came for him to return home. Hank remembered waiting with his mom and dad, and then the phone rang. It was as if a curtain had come down on the life that was. There'd been an accident. For the longest time, that was all Hank ever knew about the death of his brother. His mother and father seemed to close up and disappear. They spoke very little to one another after that, and it was only when Hank was much older that they told him how Michael—and the family he was traveling with—had been broadsided by a truck that jack-knifed on route 71. They had all died instantly, and Hank's mother and father had had to go and identify the bodies. Everything changed after that, and life would never be the same again.

The trips to the lake ended. All the treasure hunts and the endless days that ran into the next were over. His parents never recovered, and everything they did was colored by the grief of that horrible afternoon. Hank began to grow up like everybody else, and his mourning for the loss of those days was every bit as great as was his mourning for the loss of his brother.

Getting sued is more of a process than a one-time event. Soon after Hank contacted his malpractice carrier he began getting a flurry of paperwork on an almost daily basis. The language of legal forms and malpractice paperwork is a strange thing that only attorneys know. At first Hank would read it and try to understand it, but he would eventually just file it with everything else relating to the case as he tried—unsuccessfully—to carry on as if nothing had changed. But something had changed. It was difficult in the beginning for Hank to describe what it was that felt so terrible about being sued. It wasn't fear. He knew he'd done nothing wrong, although he also knew that didn't mean a thing. But he knew his million dollar coverage would handle even the worst outcome. So it wasn't fear. It was more like shame.

Hank didn't mind people knowing he'd been sued, but it took all he had to not allow it to alter his perception of himself. He also felt betrayed. He had shown only kindness to Irene Morrison and did not understand why this family felt a need to avenge her death. More importantly, he didn't think Irene would have approved at all. But it wasn't about her. And it wasn't about Hank either. It was about a system, kept alive by attorneys that pitted one attorney against another much like a good game of chess. The lives that were changed in the balance were meaningless.

Hank was astounded the first time he met with his lawyer. Jimmy Johnson was tall and had a somewhat gangly appearance, with a quick smile and eyes that seemed to dance with mischief. His sandy hair and his freckles lent him the look of an Irish seaman, and his quick, witty responses seemed to confirm the caricature to the point where Hank half-expected a jig at any moment. He was charming and gregarious, yet seemed to regard this horrible situation as though it was nothing more than a ping-pong game among friends. Hank started the meeting. "You're gonna' get this dropped, aren't you?" Mr. Johnson burst into laughter. "Yeah, sure. I'll just call the other guy and tell him to drop this. I'm sure he'll agree—since I asked him to." Jimmy smiled a wide grin and told Hank to sit back and get ready for a wild legal ride.

Hank realized then that—regardless of the merit of this thing—the entire show would have to be played out. And the attorneys were ready. One day when they were discussing things Hank asked about the potential of a trial. "Don't worry about that. Think of it as a game. Then it's a lot more fun." It occurred to Hank that Mr. Johnson was thinking of this simply as sport. And he was on Hank's side. What a long and unpleasant ordeal this was to become.

Physicians basically can be divided into two types: those who are certain of their brilliance, and those who pretend to be. The patient expects brilliance, and so you quickly become adept at displaying confidence, whether you feel it or not.

Most doctors fall into the second group. They spend a good part of their day questioning their knowledge base and their abilities, as they try desperately to keep up with the latest "current medical thinking" as well as all the new medications.

Needless to say, most doctors don't need any help to feel inadequate. In spite of intense preparation, and frequent medical education, doctors are quite aware that they don't know everything, and on any given day, might just miss something significant in a patient's care.

Hence, two months into the ordeal, when Hank received his "expert witness" evaluation, and it was less than glowing, he faced the horrible affirmation of his own inadequacy. In spite of a remarkably successful 20 years of medical practice, it all came down to an "expert witness's" critique.

The notion of the expert witness is an interesting and puzzling idea. Although one might think their job is to testify on behalf of a witness, their real purpose is to "poke holes" in the defendant's case in order to prepare the defendant for what may be used against him.

When Hank received the copy of his expert's view of his case he became incensed over the critical eye used to evaluate his care. Because he didn't understand this process, he felt quite certain that if "his" expert was this critical, then all of a sudden this meritless case had acquired merit.

For the first time since this had all begun, he began to feel bitter. He was angry and depressed at the same time. Although he tried to keep this process from affecting the rest of his life, he now saw the bitterness and anger he felt flowing into other areas.

He became short with patients and loved ones alike. The joy he had felt as he walked into his office each day was quickly becoming a thing of the past. He began to view patients as potential plaintiffs and their needs as potential lawsuits. Hank was being transformed.

Hank's first wife was still in his life, but only marginally. Their only child together—Jack—was now "grown up" and in college, and as such there was very little need for Hank and Jenny to communicate. They were, however, still friends and were concerned with one another's well-being. Hank had remarried, but his second marriage hadn't lasted long: although she was smart and quite attractive, she was not quite ready for all that marriage entailed. Besides, Hank was still in love with Jenny. Jenny knew this, but she had moved on and married again, happily, and had two lovely daughters and a beautiful new life.

Hank hesitated to call her when he needed a friend, but had now decided that he had to talk to somebody about the horrible thing that was happening to him. He reached her by telephone as she was getting ready to walk out the door.

"Jenny. It's Hank."

After a brief pause, he heard Jenny's soft voice on the other end of the phone.

"Yeah, Hank. What's up?"

Hank hesitated, then spoke quietly, as though he thought someone else might hear him. "Not much. Well, actually a lot. Can we talk?"

There was another pause. "I'm getting ready to pick up the girls to take them to dance. But I could talk afterward. Wanna' meet at O'Riley's? How 'bout 4:30?"

O'Riley's was a tavern the two of them used to frequent "in the good old days." It would be a comfortable, safe place. "That would be great," he heard himself say.

He got to O'Riley's before Jenny so he had some time to sit and remember … He ordered his requisite gin and tonic and sat and looked around. Not much had changed. Harry was still behind the bar. But Hank didn't recognize any of the waitresses.

Harry gave him a nod and a smile and Hank nodded as well. So many wonderful memories were living in this tavern. Hank smiled to himself as he thought back to those days.

He and Jenny had been so young and so very much in love. The memories of her long brown hair and her freckled face filled Hank with longing for the life they used to know.

When Jenny finally walked in Hank felt flushed and excited, as though they'd never been apart. It never ceased to amaze Hank how great Jenny always looked to him. Even when she was running errands with her hair in a pony tail and blue jeans on she still looked spectacular to Hank. He occasionally thought back to what had happened between he and Jenny. The day she left she told him they had just "grown apart." But he knew it was because of his chronic absences. As his practice grew, so did his time away from home. He'd left Jenny and Jack too many nights alone, and, even as he saw it happening he couldn't seem to stop it. His patients needed him. The hospital needed him. The nursing home needed him. Jenny and Jack had to wait …

He and Jenny sat in O'Riley's for an hour and a half as he told her the entire story. She listened intently and offered her support. Hank wished for more. But he was grateful for her friendship and told her he'd keep her informed.

On a particularly cold winter day, Hank was trying to have a quick lunch in his private office. The phone rang, the call was directed to his private phone, and he proceeded to listen as his lawyer explained the latest in the nightmare of being sued. Apparently, Jimmy had misplaced Hank's affidavit—whereby Hank attested to his innocence of any wrongdoing in his malpractice case—and had therefore missed a deadline for filing. Hank was furious. "You mean to tell me that after nearly two months of having my affidavit on hand you inadvertently missed filing the motion for dismissal? And my future is in your hands?"

"Hank, you need to sit back and prepare for a long haul. These things don't move very fast. I'm sure it's hard to understand that."

"Yeah, but what if I were to do that to one of my patients. I'm sorry, Mrs. Smith, I've misplaced your pathology report. Just give it another month. You can bet I'd need Mr. Malpractice Attorney, wouldn't I?" Hank had about had it with the entire process. He'd had a friend tell him once that lawsuits steal time and emotions away from one's family, but he'd had no idea how true that was. Not only from family, but from all things good in life.

The Fall that year was a particularly rainy one and, although Hank usually loved the rain, he found himself this year fighting with an ever present depression. It was threatening him all the time. It reminded him of how one feels when it's flu season and you always feel about one sneeze away from getting the illness that surrounds you daily.

He attempted to pursue his normal interests, tried to follow his routine, but nothing held the same joy for him. And if, for a moment, he forgot about his situation and had a laugh or a smile, he would immediately remember the horrible situation he was in and the joyful moment would be lost.

And so it was for weeks on end. The Holiday season came and went, and, even though Hank wasn't typically enthralled with the trappings of Christmas, it was particularly true this year. Jack would always make a point of stopping by on Christmas Eve, and that was about the extent of Hank's Christmas celebration. They had a drink or two, while Jack updated Hank on all that was going on in his life.

Hank listened, so happy to hear about the interesting life Jack was living, but nonetheless distracted as his mind would inadvertently drift back to his lawsuit. Hank was glad when the evening finally ended. Jack left, knowing his father was not at all himself.

Typically Hank saw New Year's Day as a way to reflect, not only on the year that has been, but on the life that has been. He found himself on New Year's Eve sitting in O'Riley's doing just that. He was on his second gin and tonic, feeling pretty miserable overall, when Jenny and Jack walked in the door. They spotted Hank sitting alone in a corner booth and proceeded in that direction.

"Ya' want some company, Dad?"

"Sure. Have a seat. What are you two doing out on New Year's Eve?"

"Just a little celebration to greet the New Year." Jenny was her usual beautiful natural self. "Jack is heading back to school tomorrow so I thought we'd have a drink before he left."

Sometimes it surprised Hank how "married" he still felt to his family. "Why are you going back to school so early?"

"I'm involved in a psych study at school and we need to do some prep work before the rest of the students come back from break. Mom filled me in on your "situation" at work. Bummer, Dad. Seems ridiculous to me'"

"Yeah, me too. Hopefully it will go away soon."

The three of them soon began chatting about other things and for a brief moment things felt good to Hank. After one more drink, and a few more words, Hank kissed the both of them and headed for the door.

He headed home, passing by Noble Manor on his way. He started thinking about how much more difficult it was becoming to enter that facility without pain and regret, and he knew that it was only a matter of time until he would be forced to make a decision. The next morning—New Year's Day—he decided to go to the nursing home and check on all of his patients. He knew the holidays were a lonely time for his residents and he felt that spending time with them might help his own soured look on life.

As he walked in the door, he was aware of how comfortable Noble Manor Nursing Home had become to him. The familiar smells and the familiar faces all greeting him at once as he walked in the door. He loved it all, but it had become painfully clear to him that so much went on at this nursing home over which he had no control. There were different Aides on different shifts and turnover was high. The RN's rotated frequently as well and there was often very little continuity among caretakers.

This resulted in an increased opportunity for errors and a decreased opportunity to identify those errors.

Hank was only one piece of that puzzle but he knew that anything that went wrong with a patient's care would be perceived to have been under his watch. And he was now painfully aware that that could very well land him in another lawsuit. He couldn't even think about that.

He went in, checked on a few of his folks, and then headed out the door. Yep, he'd have to quit his nursing home practice soon. But it certainly wouldn't be easy.

He received notification of his deposition on a Thursday afternoon. It was a busy January day—flu season had hit with a vengeance. He contacted his attorney who, once again, told him not to worry. Yeah, right.

So, Hank began preparing for his deposition much like he used to prepare for a final exam in Med School. He outlined the contents of Irene's chart from start to finish. He reviewed her meds, as well as all their potential side effects and interactions. He reviewed the nurse's notes. He reviewed the emergency room evaluations and all their testing. He reviewed all her labs and x-rays. He relearned all the rules governing restrictions on nursing home residents. Hank intended to go into this deposition as prepared as any one could be.

As he was doing all this, however, he began to notice a change in how he approached his patients in his practice. He began to document defensively. He began to order tests defensively. He began to regard them defensively. Hank was no longer medically caring for his patients, he was treating them as legally as he could. And that was a very different kind of care. Hank began to see that he would never ever treat patients the same again.

CHAPTER III

Amanda knew she had to hurry if she wanted to catch the 7:30 bus, so she threw her hair back in a pony tail, grabbed her scrubs and ran for the door. There had been a threat of rain all night and it had finally started with a vengeance. It was too late to grab an umbrella—she'd just have to be wet. Not that her patients would care—they were just thankful she had moved to Columbia and that she was willing to come to the dingy clinic just off of Blossom street.

Amanda had grown up in a place much different from where she was now. Growing up in Upper Arlington, a suburb of Columbus, Ohio, had its advantages and its disadvantages. Most of the people Amanda grew up with were from rather wealthy families, and, although she'd made some rather good friends, she felt that the wealth had given many of them a sense of superiority—that was the disadvantage. But, every door in life seemed open—Amanda always knew that the choices she made for her life would never be limited by a lack of funds.

She did learn, however, that there were other limitations life itself may place upon a person.

Amanda was an only child, her parents having gone to great lengths just to be able to have her. In vitro fertilization had only succeeded after the third try, when Amanda's mother was 42 years old.

This created a special, wonderful attachment between Amanda and her parents. They adored her and gave her a life not only filled with many possessions, but filled with love and strong values as well.

Amanda's father was in Real Estate, and was able to capitalize on the growth and development going on in Columbus, Ohio in the seventies and eighties.

His success allowed him to provide Amanda and her mother a beautiful home, and the best of everything.

And, he loved to fly. Eugene Wilson had flown planes in the Air Force and had always loved life most when he was flying through the clouds on a beautiful, sunlit day.

When his finances permitted, he bought a nice little Cessna aircraft, and proceeded to teach his wife, and eventually Amanda, how to fly.

Amanda and her mother were not nearly as fond of being behind the wheel of the airplane as her father was, but they very much enjoyed traveling with him when he took them out in the Cessna. And this they did often. Amanda remembered fondly their times in the plane, flying above the world, far removed from all that lay below. These memories were some of the best she would ever know and she would revisit them often when she needed to escape whatever pain she might have in her world.

When Amanda graduated from high school, she elected to go to Smith College out East, to begin her premed studies. She had always wanted to be a doctor, from the time she was little and would go to her pediatrician who would always make her laugh, and would always make her better when she was sick. Helping people in this way had become Amanda's dream and she set a course to be able to do that very thing.

She headed to Smith in late August, and found herself comfortably moved in and involved in college life rather quickly. Most of the individuals at this college were like her well-to-do friends back home, having had few true struggles in their lives. Amanda felt as though she hadn't even left the comforts of Upper Arlington and her protected life back home.

But, she desperately missed her parents. She called them daily and counted down the days until Thanksgiving break when she could return home and see them.

November of her freshman year was colder than usual. Amanda often remembered sitting in her Biology classroom—at 8:00 in the morning—with her coat still on as she tried to get warm and listen to the lecturer all at the same time.

Three days prior to the day Amanda was scheduled to head home for Thanksgiving break she was sitting in that same classroom—with her coat on—when a stranger walked into the classroom soon after the lecture had begun.

She will never forget how the instructor scanned the room and then stopped when his eyes fell on her. He spoke to the stranger and pointed at Amanda. Then, in a voice that seemed all-of-a-sudden very loud and ominous, the instructor asked Amanda to come to the front of the room.

Amanda immediately jumped up and headed toward the front. The instructor stopped her—advising her to grab her books and hat and gloves as well.

Amanda's heart sank. Whatever this was about, it couldn't be good. She quickly retrieved her items and headed to the front of the lecture hall.

She and the stranger walked out the door and into the hallway. Amanda felt her legs shaking beneath her. The stranger wore a perpetual frown on his face, and he appeared to be quite uncomfortable, shifting his weight back and forth on his long legs. He wouldn't look at Amanda, and she felt the long hallway closing in on her as she stood there feeling like she was being smothered.

When they were several feet away from the classroom, the stranger turned, gently grabbed Amanda's arm, and spoke in a voice so soft that Amanda had to strain to hear him.

"There's been an accident."

Amanda remembered very little of what followed in the days and weeks ahead.

Her parents had been flying in the Cessna, when—from what can be gathered—her father suffered a heart attack—and the small plane crashed into a field outside of Columbus. He—or his wife—had somehow managed to get the plane low enough to the ground that the damage was not as severe as it might have been. Her father had survived—though barely—but her mother had been killed instantly.

Amanda would never forget what she felt when she first saw her father laying in that hospital bed, struggling for his life, with tubes everywhere and an incessant beeping noise ringing throughout the small hospital room. She rushed to his side and squeezed his hand. He opened his eyes, and Amanda could immediately see the incredible amount of pain and sadness her father was feeling. Her heart broke—not only for her own loss, but for his as well. She knew he would never recover from this.

She immediately made the decision to transfer back to Columbus—to Ohio State University—so she could be near to her father, as well as take care of the affairs at home.

The move back was traumatic for Amanda. She had been quite comfortable at Smith College, and she knew Ohio State would be very different from what she was used to.

And so it was. At Smith College, most of the students were from wealthy backgrounds. It wasn't until she went to Ohio State University that she actually got a sense of how "other people" lived. A college like OSU is a great equalizer in many ways. Whether one is rich or poor they wind up in the same freshman dormitories, with the same class loads, and the same cafeteria food. They order pizzas from the same pizza place, and they listen to pretty much the same music.

Although at first Amanda was unsettled by all the "exposure" to other life-styles, she quickly began to embrace all the differences in people and the different worlds they had come from.

She especially enjoyed those individuals who had to work so hard for their opportunity to go to college. Amanda had been raised well, and in no way was cocky or arrogant about her wealth, but she knew that there were lessons in life that others had learned—and she had not.

She found herself gravitating to these types of individuals, almost as though she could vicariously learn those life lessons just by spending time with those to whom the teachings had been given.

Amanda eventually came to love Ohio State University. She was studying pre-med, and had hoped and dreamed of becoming a Family Practitioner and starting a medical practice in Upper Arlington, creating a life for herself much like the one she had always known.

She would visit her father nearly every day at their home, where a 24-hour nurse was attending to the majority of his needs. It broke her heart every time she saw him. His face was like a book that told of all the guilt and all the pain he felt. He was no longer anything at all like the man Amanda had known and loved throughout her life.

Eugene became weaker and weaker—he had not ever recovered from the Cessna accident—and his heart and lungs had been severely weakened by the trauma. It seemed to Amanda that his heart had been broken—the physical changes reflecting the emotional destruction—and day by day she saw his life leaving him.

Eugene Wilson passed away during Amanda's senior year at OSU, she felt a mixture of sadness and relief, as she knew an overwhelming amount of grief, guilt and pain died with him.

It wasn't until she walked away from the grave sight—where her two wonderful parents were now together again—that she realized that she was all alone in the world.

At first this realization was overwhelming and frightening to Amanda, and she withdrew from life at school and allowed her studies to suffer. But soon she realized that the best way to fight the incredible sense of loneliness and fear was to immerse herself in her studies and her friends. This she did, and she was certain that that is what saved her.

Amanda was now also responsible for their large home and all their attached wealth. Her father's brother assisted her with the sale of the home and the reassignment of all the assets, and—except for what Amanda would need for medical school—she had her uncle put all the funds in a trust—far removed from her current life. Amanda was going to live her own life and make her own way in the world. She was going to learn some of those life lessons that she felt she had missed.

When it came time to apply to medical school Amanda applied and was accepted to eight different schools. Ohio State was one of them, but Amanda was unsure if she wanted to stay or if she should get far away from Columbus and her world there.

She wasn't quite sure what compelled her to stay—perhaps because it was her only home—but, whatever the reason, Amanda never regretted the decision.

But now she could go anywhere. She was alone and disconnected from all that was and the entire world lay before her. She wanted to explore something different—a way of life much removed from the way she'd always lived. She elected to do her residency training in Columbia, South Carolina, where a part of her rotation involved spending time at the Clinic in the downtown area, just three blocks from the State House.

Amanda remembered the first time she ran and grabbed that bus that took her to the Clinic. It was spring, and the smell of the flowers blooming on the trees was the most magnificent thing Amanda had ever experienced. She fell in love with Columbia right then and there.

Amanda would walk down the streets in the downtown area, the horseshoe of the University of South Carolina not far from where her clinic sat, and just revel in the beauty and the history that surrounded her. The antebellum buildings, with their angry past, made Amanda feel at home as she reflected on her own conflicts between the past and the present. Just as the city itself rose from the ashes of the Civil War, Amanda, too, had awakened from the ashes of the loss of her parents and their wonderful, comfortable life, and was reborn in this resilient city.

Everywhere she would look she would find beauty and restoration. Nearby to her clinic was the magnificent State House with its illuminating copper dome, allowing it to stand out for all to see, a beacon for those who might want—or need—to gain inspiration from the story of its survival and rebirth.

Amanda loved Columbia, and felt that the city loved her back, accepting her as she tried to find her way in the world.

Amanda quickly fell in love with the patients at the Columbia Clinic. Although they weren't quite sure of Amanda in the first few days, they quickly warmed up to her kindness and her convincing way of caring about them. Each and every one of them.

Even Old Jimmy Smith, with his dirty hair and his smelly clothes and his horribly gruff demeanor. Amanda walked into the treatment room where Jimmy sat and asked him how he was.

"How do you think I am, lady? My head hurts all the time, and my skin feels like there's something crawlin' all over it, and I'm vomitin' up most of what I eat."

"How long has this been going on, Mr. Smith?"

"Long as I can remember. So, whatcha gonna do about it, fancy lady doctor? Yer probly just here to make yourself feel better about all your money and all your fancy clothes and shit. If that's the case, just pack up your pretty ass and take yerself back where you came from. We don't need yer pity."

"OK, Mr. Smith. I'll pack it all up and go, after I take care of your liver disease. When is the last time you had a drink? I know it wasn't long ago, because I smell it all over this room. So let's just see if you and I can maybe get you feeling better, then if you still want me out of here, I promise you I'll go."

It's hard to say what exactly sold Mr. Smith on Amanda, but from then on he was definitely sold. As were all the other patients at the Clinic. Amanda had started there in the Spring of 1986, thinking she would spend about six months there, before she went out into the "real world" of practice in a safe suburb back home.

She couldn't go home without doing this however, and she wasn't sure why. She knew she had to see something different than townhouses and comfortable cars. Or maybe she just had to see something more real than what awaited her at home.

Nonetheless, that was 20 years ago and here she was—in a God-forsaken clinic in Columbia, South Carolina, with a bunch of folks that were all but forgotten, and Amanda loved every minute of it.

Occasionally she would talk to one of her friends from Med School and listen to them moan and groan about HMO's and Business Overhead, and how bored they were with Cholesterol and Hormone Therapy, and she would think silently to herself, "Thank God I'm here, actually making a difference."

Amanda loved her days—she loved the people, the problems that they had that were real. She was always busy but never hurried. She would often think about how she needed to "move on" to her "real" future, but then she would talk to one of her colleagues and be quite content staying right where she was.

One of her favorite patients was Lois. Lois was a 49 year old alcoholic, who couldn't seem to quit drinking. She had made many valiant attempts, and had even returned to her rather fine home in North Carolina once—but she would always show up—back at the Clinic.

Lois didn't talk much about her family, but one got the sense that they really didn't want her to come home. Finally, she just decided to stay.

Lois offered to help out, and so the caretakers of the clinic found a job for her cleaning the treatment rooms and emptying garbage. This became sufficient for her to stay "on the premises" in a small studio apartment which had been used for storage. Lois had been a fixture at the clinic since Amanda had arrived. In the 20 years that Amanda had been there, she'd never seen anyone come to visit Lois. She asked her about it one day.

"I don't want them to come see me here. They just assume I'm dead—and it's better that way. They don't have to feel guilty now."

"Feel guilty about what?" asked Amanda.

"Oh, nothin.' You wouldn't understand anyway."

"Sure I would—try me." But Lois never did confide in Amanda as to what her family should feel guilty about.

Lois had multiple medical problems. The most significant was the alcoholism, but she was also a diabetic and had high blood pressure as well. She was marginally compliant with treatment, and—no matter how hard Amanda tried to get Lois on track—she couldn't. They had had many conversations about her medicines—particularly her insulin.

"Lois, if you don't take your medicines you're going to get really sick and you're going to die." Amanda would say.

"Oh well, ya' gotta' die from somethin' don't ya'?" Lois would chuckle dismissively.

"Not on my watch you don't." But none of these conversations ever changed anything.

One hot summer day, Lois came into Amanda's office with perspiration pouring off of her forehead, having difficulty walking once she got into the room.

"Oh my God, what's wrong, Lois?"

Struggling to speak, Lois muttered something about feeling cold and "crazy" inside. As she was trying to tell Amanda what was going on, she collapsed on the floor in front of where Amanda was standing. Amanda rushed to her and began to check for a pulse.

"Somebody call an ambulance! Hurry!" Lois was barely breathing, and Amanda began to go through her check list for what could be happening to Lois. She grabbed the blood pressure cuff and her stethoscope from her desk and tried to get a blood pressure. She was unable to obtain a pressure or a pulse. She went into the central supply and grabbed a lancet and quickly obtained a blood sugar. "Hi" was all it said. By this time, there was a nurse and a receptionist standing by. "Go look and see if you can tell the last time Lois had her insulin."

What seemed like an eternity later, the RN returned. "There are 2 full vials of insulin in her room, neither has been touched. It looks like Lois hasn't had her insulin for quite a while."

The ambulance showed up, and Amanda filled them in on what had transpired. Lois was quickly taken to the nearest Emergency Department. Despite their best efforts, Lois died en route. Amanda was notified by telephone that night. She wept in the privacy of her room.

Lois Skycroft was born in an upscale neighborhood on the outskirts of Charlotte, North Carolina. She was the youngest of three children born to Mr. And Mrs. Wayne Skycroft—descendants of Thomas Jefferson—so they said.

She grew up with the best of everything and was marching down the path of "successful child," when—at the age of 11—she was raped by a neighbor boy, Jimmy Clayton, while her parents were at the local Country Club for dinner one night. Her brothers were both at basketball practice in "the city," so her parents had asked this neighbor boy to watch Lois while they went out for the evening.

The Skycrofts had known the Claytons since they'd moved there four years earlier, and were quite certain they could trust Jimmy to watch over things while they were away. He was from a "good" family. His father was a Congressman in Washington, and his mother administered one of the local foundations. The Skycrofts were thrilled to be their neighbors and quickly made the Claytons their best friends when they moved in four years ago. Jimmy was older than the Skycroft children but seemed to really enjoy coming over and playing—especially with Lois. Lois wasn't nearly as interested in Jimmy as he was in her, but she tolerated him well enough. He had never "babysat" for the

Skycrofts however, but Mrs. Skycroft was certain that Jimmy would do an excellent job.

He came over that night acting stranger than usual. He encouraged Lois to lie on her bed and he wanted to read to her. She really didn't want to, but decided to go ahead—what else was she going to do? Quickly Lois realized she had made a mistake. Jimmy approached her, got on top of her and began to carry out his intentions. Lois resisted and started screaming. "No! Stop Jimmy, I said No!" But this only made Jimmy more aggressive. After what seemed like an eternity, Jimmy was finished. He got off of Lois, spat out something to the effect of "you better not tell anyone," and walked home.

When the Skycrofts came back from dinner, Lois was alone in her bedroom, and refused to tell them what had happened.

"Where's Jimmy?" Lois wouldn't answer. They phoned over to the Clayton's and Mrs. Clayton answered the phone. "Oh, Jimmy just came home a few minutes ago. He must have known you'd be home soon."

The Skycrofts could tell something had happened—but had no idea exactly what. Lois wouldn't eat or go to school for days. Her parents stood helplessly by as they watched Lois descend deeper and deeper into a very dark and very frightening depression.

Finally, they took her to a friend of theirs who at one time had been a counselor. At first she refused to talk to this "friend of the family," but eventually broke down and told her what had happened. The ex-counselor eventually convinced Lois to tell her family what had occurred on that dreadful night.

Lois finally got up the nerve to tell her parents everything about that night and she approached both of them after dinner one evening.

"Mom, Dad, I have something to tell you. A dreadful thing happened to me that night you two went to dinner at the club." And with that, Lois proceeded to tell her parents everything. She told them about Jimmy and what he had done that night. She left out nothing. Every detail of that horrible night came pouring out of Lois' mouth. She didn't leave out anything, and she didn't stop talking until everything had been told.

When she was done she sat down in front of both of her parents and waited. Many seconds went by. Time seemed to have stood still as Lois waited for her parents to comment. Finally, her mother looked at her, smiled sweetly and said "Lois Dear, that just can't be."

Her father chimed in. "Yes Honey, the Clayton boy wouldn't do that—his dad's a Congressman for God's sake. You must have dreamed it. Were you watching something nasty on T.V?"

Lois couldn't believe what she was hearing. They didn't believe her! Her incredible, loving parents thought she had imagined the most horrible event in her life.

She wasn't quite sure what to do with this. She could argue with them—but she was quite sure it wouldn't matter in the least. Lois had dared to challenge their happy little social scene—and they weren't going to have it.

Lois just looked at them both. "Believe what you choose."

And then she slowly walked out of the bedroom. From then on, things were different for Lois. Her grades slipped, her social activities all but stopped, and she began to spend a great deal of time alone in her bedroom. Her parents never spoke of the incident again. Neither did Lois.

Amanda was assisting the Clinic Administrator in trying to obtain information about Lois' family. They needed to tell someone that she had died. Amanda remembered Lois mentioning Charlotte, so they began there. They had a photo of Lois with a man—a boyfriend? A brother? They also knew that at one time she had attended a Catholic school in Charlotte, known as Saint Michael's. Amanda set out 2 days after Lois' death, with the few remnants of her life that existed. The picture, a trunk filled with old paperback books, and a few items of clothing.

It only took her one and one half hours to get to Charlotte, and once there, she asked about Saint Michael's. She was given directions and—40 minutes later—parked the car in front of Saint Michael's Catholic School for Girls. Amanda walked in and asked to speak with the principal. He was an older man, which was good—he might have actually been there when Lois was. She showed him the photo.

"Hmmm. Let me see now. She does sort of look familiar. I remember her brothers. Yeah, the Skycroft boys. Good athletes. And the mother was some kind of charity worker. "He thought for a moment more. "Lois! That's it! Lois Skycroft." Amanda was thrilled. This was too easy.

"Do you happen to know where her family is now?"

"Well, I think they probably still live over on Beaumont Street. There with all those fine fine homes." He proceeded to tell her how to get to Beaumont Street.

Amanda jumped back in her car and started driving. As she got closer she began to feel uneasy. What was she going to tell them? Would they even be sad? What about the brothers? Were they still around? Had Lois stayed in touch with any of them?

She arrived on Beaumont Street just before dusk, and began checking the mailboxes for clues to the owners of the beautiful homes that lined the street. Soon she came to 5498 Beaumont Street. There was a sign above the door which said "The Skycroft Residence." Amanda slowly stepped out of the car and proceeded to the door. She stood there for many minutes trying to figure out what to say. She was just getting ready to knock on the door when suddenly it opened, and there in front of her stood a small, Hispanic woman. 'Can I help you?" she asked.

Amanda began. "Yes, my name is Amanda McKinney, and I'm a physician in Columbia. I'm here to speak to the Skycrofts about Lois?"

The woman frowned and looked closer at Amanda. "Just a moment please."

Soon a very tall, elegant woman waltzed to the door. "I'm Mrs Skycroft. I understand you're here about Lois?"

"Yes I am" said Amanda. "Lois was staying at a clinic in Columbia, and I'm sorry to inform you that she died two days ago. I needed to let someone know."

Mrs. Skycroft stared at Amanda for what seemed like an eternity. "How did she die?" she asked.

"We're not quite sure, but we think it was from a diabetic coma."

"Were you her doctor?"

"Yes, I was."

"Was Lois sober?" This comment made Amanda uncomfortable, but she continued on.

"Yes, she was. She'd actually been sober for several months. We think Lois had quit taking her insulin, and gradually her blood sugar built up to the point where she went into a coma. We won't know for sure, I suppose."

"What do you mean, you won't know for sure?"

Lois was surprised by this remark. "Well, we have to assume because the cause of death is unclear. We wouldn't know unless we did an autopsy, and there really isn't any reason—"

"I want that done" Mrs. Skycroft interrupted. "I need to know what killed Lois, and I want an autopsy done."

This entire line of reasoning was baffling to Amanda. "Lois had multiple medical problems. I'm quite comfortable calling this a natural death and letting that be the end of it."

"I'll bet you are comfortable with that. For all I know, you and your colleagues at that "Clinic" killed Lois." She emphasized the word 'clinic,' almost snarling as she spoke.

Amanda was at a complete loss for words. All she had ever done was taken care of Lois and be kind to her. She liked Lois and Lois liked her. The implication that Amanda—or the Clinic—had somehow failed Lois was the furthest thing from the truth, and it angered Amanda.

"I assure you, Mrs. Skycroft. We did all we could for Lois. She often was poorly compliant with her medications."

"Wasn't it your job to make sure Lois took her medicines? After all, I'm assuming she lived at that "Clinic" because she was unable to care for herself or make any kind of meaningful life for herself. It sounds to me like you failed Lois."

And, with that comment, she slammed the door. Amanda stood there for several minutes, trying to figure out what just happened.

Finally, she grabbed the few remnants of Lois that she had intended to give to the Skycrofts, and turned toward her car. She walked slowly down the driveway, and slid into the driver's seat of her Honda, turned the key, and headed for home. Columbia. Where she worked at a clinic for indigent folks who needed a doctor with compassion and caring, who didn't have a desire for wealth. Amanda headed back to her life.

The autopsy took weeks to obtain, and the report took several weeks after that. Basically, it confirmed that Lois died from a diabetic coma, caused by insufficient insulin. Beyond that, nothing more could be ascertained.

This information was provided to the Skycrofts in Charlotte. There was no word in reply from them. Amanda slowly began to get back to the business of taking care of the folks in Columbia—that had been all but forgotten. Gradually things began to feel like they used to. Some new and delightful individuals had trickled in to the clinic, and Amanda was once again getting happily caught up in their care.

The certified letter came on a Thursday afternoon. With very little fanfare. Amanda was just finishing a very challenging day full of interesting, horrific problems, when the receptionist came back to her office and handed her the letter.

"What's this?" asked Amanda.

"I dunno.' Just some letter some man dropped off. I had to sign for it."

Amanda proceeded to open it. Her jaw dropped. Her stomach—and her heart—sank. Those ridiculous people in Charlotte, North Carolina, were suing Amanda—and the Clinic—for negligence in the death of Lois Skycroft.

CHAPTER IV

Jeremy awakened once again covered in sweat, as his thoughts wandered back to that village in South Africa. Always the little face of Boti staring back at him with those beautiful eyes, buried in hollowed-out sockets, reflecting life-long hunger and need.

And there was the AIDS. Everywhere he looked he saw lives ravaged by the disease. Mothers and their small children. Men in the prime of their lives. All taken down by a simple virus. How could this happen? Why couldn't more be done?

Jeremy would often wake up from a sound sleep seeing the image of a beautiful African woman with a small child at her wrinkled, sagging breast, both mere shells of who they were meant to be, dying a slow death as the world looked on and did nothing.

One particular incident played itself over again and again in his mind, and he would immediately be filled with the pain and heartache which exemplified so much of his experience in South Africa.

Boti was only five years old when Jeremy met her. She had come to the clinic, trying to get help for her mother who was dying from AIDS. Her mother had apparently contracted the virus from a young man who had died several years earlier from the merciless disease.

Boti had beautiful dark eyes—set like two onyx in her magnificent black-skinned face. She was very small and thin, likely suffering from chronic calorie depravation, but full of love and hope like every child should be. Jeremy remembered her illuminating smile, so infectious and inspiring. That smile would often bring beauty to the ugliness surrounding him. She had singled him out that very first day in the clinic, and the two of them had become friends almost immediately.

She had asked Jeremy to follow her to where her mother was sick and dying, hoping he could provide whatever was needed to make her well again. They walked the three miles to her small village east of the clinic.

Boti spoke very little at first, but as they neared her home she began telling Jeremy stories and information about the people and places where she grew up. Jeremy enjoyed hearing about her life—so challenging, but still full of the magic and wonder of childhood, even in this desolate countryside.

Once they arrived at her small home they walked inside and went to her mother's bed. Jeremy took one look at Boti's mother and knew he was too late. Flies were enjoying a feast on her open sores, and her ravaged body didn't even have the strength to allow her to raise her head when Boti bounced into the small abode.

"Mommy, mommy, I have a doctor. A doctor to fix you. Look up, Mommy!"

Boti's mother moved her eyes in Jeremy's direction, and Jeremy saw a small flicker of fire and life left inside the poor, ravaged woman. He smiled at her with great effort as he knew he was witnessing her final moments on this earth. He was immediately overwhelmed by the knowledge that he had nothing to offer her, nothing that could save her from this devastating disease.

Boti ran back to where he stood and pulled him to her mother's side.

"Fix her doctor. Please." Boti's eyes—full of life and hope—stared up at him pleadingly, and he looked back at her, his heart heavy with the knowledge of her mother's approaching death.

"Boti, I don't know what I can do. She is very sick."

Boti gave him a long hard look, her eyes narrowing to mere slits, as she weighed what he had just told her. She stood up and went over to the bag he kept with him which held medicines and other tools of his trade. She pointed to the bag, and spoke again, only this time the hope and joy were nearly gone.

"In your bag. You have medicines. Help my momma. Medicines from your bag."

Jeremy knew he had to try to do something for this poor woman—if for no other reason than that Boti expected—and needed—it done.

He walked over to the bag and began to rummage through it. He grabbed his stethoscope, a syringe, and a vial of Demerol, and walked back toward Boti's mother. He bent down beside her and grabbed her frail hand, appreciating immediately its skeletal qualities.

Jeremy gently bent low toward her face and very quietly told her that he was there to help her. She was looking at him with seemingly over-sized eyes, staring up at him from sunken sockets in an emaciated face. She made her best effort to smile, and a small flicker of life danced from her eyes for a brief moment.

She tried to squeeze Jeremy's hand, and he felt the subtle increase in pressure and squeezed a bit harder himself, careful not to hurt this frail, breakable woman.

He listened to her bony chest, barely hearing the breath exchanged in her dying lungs, and a heart that seemed to be struggling for every beat.

He sat up and looked over at Boti. He saw the sorrow in her beautiful eyes intermingled with the hope he had seen earlier. He noticed tears starting to form and he immediately began to draw up the Demerol into a small syringe. He quickly found a small area of flesh and proceeded to inject the calming medicine into what remained of this poor dying woman.

For a moment Jeremy imagined what Boti's mother must have looked like before the AIDS had its way with her. She appeared to have been tall, with distinctly beautiful features, and magnificent ebony skin. Jeremy was certain that she had been a strong, attractive woman at one time. Suddenly tears filled his eyes, and he quickly turned away so that Boti wouldn't see him cry.

Boti walked over to him and knelt down beside him. She placed one hand on his shoulder, and another on her mother's dying body.

Her mother slowly closed her eyes, and—for what Jeremy imagined was the first time in a long time—a peace seemed to take over her stark features. Her beauty was briefly restored as she quietly took her last breath. The three of them sat there in silence for several minutes, as the sun slowly set over the horizon.

Jeremy Bourne was born the day John Kennedy was shot. He was a product of that volatile time, and a true believer in the ideals of that generation. He'd entered the Peace Corp upon graduation from college wanting desperately to change the world. He stayed for seven years and loved every minute of it. He'd elected to go to South Africa and had learned a great deal about South Africans, and humanity while he was there. He'd seen first-hand how dreadfully poor and needy many people on this earth lived. He was astounded at what they were forced to live without and he vowed to make a difference in whatever way he could. His experience with Boti and her mother was one of many which shaped his perspective and his goals for the remainder of his life.

When Jeremy finally returned to the states he applied for Medical School. He was accepted 6 months later at the University of Oklahoma. He finished in the middle of his class, and went on to a residency in family practice, always with the knowledge and commitment that he would dedicate his life to helping others improve their health and their lives.

Jeremy chose to begin his mission on an Indian Reservation in Arizona. When he arrived at the Pima reservation outside Phoenix, he knew he had chosen his life mission well. He just felt at home there. And so much work to do.

The Pima Indians had a very significant problem with diabetes, and like many other Native Americans, were also dealing with alcoholism on a grand scale.

Jeremy was welcomed on the reservation by an elderly white man who referred to himself as "Doc Jones." He immediately made Jeremy feel at home, and offered him a room at his small house. Doc Jones lived alone and welcomed the company. Jeremy was totally alone and was glad to have a place to stay. The two men quickly became friends and Doc Jones introduced Jeremy to the people and the places that were important on the Pima Reservation.

It didn't take long for Jeremy to feel a part of things on the reservation. The people there were very welcoming and in great need of another doctor. Jeremy began working soon after arriving, and loved every minute of it. The clinic was very busy every day, and it didn't take Jeremy long to find a rhythm and a pace that was comfortable for him. He began to get to know folks, and find comfort in some familiar faces. Mabel, the very overweight but delightful Pima who essentially ran the clinic, and Katy—the RN who was of Pima heritage, who assisted Jeremy in the clinic.

Katy was approximately 28 years old, and possessed the dark and appealing features of Native Americans. Jeremy found her quite attractive and very likeable. He and Katy slowly became comfortable with one another and found a unity in their desire to help the Pima population.

Diabetes was the predominant illness, and Jeremy was very aggressive in approaching the problem. Doc Jones had been unwilling to try much in the way of new medications, but Jeremy was quite willing—and anxious—to put some of the newer medicines to work, and hopefully turn some of these poorly-controlled diabetics around.

He began by converting many of the non-insulin patients to a new medication called Diacam. It had recently been released, and was found to offer many advantages over some of the earlier medications, especially with regard to low blood sugar reactions.

Jeremy liked it because he could be more aggressive with a patient's blood sugar without the fear of a severe hypoglycemic reaction. He soon had nearly all of the non-insulin-dependent diabetics on Diacam, and he was seeing some tremendous results. Patients were not only achieving blood sugar control like they never had before, but they were feeling better and becoming more interested in their illness and its management. Jeremy and Doc Jones were thrilled.

One hot, dry summer day Jeremy was taking a break in the back room of the clinic, scanning through his journals. He saw an article on Diacam and began glancing through it. The gist of the article was that there was a newly discovered concern about a potential problem with Diacam with regards to liver function. Apparently a small number of patients were experiencing liver enzyme increases and subsequent liver disease. Jeremy read on with interest. Currently there was no recommendation to stop the medication, but it should now be used with renewed caution, and with frequent liver function testing.

The next morning Jeremy began liver function testing on every one of his patients. There was no laboratory on the premises, so Jeremy had to draw the labs and send them off to be processed at the lab in Phoenix. He expected results within 72 hours. In the meantime, he questioned all his patients as to any side effects they may have been having. They consistently denied any problems.

Three days later, the lab results were in. Jeremy was dumbfounded. Every single patient was experiencing mild liver function elevations. He was faced with a choice—take the patients off their Diacam and revert to their old lack-of-control status—or use insulin to achieve the same thing. Or, he could continue the Diacam, watch the liver function values closely, and see if the numbers continued to rise.

He decided to allow the patients to help him with this decision. A few were frightened enough that they immediately stopped their Diacam. But, they refused insulin, and therefore became poorly-managed diabetics once again. Many of the patients, however, wanted to continue the Diacam. Jeremy made sure they understood that routine lab tests were essential, and that they absolutely must refrain from any alcohol due to its toxic effects on the liver as well. They agreed to both the lab tests and the avoidance of alcohol.

Many months passed and Jeremy continued his quest to make the Pima Indians a healthy, happy population. He had started a softball team and had found some leagues in Phoenix for them to play against. This had generated an incredible amount of enthusiasm. His diabetics were thriving and Jeremy was feeling quite good about the impact he was making on this small Indian Reservation. He continued to do routine liver function testing, but no further increases were noted. The patients were kept on their Diacam and their diabetes continued to be much better controlled.

The lawyers came 2 weeks later. A group of them. It occurred to Jeremy that lawyers seem to prefer groups. Perhaps something to do with their unholy missions and comfort in numbers—who knows? They drove up in two separate vehicles—large black sedans. There were four altogether, in dark suits and ties, and large grins on their faces as they approached the small clinic building on the reservation. They burst through the door and handed Mabel a folded up letter and spit out the following words:

"This is a request for records. It must be adhered to, and we need the records now, please, as we have an active investigation going on and the records are needed to further the investigation."

Jeremy was listening to all this from his room in the back and finally walked out as they were finishing their statement.

"What appears to be the problem here, gentlemen?"

"No problem, sir, just comply with the subpoena."

"What are you investigating?" asked Jeremy.

The lawyers shrugged in unison, as the spokesman for the group said "we think someone in this clinic has prescribed a medication inappropriately and we have some complaints from various individuals substantiating the same."

"Where do lawyers learn to talk like that?" Jeremy wondered to himself.

Out loud, Jeremy questioned the attorney who had just spoken. "What medication, if I might ask?" By now, Jeremy was aware of several beads of sweat pouring down his back.

"You actually should speak with your attorney. But I'll tell you this much—Diacam is about to be taken off the market."

Jeremy and Doc Jones immediately began researching the situation, and soon found out that one of the patients he had on Diacam had recently traveled to New Mexico to visit some distant relatives and had been admitted to a hospital there due to severe abdominal pain. The patient was quite distended and lab work revealed liver enzymes that were significantly elevated. The man was still hospitalized, but his wife immediately contacted some of her friends back on the reservation, and informed them of what had happened to her husband.

Some of these individuals, many of whom had been poorly compliant with obtaining their lab work, then proceeded to Phoenix for testing. They also were found to have significantly elevated liver enzymes.

One of the lab technicians in the Phoenix hospital advised them to get a lawyer because their physician had "prescribed the wrong medicine." This they did.

The four attorneys who had come into the clinic were from the firm of Wyatt, Hanson, Richards, and Schultz—a very prominent firm in Phoenix, who—by coincidence—were working with some other clients who were taking Diacam and had had similar liver function abnormalities.

Jeremy was devastated. His first action was to call all his patients and immediately advise them to discontinue their Diacam. Secondly, he insisted they all come in for repeat blood work. He looked through each of his files and tried to anticipate what the attorneys would look at, how they would look at it, and what they would try to use against him. He lost himself in this process, and cancelled the normal clinic hours for the next several days. He slept only briefly and ate very minimally. The love he felt for what he was doing changed overnight. Jeremy was being transformed.

There was a tavern on the Reservation known as "The Coyote." It served fairly good food, and lots and lots of alcohol. Old Jimmy Crow was a regular there. He ate a little, and he drank a lot. He had been drinking a little more lately because his life was such a mess. His wife had divorced him six months earlier, and had taken the two children with her. Some crazy judge had decided that Jimmy needed to pay her $40 a week to take care of the children, and Jimmy couldn't come up with the money. All his efforts in the casino had failed. He wasn't sure what he was going to do.

His letter came by registered mail, late on a Friday afternoon. His neighbor signed for it and brought it to the tavern—where she knew he would be—and he opened it slowly and read carefully.

∾

Dear Mr. Crow,

Your health insurance company, in the interest of your health, has made us aware of your prescription history. It appears that you are on a dangerous medication that has recently come under question. If you are currently taking Diacam, we—and your health insurer—recommend that you stop it immediately.

We also encourage you to obtain labs to see if any damage has occurred to your liver as a result of this medication. To facilitate your obtaining these labs, we are setting up a portable lab to draw your blood in the local tavern this Saturday. If you are concerned about your future health, please arrive at The Coyote on Saturday morning between 10:00 and 12:00 and we will take your blood and see if Diacam has impacted your liver.

All results will be confidential and shared only with you. In the event that there is evidence of damage, you will be in a position to obtain compensation to assist you in your management of the diseased liver. Our law firm is committed to seeing that you acquire all that is due you as a result of this negligence. If you have any questions, please feel free to contact our hotline at: 1-800—555—LAWS (5297). Someone is available 24 hours a day to assist you as you pursue this claim.

We, the lawyers at Wyatt, Hanson, Richards, and Schultz, want to help you in any way possible as you go through this difficult time. We are here for you. We will contact you soon after your labs have been obtained to tell you what you need to do next. Once again, please be at The Coyote on Saturday morning, between 10:00 and 12:00. Thank you, and have a nice day.

Sincerely,

Becky Robinson, attorney-at-law.

What an opportunity for old Jimmy Crow. He immediately finished his eighth or ninth beer. Tomorrow was Saturday, and Jimmy would be there.

Maureen Robinson received her letter on a bright, very hot Tuesday afternoon. She had just picked up her children from school and was unloading groceries. A gentleman approached her and asked her to sign for a letter.
"Who's it from?"
"Don't know. I've been handing out several of these letters, though."
Maureen signed for the letter and walked inside with it. She opened it and read it carefully. She never thought much of those lawyers who always seemed to be looking for a case. And she had read enough Grisham books to know that—in the end—the lawyers got rich and the "regular folk" didn't get much more than some headaches.

But one part of the letter held her attention. Her father had died from a "diseased liver," cirrhosis of the liver, to be exact. He had a bit of a drinking problem and it was felt that that is what caused it. But it was a terrible thing to watch. Her dad, dying like that. She certainly didn't want that to happen to her. So, lawsuit or not, she needed to know what her situation was. She would go to The Coyote on Saturday.

There were 36 other letters that were hand delivered in the same fashion. All concerning the medication Diacam, and all interested in a lawsuit. Gradually, word came back to Jeremy and Doc Jones. The clinic, and Dr. Jeremy Bourne, were under attack.

CHAPTER V

Wilson Jackson, III, went into medicine on the inspiration of his uncle Robert. Robert Jackson was one of the first African Americans to graduate from Harvard medical school, and the entire Jackson family was proud of his accomplishments. He was a fine doctor, and kind and charitable as well. He took care of many of the inner city kids in Boston, and Wilson learned early on that he wanted to try to do something good and kind—and important—just like his uncle Robert had done.

Wilson's fondest memories were of his family—all seven children, mom and dad, and Uncle Robert—sitting around the huge kitchen table in their beautiful home in Boston proper.

Uncle Robert had never found time to marry, and he spent much of his free time over at Wilson's family's home. He was ten feet tall in Wilson's mind, and he knew absolutely everything a man could ever know. He was kind, thoughtful and wise, and Wilson respected him every bit as much as he did his own father.

Wilson recalled an incident when he was fourteen years old and he got bored with doing things right. He decided to spend a little time "on the other side."

Although the Jackson's were by no means wealthy, they were doing much better than many of the neighbors and the kids Wilson went to school with. It was sometimes tough to be a well-to-do black man surrounded by folks who seemed to be so different.

He started hanging with a gang of kids who came from a much different world than he did—but they were definitely "cool." Wilson wanted desperately to be "cool" as well, and he was eager to impress these boys.

Although they were reluctant at first, they finally decided to give the "rich boy" a chance to be one of them. They asked Wilson to show his loyalty and his fortitude by having him deliver "a package" to a housing development in downtown Boston. Wilson was scared to death to do this, but he knew he had to if he wanted to impress the boys.

He picked up the package early on a Saturday morning. It was stuffed in a large duffel bag, and, although Wilson had an idea what was in the package, he tried to put it out of his mind and do his job. He grabbed the over-sized bag and quickly threw it over his shoulder. When he did so, a smaller bag filled with white powder fell to the ground. He stared at it for a moment, then quickly reached down and stuffed it into the duffel bag. He suddenly felt very frightened and confused. He wasn't sure what he should do. He couldn't disappoint the gang, but he felt so uncomfortable thinking of hauling these drugs anywhere.

He started to run. The large duffel bag bounced on his shoulder as he picked up speed, running as fast as he could to the only place he could think to go that would be safe.

He wound up at Uncle Robert's office 15 minutes later, out of breath and feeling panic growing ever stronger within him. He burst into the office, trying to talk between breaths.

"Is Uncle Robert here?" He asked breathlessly.

The receptionist was eyeing Wilson carefully.

"Hello, Wilson. What do you need your uncle for?"

"I just need to talk to him for a second. It won't take long." He attempted a feeble smile to reassure the receptionist that he wasn't up to any wrong-doing. She slowly stood, motioned Wilson to a chair, and went to the back to find Dr. Jackson.

Several minutes later she returned and motioned for Wilson to follow her. He did so, carrying the large duffel bag over his back. He was shown into his uncle's large office, and offered a seat in front of a very large oak desk. Wilson sat down, feeling quite small and insignificant in front of such a piece of furniture.

He looked around, admiring the beautiful pictures on the wall, and his eyes stopped as he saw himself staring back, with a baseball cap sitting crookedly on his small head. Suddenly he felt ashamed and alone. Maybe this wasn't a good idea. What if Uncle Robert is angry? Maybe he should just run out of that office right that minute.

He thought about that for a second, but then wondered to himself, "What would I do the next time, and the time after that?" He knew he had to stay and figure a way out of this mess. And he knew his uncle was just the man who would help him to do so.

Within moments, Uncle Robert walked into the office. He seemed even taller than Wilson remembered. Wilson felt his legs shaking. Uncle Robert stepped behind the desk and sat his large body down in the over-sized chair behind the over-sized desk.

"Hello Wilson. What a wonderful surprise!" The words were kind, but his uncle's expression seemed to indicate his awareness that something was wrong. He glanced at the duffel bag on Wilson's shoulder, frowned, and quickly turned his gaze back to Wilson.

"What brings you here to my office, Wilson?"

Wilson shifted back and forth in his seat, not knowing at all what he should say.

"Uh, well, uh, hello Uncle Robert." He paused, looking at the floor the entire time. "I think I've gotten myself in a little bit of trouble."

He slowly began telling his uncle what was going on, picking up speed as his words began rushing from his mouth, finishing with a plea for forgiveness.

When he was finished, Uncle Robert sat there with a stern expression on his face, quietly contemplating all that he had just heard. After what seemed like hours to Wilson, he began to speak.

"Wilson, you, my friend are sitting at what is commonly referred to as a "fork in the road." The direction you choose to go here and now will determine your future for years to come." He paused, coughed into his fist, and continued, still speaking quite softly.

"You can do this drug deal—pretending to yourself it will be your last—and proceed down that road. Your "gang" will think you're cool, at least for the moment, and you'll be one of them as long as you continue to do their bidding."

At this point Uncle Robert sat straight up in his chair and looked directly into Wilson's large brown eyes. He continued speaking, even softer than before.

"Or, you can decide here and now that—not only will you not participate in the action—but you will do your best to eradicate this blight from our beloved streets of Boston."

Suddenly Uncle Robert leaned forward across the desk, and was staring at Wilson with their eyes only inches apart. His voice became much louder.

"Dammit, Wilson! Do you know what I do in this office? Do you? I help take care of kids. Like you. The very kids you're about to supply drugs to are the kids I'm trying to help. At the end of the day, Wilson, we all do one or the other—we help, or we hurt. Now, what's it gonna' be for you?"

This last question was thrown at Wilson, and he sat back as though he had been physically affected. Uncle Robert leaned back in his chair, and suddenly Wilson saw a sadness creep into his eyes. Wilson knew he would remember that look for as long as he lived.

His uncle had dedicated his life to fixing the very problem Wilson was about to become a part of. No matter what, he knew he couldn't go through with it—regardless of what might happen to him.

His direction—his path—became crystal clear that Saturday morning sitting in his uncle's large office. And his love and admiration for his uncle became crystal clear as well. Wilson knew—then and there—that he would do his best to be part of the solution and not become part of the problem.

With his uncle's help, Wilson was able to tell his story to a local police officer, who just happened to be a good friend of his uncle's. The officer was able to intercede on Wilson's behalf, arranging for the other boys involved to be picked up and questioned, making it appear that Wilson had been "caught" along with the rest of them.

Wilson knew he had been given quite a gift on that day and he vowed to pay it back in some way. He began to work hard at school and at life.When it was time, he went to Harvard Medical School as his uncle had done, and graduated nearly at the top of his class. He did his internship at Massachusetts General Hospital, thinking all the while that he would become a pediatrician like his uncle Robert. But during his OB/GYN rotation he knew he had found what he wanted to do. Bringing babies into the world was something God-given and inspiring. He wanted to have a hand in such an amazing miracle.

He proceeded through his residency, and was ready to start an OB/GYN practice when he had finished all his residency requirements. He wound up joining a prominent group of physicians in Boston, and began a very successful practice.

He worked hard and volunteered often. He sponsored studies, and assisted in local clinics—for free. He lectured from time to time, and was gradually becoming one of the most prominent and respected Obstetricians in the Boston area. Whenever a magazine did a write-up about hospitals and doctors of note, Dr. Wilson Jackson, III was always mentioned with top honors.

This, however, does not have anything to do with getting sued. His first lawsuit came after he'd been in practice for three years. A child born with cerebral palsy. It was often argued at that time that Cerebral Palsy was caused by trauma during birth. And many malpractice attorneys had acquired a great amount of money as a result of that argument. Although Dr. Jackson was devastated by the lawsuit, he knew it was part of the territory—especially in Obstetrics.

His partners had reassured him that—not only was a lawsuit survivable, but that this lawsuit was only one of many he would receive throughout his time as an OB. This in fact was the case. Within the year he had been sued a second time. He was then sued again a year and a half later. By the time he had been served for his sixth lawsuit, he was getting pretty used to it.

Not that any one really gets used to it. Each lawsuit changes a person. Each person then becomes more self-protective as each lawsuit is filed. Eventually, every patient is viewed as a potential plaintiff in an unending parade of accusations and unanswered expectations.

Evelyn Wilson was pregnant with twins. It was her first pregnancy, and she was alone and very frightened. She had no idea who or where the father of her babies was. Evelyn had had a very hard life, and had developed a great distrust of most people—especially men. She needed an obstetrician—one she could trust. She had very little money and knew no doctor would see her without sufficient funds. She felt lost and forgotten.

A friend of hers had told her about Dr. Jackson. How kind he was, and how one's financial hardships only made him work harder and care more.

Although she would've preferred a female physician, she decided to take her friend's recommendation and try Dr. Jackson. She was nervous when she walked into his office. She nearly left the treatment room while waiting for him. Finally, he walked in. Amazingly, he wasn't condescending or overbearing. He treated her with dignity and respect. She felt he was the first man in her life to do so. It wasn't long at all until she knew she had made the right decision. She liked Dr. Jackson.

Her pregnancy was—for the most part—uneventful. But, having twins, especially when you're only nineteen years old is rarely routine.

Things went well until the 7th month. Evelyn came in for a routine visit, and it was discovered that her blood pressure was excessively high. A routine urinalysis revealed protein in her urine. Evelyn was preeclamptic. Fetal tones revealed that her babies were doing okay, but she certainly was not. Preeclampsia is a life-threatening illness, with the potential for convulsions and dangerously high blood pressure, and Dr. Jackson advised Evelyn to go directly to the hospital where he would arrange for her admission. This she did.

She was admitted to the labor and delivery unit for monitoring. She was given the appropriate medications, but her blood pressure and proteinuria persisted. Dr. Jackson was reluctant to take the babies so early, but he felt he could not wait any longer. Although each fetus was only 29 weeks "old," and although each one weighed just over two pounds, Dr. Jackson and the hospital staff prepared Evelyn for a cesarean-section.

Things went well, both babies appeared to be healthy, but Evelyn continued to have trouble with her blood pressure. Dr. Jackson had her on three different medications, and gradually reduced her pressure to something that was at least manageable.

The babies were kept in the NICU (neonatal intensive care unit) where they were doing well until the 5th day post-delivery, when one of the twins began to experience respiratory distress. His little lungs were simply too immature and—in spite of the surfactant and early CPAP used at the time of delivery—they were giving out. The baby was intubated. The NICU doctor was called immediately. He rushed to the baby and began to do what he could to try to keep the little boy alive. After three hours of unsuccessful efforts, the baby was declared dead. Dr. Jackson was devastated. He slowly approached Evelyn's room to tell her.

"Hello, Dr. Jackson!" she said cheerfully. "Come in and look at the beautiful little outfits my friends have brought me for my babies."

Dr. Jackson walked toward her. "Evelyn, I don't know how to tell you this. There's been a problem." Evelyn's expression immediately changed. Dr. Jackson continued. "One of the babies began to have trouble breathing."

"Yes?" Evelyn was trembling.

"Yes." Dr. Jackson was now close to tears. "And he died, Evelyn."

There was a long silence in the room. Then, all at once, a low-pitched moaning sound, followed by a very loud scream, erupted from the hospital room.

"One of my babies is dead? How could that be? "Evelyn was sobbing uncontrollably now.

"Evelyn, keep in mind, they were both so young. Their little lungs were so immature." Evelyn cried for several minutes as Dr. Jackson continued to stand beside her. Finally, her sobbing subsided, and with eyes full of tears, she looked directly at Dr. Jackson. Then she very softly spoke.

"I understand, Doctor. I know you did all you could."

Dr. Jackson spent the next 3 hours hovering over Evelyn, and her surviving twin. Her sadness was evident and Dr. Jackson felt so responsible. He knew he couldn't have made any other decision, and he couldn't have done anything any differently, but he still felt responsible.

It was 6 months later when he received the certified letter. A Thursday morning. A very typical, busy day in Dr. Jackson's office. His receptionist handed him the envelope. He opened it slowly. Although he'd been sued numerous times before, this one caused him to stop what he was doing. He quickly found a chair and sat down—his heart heavy with sadness. Evelyn Wilson was suing him for the wrongful death of her infant twin.

CHAPTER VI

Maddi was running late—again. It seemed to be the story of her life—always about 20 minutes behind. It was that way when she was practicing medicine, and it was still that way as she maneuvered through the corridors of Washington, D.C. Most of the time, it really didn't matter—meetings didn't get interesting until about 20 minutes into them anyway.

But, today, she was meeting with the Chief Justice of the Supreme Court and she really didn't want to be late. She had been trying to arrange this meeting for the last several months—and finally she had gotten it arranged for this day—and here she was—about 20 minutes late. She could blame the D.C. traffic—it was always a problem—but, somehow she knew that Chief Justice Harper wouldn't buy it. Perhaps an accident? Not unless she was willing to get bloody and put a dent in her car—and she wasn't. So, she would just have to apologize and make up for it with her charm. She had certainly done that many times in her life.

Maddi was trying to anticipate what the Chief Justice would say when she informed him of her real purpose for the interview. She had used the influence of a senate colleague—who was very good friends with the chief justice—in order to obtain the interview, under the guise of "terrorism legislation." Would he be upset when he found out she had deceived him? She hoped not. Perhaps surprised, and a little taken aback. But she also knew he would listen. He had to. Things had gotten so bad in the world of liability and medicine that something drastic was needed. And Maddi was prepared to do something drastic.

How should she greet him? "Hello, Mr. Chief Justice,your honor" No, that sounded ridiculous. How about "Hello, your honor." Yeah, that was good. "My name is Cynthia Madison. My friends call me Maddi. "So far, so good. All at once, she was pulling up to the Supreme Court of the United States, sitting so fine and regal in the very heart of Washington, D.C. Maddi looked around briefly as she stepped from her car and headed toward the Supreme Court Building. She was once again enthralled by the beauty—and the power—surrounding her.

It was springtime in Washington, D.C. The pale pink cherry blossoms from the Japanese cherry trees created an aroma and a visual panorama that left Maddi once again amazed and delighted with the nation's capitol.

Incredible landmarks—all with history coursing through them—combined with the beauty of the city itself, seemed to create the perfect backdrop for the powerful men and women who called this city home. The power seemed to engulf one's senses every bit as much as the aroma of the cherry blossoms.

Maddi loved it here, and felt invigorated and alive just being in this magnificent city. It was as though she were "plugged in" to all the importance that seemed to emanate from this, the Capitol of the Free World.

Maddi looked up at the imposing white building in front of her. Just as she was entering the building she saw above her a creed etched into the façade.

"Equal Justice Under Law."

"How ironic," she thought, smiling to herself. She quickly rushed inside. She nearly ran into a tall, lean man standing just inside the entrance. He looked at her inquisitively and then spoke.

"Senator Madison?"

Maddi nodded.

"Hello. My name is John McCargish and Chief Justice Harper has asked that I meet you here." He paused for a moment, shifted his weight, then continued, looking directly at Maddi.

"I'm sorry, Senator Madison, but Justice Harper has been detained, and he has asked that I assist you. As I said, my name is John McCargish, and I'm his assistant. Would you like to sit down?"

Maddi was so disappointed. Here she was, with a brilliant—yet drastic—plan to finally solve the malpractice crisis facing the United States and the Chief Justice had sent an underling? Oh well, she thought. I'll try it out on him. Actually, that could be a good thing—get his opinion first.

"Thank you, sir, I think I will. Sit down, that is. I'm sorry I'm late, but-

"Don't worry about that Senator, I'm sure it must have been the D.C. traffic." Was there a hint of a grin on his face? "What can we do for you today, Senator?"

Maddi smiled, and then started in. "I know I had originally scheduled this meeting to discuss issues related to international terrorism, but something just as important is currently undermining the very fiber of our nation. I am hoping to get some input from the Chief Justice on the matter."

John McCargish nodded, his dark curly hair bouncing as he did so.

Maddi continued."I've been working on some legislation dealing with tort reform within the medical industry, and—as such—I've been speaking to various entities, including local attorneys in the area. After numerous conversations with these attorneys, I have realized two very important things." Maddi was talking too fast. Slower, slower...." One, they—the lawyers—think differently from the rest of us. Two—and this is important—theirs is the only profession where their success *requires* that someone else fail. In other words, the system has been designed so that the lawyers make the laws, and they profit by these laws, and—and here's what I'm saying—they cannot do what they do under the current system unless someone else goes down. I'm thinking that this is a bad system by its very design, and I'd like to change that design."

Maddi took a big breath and let it out slowly. She looked around the great hall, noticing the busts of every great Chief Justice who had ever presided over the court. Maddi felt so small and insignificant standing among them. The Assistant to the current Chief Justice of the Supreme Court of the United States of America looked directly into Maddi's eyes.

"And how do you propose to do that?" He was grinning and Maddi noticed immediately that his smile was somewhat crooked. It seemed, however, to work perfectly with the rest of his face. He was rather dark-complexioned and had beautiful green eyes set deeply into his skull, which seemed to speak volumes.

Maddi caught herself captivated by John's green eyes and crooked smile and realized that she hadn't yet answered the question. She quickly replied, "I want to change the laws governing how and why lawyers do what they do. I want their incentives to be changed from 'hitting the big score,' to simply rectifying wrongs. Not with massive class action suits, but with simple legislative mechanisms. I want them to be paid by the work they do instead of by who they can sue that has a lot of money. I want them to acquire a desire for the truth that supersedes a desire to 'win big.' I want to help the profession of law become a noble profession once again."

John McCargish sat in silence for a few moments—just staring at Maddi. He looked at her, and once again was grinning. It appeared to Maddi that he was thinking about her words very carefully, processing the information she had given him, sifting it through his legal mind, determining its validity and its worth.

Maddi sat there, feeling quite uncomfortable. She couldn't help but notice John's incredible curly hair. Not really black, but not really brown. And she couldn't help but notice his shoes. He had on Nike gym shoes with his 3 piece suit. Maddi found herself quite taken with Mr. John McCargish. Finally he spoke, his voice soft and kind.

"Why are you telling me this? How on earth do you think that I, or the Chief Justice—can help you with this?"

Maddi stood up a bit taller, smoothing down her skirt at the same time. She took a hand and brushed across her blonde bangs, and once again took a big breath. When she spoke her words spilled out of her mouth quickly, picking up speed with every sentence, revealing Maddi's passion and enthusiasm for her cause.

"I was hoping you could give me legal guidance as to how I might propose such a thing. Legally, I mean. I'm aware that our system of jurisdiction is predicated on the Scottish System and that there are a lot of reasons for the way things are done. But, I also think that the system has become perverted. It is no longer a quest for truth, or even for justice. It is simply a mechanism for lawyers to profit on the backs of poor people with real grievances, attempting to rectify them with blood money if you will. Surely there is a way to reign in this behavior?"

Maddi was getting more and more excited.

"I have to think that the kind of law that Abraham Lincoln practiced was a far cry from the kind of law being practiced today. I look around at my physician colleagues getting pursued by hungry, greedy attorneys, and I am frustrated by the blatant attempt by these attorneys to manipulate a 'bad outcome' into a bonanza of profit for themselves.

"They no longer care about the individual they represent, only about how deep the pocket is of the individual they are trying to sue. It sickens me. And it defames the profession of Law.

"I have to believe that there are decent attorneys out there who would love to see their profession become the respected search for justice that it was meant to be. I guess I'm looking to your Chief Justice to be the voice of the 'Good Lawyer,' to help me correct and improve this system in a way that survives the scrutiny of the Constitution of the United States. Can you help me? Are you and the Chief Justice the 'Good Lawyers' that I think you are?"

Maddi exhaled slowly, waiting for John McCargish to respond. John McCargish looked directly into Maddi's eyes. While she had been speaking he had listened attentively, processing her words and analyzing their meaning. He now seemed to have a somewhat stern look on his face as he responded, the smile all but gone. "Senator Madison. I'm sure you're aware of the difficult position you've put me in—as well as Chief Justice Harper—with this request."

Maddi's heart sank. Her legs began to tremble beneath her as she anticipated the worst.

John McCargish cleared his throat and continued. "Neither the Chief Justice nor I can be seen as advocates for a position, or proponents for a legislative initiative. It is absolutely essential that the Chief Justice not have his name anywhere on this agenda of yours."

Maddi turned away, her shoulders slumped and her head down, ready to head back down the steps and steer her legislation in a different direction. She knew she didn't possess the appropriate amount of legal knowledge to advocate such drastic changes to the legal system without an expert in constitutional law. She could look elsewhere, but for now she would need to let it go. The excitement she felt just moments before had vanished.

She heard Mr. McCargish continuing, and she paused to allow him his final comments, preparing to get in her car and head back to the Senate chambers. When she turned up to look at him she was startled to see a grin creep across his face. He was walking toward her, his smile even bigger, the crooked grin more pronounced. His green eyes seemed to dance in the reflection of the light shining down in the large hall.

"I, however, acting as a private citizen—during my free time, of course—could certainly help you with your legislative proposals." He continued, looking directly at Maddi as he spoke. "And I would be delighted to do so."

Maddi couldn't believe what she was hearing. She looked up at Mr. McCargish and cocked her head sideways, a puzzled look on her face. He continued speaking, walking another step toward her. "I need to warn you, however, that I am somewhat doubtful of your success—taking on the legal matrix that dominates so much of our country, but it would certainly be fun to try, wouldn't it?" He paused as he reached her, now standing directly beside her. "Think about it—all these fat cat lawyers being asked to choose a noble path? I love it! I'm quite certain, however, that the trial lawyer PAC will be all over it—in the worst way. But do I think you have something here? Yes I do! So, Senator Madison-"

"You can call me Maddi-"

"Maddi, let's see what we can do, keeping in mind once again that Chief Justice Harper simply cannot be involved in this in any way."

Maddy was speechless as she nodded her head. This was not what she expected. She actually wasn't sure what she did expect—but she knew it wasn't that. John McCargish had responded with enthusiasm nearly equal to her own. She began smiling—almost laughing.

"Well, Mr. McCargish-"

"Call me John-"

"Okay, John—you have made me very happy. I am aware that this is an uphill climb. But I also know, that if we don't make this climb, the profession of medicine as we know it, will be over. I also think the profession of law will only continue to sink further and further away from its original purpose, and we as a society will then lose everything. Thank you again. I'll be in touch." And with that, Maddi turned and quickly jogged out of the Courthouse.

She nearly ran to her car, unsure why she was in such a hurry. The image of John McCargish, and his beautiful crooked grin, was etched forever in her mind.

Maddi was shaking when she got into her car. What an amazing experience that was. Like so many experiences since she had arrived in Washington. Everything so much bigger than life. So much bigger than the small town she came from. Bigger than the delightful little medical practice she had back home. So much bigger than the commissioner meetings to discuss whether Wal-Mart should come to town. Washington was big in every way. And Maddi loved every minute of it. But she would often think back to her time as a physician in Indiana, and all that had happened to cause her, eventually, to wind up in Washington D.C.

Maddi's fifteen years as a family physician in Evansville, Indiana, had been mostly joyful and positive. She had originally joined the practice of an older practitioner by the name of Margaret Buchanon, who had a very successful practice at the edge of town.

Margaret, or "Dr. Mo," as her patients often referred to her, had been practicing for nearly forty years, and was the only female physician for many miles.

She had been Maddi's doctor since the Madison's had moved there, when Maddi was five years old. She and Maddi had liked one another immediately.

Dr. Mo had been a life-saver for Maddi. Maddi's father, Stewart Madison, was a Greenwood police officer. He had been on the force for fifteen years when he was brutally gunned down while trying to stop two men who were robbing a jewelry store. He died at the scene. The two men responsible for his death were never found, and the investigation—and his death—had taken a toll on everyone, particularly Maddi's mother.

Jeanie Madison was never the same after his death. She had adored Stewart, and her life revolved completely around him. He seemed to be the very thing that gave her life, and when he died it was as though she died with him.

Maddi was only five when all this occurred, but she remembered it all so well. The knock on the door so very early in the morning. Two officers with their heads hanging down talking softly to her mother. Her mother then falling to the ground and moaning, in true physical pain. Her older brother Andrew was standing next to her, only twelve years old at the time, and he tried to help his mother. Through his own tears he knelt down beside her, trying to put his arm around her and help her up. But, she just pushed him away, screaming at him to leave her alone.

Maddi knew she would never forget the look on Andrew's face at that moment. Andrew was more devastated by his mother's reaction than by his father's death, and he, too, was so very changed by the events that night.

The following days were very distant and confusing in Maddi's mind, but she knew in her heart that her world and the people in it would never be the same.

The move to Evansville came soon after. Maddi's mom had grown up there and she felt a strong need to "go home" after all the suffering she had been through. Maddi had just started kindergarten in Greenwood, so for her there was very little she was leaving behind. But Andrew was in the sixth grade, with lots of friends and all his sports to say goodbye to. He was angry and he slowly began to change.

Because he was seven years older than Maddi he had, for the most part, been a delightful older brother. He would protect her when she needed protecting and comfort her when she needed comforting.

But, that all changed after the events of that fateful night. He seemed to have very little to say to Maddi or their mother, and Maddi felt as though he, too, had died.

Maddi started having stomach aches soon after the move to Evansville. Her mother had heard about Dr. Margaret Buchanan from a co-worker and began taking Maddi to see her to find out what was wrong.

From the very start, "Dr. Mo" and Maddi enjoyed one another. Dr. Mo was funny—like her dad had always been—and Maddi began relying on her to provide needed human connection—and humor—that was so lacking at home.

Over time Maddi's stomach—and life at home—settled down, as the three of them gradually adapted to life without Stewart Madison.

Her mother remained distant to both of them, and Andrew—although he finally warmed up once again to Maddi as the years went by—continued to keep his mother "locked out" of his life.

Maddi would see Dr. Mo whenever she had any sort of problem, and Dr. Mo became more like a "favorite aunt" than her family physician.

There was no doubt in Maddi's mind that—when she returned to Evansville to start her medical practice, Dr. Mo was the first place she would go.

Maddi smiled whenever she thought back to that first day when she walked in to see if Dr. Mo had a spot for her. She remembered walking into the waiting room and being greeted by Lisa, the receptionist. They all knew her there at the office, both from her time as their patient, as well as the numerous rotations she elected to do there when her schedule permitted. It had always been a "perfect fit."

Soon Dr. Mo herself walked out from a treatment room, saw Maddi, and immediately rushed over to give her a hug. Maddi hugged her back, then stepped back and shrugged her shoulders and said "Well? You ready for a partner?"

Dr. Mo's jaw dropped. This subject had never even been broached prior to that moment, and Dr. Mo had always been a solo practitioner. But she loved Maddi, and besides, she was getting older. Perhaps it was time to bring somebody else in. Some "younger, newer blood," as it were.

It took Dr. Mo all of thirty seconds to say "You betcha'!" and the partnership had been born.

Maddi began working in Dr. Mo's office three weeks later and the two of them had a wonderful and thriving practice. Their patients loved them, referring to them fondly as "Maddi and Mo." The office itself was a warm, welcoming place to be and Maddi remembered it as the most wonderful time she would spend as a physician.

Three years later, in the middle of a very busy morning at the office, Dr. Mo suffered a massive heart attack. Although she survived for several days, she never recovered consciousness, and died one week later, with Maddi sitting by her side.

Dr. Mo had never married, and her only sister had died several years earlier, so it was up to Maddi to carry out Dr. Mo's well-laid out requests for her funeral and her burial.

She had wanted to be cremated, and then have a Memorial Service, and Maddi followed her wishes to the letter.

At the Memorial, the church was overflowing with all of the folks who knew and loved Dr. Margaret Buchanan. Maddi gave the eulogy and the sad Memorial service concluded. Maddi pushed her way through the crowd and went immediately back to the office to try to figure out what she should do next.

Dr. Mo had left her everything. The practice, the patients, her life savings. Everything. Maddi knew that she would continue that practice just the way Dr. Mo would want her to.

That was sixteen years ago, and, for awhile, things went along very well. Then came the first managed-care contract, with all its rules and restrictions. Although Maddi found the entire process of managed care prohibitive and uncomfortable, she felt she could tolerate it—after all, it only affected a few of her patients.

Then came the second contract, then the third. Maddi had already been dealing with Medicaid and Medicare, but now, quickly, nearly every patient was part of some "third-party payer" agreement. And so, gradually, the complexion and feel of Maddi's—and Mo's—wonderful practice was changing.

With more insurance companies came less and less control. Maddi was increasingly being told what she could or couldn't do, what medicines she could or couldn't prescribe, and what amount of payment she would or wouldn't receive. And all the decisions were arbitrary. No justification was given for many of the decisions and it was as if none was needed.

As more restrictions were occurring, patients became increasingly frustrated and dissatisfied. It was difficult for them to accept the loss of control they felt and it was unclear to them who was responsible for this loss of control.

Gradually, their expectations changed, as did their faith in "the system" or in the doctors who were acting within "the system."

The situation was perfect for what was to come. It was as if "The Perfect Storm" had manufactured itself in the horizon of medicine, and now the final thrust of that storm was to be felt.

In came the lawyers. Gradually, at first. The very rare "million dollar verdict." Slow but steady increases in malpractice insurance costs. Defensive medicine taking the place of conservative medicine. And, soon, eight out of every ten physicians being sued at least once in their career.

Maddi cringed when she thought back to those last several years of practice. All the negatives swirling around her and all the positives fading quickly, becoming a distant memory of how practice life used to be. Maddi was becoming increasingly frustrated and less satisfied with her days in the office. She occasionally wondered how long she could continue.

Then came the case of Carla. Carla Stanze. A beautiful, twenty year old college senior with promise and enthusiasm for all that lay ahead. She had started seeing Maddi soon after her mother died, when Carla was only seven years old. She and Maddi had hit it off immediately—much like Maddi and Dr. Mo so many years before. Maddi seemed to give Carla some much-needed guidance during that painful time. She was also helpful during Carla's teenage years, serving as her "female adviser" on so many levels.

Carla came to see Maddi for birth control pills in the Fall of her senior year of college. Taking care of these young girls and their reproductive health needs, was a significant part of Maddi's practice, as she continued to be the only female physician in that area.

Carla and Maddi were always glad to see one another, and they would spend most of their visit just catching up on all that was going on in Carla's life.

Maddi did her exam while the two of them talked delightfully about Carla's plans for the future. Maddi prescribed Carla her pills and instructed her on their use. She scheduled a follow-up visit during Christmas break in order to keep tabs on how things were going.

Seven weeks later, while working out at the gym, Carla collapsed to the ground, and was immediately taken to the area hospital. She had suffered an embolic stroke—a blood clot had blocked an artery to the brain—and she died later that day.

Maddi was finishing up a busy Monday when she got the call. She was devastated. How could this have happened to a healthy twenty year old girl? She quietly sat down, tears welling up in her eyes.

Maddi quickly ran to the outer office and grabbed Carla's chart. She ran back into her office, sat down, and began thumbing through the record. Her hands were shaking as tears fell on each page of the chart that Maddi was reviewing.

Normal blood pressure. Non-smoker. Negative family history. Maddi suddenly stopped dead in her tracks. There it was. Carla's mother had suffered a deep vein thrombosis and a subsequent stroke when Carla was seven years old. How could Maddi have forgotten? There in front of her, big and bold on Carla's patient information sheet. Under family history. Right where Maddi should've seen it.

The only true contraindication to birth control pills is a strong family history of blood clots. And there it was. Staring at Maddi like a mirror reflecting her own incompetence. How could she have missed that? And what should she do now?

Carla had lived with her father, and she had a younger brother who attended the local high school. Maddi knew she needed to talk to Carla's father and let him know how sorry she was for what had happened. She also knew, however that by doing so she would be opening herself up to a probable lawsuit.

She thought for a moment. She could just sit on this information—and hope and pray it would never be revealed. She thought long and hard about how that would feel. Finally, after sitting in her small office for several hours, Maddi knew exactly what she had to do.

She walked outside, went to her car, slid into the front seat, pulled out of the parking lot, and headed straight for Carla's father's home. She anticipated that, by now, Mr. Stanze would have returned home beginning the horrible process of burying his only daughter.

Maddi was shaking as she turned onto the street where the Stanzes' lived. The last time she had been here—for Carla's graduation party—had been such a positive and uplifting time. Now, here she was, preparing to explain to Mr. Stanze that she bore partial responsibility for Carla's death.

Maddi stopped the car short of the driveway. She turned off the ignition and sat there for several minutes, trying to generate the strength to open her car door.

There were several other cars parked in the driveway—probably friends of the family.

Finally, she opened her door, stepped out of the car, and headed toward the Stanze's front door. After several more minutes she rang the bell and waited.

The door was opened by a woman unfamiliar to Maddi, who had clearly been crying.

"Yes. Can I help you?"

Maddi smoothed down the front of her jacket and cleared her throat.

"Yes. My name is Dr. Cynthia Madison, and I am—was—Carla's doctor. I would like to speak to Mr. Stanze if I could?"

The lady at the door gave Maddi a long, hard look. She said nothing, turned and walked back in to the house.

Maddi stood there shivering, not knowing if she should stand there and wait, or if she should simply run away.

Just as she was preparing to turn for her car, Mr. Stanze walked to the doorway. He looked completely lifeless and eternally sad. It was as though his face belonged to a different man than the one she had known. His eyes were slits, swollen from crying, and he frowned as he spoke to Maddi.

"Can I help you, doctor?" His voice was cold and empty, and Maddi felt a chill up and down her spine.

"Mr. Stanze, I am so sorry." Maddi began crying softly. She quickly stood a bit straighter, trying desperately to stop the tears from taking over.

"Your wife died the same way, didn't she?"

Mr. Stanze's eyes opened wider at the mention of his wife, and he looked directly into Maddi's eyes. He frowned even more, and nodded slowly. Maddi continued, being sure to select her words very carefully.

"I think it is only right to tell you that because your wife died from a blood clot and a stroke, I should never have put Carla on the birth control pills that I put her on seven weeks ago. Words cannot tell you how sorry I am, and I will live with this knowledge and this pain for the rest of my life, as will you. I am so sorry, Mr. Stanze."

Maddi bowed her head, preparing for some sort of rebuke from Mr. Stanze. None came. Suddenly, the door slammed and Maddi stood there, unsure of what to do next.

Maddi turned around, walked straight to her car, opened the door, sat down, and drove to her apartment.

She walked inside, sat down, and began to cry. She sat there for hours crying and berating herself. She knew that any attorney would have told her not to do what she just did, but she hoped that it had been the decent and right thing to do. It certainly didn't feel like it right at that moment. Maddi knew that she had just opened the door to a successful law suit.

Maddi was unable to go to work for several days, and word quickly spread in that small part of town that a patient had died, perhaps from something that Dr. Cynthia Madison had done.

Maddi felt a shame like she had never known. She could not forgive her own lapse in decision-making and she certainly didn't expect Mr. Stanze to understand it either. As reports from the emergency room visit came to her office regarding Carla's death Maddi wouldn't even read them. She didn't want her incompetence confirmed by an ER report.

Slowly, after several weeks, Maddi was getting back to work. Things felt very different, however, and Maddi wasn't sure if she could continue on. She knew, however, that if Mo were here she would want Maddi to continue. Maddi was an excellent physician who had simply made a mistake. It would be a disservice to so many others if Maddi allowed that mistake—though tragic in its consequences—to keep her from doing what she did so well.

One particularly difficult afternoon, several months later, Maddi was finishing up and trying to get home early. She seemed to require more sleep than usual these days and she couldn't wait to get home and go to bed.

Just as she was getting ready to walk out the back door she heard a knock. She opened the door and saw Mr. Stanze standing there. She began to shake from within.

"Mr. Stanze. Come in. What can I do for you?"

Mr. Stanze slowly stepped inside the small office. Maddi couldn't tell what emotion was operating within him and she tried to prepare herself for further rebuke.

They both sat down in two small chairs Maddi had positioned in front of her desk, and Maddi sat silently waiting for Mr. Stanze to speak.

He shifted several times in his seat, wringing his hands back and forth, then finally spoke, in a voice barely audible.

"Dr. Madison, there's something you need to know about Carla." He stopped for a moment, and Maddi braced herself for what might be coming next.

"Dr. Madison. Carla was adopted." Mr. Stanze continued staring down at the floor, as he allowed the words he had just spoken to sink in. He continued.

"She never knew that. We had never found the right time to tell her. Vivian died when Carla was only seven, and I just never felt there was an occasion to tell her. I kept meaning to, but I just hadn't done it yet. Carla's little brother, Sam, he was Vivian's and mine. We didn't think we could have children—which was why we adopted Carla—so, Sammy was quite a surprise. Once he was born it seemed even harder to tell Carla, and, like I said, once Vivian died, there was just never a good time to tell her. I know we should've but-"

Maddi's mind was going a million miles a minute. If Carla was adopted, then the family history—Vivian's blood clot and stroke—was irrelevant. Maddi's "mistake" was not in any way responsible for Carla's death. Maddi sat in her chair dumbfounded and unsure what next to do. She wasn't yet clear where Mr. Stanze stood with all of this, so she allowed him to continue.

"Carla thought the world of you, doctor. You were sort of like a mom—or an aunt, if you will—that she didn't have. I was always so grateful for that."

Mr. Stanze got quiet once again, this time trying to keep from crying. He got his emotions under control and went on.

"I should've told you that night, but I was just so angry—not sure at who—at God, I suppose. The ER doc had asked about a family history of a blood clot or stroke, and I absently had told him about Vivian. He started talking about how Carla should never have been on birth control pills with that history in the family. Suddenly I realized that I had given him a false impression. Before I could correct it though, the doctor had left the room and I was overwhelmed with my grief and the loss of beautiful little Carla."

At this Mr. Stanze burst into tears and Maddi sat quietly by, allowing him to cry, as he clearly needed to do. Finally, he once again pulled himself together and continued.

"I needed you to know that nothing you did or didn't do could have prevented Carla from dying—and I know she would be devastated to think you blamed yourself in any way." Mr. Stanze paused, and then concluded what he had come to say.

"I need to go now. I thank you so much for the kindness you showed to Carla throughout her life." With that, Mr. Stanze stood and walked to the door.

Maddi stood as well, opening the door for him.

"Thank you for coming by, Mr. Stanze. A burden has definitely been lifted for me, and I can't thank you enough."

Mr. Stanze simply nodded, turned, and walked out the door.

Maddi sat back down in her seat and began contemplating what had just occurred. Yes, she could now let herself "off the hook" for thinking she had contributed to Carla's death, but she knew, nonetheless, that her actions could have very well caused such a thing to occur. Suddenly she felt the huge burden she carried and the massive responsibility she bore everyday for each patient that walked in her door. Suddenly she realized it was too much. She knew—right then—that she couldn't do this job, this calling, any longer. The pain she felt the last several months had been too great. The fact that a simple mistake could put her there again was more than she could bear. This "practice" of medicine had taken a toll on her greater than she was able to give. She would have to leave this profession that she loved, somehow, and soon.

Maddi knew that she somehow had to change things not only for herself, but for the practice of medicine as well. Soon after, she was approached by the local Party Chairman about running to fill the seat of a retiring Representative. Even though Maddi had no experience with being a candidate or running an election, the Chairman felt she would be excellent. She was somewhat well-known in Evansville and she was very well-thought of by all who knew her.

At first, Maddi was hesitant, but soon the idea and the opportunity for a much-needed change captured Maddi's imagination and her enthusiasm. She decided to jump into the race and she approached the election with emotion and fire.

The election wound up being quite close—Maddi's opponent was a well-known attorney from neighboring Boonville—but Maddi somehow managed to win her seat by a narrow margin. She came to Washington two months later, ready to change the world.

Washington D.C. in January is a dreary, cold place—but the minute Maddi arrived she felt warm and invigorated. She loved everything about it—the buildings, the people, the history, and she knew she had found her place in the world. Washington D.C. is where Cynthia Madison was meant to be.

She was only a Representative for a short time before an unexpected death of one of the United States senator created an opening that Maddi was encouraged to fill. Once again, it was the local party Chairman who encouraged Maddi to run for the open Senate seat. Although she was hesitant, she decided to give it a go. Maddi knew she would have much greater influence for change as a United States Senator.

The campaign was somewhat nasty—things were brought up on both sides that had nothing to do with legislating—but somehow in the end Maddi ended up on top. Senator Madison was ready to change things. And, because of her experiences as a physician, she knew she had to start with health care. And tort reform. To do this, Senator Madison would eventually have to take on one of the largest, most powerful lobbies in Washington D.C.—the Trial Lawyers.

Maddi quickly did her homework. The American Trial Lawyers Association was created in 1946, actually starting as a group of Worker's Compensation lawyers. Their effectiveness as a group became a magnet for other attorneys with different interests and—in 1972—the lawyers all joined together to become the Association of Trial Lawyers of America—also known as ATLA. Their headquarters was located in Washington, in historic Georgetown. They stated their mission as "the promotion of justice and fairness for injured persons, safeguarding victims' rights—particularly the right to trial by jury—and strengthening the civil justice system through education and disclosure of information critical to public health and safety."

However, the most interesting thing as far as Maddi was concerned was that since 1990 the litigation industry in America had contributed a staggering

$470 million to federal campaigns. This huge amount had made the lobby very influential, and a force to be reckoned with. Taking them on was not going to be an easy task. But Maddi knew it had to be done.

CHAPTER VII

Hank couldn't believe what he was reading. The front page of a local Cleveland paper was boldly asking—"Is This How We Get Tort Reform?" Apparently, a large group of doctors in Columbus, Ohio had simply quit their practices. According to the article, 26 doctors from the Columbus area had decided to simply walk away from their life's work—from their practices that many of them had been building for decades—in an effort to protest what was rapidly becoming a no-win situation for doctors in Ohio, and throughout America.

"Doctors in the Columbus area have decided—en masse—to just walk away from their practices—many after having built those practices for decades. One doctor was quoted as saying 'I can't do this anymore. I can't wake up every morning at 3:00 am worrying about my patients, and then walk into the office the next day worrying about whether I'll be sued that day.'

"The doctors indicate that they are tired of a system that threatens their life's work and their life's savings on a daily basis. They can no longer enjoy what they are doing because the threat of liability and loss hangs over them too greatly. The same doctor put it this way: 'I know of no other profession where the threat of liability is as great, or as personal, as it is in medicine. Every day we make 50 plus decisions, each one potentially landing us in a malpractice suit. Bad outcomes are now the equivalent of negligence, and we are sitting ducks out here praying that our patients don't have bad outcomes. Of course, bad outcomes can't always be avoided. So we are essentially in a no-win situation.'

Doctors, by law, are not able to unionize or strike, so these doctors have concluded that their only course of action is to quit. They all seem to say the same thing: basically, that as much as they love the profession of medicine, they can no longer tolerate the down-side risk of liability that hangs over them so greatly these days.

Patients affected by their doctor's decision to quit are devastated. Some are saddened by a legal system gone awry, while others feel the doctors are aban-

doning them. One patient has threatened a lawsuit to that effect, failing to see the irony of such an action. Many of the doctors refused to be interviewed for this article, and it is unclear what any of them plan to do now that they have left their life's work."

Hank was stunned. He immediately understood however. He couldn't believe what he was feeling, but he knew that he too had lately considered such a move. He had already pretty much decided to quit doing the nursing home work he so loved. He had been mulling the idea around for weeks, but his decision was finalized by a happenstance internet search.

Hank was trying to understand the litigation process he was dealing with, and had done a quick internet search of trial lawyers. He wound up at the American Trial Lawyers Association website. On there he saw an entire section devoted to nursing homes and their potential for lawsuits by any enterprising young attorney. Hank was disgusted.

He also had to face the reality that in the nursing home setting there were just too many people caring for a patient and the doctor was responsible for everyone's actions. In other words, the minimally trained nursing aide was acting under the legal responsibility of the physician, who had no supervisory role to play.

He knew that the situation was perfect for a lawsuit—much like the one he was already in—and so he knew he had to quit. He hadn't told anyone yet—it was simply too painful. He also had to consult an attorney to make sure he left without "abandoning" anyone.

He was becoming more and more depressed. He had talked to Jenny a time or two, and she had encouraged him to see a counselor. He had been unwilling. But, he knew his life was suffering from his lawsuit and his depression. He just wanted it all to be over.

He contacted the nursing home director 5 days later and informed her of his decision to quit providing nursing home care, effective 90 days from the current date. The director was shocked and saddened.

"Dr. Clarkson. You are so good at what you do here. How can you leave us? And why?"

Hank just shook his head. "I don't know, Jeanie, things have just gotten out of hand. I'm so busy and I just can't seem to find the time anymore."

Jeanie and Hank both knew that was a lie. But, they both let it be.

Two weeks later, Hank was in his office going through his mail, when something caught his eye.

∾

"Are you frustrated with the liability system as it now stands? Would you like to be a part of changing this system for good? If so, I would like to hear from you. I have undertaken the massive task of changing forever the way the legal system works in this country and could use your help. If you are interested, please contact me through my senate office at. 1-202-555-3418

Sincerely,

Senator Cynthia Madison"

Hank couldn't believe it. His old friend, Maddi was pursuing meaningful tort reform! Hank had gone to med school with Maddi many years earlier. They had always liked one another and had often studied together. He knew she was interested in politics and had heard she was a Representative, but he had no idea she had become a Senator.

He wondered what her plan actually was. How could anybody ever fix this corrupt system? Most of the legislators were attorneys at one time, and many of them were still bankrolled to some degree by the Trial Lawyers of America. How on earth could that system be changed. One thing Hank did know was that if anybody could change it, Maddi could.

Maddi and Hank had first met one another in anatomy lab. They were partners and had been given a cadaver with an abdominal mesh in place, an interwoven piece of material placed in the abdomen in order to help avoid recurrent abdominal hernias. This of course made the dissection more difficult and more confusing. There were two other students with them on this cadaver, and the four of them spent many a night together dissecting and studying the cadaver.

Maddi was always the one who kept them all going when they felt they couldn't do any more.

"Come on, guys, just another few minutes. Each of us take a section and we'll educate the other three on what we've done." Eventually, with this approach, all four managed to learn gross anatomy, and quite well as it turned out. None of the four were at the top of the class, but all four did better than average. Maddi was sort of their cheerleader. She had a way of inspiring them. Perhaps she could do that now. Hank hoped so. He decided to call her office.

"Senator Madison's office. My name is Phil. Can I help you?"

"Yes. My name is Dr. Henry Clarkson, and I have recently received correspondence from the senator regarding Tort Reform. I am interested in hearing more about what the senator has in mind and possibly assisting if I can."

"Thank you so much for calling, Dr. Clarkson. I am sure the senator will be very glad to hear from you. She is currently in session, but I will give her this message and I know she will be in touch with you soon. If she were to want you to come to Washington would that be something you might be able to do?"

Hank thought for a moment, and then smiled at the thought of leaving town for a while and turning his frustration into meaningful action.

"Yes, I think I could arrange that."

"Very good. I'll let her know you called. What is the best way to reach you?"

"Well, I spend most of my time at my office," this had become more true lately, Hank was sad to think—"and that would be the easiest place to get me." Hank proceeded to give Phil his office number, as well as his home number, and left it that he would wait for Senator Madison to contact him.

He wondered if she would.

CHAPTER VIII

The lead article in a Phoenix newspaper screamed at Jeremy while he was having his coffee early on a Saturday morning. He'd overslept—he did that often anymore—having stayed up late the night before doing research and drinking beer. The lawsuit—and all that went with it—had taken a toll on Jeremy, and he was finding it more and more difficult to shut off his brain at night. The beer had seemed to help. He felt foggy this morning, but the headline immediately snapped him into focus.

"LOCAL PHYSICIAN GROUP WALKS AWAY FROM PRACTICE"

"In a surprising move, which mirrors several others made around the country of late, a large group of Phoenix physicians have simply closed their doors to a practice establishment that had been in the Phoenix area since the early 1950's. The 54 doctors and all their affiliates have simply quit their practices, reacting to what they refer to as "the impossible climate of litigation" that they say currently exists. They site statistics which show that over 50% of physicians have had at least 1 law—suit filed against them, and many have had more than one.

"As one physician, who chose to remain nameless, put it: "I know many people think that only 'bad' doctors get sued, but how on earth can anyone think that over half of us are 'bad?' It doesn't make any sense, and it is such a brutal process when it happens to you—regardless of the outcome."

"Other physicians in the practice echoed his sentiments, and one added: "What other profession carries such an incredible risk? Everyday we are put in a position of making 50 to 100 decisions—some of them life-threatening—and for every one of those decisions we could face a million dollar law—suit. It is ridiculous to think that any of us can continue to survive such a system."

"Several local attorneys were interviewed and one offered the following comment which seemed to sum up the attorney group's point of view. "It is a shame the doctors have chosen to quit and abandon their patients in this fash-

ion. Because of only a handful of bad doctors, this entire group has chosen to leave their patients without any adequate health care. It appears to me—and to my fellow attorney friends—that this move is akin to defiance of the oath that these doctors have sworn to uphold, and, by leaving their patients like this they are probably open to some form of litigation.'"

Jeremy took a big breath and let it out slowly. What he was reading was beyond belief to him. He felt both anger and humor at the actions of his colleagues. How could they quit? Didn't they—like he—sign on for the long haul? What about the patients that needed them? Where would they go? What would they do? Jeremy sat and thought for a long time. Finally, he knew what he would do. He would go talk to the Medical Director of the facility and try to understand what could make these doctors do this. When he stood up to go get ready to pursue his day, papers fell to the floor. He looked down and saw a myriad of papers related to the lawsuit involving Diacam and—of course—Jeremy Bourne. He sat back down and sighed. He didn't need to go speak with the Medical Director. He knew exactly why these doctors had chosen to do this.

Jeremy walked into an office overflowing with patients and messages and people that needed him. He was preparing to get to work and quickly glanced at his mail. Among various legal papers, and letters from specialists, and advertisements, and medical journals, he saw a letter from a Senator. Cynthia Madison, Senator from Indiana. He wasn't sure what to make of it, but quickly opened it, preparing to find an empty request for money to finance some agenda. However, the letter quickly grabbed his attention.

"I am looking for any physicians who might be interested in helping me try to change the litigation environment in this country. Having been a physician myself not too long ago, I appreciate greatly the burden that malpractice places on physicians and their practices. I am willing to take on the most powerful lobbying group in the country, and—with your help—might actually make medicine an honorable and enjoyable pursuit once again. Our country is quickly destroying itself while lawyers profit on both sides of every issue. This situation cannot continue and I have decided that I can no longer stand by idly and watch this destruction occur. I am not seeking money. I am interested in finding physicians who have the passion and the drive to assist me in my efforts. If you or a colleague of yours is interested in assisting me in this effort, please contact me at my Senate offices, at 1-

202-555-3418. I am looking forward to hearing from as many of you as I can and—together—I know we can make a difference.

Sincerely,

Senator Cynthia Madison

Late that afternoon, after Jeremy had seen all his patients, and reviewed his charts for legal mishaps, he sat back and grabbed his telephone. He dialed Senator Madison's phone number. After 3 rings, it was answered.

"This is Senator Madison's office. Phil speaking. Can I help you?"

"Yes, my name is Jeremy Bourne, and I am interested in helping the senator fix the legal system in this country."

And, with that, Jeremy Bourne had signed on.

CHAPTER IX

Dr. Jackson received his request from Senator Madison on a Saturday morning as well. It caught his eye immediately. Cynthia Madison. Maddi? It had to be. He knew Maddi from their days as interns when they both rotated through the extensive Cleveland Clinic network.

Maddi was always outgoing and well-liked by everyone and she made the difficult hours and the challenging responsibilities more tolerable and even more interesting. Wilson had always felt a little out of place, being from New England, but Maddi had made him feel so comfortable. She introduced him to the other interns and made him feel a part of things. His rotation was only a month long, and he was anxious to get back to the "East Coast," but he always felt like Maddi was a friend of his.

And here she was, a Senator, writing him a letter.

He opened the letter and began reading. He then began chuckling. What on earth was Maddi up to? How did she think she could really change anything? But then, Wilson had to think back at other major changes in the country that many doubted could occur. And he, Wilson Jackson III, being a respected Obstetrician, while being African American, was one of them.

He picked up the phone, and called the Senator's office. Wilson Jackson III had signed on.

CHAPTER X

Maddi could not believe the response she was getting to her letter. Doctors from around the country were calling in, and Maddi actually had to dedicate a second, and then a third line to handle all the calls. She was surprised to see that she recognized some of the names. She initially had intended on calling each physician personally, but soon realized that she would not have the time for such an endeavor.

Within 2 weeks of sending out her letter, she had heard from over 2000 physicians. She decided she would try to arrange a forum and get all interested physicians in one location. She settled on Indiana for the location, due to its central position in the country, as well as the fact that it was her home state. She had her staff rent out a large conference center with a hotel attached in Indianapolis. The Hyatt Regency was thrilled to cooperate, and, due to the large number of physicians—and others—expected to attend, Maddi also made sure other hotels in the area were available.

She picked a day in July—sometime after the fourth—thinking it was probably the slowest time for physicians, and they might be more apt to attend.

She had her chief of staff, Phil Mason, whom she had brought with her from Indiana, coordinate the effort. Phil recruited several other staffers to begin the process of writing each physician with details concerning the forum. They entitled the forum "Taking Back America" and began constructing invitations and directions to coordinate the effort.

Maddi's efforts were soon being discussed in circles other than those involving physicians. The media—and many attorney organizations—began taking note of what Maddi was attempting to do. An attorney group in Indianapolis had actually discussed it at their last meeting. One of the lawyers in that group worked in downtown Indianapolis, and was friends with an employee who worked directly with the Manager of the Hyatt. The two were talking one day, and the employee, Jimmy Parsons, mentioned something about the huge forum being organized by Senator Madison. The Attorney, Kevin Clayborne, was curious.

"What's the forum about?"

"I'm not sure, it's entitled "Taking Back America" and involves a bunch of doctors."

"Hmm. That's sort of interesting, don't you think?"

"I guess so. All I know, is that if it is half as big as I think it is going to be, we're gonna' make out like bandits."

Kevin than excused himself and went to phone his friend in D.C. After being put on hold, and then transferred several times his call was answered.

"Trial Lawyers of America. How can I help you?"

"Could I please speak with Roger Clairy?"

"May I ask who is calling?"

"Just tell him it's Kevin from 'back home.'" After a few moments the line was picked up. "Roger Clairy here. How can I help you?"

"Hey Roger, it's me, Kevin."

"Yeah Kevin, what can I do for you?"

"What can you tell me about a Senator Madison, and a forum she is planning with a bunch of doctors?"

"Well, I don't know much, but it's something about tort reform. You know, the same old thing. But I've got some guys on it from the Association, just in case it starts to amount to something. Don't worry, the Senator won't get anywhere with this."

"Don't you think you should shut it down?"

"Nah, let's give them all an illusion that they actually have some power. It will be easy, and much more fun, to shut them down after they've gotten some prominence."

"Allright, Roger, whatever you think. I'll go ahead and be the eyes and ears here in Indi."

"That would be great, Kevin. Let me know if anything interesting comes up, okay?"

"Yeah, okay."

Kevin hung up the phone and proceeded to contact his friend at the Hyatt. Jimmy Parsons, whom he had known since they were kids, helped run the audio visual props for all the major conventions. Kevin knew he would have an inside scoop on whatever was taking place with the forum. He dialed the number and on the third ring, the phone was anwered. Kevin heard a crisp and nasally voice on the other end. "Hello?"

"Hey, Jimmy, Kevin here. Listen, I want you to kind of keep me up to date on how that forum is coming along. Can you do that?"

"Sure Kevin. I'll let you know as it moves along."

Kevin Clayborne was following the planning of the forum eagerly. He just felt that something big was happening here and he was so excited that he was going to be the one to blow it wide open. He'd been a mediocre attorney his entire adult life and was ready for some overdue recognition. He had spent his whole life trying to achieve his potential. The fact that no one else seemed to appreciate that fact didn't ever occur to him. He'd become an attorney for the sole purpose of achieving power, and he knew his destiny was to be a very powerful and influential man someday. He'd made up his mind long ago that no one would stand in his way.

Kevin felt a little betrayed that his friend in D.C. hadn't helped him along any more than he had, but he knew that this was his chance. When Roger Clairy had been selected by the Trial Lawyer's Association for the spot in D.C. Kevin was sure it was only a matter of time before his old friend would call him to come join him. The fact that—five years later—he had not done so weighed heavy on Kevin. But this was it. His way in. And, his way out of his dull life in Indianapolis. But he knew he would need an insider's perspective. He had to somehow get involved in this forum. He tossed around several different ideas, but gradually settled on what he decided was the most brilliant of plans.

Several days later Kevin was sitting idly in his office and decided to make the phone call.

"Hello. Is this Senator Madison's office? My name is Kevin Clayborne and I'm an attorney from the Senator's home state. Now, before you hang up on this attorney-" (Kevin could be so charming when he wanted to be)—" I would love to offer my services to the senator for her upcoming forum. Although I'm an attorney, I can't help but think that we are headed in the wrong direction, and I'd love to be part of an effort to change things."

The response Kevin received on the other end was exactly what he had hoped for. Phil Mason agreed to take his name and number and agreed to communicate his desire to help to the Senator. He was certain she would be thrilled to have his input. Kevin Clayborne, Attorney-at-Law, was signed on.

CHAPTER XI

Amanda McKinney was going about her very busy day in the clinic in Columbia when her receptionist informed her she had a phone call.

"Who is it, Jane? I'm really busy right now."

"She says her name is Cynthia Madison. Senator Madison."

Amanda was surprised. She had received the letter from Maddi but did not have the energy to pursue such a quest. Actually, since the lawsuit, she barely had energy to get through her day. But now Maddi was calling her personally. Her curiosity was too great. She would take the call.

"Put her through, Jane. I'll take it in the back." She picked up the phone. "This is Dr. McKinney. What can I do for you?"

"Amanda. It's Maddi! How the hell are you?" She was always so upbeat. It was difficult for Amanda to deal with right now. She tried to sound upbeat. "I'm just great, Maddi. How are you?"

"Well, I'm overwhelmed at the moment. And I need some help. I need a clear-thinking, non-agenda person to bounce some things off of."

"Well, why call me?" That sounded stupid. Amanda was terrible at pretending everything was fine.

Maddi continued. "Because you are that person. The one who is always honest, but kind. And your agenda is always the right one. Amanda, I've taken on something bigger than I ever imagined, and I need some help. I'm one step away from being totally overwhelmed."

"But what do you want me to do? I'm really busy down here in Columbia. That's why I didn't respond to your letter" Amanda lied.

"Well, I'm planning a rather large forum to deal with malpractice and litigation issues and I would love to have your help. I know you're busy, but I just want you on board. I want to be able to pick up the phone and get your feedback. Like we used to in med school."

Amanda remembered med school and had to smile. She truly did love Maddi. And they had had so much fun together. But they had lost touch after graduation, and sometimes it had just seemed like too much of an effort to keep in touch with everyone.

"All right. I suppose you could call if you need some help. I'm not sure I'll be very useful right now. The malpractice thing is certainly a bitch. Just ask me."

"You're kidding. They've gone after you too? That is exactly what I'm trying to change. I'm so tired of seeing good doctors fall victim to this legal monster. You will be such an asset to this effort. I am so glad you are willing to help. I'll keep you posted on what is going on. And I'll give you a private number where you can get me quick if you need me." Maddi proceeded to give Amanda the cell phone number and the two of them said their goodbyes.

Amanda went back to work. But, she had to admit, she felt a little better about things. Maddi had always had that affect. And Amanda was going to help her with her valiant, though quixotic, effort. Amanda McKinney was signed on.

CHAPTER XII

The class-action lawsuit against the manufactures of Diacam, and those physicians that had prescribed it was gaining steam. The law firm of Wyatt, Hanson, Richards and Schultz was aggressively pursuing their claim. They had rounded up numerous clients through their efforts at The Coyote Tavern and were immersed in the discovery process. All their associates were busily consuming billable hours and staying into the wee hours of the night finding case law to support all their allegations. They were all giddy at the prospect of being part of such a lucrative endeavor.

Meanwhile, Jeremy and Doc Jones were trying desperately to stay above water. Half of their patients were showing up less and less as they became involved in the legal action against Dr. Bourne and the Clinic. The other half of the patients was now struggling once again with their diabetes since Diacam had been taken off the market. The enthusiasm that Jeremy had brought to this Pima community had been changed. The softball had stopped and the people were once again spending their time either in the Coyote Tavern or locked in their homes. Jeremy was devastated by the entire process. He tried not to let it affect him, but it did. It drained him of energy. And it deprived his patients of a significant part of him.

One good thing that did seem to be occurring from this situation or, perhaps in spite of it—was his relationship with Katy. They had gotten quite close through all of this and were spending more and more time together. Katy had helped Jeremy keep it together many days.

Depositions had begun and they were brutal. The lawyers approached their clients, as well as one another, with a vengeance. Then, of course, when the day was done, the lawyers left together with pats on the back and laughter accompanying them to their big sedans.

Jeremy hated them all. His hatred drove him to continue his involvement in Senator Madison's efforts. She had planned a forum, to be held in July, in Indianapolis. Jeremy couldn't wait. He had always been a dreamer, and he knew that Senator Madison's efforts would only succeed against all odds. He didn't care. He knew that if these efforts didn't succeed, he would be gone from the practice of medicine.

CHAPTER XIII

Physicians were continuing their exodus from practice at an alarming rate. It had gotten to the point where the national media was taking note. There had been two articles in the New York Times, and a major national news magazine had done a cover story with the headline "What Will You Do When Your Doctor Leaves?"

Senator Madison was getting a little bit of this press and was interviewed for a major national news magazine Article. She was quoted as saying, "What you're seeing right now is just the tip of the iceberg. Soon, not only doctors will throw up their hands and ask themselves why they are offering their services only to be attacked by the wolves known as trial attorneys. Soon, you'll not only have lost your doctor, but your teacher and your grocer as well. If we don't stop these lawyers soon, our society will no longer exist as we know it." Although this view was portrayed as "extremist" it had taken hold with a number of individuals. Politicians were being forced to discuss "The Lawyer Problem," and the President himself had actually mentioned "Tort Reform" in his State of the Union Address. A groundswell, though small, was forming.

Maddi was doing all she could to take advantage of what she saw as a once-in-a-lifetime opportunity. She knew that if she was ever going to make a change in the way lawyers operated in America that now was the time to do it. She began trying to elicit support from her fellow Senators. Most were reluctant at best to get involved—many of them were lawyers themselves. But there were a few that couldn't deny the fact that the profession of law in America had become a corrupt and conflicted pursuit. And Maddi continued to work with John McCargish. She knew she would need his help if she truly wanted things to change.

As the time was getting closer for the forum, Maddi had seven senators signed on who were strong advocates for the changes she was trying to make. She had many who supported her efforts but wanted to keep a low profile, and she had a few very vocal opponents.

Probably the most out-spoken opponent was a gentleman from Arizona by the name of Sam Richards. He felt things were just fine with the legal system in America—and, he felt that the lawyers were the only ones that kept corrupt individuals in check. He firmly believed that the "greatness of America has more to do with lawyers and their efforts than with any other group of individuals in this fine country." Maddi could see what she was up against. And, of course, not surprisingly, Senator Richards had many attorneys aligned with him, including those from his old law firm, Wyatt, Hanson, Richards, and Schultz.

Maddi talked back and forth with John McCargish about once a week, keeping him up to date on the forum and her efforts to enlist support. He was working on some of the legal specifics related to her goals and methods of attaining the changes she was setting forth. He had not come up with much, however, feeling somewhat compromised as he tried to keep the supreme court justices uninvolved. Although this was disappointing, Maddi found herself looking forward to her meetings with Mr. McCargish a little more than she thought she should. There was just something about those eyes. And the way his crooked smile made her smile, inside and out. She was curious about his life, and what he was doing in D.C. Finally, after putting it off for weeks, she asked him.

"So, John, tell me about you." That sounded so stupid, she thought. "What brought you to Washington? Why with the Supremes?"

After what seemed like way too long, John responded. "Well, there's not really much to tell. But, I'm here, and I like it—today." And that was it. John McCargish would offer nothing more, and somehow Maddi felt that that was all she was going to get from him. She would have to leave it at that—for now.

Maddi was flying back and forth to Indiana, trying to coordinate what had become a well-advertised and much-talked about forum on Malpractice Litigation in America. There was a lot of "buzz" going on about the issue, and Maddi knew she had to run a flawless convention if she wanted to advance the cause.

One day, while she was canvassing the Hyatt convention center, she was approached by a man wearing a somewhat ill-fitting suit, with mussed hair.

When he came close she could detect an abundance of aftershave and she had to step away in order to avoid the need to hold her breath.

"Can I help you?" she asked him.

"You certainly can." His voice sounded like that of a two-pack-a-day smoker—hoarse and graveled. Maddi cleared her throat. He went on. "My name is Kevin Clayborne, and I'm an attorney interested in your efforts here." Maddi recognized the name. There were only a few attorneys who had called expressing an interest in her forum and she knew Kevin Clayborne was one of them.

"What can I do for you, Kevin Clayborne?"

"Well, I was thinking that I could help you draft some of your legislative proposals. After all, nobody knows the law like a lawyer." He chuckled a deep laugh that made Maddi's skin crawl. "And I have a few ideas myself that might be useful. Perhaps you'd like to hear about them? Maybe over dinner tonight?"

Maddi was certain that she did not want to have dinner, or lunch or breakfast for that matter, with Kevin Clayborne. But she was curious what he was offering. And what his interest was for getting involved in something thought to be rather unpopular for most attorneys to involve themselves in.

"How about a cup of coffee—right now?" she offered.

"Well, if that's the best I can do, okay." he chuckled again. "There's a place next door. Let's go."

CHAPTER XIV

The Headline in a prominent Boston newspaper was larger than usual, and seemed to be screaming at Wilson

"Large Doctor's Organization Quitting in Protest"

"Last Friday, 124 doctors from the Heritage Hospital and Clinic facility here in Boston walked away from their desks—and their patients—in a show of solidarity with their fellow physicians across the country. In a move that continues to surprise and disappoint patients across the country, doctors are quitting their practices, stating that it is the only way they have to communicate their disdain for a system that threatens their very existence on a daily basis.

The Medical Director of the group, Dr. Raymond Carter, insists that this is the only avenue available to doctors to voice their objections to a system gone awry, as well as protect themselves and any current assets from future litigation.

"We are not allowed to strike in the traditional sense of the word, and we seem to be unable to effectively combat the large, lucrative industry of litigation in this country. We no longer enjoy what we do—there are too many barriers and too many risks every single day that we walk into the minute we enter the office or the hospital. It is no longer worth it—I am sorry to say—to do what we love at the risk of losing all that we have worked so hard for. This is indeed a bold step, but the only step available to us."

"Several patients were interviewed as they were leaving the facility for the last time. Once such patient was an elderly lady named Ruby Watson. She had this to say.

"It's just a shame. I understand that the doctors are frustrated, but they make lots of money and should be able to put up with the occasional lawsuit. Besides, only the bad doctors usually get sued. Leaving us in the cold like this is unacceptable."

"Another physician from the organization responded to the above comments with the following.

"We sent every patient a letter stating our intentions over 30 days ago. We offered our assistance in helping them find another physician and we reassured them that we would help in any way possible to make this easier for them. We are all aware of what it is like to change doctors and medical facilities, and we will do all we can to assist our patients in this transitional process. If it were true that "only the bad doctors got sued," then we would certainly be able to stick it out in this profession. But what we are seeing now is that any doctor is fair game for a system which rewards attorneys on both sides of the litigation battle. Any bad outcome now immediately creates thoughts of lawsuits regardless of the physician's responsibility for that bad outcome. There are an excess of very hungry lawyers looking for a way to make a living. Doctors—because of the perverseness of this system—provide them that opportunity. I can't go to work each day, make 50-plus decisions in that day, answer an endless number of questions in that day—knowing that any one of those decisions or answered questions may land me in litigation. I'm done. I'm outa' here."

Wilson Jackson III was reading the article in disbelief. "They've done it," he thought to himself. "They've actually done it. What every one of us has been thinking about of late, they've done." He knew exactly what that last doctor was talking about. He too had had it with worrying about every decision and worrying about every outcome for fear of litigation. It took all good things out of the profession and made it much more difficult to tolerate the bad things in the profession. He—Wilson Jackson III—knew it was only a matter of time before he too would be forced to quit.

But, how could he? How could he let down the legacy of his uncle before him? How could he so disappoint his family in that way? At least now, he knew he could not. So, he went to work each day, trying desperately to love what he used to love. Trying desperately to forget about the lawsuits and the people behind them. People he had cared for—well. Trusts that had been broken—not by him—but by them. Each day brought him closer to hanging it up and walking away. But he knew he couldn't do that yet. So, he anxiously awaited a forum in Indianapolis in July where he hoped and prayed things would begin to change.

CHAPTER XV

Roger Clairy had just arrived to work on a beautiful May morning in our nation's capital. The cherry blossoms were in bloom, and the magnificent buildings—the Capitol, the White House, the monuments—all surrounded him, making him a player in the biggest powerhouse in the world. He loved D.C. He was still in awe over his amazing luck in acquiring his position with the Trial Lawyer's Association. Not all luck. After all, luck is the residue of design. And Roger was all about design. He had designed things well and here he was. A scrawny little boy from the Heartland, living it up in D.C. He knew if he played his cards right, he could possibly advance and become the "important person" he knew he was always meant to be. And he would play his cards right. He always had.

He began sifting through the day's mail tossing correspondence here, and litigation advice there, when something caught his eye. A letter from Indianapolis. From an acquaintance of his. Kevin Clayborne. What could that leach want? He opened the letter. A picture fell out. Kevin was in the picture, sitting with a senator. Roger couldn't believe it. Kevin was sitting with Senator Cynthia Madison. They were having coffee together. There was a brief note on a small piece of paper included with the picture.

"Just wanted you to know, Roger. I'm IN."

Roger couldn't believe it. That pain in the ass senator was having coffee with his old friend Kevin. How interesting. He immediately saw the positive ramifications of this for his own agenda. He now had an inside source to one of the biggest thorns in the side of the ATLA. Kevin really could be his eyes and ears. And, with any cleverness, they could sabotage the whole damn thing. And, make Senator Madison look ridiculous in the process. Roger was salivating at the thought of it. The forum was only a month and a half away. Roger had to get busy.

Meanwhile, Kevin had made great use of his "coffee date" with Senator Madison. He had talked her into the picture by telling her how much his sister adored her. What he wouldn't give for a picture with her—otherwise, Lydia wouldn't believe that he had in fact had a cup of coffee with the renowned Senator Madison. Maddi agreed, although she never thought of herself as renowned. Even though Kevin had not convinced her to go to dinner with him any time soon, he did convince her that he was a supportive ally in her efforts against the "big, bad attorneys." She had given him the assignment of writing up supportive case law—along the lines of Stark from California—concerning conflict of interest issues with attorneys and their goals at trial. Whereas Stark had focused his energies on the medical community, Maddi felt confident his same arguments would be helpful in battling the abuses of the legal community.

Kevin—of course, to himself—thought this was a ridiculous approach. How were there conflict of interest issues when each lawyer was fighting for their client's rights?—but he nonetheless enthusiastically told Maddi he would check it out and write it up. They arranged to get together in 2 weeks to review what he had found. All the while, he was grinning to himself, as each conversation between the two of them would give him further ammunition to sabotage her entire effort.

He knew Roger would want to know all of this, but he certainly didn't want to give him everything. Kevin wanted to make sure he profited from this effort. He would send him the picture and let that speak for itself. His guess was that it wouldn't be long before Roger would call him and give him the responsibility—and the respect—to work on this from the inside. He would become invaluable to the ATLA.

CHAPTER XVI

Mr. Stark is a gentleman from California who apparently has had a bad experience with physicians and hospitals in the past. This is, at least, what everyone assumes, considering he seems to spend his entire legislative life—currently as a California Representative—trying to "make sure" that doctors never profit too greatly from their medical pursuits. He focuses mainly on conflict of interest issues—doctors shouldn't own xray facilities that they then send their patients to; or—doctors should never receive payment from the hospital—for even legitimate real estate ventures—that isn't consistent with "fair market value." He has actually become quite a thorn in the side of eager, profit-minded physicians.

Maddi felt that their were some good things about the Stark Laws—for example, the laws eliminated incentives based on greed that some doctors had involved themselves in. But, the laws had also altered the availability of highly specific, technical equipment that the doctors were uniquely qualified to provide. At the end of the day, like most things, there were good and bad aspects of Stark Laws.

Maddi was convinced that the legal profession would stand to gain from similar laws. She felt their moral compass could be restored if they were prohibited from doing the very things they currently do to acquire greater wealth. She felt that the fact that they were paid by "billable hours" meant that every case was better for each side if it took lots of hours to resolve. She also felt that—because their payment system was often based on contingency—they were always better off pursuing nearly every claim—no matter how ridiculous—if they were guaranteed some form of payment.

The Lawyers countered that contingency payments made the system fair by not paying them for losing. At the end of the day, however, most entities would settle, thereby providing some sort of payment to the lawyers—no matter what. Thirty to forty percent of the judgement amount, as a matter of fact.

Maddi felt that if you ended conflict of interest issues, and if you created a "loser pays" system, that you could reform—and elevate—the profession of law by leaps and bounds. Her goal was to create "Maddi Laws" that would govern the business of law in much the same way that "Stark Laws" had done for the business of medicine.

She had assigned Kevin Clayborne the task of supporting all of the above—particularly the conflict of interest issues—with case law and historical data, so as to bolster the case she was trying to make through the court system. She was confident the entire process would eventually be evaluated at the Supreme Court level and she was so glad she had John McCargish on board.

She felt she was truly creating an opportunity for these changes to occur, but, she also knew that she was going up against a system of attorneys that wanted very badly for nothing to change. Maddi knew she would have the fight of her life ahead of her.

CHAPTER XVII

More and more physicians across the country were quitting their practices. This was getting greater attention from the mainstream press, and Maddi and her forum were becoming quite famous. She was interviewed frequently on CNN and FOX News, and was also mentioned repeatedly in the New York Times and other very prominent newspapers. There was a high degree of skepticism concerning any success Maddi might have, but the potential for a very dramatic fight was everything the modern media could ever hope for. This was going to be "the fight of the century" and was being covered as such. Maddi was regularly in touch with several key physicians throughout the country—most of them friends she'd met in college or in med school—and everybody was excited about the potential for national recognition of a problem that was quickly ruining the practice of medicine across the country. The physicians—including Maddi—knew that if this effort didn't succeed then the majority of them would quit—like many doctors before them. This effort had to succeed.

Maddi decided to try to get her core group together prior to the forum. She wanted a cohesive message, and she wanted several of her friends to be showcased speakers. She had already agreed to let Kevin Clayborne have a speaking role. She continued to be surprised by his eagerness to so publicly participate in something she was sure was unpopular with his colleagues. The more she thought about it the more she was certain he had some other agenda. But, he had been working tirelessly, and it was so helpful to have the assistance of an attorney in this way. She decided to keep a closer eye on him, but wanted him to continue to be "in the loop" with his litigation knowledge.

Maddi had her assistant Phil contact Dr. Hank Clarkson, Dr. Amanda McKinney, and Dr. Wilson Jackson III to see if they could all come to Washington for the weekend. These were three of her closer friends from the medical profession, and Maddi wanted their help—and their company—as she planned for the forum. Phil called them all and Maddi was delighted that all three were able to get there. They would all stay at the Watergate Hotel, and Maddi arranged to pick them up at the airport Saturday afternoon.

Hank was thrilled with the idea of going to Washington. He had been asked many times over the years to get involved in things like this, but never had he felt so certain that such a thing might truly succeed. This felt different, and it elevated his mood greatly to think about being involved in this effort.

Hank cancelled out his patients and let Jenny know what he was doing. She was quite excited for him—she knew he needed to do something to feel some sense of control over a situation that left him so totally without control.

Hank decided to extend his vacation just a bit into the following week, hoping that he and Maddi could catch up, and also thinking that a little time away would probably help him immensely.

Amanda tried to arrange her schedule to arrive a day earlier than requested, so as to hopefully have the opportunity to spend some time with Maddi before the others came. She only knew Henry Clarkson as a fellow Medical School classmate, but they had never been close, and she didn't know Dr. Jackson at all. She had heard of him however—he was quite prominent in the Ob/Gyn world—and Amanda had read numerous articles where he had been mentioned or interviewed.

Maddi was thrilled that Amanda was coming in early, and cleared her schedule accordingly. It would be so good to see her, and it sounded as though Amanda could use some support.

Wilson Jackson III arranged to fly in Saturday afternoon. Although he practically had to move mountains to get the time away from his practice, he was eventually able to do so, and looked forward to getting together with colleagues and perhaps even making a difference.

Wilson knew one thing for sure—if this effort wasn't successful, he would sooner or later need to leave his beloved profession. The very thought of that made him horribly unhappy. Maddi and her forum must succeed; he knew his future depended on it.

CHAPTER XVIII

Roger Clairy was sitting in his D.C. office at the American Trial Lawyers Association, when his boss, Mr. Frances Buckholtz, walked in accompanied by a very short man with sandy blonde hair which fell straight on his forehead and around his ears, looking as though it needed a trim. From behind the hair, two small eyes looked out, bright green with shadows beneath them, giving him a somewhat sinister appearance.

His eyelids appeared to be half-closed, and he seemed to have a continual glare as he reached out to shake Roger's hand. He was stocky in appearance, and his handshake was strong—almost overdone, as though he was trying to show his strength. Perhaps, even making up for the deficit in his height.

Roger's first impression of this man was not a good one. Buckholtz proceeded to introduce the two men.

"Roger, this is Peter Smith. He has signed on to help us with this litigation issue that Senator Madison is drumming up. Although I don't think it is possible for her to have any real success, I have decided to enlist the help of this gentleman to perhaps persuade the Senator that what she is doing is—how do I put it—not a good idea for her. He has assured me that he can be very persuasive and I have asked him to speak to you about this. You'll be his contact person, and the one to whom he reports. After all, that little bitch is from your home town, so it's sort of your backyard where all this is going on."

Roger wasn't quite sure what to do with this. He almost laughed out loud at Buckholtz' reference to his home town, after all, Buckholtz was from Evansville as well. Besides, what the hell did they need this guy for? Roger—and Kevin—were doing just fine. Although Roger hadn't yet found an opportunity to fill Buckholtz in on their plan, perhaps he could do so soon.

Who was this guy, Smith, anyway? How did he persuade people? Why was Roger the point man on this? Was that a good thing? A compliment? An opportunity? Or, was this situation getting a bit out of hand? Roger decided that he would investigate who this guy was and what it was exactly that he did for a living. But, today was Friday, so he made a mental note to explore the issue first thing Monday morning. In the meantime, he would placate his boss.

"Sure Mr. Buckholtz. I'll be glad to handle this situation." He then made arrangements to meet with Mr. Smith on Monday afternoon. They shook hands and Roger quickly wrapped things up in his office and proceeded to his first martini of the weekend.

The American Trial Lawyers Association had begun to take note of what was going on not only with Senator Madison, but also around the country. The doctors that were quitting were creating quite a bit of commotion, and were shining an unwelcome light on the litigation process.

Articles were being written dissecting the process of a lawsuit, and numbers were being quoted concerning frivolous claims, and how much a lawyer received from a standard million-dollar settlement. Although lawyers were seldom viewed in a favorable light, different individuals and organizations were now vocally maligning them across the country—individuals and organizations that had not been critical of or paid attention to the lawyers and their methods in the past.

Frances Buckholtz knew he couldn't let this stand. He wasn't sure what was needed, but he knew that if he didn't stop Senator Madison and her posse of physicians, his job would be in jeopardy. And he really liked his job. Besides, there were things that had gone on in his past that he knew a persistent Senator might stumble upon if she got too eager. He wondered if Cynthia Madison had any idea that the two of them had "a history" of sorts. He doubted it. After all, it was with her brother, not her. And, by its very nature he doubted that her brother would share the details. Besides, the last thing Frances had heard about Maddi's brother was that he had become a hiking guide and had moved to the Canadian Tundra to live.

Frances hated thinking about Andrew Madison. He tried his best not to do so, but occasionally their history would haunt him, as he remembered what had happened many years before....

Frances Buckholz and Andrew Madison had met a long time ago, in Evansville, Indiana. They were both in high school together and were friends of sorts. During the summers the two of them would work at a state park several hours away as life guards. They were starting their third year at the park, following their senior year. Frances had a friend who was older and was willing to purchase alcohol for him and his friends. He and Andrew would often stay late at the park—after everything had shut down—and drink with a few other friends.

Mrs. Madison was somewhat aware of this, but, in spite of her protests, was unable to stop Andrew from staying after work at the park with Frances. After several lectures, she succeeded in making Andrew see that drinking and hanging out with Frances Buckholtz was leading him in the wrong direction. He finally assured her that he wouldn't let Frances get him into any trouble and that he would refrain from drinking any of the alcohol that Frances' friend brought.

Toward the middle of the summer the two boys were at the park at the end of their day. Frances' "supplier" had once again brought a case of beer for Frances and his friends and he asked Andrew if he wanted to stick around.

"Not tonight, Frances. I promised Mom that I would get in early tonight."

"Suit yourself. You always were a "mama's boy.""

Andrew ignored the comment and quickly tried to finish up with his tasks and get out of there.

There was another friend with them that night, little Bobby Duggan, and he and Frances started drinking and carrying on. They were quickly getting quite drunk over by the lake shore.

Bobby was a year younger than they were but was willing to run errands for Frances so that Frances would allow him to hang out with all of them. Bobby felt important hanging around with the older guys, and would frequently drink way too much alcohol in an effort to impress them.

Andrew finished up in the locker room and was just getting into his car when he heard a scream.

"Andy! Andy! Hurry up! Help me! I can't find Bobby!"

Andrew ran to where the boys had been drinking. "Where are you? Frances, where are you?"

"Over here!" Andrew looked out into the black night and, with the help of a near-full moon, saw Frances waving from the shore, pointing out to the middle of the lake. Andrew looked over at him, and then to where he was pointing. He saw someone struggling in the middle of the lake. He knew it must be Bobby and he jumped in the water and started swimming toward him. Frances had already jumped into the lake and had swam to where Bobby had last gone under. Frances was diving down and surfacing and diving and surfacing when

Andrew reached him. He kept doing this, and Andrew kept hollering at Frances to tell him Bobby's location.

All good lifeguards know that the first thing you do when someone goes under is to mark that spot with something stationary on land. Frances had clearly not done this. He just kept diving under the water, hoping to find his friend. He was having some trouble himself secondary to his alcohol consumption. Andrew started diving as well. After several minutes of this it became clear to both boys that Bobby Duggan had drowned.

Frances started diving for him again, frantically. Andrew screamed at him to stop. "He's drowned, Frances! He's gone!" There was a brief silence, then Frances looked at Andrew. "Holy Christ, Andy, what the hell are we gonna' do now?" Andrew thought for a moment. "We have to let someone know. We have to tell them what has happened here."

"No! We can't tell anyone," said Frances. His expression then changed as he added "besides, if you say anything to anyone about what happened here tonight I will let everyone know that you were involved and responsible just as much as I was—if not more."

Andrew looked back at Frances, the light from the moon reflecting in Frances' narrowed, dark eyes. "You wouldn't do that."

Frances looked back at him, a sinister quality evident as he glared straight back at Andrew. "Hell I wouldn't."

Somehow the scenario surrounding the drowning of Bobby Duggan stayed between the two boys. They denied having seen Bobby Duggan that night and Frances denied having any alcohol. He stated that Andrew had been with him the entire time. Not sure why, Andrew allowed this version of the truth to stand. But their friendship was never the same. Not only did Andrew see a less-favorable side of Frances, but Frances knew what Andrew saw—and, like a mirror, resented Andrew for showing him himself. The two boys went their separate ways and hadn't spoken to one another since. Over time, Frances grew to despise Andrew, simply for his knowledge of the truth.

Frances had come to the ATLA straight out of law school. Actually, he had not had much success finding a suitable job in any notable firm and took on the job with the ATLA until something better came along. But, Frances Buckholtz knew how to play the game, and it wasn't long before he had risen in the ranks of the organization and was doing quite well for himself.

While he was in charge of the organization, they had managed to obtain status and support from lawyers across the country, and were now a force to be reckoned with in Washington politics. This of course made Frances quite important in certain circles—and that was his goal. He had power in D.C.

Senator Cynthia Madison was certainly not going to do anything to diminish that in any way. Frances knew that if he could get her to back down on her "mission" that it wouldn't be long before the doctors would go back to their practices and the lawyers could go back to work suing their asses. Doctors were not good at organizing anyway, always concerned about "the greater good." This had been a disadvantage for them—and an advantage for the trial lawyers—for the last two decades. Frances Buckholz wanted to restore that balance.

He wasn't sure what Mr. Smith had in mind to "persuade" Madison to give up her quest—nor did he want to know—but Smith had been recommended to him by some guys who knew how to get things done. Regardless of Smith's methods, Frances was glad to have him on board. This issue was that important.

CHAPTER XIX

Amanda arrived in Washington on Friday morning, and had already arranged to meet with Maddi in the Watergate lobby. Maddi was there waiting when Amanda arrived, and they gave one another a long and very genuine hug. Amanda was surprised at how good it was to see Maddi. They grabbed a cab and headed down Pennsylvania avenue—past the White House—to a local eatery close to the capitol. They started talking immediately and really only stopped when the waiter took their order.

Amanda filled Maddi in on the details of her malpractice suit, and Maddi listened intently. She only spoke after Amanda had told her everything she could think of about the case.

"What bullshit, Amanda. Why on earth do they go after people like you?"

"Well, I don't suppose they have any knowledge about who I am or what I'm like. I swear, Maddi, I think they just see an opportunity and go for it. It is the ugliest thing I've ever been a part of."

Maddi and Amanda commiserated for several hours at the eatery, and eventually got to the gist of Maddi's plans for "taking back America." Maddi told Amanda about her intentions to create "Maddi Laws" to try to limit the conflict of interest issues, and about the need for "Loser Pays" rules. Amanda listened carefully, nodding approval at various points.

"What about the Trial Lawyers Association?" Amanda asked. "Aren't they gunning for you because of this?"

"You know, Amanda. It's actually been kind of puzzling. They really haven't said much at all. I'm not sure if they just think we don't have a chance, or if maybe they're up to something. Either way, they make me nervous—after all—they're an organization of LAWYERS!"

They both laughed while Maddi made a move to pay for their meals. Suddenly there was commotion in the back of the eatery. Several people screamed and someone shouted "gun!"

Amanda turned to see what was going on and suddenly heard a shot. She looked over at Maddi, who had slumped in a ball on the floor. Several gentlemen in the front of the eatery attempted to tackle the shooter before he could run out the door, but were unable to apprehend him. He slipped away—and no one followed. Amanda immediately stooped down to assist Maddi.

"She's been shot! Someone call 911. Now!"

Amanda turned Maddi over carefully and began to try to see where the bullet had hit Maddi. Fortunately, from what Amanda could tell, the bullet had only grazed Maddi's shoulder. Maddi was conscious and was trying to talk to Amanda.

"What happened?"

"Someone shot you, Maddi!" They both looked at one another, neither one believing what had just happened. "Any idea who would want to do this to you?" Amanda asked.

As much as neither one wanted to believe it, they both knew they had a good idea as to the answer to that question.

The ambulance arrived only minutes later, and the EMS techs put Maddi on a stretcher.

"I'm allright! I don't need this attention from you folks. Just let me get in by myself."

"No ma'am—you need to let us do this."

Maddi finally agreed and they proceeded to take her to the nearest hospital.

John McCargish had just finished a long and tedious day at the Supreme Court and he was heading down 3rd Street when he heard a newscaster talking about a shooting that had occurred at one of the local eating establishments in town.

"Apparently a senator was involved in a shooting which took place only moments ago at Max's Tavern. We are currently unclear on the Senator's name, but we have word that the Senator has been taken to Arlington Hospital by ambulance. Wait a minute—we now have confirmation that the senator is Senator Cynthia Madison. The senator has become rather well-known lately for her efforts at litigation reform. We have no word on the current condition of the senator."

John did not know what to do. He nearly hit the car in front of him, quickly applying the breaks. He knew he had to see Maddi. He made a sharp left and headed down A street to try to avoid the major thoroughfare traffic. He finally reached Arlington Hospital and rushed inside. After several inquiries he located Maddi's room. He rushed in.

"Oh my God, Maddi! Who the hell did this?"

Maddi couldn't believe how excited she was to see John McCargish. Suddenly she was aware of how terrible she must look. Her good hand reached up to brush her hair back. She turned a bit and immediately groaned in pain.

"I don't know, John. Amanda here and I think we might have an idea though. John, meet an old friend of mine from med school, Amanda McKinney. Amanda, this is John McCargish from the Supreme Court."

Amanda reached her hand out to shake John's hand and they smiled at one another. John continued questioning Maddi. His green eyes had become dark and angry.

"Who do you two think this was? I heard on the news that he escaped. Was anyone pursuing him?

"I don't know. I haven't heard much yet myself. I'm currently trying to talk the doctor into letting me leave here in the next few minutes. I really am fine, and I'm anxious to learn more about what has happened here and why"

John was silent for a moment. There was a hint of sadness in his eyes. "Maddi. I want you to have protection from now on. Whoever did this won't be satisfied with grazing your shoulder. They'll try again."

Amanda pitched in. "I agree, Maddi. If it's who we think it is, then this is their plan for attacking your efforts, and they certainly won't stop at this."

Maddi made a meager attempt at a chuckle. "I really think they probably just wanted to scare me. And they have. Not that I'll stop my efforts."

"That's just it, Maddi. You won't stop your efforts. So they won't stop theirs. Mr. McCargish is right."

"Amanda, please call me John. Maddi, I'll just have one of my friends from the Secret Service put a detail on you. They often do that for certain senators—the ones with more notoriety. And now that describes you."

Maddi knew that neither Amanda nor John were going to accept anything other than yes, so she finally agreed.

Several hours later the three of them were getting into John's car and heading to the local police station to try to get some information concerning the shooter.

They pulled up to the Washington Metro police station at about 10:30 pm and rushed inside.

John did most of the talking. "Who's in charge here? I have Senator Madison with me and we are anxious to hear any information you all may have regarding the shooting that occurred this evening."

A large man came from behind the desk. He said his name was officer Perkins. He would assist in any way he could. He then proceeded to the back room, and eventually came out with another gentleman whom he introduced as Detective Horton.

"How can I help you, Senator?"

Maddi and Amanda and John filled the detective in on why they were there. The detective listened intently. After a brief pause he began to ask Maddi some questions.

"Is there anyone in particular, Senator, who would be interested in hurting you?"

Maddi explained to the detective that she was involved in some rather "hot" legislation, that had rubbed some individuals and some groups the wrong way. She told him of her and Amanda's thoughts about the possibility of the American Trial Lawyers Association perhaps having an interest in silencing Maddi.

The detective smirked. "You don't really think they would stoop to this level to protest any legislative agenda you might have?"

Maddi responded. "I certainly don't want to think so. But, you asked."

The detective proceeded to take a statement from Maddi, and soon they were finished with anything they could do there. The detective assured Maddi that he would keep her posted as to his progress, but he let her know that the shooter had been very careful to cover his tracks. The bullet casing at the scene was from a .38 pistol, a very common weapon. The man had not ordered anything to eat or drink, and had apparently spoken to no one. There were several eye witness reports from others at the restaurant but they all disagreed more than they agreed on the specifics of the man's features. The only commonality that was expressed was that the man had "beady little eyes." Not much of a lead, but he'd do his best with it he assured her.

John McCargish had made some calls to his friend at the Secret Service to obtain a couple of men to keep an eye on Maddi, and they were to meet them tomorrow morning at Maddi's apartment.

"I'm uncomfortable leaving you alone tonight, Maddi."

"Don't worry, John, I'll go back with Amanda to her hotel room and we'll stay there."

Maddi wondered if she noted some disappointment on John's face? Maybe not. He did seem somewhat relieved that Maddi was taken care of for the night.

Amanda and Maddi headed back to the Watergate and up to Amanda's room. They ordered some room service, and a couple of beers, and sat back to review the events of the day. Maddi was still quite shaken up, and found it so helpful to sit and talk with Amanda. They also took some time to get reacquainted and caught up on each other and friends from med school.

At about 3:00 am, Maddi informed Amanda that they both needed to get some sleep—tomorrow would be another big day with Hank and Wilson arriving in D.C.

They both laid down—Maddi on the couch—and quickly fell asleep.

Maddi was awakened at around 7:00 am by the telephone ringing on the nightstand. She went over and answered it.

"Hello?"

"Maddi? It's John. Your agents are going to meet you at your apartment at 8:00am. If you would like, I could swing by to get you in about a half hour?"

Maddi was thrilled. "That would be great, John. I'll be down in the lobby." She had a lot of work to do in a short period of time if she wanted to look halfway decent to meet John. She hopped in the shower and quickly got herself cleaned up and ready to go.

She left a quick note for Amanda, telling her when Hank and Wilson were coming in and that perhaps she and Amanda could meet up at 4:30 pm, head for the airport together, and wait for them to arrive. She then slipped out through the door.

John was obviously a morning kind of guy, looking bright-eyed and alert, as though he had gotten a good night's sleep. Maddi didn't imagine that he had done that however and was amazed at how great he looked.

"Do you always look this good first thing in the morning?" he asked.

"I was about to say the same thing to you." Maddi smiled.

They proceeded to discuss the prior evening's events. Maddi was clearly shaken by what had happened. John wanted to comfort her even though he, too, was unnerved by the events of the night before.

"Don't worry, Maddi. The guy who did this will be found soon, I'm sure," he said halfheartedly. "Have you had anything to eat?"

They ran through a drive-through and grabbed some breakfast sandwiches and headed for Maddi's townhouse apartment. Once there, Maddi asked John to come on in and the two of them waited for the two agents who were going to be looking after Maddi. The agents were late, and it gave Maddi and John a chance to talk. They talked about Washington, and about their lives before Washington. Maddi noticed, however, that John stopped short of telling her anything about himself other than that he grew up in Philadelphia, and that his father had traveled often, leaving John and his mother pretty much on their own. He didn't seem particularly pleased with his father for that, but Maddi was unable to elicit anything more from him.

The two agents showed up several minutes late, and explained that the British Prime Minister had arrived and traffic was somewhat snarled. No surprise, both Maddi and John responded.

After a few perfunctory statements, John informed Maddi that he needed to get over to the Supreme Court to work on some cases that were pending before the court. They agreed to try to meet up sometime later that weekend—to discuss the disposition of Maddi's shooter—and he told her he would call. The minute he was gone, Maddi felt alone—for the first time in a long time.

Maddi tried to make herself comfortable with the two agents sitting outside watching her from their car, and she proceeded to change her clothes and sit down and get some business done. The other two doctors were arriving today, and once they got there, Maddi knew that she would be tied up with them and the forum for the remainder of the weekend. Hank had e-mailed her and let her know he was staying through Monday, and Maddi had made some changes to her schedule so as to spend the better part of Monday with Hank.

Hank and Maddi had met at med school and had become friends almost instantly. They were both from the Midwest and as such shared similar points of view. They had a common outlook on life, on people and on what it was that was important in life. Maddi had always felt comforted by Hank's presence, and she had sensed that he had felt the same.

They had spent a lot of time together during those days, and at one point had danced around the idea of becoming something more than friends. But, for whatever reason, neither one had vocalized anything, and therefore, nothing had ever come of it. Sometimes Maddi wondered what her life would have been like if something had. She was looking very forward to seeing Hank Clarkson again.

CHAPTER XX

Roger Clairy was somewhat hungover from a night of far too many martinis, and he was aggressively trying to get up out of bed. While at the bar last night he had heard mention of a shooting of a local official, but he didn't recall much of anything after that. He was intent on hooking up with a fairly good-looking waitress at the bar. She would have nothing to do with him however, and that had not changed by the end of the evening.

He now decided to turn on the TV just to look at something and try to clear his head. What he heard made him immediately sit up and pay attention.

"Early last evening, Senator Cynthia Madison was shot in the shoulder while dining at Max's restaurant. Although the senator was not seriously injured, the shooting is being thouroughly investigated by local law enforcement. The man responsible for the shooting escaped, and there appear to be very few leads available as to his identity."

"Oh my God!" Roger thought out loud. "No, it can't be. Even Mr. Buckholtz wouldn't stoop to that level. Was Mr. Smith—no, no there is no way." His thoughts went on and on. Finally, he knew he couldn't stand it any longer and he looked up Frances Buckholtz' number in the phone book. There were 26 listings for an F. Buckholz. Roger was not dissuaded. He called over to the ATLA building.

"Hey Lori. It's Roger. You know, Roger Clairy from upstairs." There was silence on the other end of the line. "I really need to speak to Mr. Buckholtz. He doesn't happen to be there this morning, does he?"

"Just a moment, sir, and I'll ring his office." After what seemed liked 15 minutes the young lady got back on the line.

"I'm sorry sir, but he isn't answering his line. Would you like his voice-mail?" Roger was becoming inpatient.

"No. No, I don't need to leave him a message, I need to speak to him! Can you give me his home number?"

"I'm sorry sir, but Mr. Buckholtz has indicated that he doesn't want his number given out."

Roger was coming unglued. "But I know he would want me to have his number! I am an important person to him—you need to give me that number!" By now Roger was shouting.

"Please calm down Mr. Clairy. I have specific instructions regarding Mr. Buckholtz' phone number—and I am not going to give the number to you. Is that clear?" Roger concluded it was futile to continue to try to convince this hard-ass secretary to give up Buckholtz' number. He did his best to calm down and then thanked the secretary and hung up.

He then tried to call the number that was given to him by the mysterious Mr. Smith. There was no answer there, and no machine to leave a message.

Roger had to know what happened last night. And, whether the ATLA had anything to do with it or not. He found it hard to believe that the organization—or Mr. Buckholtz—would truly stoop to that level, but deep down inside, he knew his instincts were right. That old bastard Buckholtz hired a hit man! And put Roger in charge of him! "Oh my god!" thought Roger. "If this gets out, I'm gonna' be the one to take the fall! What a shithead that Buckholtz is." But, before Roger went on with that thinking, he knew he had to speak with Buckholtz and hear it for himself. He decided to call each and every one of the F. Buckholz numbers.

He dialed the first number listed.

"Hello, my name is Roger, and I'm from the American Trial Lawyer's Association. I'm looking for Frances. Is this the correct number?"

"You're who?"

"Roger Clairey, from the ATLA."

"Well, Mr. Roger Clairey, there isn't anyone here with the name Frances. Francene is here though. She works at the Safeway down the street. Would you like to speak with her?"

"No thank you."

After the 14th call—all calls resembling the first one, Roger was about to give up. "I'll try once more," he thought.

"Hello?"

"Yes, hello, my name is Roger and I'm from the American Trial Lawyer's Association. Is Frances available?"

"One moment sir and I will get him."

"Finally!" thought Roger. "Now, at least, I can find out the truth."

After a very long wait, the man who answered the phone got back on the line. "I'm sorry sir, but Mr. Buckholtz is indisposed at the current time. Would he be able to call you back?"

"Indisposed!" thought Roger. He wanted to scream at the guy to just go get the son-of-a-bitch, but instead calmly said "that would be fine." He proceeded to give the man his cell phone number, and then headed for the shower.

CHAPTER XXI

Peter Smith was staying at a Holiday Inn outside of D.C.

"Damn!" he was thinking. "I can't believe I only winged that bitch! I'm just lucky I was able to get out of there without anybody chasing me."

Peter had left the eatery and ran as fast as he could toward the Mall, where he knew he could easily blend in with others. He then decided to "lay low" for a few days and try again when things had calmed down.

He knew Buckholtz would be pissed. But, he would reassure him that the senator was probably quite scared and would likely back off whatever it was she was doing. If not, he—Peter Smith—would simply kill her.

He was sometimes amazed at how much he loved this type of work. He hadn't started out this way, but his life had lead him here. He'd been wronged by a very prominent person, and eventually had resorted to murder in order to make things right.

After all, it was just a simple DUI. What was all the fuss? So what if he had had three DUI's prior to this one? The judge should've let him go. Instead, he took away his license and shamed him in front of his wife and family. He had to attend some ridiculous dependency class, and—as a result of all of this—he lost his job, and eventually his family. All because that asshole judge had to prove a point.

Peter had gotten himself what he thought was a pretty good lawyer, but the inexperienced lawyer couldn't get him out of his mess. So, finally, after Peter had lost nearly everything, he decided to make the judge pay.

He planned his murder so carefully. He knew he would be a suspect, so he had to throw suspicion to someone else. He methodically carried out the deception and the murder, and couldn't believe the buzz he got from the whole thing. He succeeded, having effectively thrown suspicion on a recently-released inmate who had been "put away" by the Judge. Peter then left town, eventually connecting up with a friend of his in D.C. His friend worked for a congressman, and he would occasionally call Peter when he needed something unpleasant done. It wasn't long until Peter had established himself as the "go-to guy" for messy problems to be solved.

He certainly wasn't going to allow Senator Madison to be his undoing. He knew his reputation was on the line, and he knew that he would likely have to kill the bitch soon. He smiled to himself as he thought through his options. God, he loved this work.

Roger never did get a call back from Mr. Buckholtz. "That self-righteous prick," he thought to himself. "Trying to pin this on me." Mr. Buckholtz hadn't done it yet, but Roger knew how his boss worked. He knew that if Mr. Buckholtz were threatened in any way he would make Roger the fall guy. Well, Roger wasn't going to have any part of it. He'd confront him on Monday, in the privacy of Mr. B's office, and he would tape the whole conversation. Brilliant! That is exactly what he would do. "Roger Boy, you've still got it" he said to himself. "I'll make it so Mr. Buckholtz owes me one. How perfect is that!"

Roger proceeded to grab his phone book and find a location that sold the taping gear he would need.

Frances Buckholtz had watched the night's events with disbelief. He hadn't really expected Smith to hurt Maddi—only scare her. Hey, but maybe that's what it would take to get the bitch to stop her bullshit. And, hey, it's not like Smith killed her. He felt quite confident that this would end Maddi's crusade and that he could get back to running the ATLA without any outside threats. If not, well, Smith would just have to be more accurate next time.

On rare occasions Frances would think back to that night at the lake. He would remember seeing Bobby struggle. He would remember that split second when he saw Bobby's face—full of panic and fear. He would think about Andrew—all full of himself and smug. The Great Andrew Madison who could do no wrong. He hated that son-of-a-bitch. After all, it was Bobby's fault that he didn't know how to handle alcohol. And then he decided to go swimming. What an idiot! He knew that Andrew blamed him. But, that was just wrong. If Andrew hadn't needed to get home to Mommy maybe none of it would have happened. Hell, Andrew had some responsibility in the whole thing, too. If—or when—Andrew ever opens his big mouth, Frances Buckholtz—Attorney-at-Law—knew he could pin that night on his ass without any difficulty whatsoever. But, Andy won't say anything. He's hiking somewhere in the wilderness of Canada, and that's where he better stay.

CHAPTER XXII

Andrew Madison had been in Canada now for 13 years. And, he loved every day there as much as the first time when he set foot there. He had come that first time to hunt caribou. And he never left.

Andrew had been a physician in Montana before coming to Canada. He was considered an exceptional physician. He was several years older than Maddi and was the first in the family to become a physician. Andrew had an instinct about people and their illnesses. He knew when he needed to look further, and he knew when to send them on to a specialist. He loved medicine—in the beginning.

When he started out in the profession, there were very few HMO's, and the Internet was barely off the ground. Drug companies didn't advertise on TV. Patients and doctors created a relationship of trust and goodwill. Doctors felt like advocates for their patients, and patients—in return—bestowed respect and appreciation upon their doctors.

Then things began to change. HMO's became ubiquitous. The Internet came crashing into our lives and created a sense that all the answers were there and the doctor was simply available to facilitate what the Internet had stated was needed. Drug companies began to advertise their drugs on TV—just like McDonald's or Wal-Mart. Patients now walked into the office demanding this drug or that drug—like they'd seen on TV. The relationship between patient and doctor began to change.

The biggest change, however, were the lawyers. No—not the lawyers—they were still the ruthless predators they'd always been—but their approach changed. It became easier for them to turn a bad outcome into intent. It became easier for them to take an obscure—but lethal—diagnosis, and blame the physician for failing to find it. "Failure to diagnose" they called it. Soon,

Andrew felt like his patients were potentially "the enemy" instead of someone whom he could trust. The system had become broken and perverse.

Andrew had lived with it for a time, but something happened on his trip to hunt caribou. When he woke up that first morning in the middle of the Canadian Tundra, somewhere north of Vancouver, he felt like he used to feel. There was joy in his heart. He noticed the crisp air and the sunshine for the first time in a long time. Everywhere he looked he saw nothing but pure, unadulterated beauty. Endless water, broken up with the occasional body of land, completely untouched and pure. And, the world made sense again. Andrew knew he couldn't go back.

Andrew had always known that he wouldn't practice medicine in Indiana. His time in Greenwood, and in Evansville had not been pleasant and he knew that the further away he could get from there the better.

His decision to go into medicine surprised everyone, but no one more than himself. Following the family footsteps—becoming a cop—was totally out of the question. He liked to fix things. And he was so bright. So, with a little encouragement and a few lucky breaks, he eventually found himself in Medical School at Purdue.

From there he went to Florida, to do a residency, and to do some fishing. This was truly his passion. Fishing, hunting, and living off the land had always been Andrew's way to recover from any of life's pain. He had made several trips to Florida with friends and decided to spend some time there.

Shand's Memorial Hospital sat in the heart of Gainesville, and Andrew fit in nicely with all the transplanted people who resided in this part of Florida.

When he was finished, and it was time to actually begin his practice, he elected to join a group in Montana, where he could hunt bear and take some trips into Canada's wilderness. He did well in practice and soon had become the picture of a busy, successful physician.

But, he wasn't happy. Whether it was the long hours, the frequent call, the managed care, or the lawyers, he wasn't sure. He increasingly fought a daily depression.

He tried shortening his hours, and reducing his call, but the dissatisfaction and the depression persisted.

He and his mother rarely spoke, but he would call Maddi periodically, pretending to be fine. She knew he wasn't fine. The two would talk for hours about how much the practice of medicine had changed and how miserable many of the doctors were becoming, but Maddi knew that Andrew was fighting other demons as well.

She encouraged Andrew to get some help, but he refused, saying only that there was no cure for all that was wrong with him. He would often tell Maddi that his cynicism was well-founded, his pragmatism well-earned, and as a result he was a "cynicmatist." This would make them both laugh, but Maddi knew that Andrew needed to do something or he would wind up in serious trouble.

His trip to the Tundra had started out as a simple vacation. He'd never been up that far in Canada, and the thought of hunting caribou in the Canadian Tundra was alluring and a little more rugged than anything he had ever done.

He left on a Saturday morning, expecting to return the following Saturday night. But, when Maddi got his phone call on Thursday, she knew he wouldn't be back.

"Maddi, it's Andrew. I have found utopia." He proceeded to tell her about his trip, and the Tundra itself, and Maddi heard a thrill in his voice that she hadn't heard in many years. It was clear that the joy and invigoration he had felt that first morning in the Tundra was like something he had thought he would never feel again.

Each morning felt better than the one before it, and by Thursday Andrew knew that to leave this and return home would be to eventually sign his own death sentence.

So he stayed. And he found work as a guide. And he smiled more each day, as he saw the colors of the Tundra grow stronger every time he woke.

Now, thirteen years later, here he sat with joy in his heart. He ran backpacking trips and led caribou hunts to earn enough money to live and he was thoroughly happy. No more worries about medicine. No more worries about things in his past. Andrew had escaped it all, here in the beautiful, god-forsaken Canadian Tundra.

The summer days were endless, the winter nights—the same. But Andrew loved every bit of it, and felt certain he would never leave. He noticed that—each time he looked out at the gray sky and the endless horizon he would see more and more color—like his eyes were opening again—as a newborn learning to see.

He was drinking his morning coffee and looking out at the Canadian horizon in the distance. He had just started reading his newspaper. Yellowknife, the local community where Andrew spent his time off, would receive a selection of newspapers periodically, and Andrew would grab one for the occasional update on all that was going on in "that other world." It was amazing how little anything truly changed—much like a soap opera. You can not watch it for months, but when you get back to it you easily catch up.

Today was Saturday and he was reading a section entitled "Washington Events." He was wondering what Maddi was up to these days. He knew she was working on tort reform—weren't all doctors? Suddenly he sat straight up and started to read faster.

> "SENATOR SHOT BY UNKNOWN ASSAILANT
>
> Senator Cynthia Madison, R-IND, was shot in the shoulder last night by an unknown gunman who escaped capture. The senator was taken to Arlington Hospital where she was treated and released. The motive for the shooting is not currently known, but it is of interest to note that the senator has received nationwide attention lately for her attempts at litigation reform. Whether or not this had any bearing on the shooting remains unknown at this time."

Andrew couldn't believe what he was reading. Who on earth would ever want to shoot Maddi? He had no idea, but he knew he had to go to D.C. to find out, and to take care of his little sister. Andrew started packing his bag while he was calling for a plane reservation.

CHAPTER XXIII

By Saturday afternoon, Maddi was feeling much better—physically; and was trying her hardest to refocus on the task at hand. She had Amanda there with her, Wilson and Hank on their way. There was a lot of work to do, and—clearly—a lot of obstacles to overcome. She and Amanda were sitting in the living room having tea and making some plans for the convention.

"Do you think that guy was really trying to kill me?" Maddi asked.

"Maddi, as much as I hate to say it—I think so." Amanda went on. "We've all known for a long time that if we truly cleaned up the litigation industry in this country there would be hell to pay with trial lawyers who were profiting so greatly from this current system. Just think about all the money involved. If it suddenly become much more difficult to sue doctors indescriminately, a major part of lawyers' income will be eliminated.

"And, if I am hearing you correctly, you're actually going after more than just malpractice. You're doing a cleaning up of all litigation in this country. Millions and millions of dollars will be lost by attorneys unable to profit by the misfortunes of others. With all that to lose, it isn't farfetched to think someone put a hit on you."

Maddi nodded her head and they both sat in silence. After a period of time Maddi said "Well, I'll not let it stop me. It needs to be done, and Amanda, we're going to do it."

The women proceeded to map out the upcoming convention. They jotted down the names of effective, prominent speakers, physicians, politicians, and—hopefully—an attorney by the name of Clarence Morrow. Maddi had been trying—unsuccessfully to speak with Mr. Morrow for weeks but he wouldn't return her calls. She had been told he was out of the country for several weeks, and Maddi had no reason to doubt this was true.

Clarence Morrow was a very prominent attorney who lived in Philadelphia. He had started as a prosecutor for Buck's County, and had gradually worked his way over to Philly to work as Assistant D.A. for the county. He enjoyed his work, but one day was approached by a friend, who brought with him a very prominent business owner who had been sued by a former employee. The business owner had explained the case to Clarence and had wanted his help.

Apparently the employee had been fired for stealing thousands of dollars from his employer, and had been caught red-handed in the act. He was now claiming that the employer had not paid him for his work and had harassed him to the point where he felt he had no choice but to take the money from the employer. He had hired a top-gun attorney who was making a case from this ridiculous complaint and the case was gaining momentum. The employer wanted Clarence to get him out of this horrible, unjust mess.

Clarence was infuriated at the gall of the plaintiff's case. In spite of records substantiating payment by the employer, they were claiming that the employee had done much more work than stated, and had not been paid for such. They were suing the employer for 3.5 million dollars, for redress of wrongs perpetrated by the employer against the employee.

Clarence was happy to help his friend, especially over such a ridiculous claim. After eight months of motions and depositions Clarence was able to have the claim dismissed. His internal fire had been lit by this experience and he began to seek out other ridiculous claims that were pending in the courts. They were abundant. He successfully fought off the majority of these claims and quickly acquired a reputation as a no-nonsense attorney, who was practicing on the "right" side of the law. Maddi knew she had to have him at her forum.

John McCargish had become acquainted with Mr. Morrow somewhere in his mysterious past, and he agreed to speak to Mr. Morrow about possibly joining Maddi's crusade. Maddi was hopeful he would sign on—he would be the perfect spokesman.

As for physicians to speak, there were a plethora of prominent physicians who had been the target of a law-suit over the course of their careers. Most physicians would be sued at least once in their career, and over 50% would be sued more than once.

Maddi and Amanda began formulating a list of those doctors they thought would be most effective. Amanda suggested that Hank Clarkson should be one of them. She remembered him from Medical School, as the guy always selected to speak at all major functions and events. And she knew he and Maddi had been friends. Maddi wasn't sure if Hank had been sued, but any doctor who was anxious to get on board with this effort had probably had a personal experience which led them to such a cause. Maddi would address this with Hank when he arrived that afternoon.

Politicians always loved an opportunity to speak, and Maddi knew a few who would be helpful in advancing the cause. She was also trying very hard to get the President of the United States to make an appearance at her forum as well. This was a long-shot she knew. The power in the U.S. is concentrated in only a few places, and the "successful" politicians learned not to piss off the power factions if at all possible. But, this president was a bit different. He seemed to follow his own mind, and he had already indicated his desire for tort reform. Maddi would continue to try to persuade him to join her effort.

She and Amanda continued to plan various other aspects of the forum, including brochures and reservation options, as well as an outline of lectures and featured speakers. They were both very anxious to get some help from Hank and Wilson later on that day.

Peter Smith was still quite angry with himself. "You stupid shit," he was saying over and over again. "She was sitting right there in front of you, and you missed her. You are a pathetic, useless screw-up."

The self-loathing had been going on for two days now. Lots of alcohol and two sleepless nights later, and Peter was still angry. He kept thinking to himself, "I know I can kill that bitch. In spite of that detail of secret service guys that that candy-assed Supremes clerk had assigned her, I'll wait for my opportunity, and I will kill her." Peter knew his reputation depended on it.

Hank and Wilson's planes were arriving within 45 minutes of one another, so Maddi and Amanda were "camping out" in a Dulles airport Friday's. They had each ordered a beer and were anxiously awaiting the guys arrivals.

Wilson arrived first—a straight shot from Boston to Dulles. Maddi was very glad to see him and gave him a brief, but meaningful hug.

"Wilson, you look great! How was the flight?"

"Not too bad. I'm just glad to be here—and away from Boston for awhile. What's with the sling?"

Maddi proceeded to fill Wilson in on the details of the last 24 hours. He listened in disbelief as she related the series of events that had occurred.

"I can't believe they would go that far."

"I couldn't myself, at first" said Maddi.

They all proceeded to get acquainted or to get caught up, and, by the time Hank's plane arrived the other three had gotten very comfortable with one another.

Maddi saw Hank before he saw her. She couldn't believe how wonderful it was to see him. He looked about the same—but a little older—perhaps more distinguished? She suddenly became very self-conscious of her own appearance. She quickly messed with her hair and straightened her shirt. She was still wearing her sling and decided she probably looked quite ridiculous.

Hank suddenly saw Maddi and his face lit up. He was quite surprised with his own reaction. He ran toward her and the two embraced in a very genuine hug.

"Oh my god, Maddi—you look absolutely wonderful!" Hank exclaimed. "Who did you take out with that arm?"

"Hank, it is so good to see you. Things can get pretty tough her in D.C., and a girl has to defend herself." They both laughed and Maddi then told Hank—quickly—all that had happened. They met up with Amanda and Wilson and all four proceeded to catch a cab and head for the Watergate Hotel.

Once there, Maddi left the three of them to get ready for drinks and dinner and forum arranging. She would meet them all there in an hour.

Maddi got back in the cab and had the driver—followed by the secret service guys—take her back to her townhouse. It was a 25-minute drive and Maddi sat back and began to think.

She couldn't believe someone would try to kill her. Little Cynthia Madison from Evansville, Indiana. Amazing. And, frightening. Oh well, she would be safe with that detail following her all the time. Right?

And what about Hank. My god, he looked great. Older, maybe sadder, but great. Go figure. Maddi wasn't sure what she expected, but she was quite surprised at how happy she was to see Hank again. And she thought he seemed happy to see her as well. She'd have to see how things went. Who knows?

Her mind immediately went to John McCargish. There was something there, she knew. But what? Time would tell. She just needed to give everything a little bit of time. Soon Maddi fell asleep in the back of the cab.

Peter Smith was watching. He was watching Maddi as she dropped off the other doctors. He was watching her as she got back into the cab. He was watching her as she headed for her home in D.C. He saw the secret service detail following her, and he chuckled to himself. "Little they can do to save you," he thought. He watched Maddi get out of her car and his eyes followed her up the steps and through the front door of her home. He would watch her a bit longer and he would wait. He knew his opportunity would come. It had to, or he would have to make it happen. He couldn't afford to fail.

Hank checked into his room at the Watergate and started the shower and unpacked his bag. He sat on the bed for just a moment and began to think. Maddi looked wonderful. He couldn't believe how great she could look after all this time. And still her bright, cheerful self. It was so great to see her. He wondered if she felt that way as well. He thought she seemed to.

Hank thought back to med school. To the Anatomy Lab and the cadaver with the damned abdominal mesh. And Maddi. She was the only thing that kept him going through that first horrible semester. Always upbeat and positive. And funny. She could always make him laugh. Why hadn't the two of them ever gotten together, he wondered.

He recalled wanting to ask her to the annual Fall Harvest Party at the Medical school. He chickened out. Instead, he asked all four of the students working on the cadaver if they all wanted to go together. Three of them said yes. He, Maddi and Phil ended up having an incredibly good time at the party and they all walked home to their rooms together. Phil's apartment was first and they both told him goodnight and continued on. When they came to Maddi's apartment, Hank stopped and looked straight into Maddi's eyes.

"So, Maddi, what are you going to do now?"

"Probably go to bed. How about you"

"I don't know. I was thinking maybe...." Hank paused. He couldn't do it. He had tried, but he couldn't do it. "Maybe I'll go home and go to bed too." Did he sense that Maddi was disappointed? He wondered.

"Okay," she said. "I"ll see you tomorrow in the lab."

And with that, the opportunity was lost—and it never came again. Now here he was, in Maddi's town, and he wondered. He would have to think about it—maybe now it could work with the two of them. He knew he would at least have to try.

CHAPTER XXIV

Frances Buckholtz was angry. His mind was going round and round as he kept wondering to himself, "what was that idiot Smith doing, anyway?" Frances had been assured he was the best. Hell, the guy couldn't even get a good shot in within 30 feet of the target? And where was he, anyway? Frances had tried the two numbers that Smith had given him and neither one was even operational. He knew he would have to just wait for Smith to contact him. And, he knew Smith would—if he wanted to be paid.

He decided to try to get back to work and see if the good senator had maybe been scared off of the whole thing. He hoped so. He wondered if that shit-head Clairy would know anything. He said he had a guy "on the inside" who could keep the organization abreast of things. He paged his secretary and asked her to find Roger Clairy for him, and to have him come to the office.

Ten minutes later Frances heard a knock on the door. He opened it and saw Roger standing there.

"You wanted me?" Roger looked terrible, Frances thought. Like maybe he hadn't been sleeping well?

"Yeah. Didn't you tell me recently that you had somebody working on the inside for Senator Madison's Doctor Forum?"

Roger grinned. This was the opportunity he was waiting for. "Yeah. His name is Kevin and he's "helping" the senator with some of her research. I haven't heard from him lately, but I could give him a call."

Frances cocked his eyebrows, obviously impressed.

"Working directly with the senator on her stupid forum?" Roger nodded. Frances seemed genuinely pleased.

"That is great. We need to know where she is with this forum of hers. Maybe she is even thinking of calling it off. After all, somebody did take a shot at her." The two men exchanged glances. Roger quickly looked away.

"I'll call him now and let you know what's up." Roger felt the bulge in his pocket—his taping device—and knew he needed to get something on tape concerning Frances' role in hiring the hit man.

"Mr. Buckholtz" he sputtered. Buckholtz turned and looked at him.

"Yeah?"

"What exactly is Peter Smith supposed to be doing?"

Buckholtz eyed Roger slowly and carefully. He thought quickly for a moment before he responded.

"Who's Peter Smith?" he asked. He then turned and walked away, a subtle grin appearing on his face as he left the room.

Roger stood there—quite angry with his deceitful boss. He finally turned and left the room as well. He'd have to work this another way. He proceeded to his own smaller office on the 4th floor. He looked through his rolodex and finally found Kevin's name. He dialed the number and waited. Soon the phone was answered.

"Hello?"

"Kevin?"

"Yeah?"

"This is Roger. How's it going out there in Indiana?"

Kevin was eager to tell Roger every detail of what was going on with the forum, but decided to play his hand close to his chest. "I don't really have a lot of info right now. But I know that in spite of the recent shot she took to the shoulder she is still proceeding ahead. Perhaps I would be in a position of learning more information if I had some more clout behind my name." Kevin was definitely going to get something out of this arrangement.

Roger was curious what Kevin had in mind. "What do you mean—clout?"

"You know. An important affiliation or an important title to my name."

Roger saw the writing on the wall. "Like what, Kevin?"

"Oh, you know, maybe something like Assistant Director for the American Trial Lawyers Association. Maybe something like that."

"I don't have the power to do that. Besides, I'm the Assistant Director."

"Well, maybe we'll just sit back and let the senator run with her forum. I'll do my best to obtain info. But, you may want to consider my offer. It seems to me we both have something we could gain from this."

Roger was puzzled. "What can I gain from you acquiring a position in the ATLA?"

"I'll leave that to you to figure out. Let me know if you can help me. Then perhaps I'll be able to let you know if I can help you." Kevin hung up the phone.

Roger was angry. "That little piss ant," he said to himself. But he knew that he needed Kevin's help, so he would have to try to come up with a way to put him into the organization somehow. He'd have to work on Mr. Buckholtz and see what he could do.

Maddi and her friends had arranged to meet in the hotel lobby at 7:00 that evening, and—true to form—Maddi was about 20 minutes late. When she finally walked into the lobby the other three were waiting for her. They all laughed—Maddi had always run about 20 minutes late.

They got in the back of two cabs and headed for a restaurant several blocks away that Maddi loved for its privacy. She felt the four of them could talk without risk of being overheard, and she knew she would have her "body guards" with her and thus would be safe from whoever the crazy guy was who was out to get her.

They arrived at the restaurant and were quickly seated at a table toward the back of the restaurant. They ordered drinks and were glancing through the menu.

"All right gang. Here we are. Let's say we get started with some 'strategizing.'" They all four chuckled. Maddi was having a wonderful time with her three friends and it showed. She was animated while she spoke of her plans for the forum. "I've got several speakers lined up, and I would love it if each one of you would say something." She had already spoken to Hank, who had agreed to be a speaker. They had all briefly shared their "lawsuit" stories and Maddi knew that their experiences were all too common in medicine today. The others reluctantly agreed to give small speeches as well and Maddi continued on with her agenda.

"I've arranged for everyone to stay at four different hotels close to the convention center. I've already booked the rooms because I know the press will want some accommodations and I didn't want anyone to not have a place to stay. So far we've got over 2600 doctors coming to the forum. I'm hoping to launch some legislation at the forum to introduce "Maddi's Laws" for consideration by the Congress. The forum will be a great place to see how the Laws are going to play."

Maddi proceeded to tell them about her idea for Maddi's Laws to rival Representative Stark in California and his batch of laws governing how doctors profit from medicine. She explained her notion of eliminating conflict of inter-est issues, as well as her idea of changing the pay structure for attorneys so that their mission and their means would not be incongruous with one another. The other three listened intently, often nodding their heads in agreement. After they had ordered their meals they began to discuss other aspects of the forum, as well as issues related to the practice of medicine.

Amanda shared her story about Lois Skycroft and the details surrounding her lawsuit. She also shared what the lawsuit had done to her emotionally. There were tears in her eyes as she shared her feelings about her patients, and how much she loved her work, but how much she hated the current system that was so terribly broken. The other three listened intently and it was clear from their expressions that they knew exactly what Amanda was talking about.

Wilson then began his story. He told them all of the shy young girl who had come to him so frightened, pregnant with twins. He told them of the terrible details surrounding the death of one of the twins, and he told them how kind—but devastated—the young girl had been. He felt so attached to her, and had given so much emotionally to her. The betrayal he felt when she sued him was almost more than he could bear. Once again the other three nodded understandingly. They knew that same sense of betrayal.

Hank was the last one to share his story. He was reluctant at first, but then began to see that it felt very good to talk to others—whom he knew, and whom he knew to be good at what they did—and have them understand his pain. Even when he had talked to Jenny he knew she didn't know what it was like to be in the position he was in. She was so supportive and so understanding—but she couldn't know how it felt to dedicate your life—and your every day—to trying to help people in any way you could; and then have one of those peo-ple—or their family—betray you in such a cold, impersonal way. These people here at this table understood. Gradually, Hank told everything about his case. He shared every detail and every emotion. He too had tears in his eyes at vari-ous times as he shared his fondness for Irene Morrison, and his fondness for all his wonderful patients at the Nursing Home, whom he had recently quit seeing because of the risk of further liability. They all ached when he told them how he finally had quit the Nursing Home, and how close he was to quitting his current practice. They had all entertained the same idea. And they were all offended by it. Talking about it was so incredibly comforting for each one of them.

The evening continued on with more wine and wonderful food and the four of them continued talking about so many things that needed to change in the profession of medicine. They eagerly planned for the forum and by the time dessert came they had pretty much gotten the forum ready and had found their way back to memories of college and medical school and were having a most delightful evening.

Suddenly Maddi's cell phone was ringing. Several other phones rang at the same time in the restaurant. Maddi looked down at the number. It was Phil from her office. She excused herself and went to a hallway in the restaurant to call him back.

"Phil, it's Maddi. What's up?"

"You won't believe it, Maddi. You need to find a TV and tune in to the news."

"Why? What's happened?" Maddi was getting concerned.

"A group of lawyers from Arizona have just filed a class-action suit against over 3000 doctors from around the country. They are accusing them of knowingly treating patients with a dangerous drug. They are seeking one billion dollars in damages!"

Maddi couldn't believe it. That was a bit much—even for lawyers. "Phil, that's horrible!"

"That's not all, Maddi. Most of the doctors named in the suit are threatening to quit. Over 3000 doctors, Maddi. Threatening to quit. This is getting way out of control."

Maddi didn't know what to think. She quickly told Phil that she would get back with him later and she then headed back to her table to tell the others what was happening.

On her way, she failed to see the lone diner sitting off to the side of the restaurant. But his shaded green eyes had seen her. As a matter of fact, Peter Smith had been watching her all evening. Waiting. Just waiting for his opportunity. And this time, he wouldn't miss.

CHAPTER XXV

Andrew Madison had had a difficult time getting out of Canada and anywhere close to Washington D.C. There were storms in the Midwest, and there were delays across the country. He was as far as Chicago, when his flight to Dulles was cancelled. He was about to drive to D.C., but arranged to catch the 5:30 am flight out and decided he would get some sleep and get to D.C. in the morning. He booked a room at an airport hotel and proceeded to settle in for the night. He turned on the TV, and a major cable news program came on. He was half-listening when suddenly he was aware that they were talking about doctors and an apparently huge exodus from their practices. He turned it up.

"Late yesterday afternoon a class action lawsuit was filed in Philadelphia naming three thousand four hundred and thirty two physicians. They are accused of knowingly prescribing a dangerous medication. The medica-tion—known as Diacam—was recently pulled from the market place, but not before several hundred people had died from liver failure allegedly caused by this medication. The medicine was originally thought to be something of a miracle drug for diabetics and, as such, had been prescribed enthusiastically.

"The law firm filing this claim states that the doctors involved had ample opportunity and sufficient knowledge to know that Diacam was unsafe and may contribute to death. The law firm of Wyatt, Hanson, Richards, and Schultz states that—although they hate to involve this many physicians in liti-gation—it is their public duty to punish such carelessness.

"In response to this class action suit, many of the named physicians have stated that they will quit their practices in response to what they consider a sys-tem gone awry. Their representative stated earlier to this reporter that they can no longer in good conscience practice medicine in an environment where they are continually pursued with legal action. The thought of this many physicians leaving the practice of medicine—along with the hundreds who have already recently walked away from their practices—is alarming and is causing some grave concerns across the country as people try to figure out who will take care of them if doctors continue to leave the profession in such numbers.

"When asked about this, the representative from Wyatt, Hanson, Richards, and Schultz said only that their leaving is indicative of their guilt."

Andrew Madison was listening in disbelief. Then, all at once, he began to laugh. "Finally," he thought. "They have gone too far."

CHAPTER XXVI

Across the country the headlines were screaming about the mass-exodus of physicians across the United States. The New York Times referred to it as "Physicians jumping ship." The Washington Post called it "Doctors Finally Fighting Back." And the Wall Street Journal asked the question "Who Will They Sue Now?"

Maddi found herself in the spotlight—as well as her upcoming forum—because of her close connection to the litigation battle. She and her friends had left the restaurant upon hearing the announcement, and they all proceeded to Maddi's townhouse to continue watching coverage—and to see how the media was portraying this.

Maddi's phone was ringing off the hook—and, she finally left it off the hook. A cable news network was interviewing one of the attornies from the law firm of Wyatt, Hanson, Richards and Schultz.

"Tell me, Mr. Wyatt, what compelled you to sue so many doctors at one time?"

Mr. Wyatt, who was quite small with sparse white hair above each ear, responded. "Well sir, we simply couldn't sit by idly while these doctors carelessly endangered so many patients. They were adequately warned of the dangers of this medication, but elected to proceed to use it anyway, with disastrous results." Mr. Wyatt then coughed, and cleared his throat. His gravelly voice continued. "Doctors have for too long ignored their obligation to 'do no harm' and the public continually suffers the consequences. We at the law firm of Wyatt, Hanson, Richards and Schultz could no longer allow this to proceed unchallenged."

The interviewer continued. "But, now that so many doctors are quitting the profession, do you or your colleagues feel some sense of responsibility for their exodus? Do you feel that your aggressive pursuit of physicians may impact future health care in America?"

Once again Mr. Wyatt coughed. "Those who have chosen to quit are simply showing their guilt. An innocent man or woman would simply call their malpractice carrier and allow them to handle this lawsuit. After all, that is why they have insurance, right?" Mr. Wyatt let out a low chuckle and proceeded on. "We are hoping to improve healthcare in America by exposing those doctors who so carelessly jump on new medications without regard for their consequences. If we can hold those doctors accountable, perhaps we can improve healthcare in this country and will have ultimately saved hundreds of thousands of lives."

Maddi and her friends burst into laughter.

"What nonsense," said Hank. "Those lawyers don't make anything better for anyone except themselves and their partners. I really can't stand it any more. I really can't."

Amanda jumped in. "I know, Hank. Me either. Don't they see what they are doing. They are single-handedly crushing the spirit of physicians across the land, and soon there will be no one left."

"That's what I'm afraid of" chimed in Wilson. "I wonder who it is that takes care of them? I read an article recently where doctors were asking if it was unethical to refuse to care for lawyers. At the time I was appalled at the obvious unethical quality of such a request. But now, I don't know."

The four continued on for several hours, eventually getting back to finalizing the forum agenda. By 2:00 in the morning they had pretty much gotten the speakers and the content agreed upon, and decided to finish up in the morning. Maddi called a cab for the three of them. As they were leaving Hank gave Maddi a very long look. She caught his glance and returned the gaze—both of them longingly wondering if the other was thinking what they were. Amanda and Wilson hollered for Hank to come in and get in the cab. He gave Maddi a small nod and turned for the cab. Maddi was about to say something and then simply waved to the three of them and proceeded back into her lonely townhouse apartment.

John McCargish was exhausted. He hated it sometimes when the Supreme Court was in session. There weren't enough hours in the day to do all that needed done to research the various issues that came before the Justices. He had tried to call Maddi several times but by the time she would call back he would be unavailable once again. He knew she was busy with everything going on, but he so wanted to see her. He also found himself very worried about her safety, in spite of the two guys he had arranged to keep an eye on her.

He found himself thinking about Maddi more and more. He had promised himself that he would never again have a romantic relationship with a prominent individual. It wasn't that he minded being in their shadow so much as he knew that the prominence would eventually ruin the relationship. It had happened to him once, and he wasn't about to let it happen again.

But he was having a very difficult time keeping Maddi out of his thoughts. Maybe he should tell her about himself. And about the life he used to have. Maybe if he told her then somehow the relationship could survive against the odds. Maybe that's what he needed to do. Maybe.

John McCargish grew up in a family that traveled often. His father was a Military Man and was moved frequently while John was growing up. John hated his father. His experiences in the military had left him empty and unable to communicate love. Discipline replaced love. At least that is how John saw it. His father was never able to come to any of his sporting events and John got the impression that he didn't really want to. John was 14 when they moved to Philadelphia, and John decided then that he was done moving. He made friends, joined ball teams and spent as much time as he could away from home.

His mother was very passive and withdrawn, and looking back, John had decided she was probably a deeply depressed lady. He did not feel very close to her. She died on John's fifteenth birthday and he didn't recall that he even cried at the funeral. Nor did his father, as he remembered it.

He had no brothers or sisters, and because his father traveled all the time he was unsure what to do after his mother's death. His best friend offered for him to stay there and John decided to do so. He was done moving around, and he was on his own.

He became very self-reliant and worked extra hard at everything he did. His drive strengthened and he eventually wound up at Temple University where he pursued a pre-law degree. He followed this with a law degree from Harvard. He received top honors in his class, and returned to Philadelphia to begin the practice of law. Eventually, he wound up being an assistant district attorney, where he met two people that would impact his life greatly. The first was Evelyn Marker, another assistant District Attorney.

Evelyn was a go-getter, and had her sights set on being District Attorney at some point. She involved herself in the Political Game and was very successful in that arena. John had fallen for her almost the minute he met her, and she had felt the same about him.

John, however, was not nearly as savvy as Evelyn and little by little their different ambitions became a problem. Evelyn was always looking for an opportunity to "put herself out there," while John was more comfortable being "behind the scenes." They tried their best to keep the relationship together but soon Evelyn became more and more distant. Their last night together John remembered well as she told him that he wasn't ambitious enough for where she wanted to go. John gave her one long last look and left her then, never looking back. But his heart had been broken.

The other significant person he met while assistant DA in Philly, was a man by the name of Clarence Morrow.

Clarence Morrow was one of the most impressive attorneys John had ever known. And he was a man with some integrity, which, as John was discovering, was in short supply among lawyers. They quickly became friends and found themselves spending quite a bit of time together during those days when they both worked at the DA's office.

Clarence eventually moved on and made quite a name for himself taking on seemingly impossible cases and winning them. He had a strong dislike for what he considered frivolous lawsuits, and he felt they were becoming all too common in America. He more or less made it his mission to do his part to fight back and defend against any and all frivolous suits he encountered. And he nearly always won.

He and John had kept in touch however, and John would call him on occasion when he needed to bounce something off another brilliant legal mind. When they spoke to one another it was as if no time had passed and the two men always swore they would get together soon and catch up. They had been swearing that now for about 15 years, but they knew someday they truly would make the effort.

Andrew Madison was angry. He was waiting for his flight to leave for Dulles, and was watching CNN as they paraded endless lawyers one after another talking about "those careless doctors" and the damage they had done. He was so glad he had gotten out of medicine when he had, but he nonetheless was troubled by watching the profession fall into such disarray at the hands of greedy malpractice attorneys. He had always known it would come to this, but he hated to see it nonetheless.

Finally his flight boarded and he got settled in his seat. He pulled out the Wall street Journal and began to read. Suddenly an article caught his attention. It was an article concerning the American Trial Lawyers Association and their efforts to combat any and all efforts at tort reform in America. The article had tried to present various points of view concerning litigation reform and the paper had made an effort to interview several different factions. As he was reading he was startled to see Maddi's name in reference to one of the factions trying to "clean up" litigation in the United States. He enjoyed seeing his baby sister quoted and referenced in such a significant way. He kept reading, and then suddenly sat straight up in his seat. They were quoting the president of the ATLA—Frances Buckholtz.

"No way!" Andrew said to himself. "No way that could be the same Frances Buckholtz who was such a little shit back in high school." He continued his reading, looking for something personal about Mr. Buckholtz that would indicate if it was in fact his "old friend" from Evansville, Indiana. Then he saw it.

"Mr. Buckholtz oftens comments about his efforts for the 'little guy,' stating that he identifies with those folks from his days in Indiana."

The words jumped out at Andrew and made him feel sick to his stomach. He couldn't continue reading. All he could do was think back to that terrible night when little Bobby Duggan had drowned. What a snake Buckholtz had been. Not only did he refuse to take any responsibility for the accident, but Andrew knew full well that he would do his damnedest to pin it on Andrew if he could. And Andrew had stood by and allowed the silence. Why? Was he afraid? Did he feel guilty because he hadn't stuck around—perhaps if he had Bobby wouldn't have died? He wasn't sure; he only knew that just thinking about it made him sick to his stomach. He continued thinking about Maddi. All of a sudden he realized what Maddi was up against. That creep, Frances Buckholtz. He wondered if Maddi had any idea who she was battling here. He doubted it. She was nearly seven years younger than Andrew and he didn't think she knew anything about what had happened at the beach that night.

Suddenly he couldn't get to Washington D.C. fast enough. He had to warn Maddi. He had to let her know what a creep she was dealing with. He had to save his little sister.

CHAPTER XXVII

Maddi was having a tough time waking up. She was somewhere in between her dreams and her reality, and she was running as fast as she could. She kept hearing footsteps following her and she was panicked as she tried to run faster and faster. Suddenly she heard a tapping—which sounded like it was directly behind her. She sat straight up and realized that what she heard was a knocking on her door. She felt afraid and didn't know why. She wondered where her two "brutes" were.

She quickly jumped out of bed and grabbed her sweatshirt and headed to her door to answer it. She peaked through the window and couldn't believe her eyes. There before her stood her wonderful big brother Andrew—here in D.C! What was he doing here? The last she knew, he was still up in the Canadian Tundra.

She opened the door.

Suddenly, the two secret service men were at the door—their guns pulled and leveled directly at Andrew.

"He's my brother!" Maddi hollered. They looked questioningly at both Maddi and Andrew, then slowly lowered their guns. Maddi quickly made introductions, and the two men proceeded back to their car. Maddi turned to Andrew and they both started laughing.

"Just an extra precaution a friend of mine set up."

Andrew smiled and nodded his head.

"I'm glad someone is looking out for you."

Maddi reached out and hugged Andrew.

"I can't believe you're here!" Maddi said. "What on earth are you doing here?"

Andrew was grinning from ear to ear. "I came to save my little sister from the Assholes of the world."

Maddi laughed. "Ha! Good Luck. I used to think we could match them but I'm beginning to think their numbers are too great."

"Well, perhaps, but I'm convinced that eventually 'right' wins. So … let's do it."

Maddi began filling in all the pieces of her current situation, trying very hard to leave out nothing. Andrew listened intently, only interrupting when he needed to. Eventually he knew about as much as there was to know, and the conversation drifted to matters of home, Mom, and the Canadian Tundra. After several hours of talk, and several cups of coffee, Maddi jumped up. "I've got to get ready to meet with the others. We're finalizing the forum plans, and Amanda and Wilson are leaving this afternoon. I'd love you to meet all of them—I know they would love you. So, you'll come with me, right?"

"Maddi, I have nothing else to do but hang out with you and keep you safe from Assholes." They both laughed and Maddi proceeded to clean up and get ready to call a cab and run over to the Watergate and grab the others.

While she was getting ready, Andrew made himself at home and began looking around. He saw newspapers scattered all around the flat and started to read the various articles concerning doctors leaving medicine. He thought back to when he made the decision to leave the profession. He had gotten so frustrated with everything. So many things had changed from the time he had started. It was overwhelming. Patients had much higher expectations for their physicians and much lower expectations for their role in their own care. This required doing so many more tests to reassure patients that you were doing all you could. The insurance companies then began to require that you 'preauthorize' everything—which took additional staff, which increased overhead. Lawyers became much more sophisticated about medicine and what was involved and therefore became much more effective at suing doctors. This increased malpractice insurance costs which increased overhead. If the doctor then tried to raise his fees, the insurance companies simply said "no, we're not going to pay them." Pretty soon you had a situation where costs were doubling, income was being cut in half, and patients were no longer appreciative of any of your efforts to help them. Andrew finally woke up one day—in a tundra in Canada—and thought to himself: "What self-respecting individual would put themself through such a thing day after day?" He answered his own question then and there by simply deciding to not go back.

He often wondered about things back home, however. It really is hard to leave everybody and everything you ever knew. But, then, whenever he thought about returning to his former life he knew immediately that he just couldn't do it. He rarely went home even for family gatherings, usually getting home only once a year at Christmas time.

When Maddi had left the profession to go into politics he felt he finally had a comrade who would now know how good it felt to leave the overwhelming responsibility of practicing medicine in America. They really hadn't had a lot of time to discuss their observations since the two of them had left the profession, but he was hoping that maybe now they could do so. He was looking forward to such a conversation.

Maddi came out of her bedroom looking quite refreshed and ready for the day. "I'll call the cab and we can go get the others. My cohort can follow us." Maddi had already filled Andrew in on the Secret Service guys, but had not told him much about John McCargish. She wasn't sure what she would've said had she talked about him anyway.

The cab arrived quickly and Maddi and Andrew hopped in. They chatted about Washington D.C. during much of the 25-minute cab ride. Andrew had lots of questions about Maddi's life, and she had lots of interesting things to share with him concerning her life in Washington.

The ride seemed like it went by very quickly and soon they were pulling up at the Watergate. Maddi asked the cab driver to wait while she and Andrew ran into the lobby to grab the others.

Amanda, Wilson, and Hank were all standing there laughing about something that Hank had said when they saw Maddi and a man they weren't familiar with walk into the lobby.

Maddi made introductions and soon they had all decided to head to a diner that Maddi knew of off the beaten path. They headed outside and hailed a second cab and all proceeded to the diner.

The Secret Service agents followed the two cabs, and—far back behind them was a small blue Toyota making its way cautiously between the traffic, with the driver never taking his dark green eyes off of the cab with the senator and the others inside.

CHAPTER XXVIII

The Diacam case continued to dominate the 24-hour news cycle, and the attorneys were doing their best to dominate the spin. They continued to discuss the carelessness and callousness of physicians in America, belaboring the point that if doctors would only worry more about their patients and less about their wallets none of this would have happened.

The doctors meanwhile, having gotten a late start on the spin machine, were finally having several individuals state their version of events. They detailed the events that occurred, including the FDA approval given to Diacam, culminating with the fact that—if the attorneys weren't so anxious to profit from this misfortune—perhaps more could be done to assist those who were inadvertently injured by Diacam and more could be done to insure the safety of future medications.

FOX News and CNN ran nightly stories concerning various individuals affected by Diacam, and had their prospective "experts" discuss the merit of the case and/or the defense of the doctors.

Meanwhile, across America, there was an increasing awareness of an impending doctor shortage as more and more physicians were displaying their frustration with a system gone haywire. Many doctors continued the exodus from medicine, while others simply began refusing to do any procedures that put them at greater risk from a liability system that was unmistakably out to get them.

This of course affected things such as neurosurgery and cardiothoracic surgery, putting many people in a terrible bind as more and more serious cases were being handled by fewer and fewer physicians. Also greatly affected were pregnant women, whose Obstetricians were simply not willing to continue to deliver babies anymore. There was a steady outrage building across the nation as more and more people felt the effects of doctors leaving their practices.

All the while, insurance companies kept up a steady attempt to cover fewer seriously ill individuals, and pay less and less for services. Their profit margins were growing dramatically as they insured only those individuals who were healthiest, subtly blaming the physicians for not being available to those sicker patients. This allowed their stock and their bottom line to flourish in a climate where more and more Americans were being denied healthcare.

Blame was being assessed everywhere by everyone and no one was willing to except responsibility for the impending disaster. Congress had decided to form a committee to explore and attempt to solve this crisis, but the committee was bogged down by two senators who were at complete odds with one another concerning what the crisis actually constituted.

Senator Richards, (D) Arizona, felt that the doctors were mostly to blame for a system that robbed patients of their protections while the physicians were recording large incomes and having second homes. He felt that the solution lay mostly with socialized medicine, thereby assuring that all Americans would be covered, and physicians would no longer have much individual power at all. He felt that by taking the doctors' power away, you would then be able to offer healthcare to patients without an ulterior motive. The doctors would serve at the Government's behest, and this would restore what should be the doctors' willingness to take care of sick people without requiring a large income. The physicians would still receive "adequate" reimbursement from the Government and all Americans would be covered.

Senator Madison, (R) Indiana, felt much the opposite. She believed that the root of the problem lay in a system where responsibility was no longer expected from individuals, and that anything that went wrong deserved a financial compensation. She felt lawyers kept that thinking alive, actively encouraging what she referred to as "The Victim Mentality." She believed lawyers to be gifted at exploiting victim-hood and making it seem not only acceptable but obligatory. She blamed the legal industry for profiting on both sides of every issue, and she felt strongly that the lawyers designed the law so that attorneys were essential for every dispute.

Maddi had already had ample opportunity to share her impressions of this system and her forum had already been discussed nationally. The current situation with Diacam and the law firm of Wyatt, Hanson, Richards and Schultz made her position that much more relevant and thus more newsworthy. Maddi was being interviewed daily and her forum was becoming a very big deal.

She and her friends had finished up their plans for the forum on Sunday morning and she and Hank and Andrew had taken Amanda and Wilson to the airport and sent them on their way. They were both planning to attend the forum and thus would see Maddi and Hank again soon.

Hank, Andrew and Maddi had then done some sight-seeing and discussed nearly non-stop the issues facing physicians. Hank and Andrew took an immediate liking to one another and the three of them had a delightful afternoon together.

Andrew had arranged to take the first flight Monday morning back to Detroit, then back to the Tundra. He knew he had to talk to Maddi about Frances Buckholtz and, although he would've preferred to discuss the history surrounding Buckholtz with Maddi alone, he decided that Hank was trustworthy. He informed Maddi and Hank that he was taking them both to dinner and plans were made. They stopped by the Watergate and waited for Hank to change and then the three of them proceeded to Fran O'Brien's Steakhouse for dinner and drinks.

Once they had ordered their cocktails, Andrew proceeded to tell the story of Little Bobby Duggan's death so many years ago.

He slowly introduced the characters of his story, and—one by one—allowed Maddi and Hank to appreciate the role of each individual in the drama he was unfolding before them.

He refrained from connecting Frances Buckholtz to the current situation by simply referring to him as Frances. Maddi was not very well acquainted with the individuals involved, although she did know Bobby Duggan's little sister fairly well when they were in school. The sister would never say much about what had happened to her brother however; only that he had drowned.

As Andrew proceeded to tell Hank and Maddi about "that night" out on the lake, Maddi could feel her heart beating faster. She had no idea where Andrew was heading with this story, but she knew she wasn't going to like it.

Finally, Andrew had gotten to the part of his story involving the actual drowning of Bobby Duggan. Maddi and Hank were on the edge of their seats, as Andrew continued.

"I'm about out of there, no longer wanting to sit around and drink alcohol with these silly losers, when I hear someone screaming. I ran toward the screaming and saw Frances quickly running into the lake. I yelled at him to stop—I knew he was already well into the night's booze—and he turned around to me." Andrew paused. It was clear to Maddi and Hank that this story was a very difficult story for Andrew to think about, let alone share with them. He proceeded, but much more quietly.

"Frances started screaming something along the lines of 'we have to help him Andy. He's drunk and he's out there somewhere.' I asked him who we had to help. He screamed out Bobby. I knew he meant little Bobby Duggan, who often joined in on the drinking by the lake. So, I jumped in the lake with Frances and we swam toward where Bobby had supposedly gone under. I asked Frances if he had visually marked the spot where Bobby had gone under with a stationary object on land and he simply ignored me and continued diving for Bobby. I knew then that we were essentially looking for a needle in a haystack without any land markings, but I also began diving and looking for Bobby.

"After several minutes, I knew that we weren't going to find him. I grabbed at Frances, but he ignored me. Finally, I grabbed him and wouldn't let him go. I told him we had to stop and go to shore and let someone know what had happened. He looked at me with his eyes wilder than I've ever seen anyone's, and he said 'No! We can't tell anybody, ever!'

Andrew's upper lip was perspiring and he was visibly shaking in his chair. He looked as though he was trying to keep from crying. He continued on. "I kept trying to convince him that we needed to call someone. He tried to tell me that we would be blamed. He kept including me in the situation, as though I too had played a role. He insisted that if the police did get involved he would make sure they knew that I had been there as well. He also told me that he would tell them I had been drinking along with he and Bobby." Andrew got a very sad look on his face. It was evident that he regretted that night more than he could ever say.

"I guess I was scared. I'm not really sure. For whatever reason, though, I went along with him and never told anyone—until now—about the events of that evening."

Maddi was watching him very closely. She felt his pain and watched as he trembled with just the memory of that night. "Andrew. How did they finally find out about him drowning?" she asked.

"Several days later his body drifted to the shoreline. Although there were suspicions about what had happened, the people involved chose—for what-ever reason—to let it go, and they classified it as a drowning. No autopsy was performed, and the fact that he was drunk was never uncovered. I have never fully forgiven myself for the entire thing."

The three of them sat in silence for several minutes. It appeared once again as though Andrew wanted to cry, but he didn't. Maddi and Hank exchanged glances, and then Maddi reached over and grabbed Andrew's arm.

"I think that any 17 year old boy would've done the same. Besides, your telling of the truth would not have changed anything." She paused a moment and then continued. "I am curious though why you're telling us this story here and now."

Andrew looked at them both and shrugged his shoulders. "The truth of it is, Maddi, Frances knew that I knew the truth. He also had shown me his true colors that night, and he knew that I saw him for how he really was. A very shallow, calloused, self-serving man who had no other interests in mind but to save his own ass." Andrew was speaking much faster now, clearly upset and angry. "He told me that night that if I ever told anyone what really happened he would see to it that I would be blamed along with him. I think as time went on, he began to despise me for what I knew about that night, and for what I knew about his character. I believe it safe to say that the hatred he felt for me has probably magnified itself through the years."

Maddi jumped in. "But I still don't see its relevance to now."

Andrew cleared his throat. "Maddi. Frances' last name is Buckholtz." He paused waiting to see if Maddi comprehended the significance of what he had just told her. When she continued looking at him clearly puzzled, he spoke again. "Frances Buckholtz. As in the president of the American Trial Lawyer's Association."

Maddi gasped. She reached her hand up over her mouth, spilling her water in the process. She began cleaning it up and shaking her head. "Oh my god, Andy. You don't think there is any connection between what happened to you 30 years ago and what is happening to me now, do you?" She was trembling as she continued to clean up her water spill.

"I would certainly like to think there is no connection, Maddi. But, ya' know? I wouldn't put it past him at all. Face it, Maddi, he's a Creep. He always was and he continues to be. So, why wouldn't this play a role?"

Hank, having remained silent during the telling of the entire story, now interjected. "Do you think he even knows that Maddi is your sister?"

"Of course he does," Andrew replied. "I mean, we grew up together, dammit! I'm sure he has known it all along. Whether or not it has anything to do with Maddi getting shot at—now that, I don't know."

Maddi looked at Andrew with disbelief. "There is no way you think his hatred for you would cause him to hire a hit man to shoot me! No one is that evil."

"Well, Maddi. I'm here to tell you that Frances Buckholtz is quite capable of such a thing. Just think what he was capable of at the age of 17. I'm almost sure he could do it—if it suited his needs."

The three of them continued to discuss the story of Frances Buckholtz and how it might be related to current events. Their dinner finally came and they all three picked at it, talking avidly the entire time. Eventually they had all refused dessert, and were sipping on after-dinner drinks. They talked awhile longer, then Andrew mentioned that he had a very early flight and so the three of them headed back toward the Watergate to drop off Hank. He and Maddi had made arrangements to meet for brunch around 10:30 and they said good-night.

Andrew and Maddi headed back toward her townhouse. They were engrossed in conversation concerning the Forum and Maddi's legislation for the laws to govern attorneys, when the cab driver spoke from the front of the cab.

"Do either of you know someone in a small, blue Toyota?"

Andrew and Maddi looked at one another with puzzled expressions. Maddi responded. "No sir, we don't. Why do you ask?"

"Well, ma'am. There is someone behind us in a small, blue Toyota who has been following us since we left the Watergate."

Maddi and Andrew quickly turned around and could see, hiding behind a large black SUV, the small blue Toyota the cabby was referring to. Maddi looked at Andrew, and he looked back reading her mind.

"You don't think-" she said.

"Maddi, I think we need to let your Secret Service guys know what's up. Where are they and how do you get a hold of them?"

Maddi replied. "I don't know where they are. Come to think of it, I haven't seen them since we left the restaurant."

Maddi and Andrew exchanged fearful glances. Andrew spoke first.

"Cabby. Pull over. Now."

"But Sir, I'm in the middle of Constitution Avenue. I can't very well stop here."

"Well. Stop and pull over as soon as it is feasible. Wait! On the other hand, what is that road over there?" Andrew pointed to his left to a small side road barely visible off of the busy thoroughfare.

"That is Wilson Avenue. There's not much down there but some homeless folks. It leads to the river."

"Take it," said Andrew.

The cabby quickly slid over into the left lane, and then, just as quickly took the turn to the left down Wilson Avenue. They proceeded down the Avenue as quickly as the cabby was able to drive. About a mile further down the road Andrew yelled out. "Quick, turn here."

"But sir-"

"Just do it, dammit."

The cabby turned right at the next road, a very small alley-like road which appeared to go absolutely nowhere. They continued about 4/5 of a mile further when the road became a dirt access road leading behind a water tower.

"Stop here." Andrew and Maddi turned to look at the same time, desperately hoping that they wouldn't see a small, blue Toyota.

After several minutes, with no sighting of the Toyota, they both began to relax. Maddi spoke first. "Andrew. If that is the guy who took a shot at me I'm sure he knows where I live. So, what's the use of out-running him this time when all he really has to do is wait for me to go home?"

"Maddi. We have to find your Secret Service detail. Do you have a number you can call?"

Maddi thought for a moment. "Actually, I've never needed to call them—they were always there. I have no idea how to get in touch with them. Besides, aren't they supposed to follow me everywhere?"

Andrew had a very concerned look on his face. "That's just it, Maddi. I'm afraid something must have happened to them. We have to find out. And if it has, we have to report it immediately."

"I'll call John" Maddi said. "John McCargish. He's the one who assigned them to me in the first place."

Maddi proceeded to find John's name in her cell phone directory. She dialed the number. After several rings, John's answering machine picked up. "Damn!" Maddi said. "His machine." She quickly left a message simply asking John to call her as soon as possible, and hung up the phone. The three of them—Andrew, herself and the cabby—continued watching behind them for the Toyota. It never came.

After several more minutes, they decided to head back to Maddi's townhouse, and they would try to call John McCargish again. The cabby tried to make conversation, and inquired as to who the guy in the Toyota might be, but Andrew and Maddi didn't respond. They were both lost in thought. Andrew thinking about Frances Buckholtz's role in all this, and Maddi thinking about whether it was even safe for her to go home tonight.

Peter Smith couldn't believe it. He'd lost them. How on earth had they gotten out of his sight? He was the best in the business, and that crazy cabby had given him the slip. He was starting to get just a bit annoyed with this situation. He'd have to kill the senator soon, because he couldn't stand failing at something he normally did so well.

He grinned to himself. He had, however, taken care of the Secret Service guys. He had been so clever. He knew they wouldn't be found for days. He tore off some of their clothes, stuck a bottle of liquor in each guy's hands, and laid them behind some trash cans in the middle of a forgotten alley. No one would find them any time soon. They were so easy. Simply let down their guard. He was almost disappointed at the lack of challenge killing them had been.

This meant that the senator would be an easy target. Perhaps tonight. While she was sleeping. He didn't even care if he got paid for this now. He had to do it for his reputation. If he didn't kill this senator, he knew he would no longer be the go-to guy. He'd have to do it, and he'd have to do it soon.

CHAPTER XXIX

John McCargish finally left the Supreme Court, where he'd been all day. He was exhausted. Although he loved what he did there for the court and Chief Justice Harper, he always dreaded these kinds of days—they went on forever, and left him totally spent. He got nothing else done during this time; it was as if he wasn't part of the world …

… The world with Maddi. He found himself thinking of her more and more. He so wanted to get closer to her. To know her—what she was made of—her past, her dreams, what she wanted to do in the future. He had decided to call her once he left the Court and try to arrange for an actual date. He grabbed his cell phone from his briefcase where he kept it because one of the Justices despised "those intrusive devices-" and quickly checked for messages. He had several. He began to review them.

The first was from his aunt—he would call her later. The second, from the Secret Service men following Maddi. It was very out-of-the-ordinary for them to be calling him. He anxiously played the message.

"John. This is Kent Williams—I'm one of the detail on Senator Madison. Something's up. There's this small, blue Toyota that I think has been following her. I'll check it out and get back to you."

Time—9:27pm.

John was concerned. He continued to review his messages. The next was from the Sheriff's Departement. John played the message.

"Mr. McCargish. This is Sheriff Rutherford. I need you to come down to the station to assist us with the identification of two bodies. I believe these men may have known you. We've found your card in some of their belongings. At first they were dismissed as drunks, but then one of our officers found your card in a back pocket. We have now determined that they are with the Secret Service. We've contacted the Secret Service and they are on their way."

Time—10:32 pm.

John started to shake. He felt panicked. He knew he had to speak to Maddi. He looked down—he had only 1 more message to play. It was from Maddi.

"Hey John. It's Maddi. Call me the minute you get this message."

Time—10:37 pm.

John looked at his watch. 1:07am. John tried to dial his phone. His hands were shaking and he had to keep starting over. Finally, he dialed Maddi's cell phone number correctly and waited for Maddi to pick up. After several rings he heard her message. "This is Maddi. Leave a message. Thanks."

"Shit!" he muttered under his breath. He thought he had her home phone number in his cell directory. He scrolled through, but couldn't find it. "Shit!" he said again. He decided to just head to her home. While on the way, he called the Sheriff's office.

"This is John McCargish. I was contacted earlier by the Sheriff to come in and ID some men who were found several hours ago. Secret Service men. Would the sheriff be available for me to speak with?"

"One moment, sir, and I'll check."

After what seemed like hours, the secretary got back on the line. "The sheriff is unavailable at the current time. If you would like to-" John hung up the phone.

He continued to head toward Maddi's house. He arrived 17 minutes later. He began walking quickly toward Maddi's front steps. As he neared her residence he stopped suddenly in his tracks. There silhouetted in the darkness, stood a man holding a shotgun to his shoulder—aimed and ready to go.

Andrew knew he would be unable to sleep that night. Maddi was in trouble and he knew it. Fortunately, Maddi had a shot gun in the attic, which had belonged to their father. She'd taken it at her mother's request, because—as she put it—"you're living amongst some pretty dark elements out there in D.C."

Maddi had intended to eventually obtain a license and learn how to shoot the gun—but she hadn't yet found the time, so there it sat in the attic where she had put it when it had been given to her over a year ago.

All this came out when they got in the house. Andrew made a comment about wishing he had his gun with him and Maddi informed him of the shotgun in the attic. Andrew immediately climbed up and found the shotgun. He looked it over and grabbed some shells which were sitting along side of it. He brought the gun and the shells down the steps and looked it over quickly while sitting in Maddi's living room.

He knew the gun well. He had fired it on numerous occasions. It was the gun his father had used to teach him to shoot when he was eight years old. He was suddenly back in time. Remembering the hunting lodge where his dad taught him to shoot and to hunt. The nights by the fire, and the early morning sunshine. The way it smelled when the dawn was breaking, and the sun was echoing through the trees, light reflecting like a prism in the early morning dew.

Then, all at once he was twelve years old, watching as two very sad policemen told his mother that his father was dead. Suddenly Andrew felt anger. He was full of bitterness at the memory of his mother and her refusal to let him help her. How she shut him out of all he needed to be part of. He had never forgiven her for this, and the memory of it filled him with sadness and anger, even 40 years later.

Maddi was watching Andrew as he traveled back, and she could see all the hurt and the anger rising up within him. She softly touched him on the shoulder.

Andrew quickly put his memories back in their prison deep inside him, and tried to focus on the problem at hand.

As he prepared the gun, he and Maddi exchanged concerned glances. Neither one said a word, however, as they both knew that whoever it was that had taken a shot at Maddi wasn't kidding around. And, they both also knew that Maddi's secret service men were no longer with her.

Maddi elected to try to go to bed, while Andrew agreed to stay up and keep watch. He took the gun and headed to the front porch where he found a place in the corner hidden by the shadows where he could keep watch.

Andrew sat watch for several hours. He had plenty to think about and much to reflect on. Andrew enjoyed being alone. He enjoyed thinking and analyzing things. And, as on so many other occasions when he found himself with time to think, he eventually began replaying in his mind the events that occurred on that night long ago when Bobby Duggan died. He'd never been able to forgive himself for what had happened, even though he really had nothing to do with the drowning. He wasn't sure why, but he knew that just thinking about the fact that he allowed Frances Buckholtz to orchestrate how the tragedy was handled made his blood boil. It was as if Bobby never really got his due. Everyone was allowed to think that he'd been foolish—swimming alone in the lake at night—and had paid the ultimate price. They had no idea that Frances had provided the alcohol and the incentive for Bobby to go out into that lake in the first place. Why hadn't he—Andrew—told anyone the truth? Was he afraid? If so, why?

Andrew was lost in his thinking when all at once he heard a sound a few feet away. He crouched down even lower than he was and waited. He heard another sound. He knew it was a footstep. He tensed up and continued to listen, looking into the night to see who it was that was approaching. He was just getting ready to yell out when all at once he saw a smaller man, with a ball cap pulled low over his forehead. The minute Andrew spotted him the man saw Andrew. Andrew looked directly into the man's eyes. The man reached into his jacket and appeared to be pulling out a gun. Andrew had drawn his own gun to his shoulder and was preparing to shoot. The man suddenly tripped and nearly fell, and Andrew let off a shot. There was a groan, and then a quick shuffle of footsteps heading away from the house.

Andrew was shocked. He had never fired at a human being in his life. And, although Andrew had killed many an animal for sport, shooting at another human being—even an armed, evil one—was very different and very unsettling.

Suddenly Andrew heard another sound from the other side of the yard. He was about to draw his shotgun up to fire again when he heard a voice.

"Hey! Don't shoot!"

Andrew wasn't sure what to do. He yelled back. "Who are you?"

The voice replied. "Please don't shoot me. My name is John McCargish and I'm a friend of Maddi's. I'm the one who got the Secret Service guys for her."

Andrew thought for just a moment and decided that this man sounded legitimate. "All right, but listen. The guy's got a gun, and I think I may have hit him in the shoulder. If you can go after him, I'll call the police and stay here to protect Maddi. But keep out of sight, like I said, the guy's got a gun."

John McCargish nodded his head, then turned and ran down the alley. Andrew heard him as his steps faded into the night. Andrew sat down, and realized he was shaking. He couldn't believe what was happening here. Somebody had just tried—once again—to kill his little sister. There was no way on earth that he was going to leave her now. He had to find the guy and find out why he wanted Maddi dead. He knew someone must have hired that man to do this, but who? He knew he had to find out. He sat back down and waited. He'd wait until he had the answers he needed.

John McCargish was scared to death. What the hell was he doing? Chasing an armed man through the night with absolutely no protection of his own. But he had to do it. This man had tried to kill Maddi. Again. Why? He didn't know, but he continued running, trying hard to keep up with the man several hundred yards in front of him.

They were running for what seemed like miles, when all of a sudden the man stopped and turned around. John froze. The man raised his gun up and pointed it directly at John. John quickly looked from side to side, and—as he heard the "pop" from the pistol—he jumped to his left behind several piled up trash cans. The shot missed him and ricocheted off one of the cans on his right. He quickly got up and glanced around from behind the cans. He saw no sign of the man anywhere. He shook himself off and hesitantly stepped out into the alley. He still did not see the man anywhere. He listened for a sound, but heard nothing. This alley ran into a very busy intersection, and John knew that whoever this guy was, he had gotten away again. He finally decided to turn around and go back and check on Maddi.

When he stepped back from the alley to the front of the house he heard Andrew cock his gun and he saw him aim at him.

"Sir. It's me. The same man who just went to look for the shooter."

Andrew relaxed and allowed the gun to fall to his side. "Did you find him? Or, see where he went?" Andrew knew the answer by the look on the man's face.

"No sir, I didn't. He took a shot at me and then slipped away somewhere beyond the alley. I'll get some of my friends to work on this in the morning. Did you get a good look at him?"

Andrew told him that he saw only that he was a smaller man, and that he had a ball cap pulled over his forehead. He did mention that when the man looked his way his eyes were very small and sunk way back into his head, and that his hair seemed to fall over his eyes, nearly hiding them from view. He was certain that if he saw him again he would recognize him.

John realized then that he had no idea who it was he was talking to. Who was this man keeping watch over Maddi? He proceeded to introduce himself. "I'm John McCargish. I work at the Supreme Court. I am sort of helping Maddi with her litigation reform efforts." He stuck out his hand.

Andrew reached out and shook John's hand. "I'm Andrew Madison, Maddi's brother. I flew in yesterday to look after my little sister. I'm glad I did."

"Me too." John walked up onto the porch and both men sat and began to get acquainted. They mostly discussed Maddi's legislation efforts, and who might be threatened by those efforts. After an hour or two, they realized how late it was, and how tired they both were and John excused himself.

"Hey Andrew. Let Maddi know that I came by. I can't believe she slept through all of that, but I'm really glad she did."

"Yeah, me too. I'll let her know."

Both men nodded to one another and John headed for his car. He got in, turned the key, put his hands on the wheel and pulled away from the curb. He was shaking, and felt panic from within. Who the hell was trying to kill Maddi? His heart ached at the thought of something happening to her. He continued driving into the darkness of early dawn.

Peter was hurt. "That asshole hit me in the shoulder." He wondered who he was. Where did he come from? And who was the jerk that was following him down the alley. He wasn't sure if the shot he'd fired had hit him—but he sure hoped so.

Peter knew he had to get some medical attention for his shoulder. He also knew that there would be lots of people looking for him. Peter felt lucky because his unanticipated fall kept him from receiving the brunt of the shotgun's blast, and the few pellets that had hit him had done so at an angle, and had not lodged themselves deep in his shoulder. This was good. And, he had managed to stop the bleeding, which was even better. Maybe he could avoid a doctor. He would try.

He couldn't believe that that Senator Madison had survived again. This could not stand. Peter knew he had to succeed—and fast. He needed the money that Buckholtz was going to pay him—and he needed his reputation to remain intact. That was the most important thing.

It seemed the senator always had somebody with her. Peter had to figure out a way to get to her when nobody was around. He kept thinking about it. When would that be? How would he know? He thought she was alone tonight. He really got that wrong.

Then it occurred to him that perhaps the best way to get the senator would be when she was in a very public place. Not a restaurant, or a museum, but before a huge crowd of people. Where he could shoot her and then immediately get lost amongst the crowd. This was what he needed to do—a much better plan.

Peter began planning his strategy. He knew that sooner or later Senator Madison would speak before a large crowd of people. He knew that that would be his last best chance to take her out. He knew that she had orchestrated a forum of some sort—that was the reason he was hired in the first place. He would kill her at her own forum. Brilliant.

John left Maddi's house and went directly to the police station. He knew he wasn't going to get any sleep if he went home. Besides, he had to see who the two men were that the Sheriff had called him about; although, he already knew it was the secret service men he'd assigned to Maddi. And he was certain—if it was them—that the man he chased down the alley was the man responsible for their death. He would tell the officers all of this.

He got to the station around 4:00am. He spoke with the officer in charge, filling him in on the attempted murder of Senator Madison once again, as well as his suspicions concerning the deaths of his secret service guys. He confirmed that the two dead men were in fact working at his request to protect Maddi from the very thing that had been attempted this past evening. He provided the officer with the sparse description of the shooter that had been given to him by Andrew. They assured him that they would commence a man-hunt immediately, and keep him abreast of all that went on.

Once John was satisfied that everything was being done that could be done, he headed back to his apartment. He knew he wouldn't be able to sleep, so he sat down and began to think through all that had occurred. Could it really be true that the Trial Lawyers Association had hired a hit-man for Maddi? He found that hard to believe—even for trial lawyers. He knew, however, that millions of dollars were at stake if Maddi succeeded. Lawsuit money that would never be "earned" by trial lawyers across the land. Perhaps it was enough to justify to them the need to stop her, whatever it took…. John finally fell asleep at 5:30 in the morning, sitting in his chair.

Maddi awakened bright and early, ready to take Andrew to the airport. She took one look at his face and knew that things had changed.

"Andrew. You look terrible! Didn't you sleep well?"

Andrew chuckled, and then proceeded to update Maddi on the events of the prior evening. Maddi listened with disbelief. She couldn't believe that someone had actually tried to kill her again. And, she couldn't believe that John McCargish had come to protect her. Finally, when Andrew had finished his narrative, Maddi looked him straight in the eyes and grabbed his hand. "Andrew. You've got to get back home. I'll be fine. I know you feel you need to protect me—but I'll be okay. I have lots of friends here who are watching over me, and I don't want you to feel as though you need to stay."

Andrew laughed. "Maddi. It's a done deal. I've already contacted the outpost in Canada and they have arranged replacements for me for the next 4 weeks."

"Four weeks! You can't do that!"

"Sure I can. I have. That way I can keep an eye on you through the Forum. I think once that is done, you will be okay. So, no further discussion—I'm your roommate until this thing is done."

Maddi smiled at Andrew slowly, knowing that she felt so much more comfortable with him there. She let him know that she was meeting up with Hank around 11:00am and that he was welcome to join them, but he bowed out. He wanted to look into a gun purchase—an upgrade to the shotgun he said. He had some friends in D.C. who could help him and he was going to look them up.

There was news of the attempted shooting all over the TV set and Andrew and Maddi watched a bit of it over coffee. A manhunt was underway, and Andrew's description of the assailant was played over and over again. John had arranged for another secret service detail for Maddi, and this made both Maddi and John feel a bit better about things. Maddi finished her coffee and headed for her bedroom to get ready to go for the day.

Andrew tidied up the kitchen and got ready to go himself. He had a lot to do if he was going to protect his little sister properly.

Maddi hailed a cab at around 11:00am—which would make her about 20 minutes late to meet Hank—but she knew he'd understand. Hank was that kind of guy. He always had been. Just a nice, easy guy. Comfortable to be around. Interesting without being overbearing. Maddi was anxious to spend the day with him.

Then she thought about John. He'd come there last night to look after her. To protect her. She hadn't heard from him in several days and thought perhaps she had read his signals wrong. But there he was last night. And he must be devastated about the two men he had assigned her. She wanted to talk to him. She'd have to try to see him after she got Hank on the plane.

Maddi felt confused. She had never wanted to allow a relationship to get in her way. She had always felt that her satisfaction in life would not come from a man but from her accomplishments, and she knew if she got tangled up in a relationship it was very likely that she would forego her accomplishments. She would end up living a boring, content life, having done nothing useful or important.

Yet here she was. With not one but two relationships knocking at her door. Both very good men. But the timing was all wrong. She couldn't allow anything to happen with either man. At least not now. She had to get her forum going and succeed with making "Maddi's Laws" as prevalent as Stark Laws. She had to fix the industries of both medicine and law. It was important and essential that she do this. She had to allow relationships to be put on hold. She would have to find a way to make this clear to both men. Soon.

Maddi's cab pulled up to the Watergate, with her Secret Service detail in tow, and Maddi jumped out and headed for the door. She had already planned what she would say to Hank. Something along the lines of "Hank, I so enjoy being with you. Perhaps when this forum is over …"

Then, she saw Hank standing in the Lobby reading a newspaper. She felt something very strong within her—almost like a giddy feeling—and she knew this was going to be tougher than she thought.

When she walked into the lobby, Hank immediately caught sight of her and ran toward her. He hugged her and exclaimed "My god, Maddi. Someone tried to kill you last night."

Maddi could feel Hank shaking and she knew that she was shaking as well. She realized then that she really hadn't reacted to the events that had occurred, but somehow here with Hank she felt she could. In spite of her best efforts, Maddi began to cry. They both stood there like that—embraced, with Maddi crying, for quite a while. Finally, Maddi pulled away just a bit and looked up at Hank. He was smiling. Maddi knew then that she was not going to be able to set this relationship aside—like one might a book they were reading—until after the forum. She knew right then and there that she and Hank were falling in love.

She felt suddenly as though she had known Hank her entire life. She was comforted by his very presence and she could tell in his eyes that he felt the same. She hugged him again, this time tighter. He hugged her back and she hoped that moment would never end.

Finally, he spoke. "Maddi. I've seen Washington D.C. before. I've been to the Smithsonian, walked along the Mall, and stood before the White House in awe. How about we forego the D.C. tour and you and I enjoy the very expensive room I've got here at this historic hotel?"

Maddi was so confused. Should she say "yes?" This wasn't in her original plan, and she knew she would regret it if she got off track. But she wanted to be with Hank right then like she had never wanted to be with anyone. Maybe she could make it work. Maybe she could allow this relationship to happen and still do something useful and important. She wasn't sure. All she really knew for sure is that she wanted to go upstairs with Hank right now. For the first time in her life, she decided to just do it.

"I think that would be a wonderful idea, Hank." With that, she ran out and waved away her cabby, and ran back inside. She saw the car with the Secret Service, parked to the side. She and Hank proceeded to the elevator.

CHAPTER XXX

The Forum was rapidly approaching. News media were speaking about it on a daily basis, and doctors continued exiting their practices across the nation. This continued to provide fuel for the forum.

The most recent exodus occurred in New York City, thus creating an incredibly busy news day. Forty doctors left their practices which were part of the much larger organization known as "New York Medical." This was an organization with over 100 physicians from multiple specialties. They had an affiliation with several area hospitals, and were well thought of throughout the northeast. Several dignitaries from various countries had utilized their services while in New York for United Nations events or other concerns. The mayor of New York was also a patient in their facility. This notoriety caused their exodus to be front page news, and therefore put the issue back in the media spotlight just in time for Maddi's forum to benefit.

To date Maddi had 2,784 physicians registered to attend the forum. She had 14 speakers, and 2 large gala dinners arranged. Several attorneys from around the country had expressed interest, the most notable being Clarence Morrow. He was back in the States and John McCargish had facilitated his involvement. He was proving to be quite an asset. He understood lawyers well, but had grown weary of their diversion into greed. He agreed with Maddi that the noble profession of law had taken a very wrong turn and that it was time to put things back on track.

Maddi and Clarence Morrow hit it off immediately. Maddi knew something of Mr. Morrow from following his involvement in the class action lawsuit being conducted against the 3000-plus physicians who had prescribed Diacam. He had been asked—and bank-rolled—by a retired doctor from Philadelphia to oversee the doctors' defense in the Diacam case. Mr. Morrow had already proposed some interesting motions in his challenge of the suit. He had kept the law firm of Wyatt, Hanson, Richards and Shultz on the run since his involvement. Maddi delighted in watching the large, overbearing firm respond to each motion with near-exasperation. She felt that Clarence Morrow was definitely up to the task of taking them on.

Originally, Maddi had asked that Mr. Morrow work with Kevin Clayborne, who was helping her with "Maddi Laws." Mr. Morrow approached Kevin about this and was greeted with what at first appeared to be warmth and openness. However, it didn't take Clarence long at all to figure out that Kevin might not be what he seemed. Clarence had spent a life time working with—and getting to know—all aspects of people and their natures and something about Kevin and his role in Maddi's forum didn't seem right at all to him. He decided to watch Kevin closely and keep an eye on the situation. He would only bother Maddi with it if his suspicions proved to be correct. In the meantime, he pretended to cooperate with Kevin fully.

Kevin, in the meantime had been doing as much as possible to undermind Maddi's efforts with "Maddi's Laws." He wrote up his ideas, fully aware that they were bad law at best, and unconstitutional at worst. He felt he could sucker them past her, and then when she actually tried to get the Laws legislated she would be mocked for her inexperience and ignorance. He knew he would have to keep Clarence Morrow away from this of course.

Kevin was delighted with himself. His cleverness had always been unappreciated, and he knew this was his opportunity to finally be recognized as the genius he knew he was. He was in Mensa, after all.

He'd kept Roger Clairy in the loop, and now had direct access to Roger at the ATLA. He was finally working his way up the proverbial ladder.

Roger meanwhile had been doing his best from his post in Washington to publicly denounce not only Maddi's efforts but denounce her personally as well. He had hired a private investigator to dig up dirt on Maddi, and had published some commentary articles—under other names—denouncing her ideas as foolhardy and politically motivated. He tried to make the connection that Maddi was working for "big business," and that doctors had become "big business" as a result of their huge incomes. Maddi was able to combat this quite easily by publishing average income for physicians, versus average income for successful trial lawyers, as well as the income for HMO executives. She also was able to find example after example of frivolous lawsuits, not only against physicians, but against other small business owners as well.

Roger continually checked with his private investigator as to any dirt on Maddi, but was told repeatedly that he couldn't find any dirt on her whatsoever. Not only that, but it appeared that Maddi was quite respected on Capitol Hill and by the public at large. She was seen as a reformer trying with full sincerity to improve this nation. Her efforts were perceived as quixotic, but noble, and she had become a favorite underdog of sorts. Maddi was becoming a symbol for Good.

Frances Buckholtz was lying very low the last several weeks. He knew his "man" was on the loose and wanted, and he knew that this man could tie him to the attempted murder of the senator. He had hoped by now to simply have Senator Madison scared away from her effort and this guy paid off. Now that things had escalated, Frances was in a potential nightmare if the hitman was found. He was closely watching the news for any sign of the missing man, praying that no one would find him and that he would just disappear from the scene. Frances knew however, that Peter Smith—or whoever the hell he was—was not going to stop until he had completed his task. The only thing Frances could hope for was that somehow Peter himself would be killed as well. That would make everything work out great. As a matter of fact, that was a wonderful idea. If Peter died, after successfully killing Maddi, all of Frances' troubles would be over.

Then he remembered Roger. He had made the mistake of introducing Peter to Roger. What if somehow Roger made that connection? Was there any real evidence tying Peter to Frances? He could say they were acquaintances. And that he had only hired Peter to intimidate Maddi—not to kill her. Which would be true—sort of. He would have to think about this—and try to decide what he needed to do about Roger. But, in the meantime, he was just going to lay low.

He stood quietly by as Senator Madison's Forum monopolized the media. He watched the senator get positive press and watched as she seemed to gain public support. He wasn't sure what to do, but he knew he had to do something big. If her forum was successful, it would do irreparable harm to tort law for decades. Not on his watch. He couldn't allow it. He'd have to think of something to bring her down.

Buckholtz' thoughts were racing through his mind. He hated that bitch. And her brother too. Self-righteous prick. If people only knew what an arrogant asshole the senator's brother was. Perhaps they'd think twice about embracing Ms. Cynthia Madison. It would be fun to expose Andrew Madison for who he really was. But how could Frances do that without opening himself up to criticism? He learned long ago that the best defense was a good offense.

What if he told that story about the lake a bit differently? What if he suggested that it was Andrew who had done the drinking and encouraged the night swim? Who would know? When Andy started to deny it, he would look like a guilty man. And Frances could talk about how he was the one who tried to save Bobby Duggan. And that Andrew begged him to keep it quiet. And that out of mistaken loyalty for a friend he agreed. And now was regretful and wanted to clear the air. This was a brilliant idea. He could come out with this announcement and get the senator off of the front pages and into the "irrelevant section" of the paper. He would also cast doubt on who she was and what she was made of. The Wonderful Senator Madison would be taken down a peg or two. And with that, Frances had a plan.

The news story broke the day before the forum was set to begin. Maddi had been staying in Indianapolis for the last 3 days, working on last minute coordinations. Her speakers had all arrived and checked in and her doctors had started arriving from across the country. News media from the major stations were all well-represented and Maddi knew that this was going to be a big event, and must be done well.

She was taking a break from her responsibilities, sipping on coffee and glancing at a local Indianapolis paper when she suddenly stopped what she was doing, nearly spilling her coffee. On the front page of the Star screamed the following headline:

"Senator Madison's Brother with Problems of His Own"

Maddi was stunned. She read on.

> *"Senator Cynthia Madison, currently well-known for her efforts at tort reform, apparently has a brother who has failed the ethics test himself. Andrew Madison, the senator's older brother by seven years apparently has a history that both he and the senator have tried to keep hidden.*
> *"It seems that nearly 40 years ago Andrew Madison had a problem with alcohol. Although this in and of itself is not an ethical issue, the loss of life connected to it certainly is. Our source tells us the following.*
> *"Andrew, who was a life guard at the time, would often drink alcohol late at night by nearby Kentucky Lake outside Evansville. He would always try to encourage his friends to join him. Apparently one of those friends was Frances Buckholtz, also a life guard, who is currently in charge of the American Trial Lawyers Association. Mr. Buckholtz has recently come forward in what he says is an attempt to clear his conscience.*

"According to Mr. Buckholtz there was an event involving Andrew and himself out at Lake Heuston when the boys were 17 years old. Mr. Buckholtz states that Andrew was doing what he always did—drinking large amounts of alcohol out by the Lake. He had tried to get Mr. Buckholtz to join him but he had told him no.

"Mr. Buckholtz then states that as he was trying to leave the Lake for the day, he heard Andrew holler at him. He rushed to where Andrew and another boy had been drinking and looked out into the lake and saw Andrew screaming wildly for someone to come and help them. Mr. Buckholtz immediately jumped in—not concerned for his own safety—and swam toward Andrew Madison. Andrew was breathless and started gesturing beneath the water. He told Mr. Buckholtz that their good friend Bobby Duggan was swimming and went underneath the water and wasn't coming back up. Mr. Buckholtz states that he then asked Andrew if Bobby had been drinking. Andrew sheepishly replied that they both had.

"Mr. Buckholtz then began diving down looking for Bobby but was unsuccessful in finding him. Finally, they both knew that Bobby was gone. They swam back to shore and just as Mr. Buckholtz was preparing to call the police Andrew stopped him. According to Mr. Buckholtz, Andrew Madison begged for Frances Buckholtz not to call the police or ever tell anyone. Although Mr. Buckholtz states he knew better, he felt sorry for his friend and agreed to not ever tell what had gone on that night by the lake.

"Until now. Mr. Buckholtz states that his conscience got the best of him and he could no longer sit by quietly when he knew what had happened to poor Bobby Duggan so many years ago. He felt a need to make things right and to tell the world what had occurred. To quote Mr. Buckholtz: "It was time that Bobby got his due."

"Attempts to interview the Duggan family have failed. This paper is trying to verify the facts in this case and will certainly be speaking with Andrew Madison at a later date."

Maddi was so angry. She couldn't believe what she had just read. "What a creep," she said, as she shook her head back and forth. She couldn't imagine what kind of person would turn a story around like he had done, just for personal gain. Especially since Andrew—against his better judgement—had remained silent all these years.

She attempted to get hold of Andrew. He had his cell phone turned off, and Maddi wondered if he knew about the article.

She had to talk to someone—she was bursting inside. She thought of Hank. Hank had been there when Andrew had told his story, and Hank would likely be just as outraged as Maddi.

Maddi and Hank had spoken daily since that afternoon in the Watergate. It had been a magnificent afternoon for both of them, and they left one another with difficulty at the airport that evening.

Each day Maddi would call Hank before he left for the office, just to wish him a happy day, and each evening Hank would call Maddi when he got home just to check on her and make sure she was safe. He was very glad that Andrew had elected to stay on, and he was also quite comforted by the secret service unit assigned to Maddi. He wasn't quite sure of the connection between Maddi and John McCargish—he knew however that it was complicated by her and Hank's relationship. He didn't care. He would give her the space she needed to work it all out, but he would definitely be there if she continued to want that. Hank was falling in love with Maddi.

Maddi felt the same way about Hank. She too wasn't sure what to do with her feelings for John McCargish. He was just so hard to get to know. But Maddi had liked so very much what she had already seen. She elected to simply not think about it any further and enjoy the feelings she was experiencing with Hank.

She dialed his number at the office, and was placed on hold. Soon Hank's voice came over the phone line. "Maddi! It's great to hear from you! Twice in one day. What's up?"

Maddi was shaking. "Hank. You won't believe what Buckholtz is up to!"

"Buckholtz?" Hank was trying to remember where he had heard the name.

Maddi responded quickly. "The jerk who runs the ATLA."

"Oh yeah, go ahead. What did he do now?"

Maddi proceeded. "Do you remember the story Andrew told us about that night a long time ago by the lake with him and Mr. Buckholtz?"

"Yeah."

"Well. Buckholtz has decided to turn it around and make it an indictment of Andrew and his 'ethical problems' in an attempt to undermind my efforts. What a horrible man!"

"Oh my god, Maddi. How did he do that?"

"He spoke with a reporter from a local Indianapolis paper. They were hungry for anything related to me or this forum, so they ate it up. It's terrible! It makes Andrew sound awful. Spineless and weak. Like Buckholtz!" Maddi was speaking quickly and breathlessly. "I don't know what to do, but I need to put a stop to it—now!"

There was silence for a moment, and then Hank spoke. "You know Maddi, these things have a way of working out eventually. I mean, the truth usually reveals itself."

Maddi was frustrated. "Yeah, but I don't have until eventually to clear my brother's name. This was done because of me and my efforts, and Andrew should be kept out of it."

The two of them continued talking for a while longer, and finally Maddi told Hank that she would talk to him later and should be going. Hank agreed to call her that night after he finished office hours. He was flying in the next morning for the start of the forum and both were anxiously awaiting their opportunity to be together again.

Maddi spent the remainder of the morning trying to locate Andrew. She was unsuccessful, however, and headed back over to the convention center to finalize plans for the convention. The forum started tomorrow and Maddi knew it needed to go on without a hitch. So much depended on it. Everything she knew and loved was involved in what this forum represented. If it was successful, Maddi could once again be optimistic about the future of the country and its direction. If her forum failed, and litigation reform failed, Maddi knew that the country and so many good and decent people would suffer needless harm in a society where goodness and decency were not valued or rewarded. Maddi had to succeed.

Since coming home from Washington, Hank had felt like a new man. Actually he felt much more like he used to feel before the lawsuit. He was happy to get up in the morning, and was even looking forward to his day at the office. As much as he was missing his nursing home practice, he was enjoying the increase in free time. He started going hiking again and reading for pleasure—both things he had abandoned as he sunk into his ever-deeper depression after the lawsuit.

His lawsuit was continuing on however, and the depositions were now underway. Hank refused to take any time from seeing patients in order to prepare or conduct the depositions, so the majority of the work in preparing and conducting the depositions occurred on Saturday afternoons in Hank's office.

At first he nearly became ill at the thought of the depositions and all that went with them, but eventually resigned himself to the situation. He realized that this was now a part of medicine. This was something as integral to the practice of medicine as staffing an office and taking call on the weekends. It was unpleasant but a necessary evil if you wanted to be a physician this day and age. He often reminded himself that he should not take it personally, but should look at all the fine company he has with other great physicians being sued daily around him. For the most part, this thinking was helpful. But, there were still times when Hank knew—deep down in his soul—that his love for medicine had been forever changed, and that soon he would have to leave. This saddened him greatly. He had so loved his calling. He had so loved his patients. He had so loved everything about the practice of medicine. He no longer loved it, and so he would leave. Soon.

Hank had recently told a colleague how he felt about his practice and his profession, now that he'd been sued. "Medicine is one of those things that takes all your heart and soul. You can't just "sort of" do medicine. You have to be all there—fully invested. If you are, the rewards are tremendous, both for your patients and for yourself. But, if the patient becomes the plaintiff, and the physician becomes the defendant, the perfect and pure relationship between physician and patient is destroyed and the energy is transformed to something akin to fear and resentment. Medicine then becomes a prison, not a calling." Hank knew these feelings all too well. He understood fully why doctors were leaving across the country. He understood fully that he too would soon leave.

For now however, he would throw his energies into Maddi's forum. It was medicine's last best hope and so many physicians knew it. It had to succeed. Maddi had to succeed. And Hank planned on helping her any way that he could.

He had a 7:30am flight out the next morning to take him to Indianapolis and the thought of seeing Maddi again made him so very happy. He desperately hoped she was feeling the same; he felt sure she was.

The Indianapolis airport was a zoo. There were doctors flying in from everywhere and most of them had arranged to fly in that first morning. Hank's flight was mercifully on time and Maddi met him at the airport. She spotted him walking through the door immediately and ran past several others as she eagerly embraced him. They were like teenagers, full of excitement and passion, and they were each as surprised as the other by their enthusiasm.

It was Hank who spoke first. "Maddi, it is so good to see you. I missed you—so much more than I ever thought I would."

Maddi looked up into Hank's eyes and smiled her best smile. "Hank, I can't explain it, but now that you're here everything feels right."

They hugged one another again and Maddi led Hank to the waiting taxi cab. Hank glanced back as they were getting inside and noticed—happily—that the two secret service guys were right where they were supposed to be.

Amanda and Wilson had both arranged to fly in Friday morning as well, and their flights intersected in Pittsburg. They saw one another and quickly made their way to an airport eatery to have something to drink while waiting for the connecting flight that would take them both to Indianapolis.

They caught up on things, mostly discussing the status of the lawsuits they were both involved in. Wilson informed Amanda that he felt his lawsuit may be settled out of court. As much as he hated that—it felt like an admission of guilt—he knew it was best in order to make sure he continued to have insurance coverage. A settlement was far less expensive than a trial, unless he won. The odds of that were not good enough to justify the risk, and so the insurance company had urged him to settle.

Amanda was in a similar situation, but was fighting her insurance company on a similar recommendation. She and Wilson continued to talk back and forth about which course was a better, more noble course to take and eventually found themselves once again commiserating about what had happened to medicine and its joy.

They were saved from going ever deeper into their sorrow by the announcement of their flight for Indianapolis. They both boarded the plane, and agreed to try to join one another at the Gala dinner that evening.

Jeremy Bourne was desperately trying to finish up his early morning in the office and catch his 11:30 flight for Indianapolis. Per usual, his day had gotten completely away from him with emergencies of one kind or another. He'd had a fracture walk in at the last moment, and while he was waiting for the x-ray, he received an abnormal ekg taken on a patient he had seen earlier in the day. Doc Jones had fortunately come in to help him, and he was able to hand both cases off to him at the last minute and jump in his old Wrangler and head for the airport.

He barely made his flight, but once on board began slowly relaxing. The flight was a two-and-a-half-hour flight, and this gave Jeremy plenty of time to reflect. He had been very excited about the forum, knowing that if it wasn't successful, at least in spirit, then he would soon find himself joining those colleagues who had elected to quit their practices. He so didn't want to leave the Pimas. He loved what he did. But he couldn't sit by and watch his efforts be perverted by a system that seeks to gain at someone else's loss. Jeremy had thought long and hard about his options and he knew that—if medicine didn't solve what lawyers had caused, he would be forced to look elsewhere for his calling. For now, however, he was committed to the cause of saving medicine itself.

He reviewed in his mind the recent deposition he had been forced to give to those delightful attorneys representing Wyatt, Hanson, Richards and Shultz. What a bunch of clowns. All self-important with their lawyer phrases and their fancy suits, talking down to those poor Pimas who had been misguided by their promises. It sickened Jeremy beyond belief, and it saddened him greatly. He felt he had done fairly well in his deposition—but who could tell. Who could tell what those vultures would do with an honest man's testimony, and an honest man's efforts to improve the lives of those around him.

At one point during the deposition, Jeremy was asked by one of the "suits" to explain why on earth he had felt it was acceptable to expose these less fortunate individuals to a potentially fatal drug. Jeremy adjusted himself in his seat, cleared his throat, and proceeded to explain himself.

"You ask why on earth I felt it was acceptable to expose these poor folks to a potentially fatal drug. There are many things I could say right now to address that question, but probably the clearest answer I can give is to ask you to look at the Pima Indians prior to my arrival. These are a forgotten people living a very poor, simple life out there on the Reservation. They are a delightful and giving people, who have been left behind by a society that values profit over people and economic growth over the growth of one's soul.

"These people understand this. They know that what that had always held most dear is not what is valued by our society—the society they now live in. So, they have elected to continue on, trying somehow to 'fit' in a culture that is in many ways beneath them.

"I came to their world full of grand ideas and strong, sincere desires to help them. They had significant medical needs as well as significant medical neglect. They had been all but forgotten on their reservation. Well over half of these people are diabetics, the majority poorly controlled. Although they were familiar with insulin I found that most of them were not just reluctant but absolutely against injecting themselves daily with a substance such as insulin.

"Along comes Diacam. A miracle drug from where I sat. This was the answer to helping these wonderful people who had been all but forgotten by society. A medicine that controlled their diabetes and allowed them to avoid the injections that they loathed. And, the medicine, and the Pimas, were successful. They finally achieved success in controlling their diabetes. For the first time for many of them, they actually felt good enough to become active and involved in their world.

"And this they did. They began a softball league. They started projects to improve their lands and their surroundings. They were doing great. When it became clear that Diacam might have some problems I let all of these people know that, and I assured them I would monitor them.

"This I did. Frequently and faithfully. The only thing I asked of them was to refrain from drinking alcohol. The combination was apt to be more toxic to their liver and I informed them of that fact. From what I have read concerning the bad outcomes with diacam, nearly every one involved with a bad outcome had participated in the inappropriate use of alcohol. As much as I regret that anyone suffered ill consequences because of this drug,I do believe that these people need to assume responsibility for their abuse of a substance known to affect the liver fatally, without any help from any medicine whatsoever.

"I'm aware that your response to that is that we should know who is drinking and therefore withhold any drug which may interfere. Perhaps so. But one thing comes to mind. These people will die from their liver disease secondary to their alcohol abuse with or without Diacam. In the meantime, Diacam allowed them the opportunity to treat their other chronic illness—diabetes—well. This can't be a bad thing. Of course, you will try to make it such. I will never claim that responsibility however."

A couple of the people in the room during Jeremy's deposition gave him a nod and a thumbs up, but for the most part his words were ignored as the lawyers continued to try to score points with their cleverness.

Jeremy no longer cared. To hell with all of them and their bullshit. He'd had it. Do whatever you need to do, he felt. He was done.

The Diacam lawsuit had acquired its own life and was spiraling completely out of control as far as Jeremy was concerned. He knew his part in the entire thing was relatively small, but he also knew he—or his malpractice carrier—could be on the hook for millions of dollars because so many Pima Indians had attached themselves to the suit. Interestingly, Jeremy didn't blame them for that. A bunch of clever, well-spoken attorneys had convinced them that "justice" was being served and that they could play a role in that, and gain some much-needed cash in the process. He didn't blame them, but it sickened him nonetheless.

He watched the trial as it geared up in Philadelphia and he delighted—to the extent that he delighted in anything anymore—in watching the clever Clarence Morrow take on the Big, Bad law firm of Wyatt, Hanson, Richards, and Shultz. It definitely made for good theatre—if only the consequences weren't so tragic.

Jeremy continued to think about such things and gradually drifted off to sleep. Boti's face—and the stark landscape of South Africa—appeared once again. All the pain, all the suffering. Boti's endearing spirit.

He woke when his plane landed in Indianapolis, and got up and prepared to participate in what he hoped was the saving of America.

Peter was watching Maddi read the paper. He saw her surprised look, and he saw her nearly spill her coffee. He watched her dial several numbers frantically, and speak briefly to someone on the other end. He was amused. "There she is," he thought, "all full of her self-importance. Just wait, pretty lady. I'll take you out when the whole world is watching. And I'll be the one they're writing about. I'll be the one with the reputation."

He had decided that this forum was the perfect opportunity to do the job for which he had been hired. And what a jackass that Buckholtz was turning out to be. Weak-kneed and nowhere to be found. Peter was thinking that he might just take him out for the fun of it. But first came Senator Madison. And soon.

John McCargish had decided at the last minute to go to Maddi's forum. He had finished most of what needed done for the Chief Justice, and he really wanted to be with Maddi and watch her pull off one of the biggest grass roots efforts to come along in America in a long time. He hoped she could do it. He was fearful where things would end up if she couldn't.

John regretted that he had not found a way to speak to Maddi since the second shooting attempt. He was always busy at the Supreme Court and she was always busy with Congress. He wasn't even sure if she would be interested in having a relationship with him, but he felt he may regret it forever if he didn't at least try. He admired and cared about her so much. She had such strength. But was still so kind. And good. He knew that if he wasn't careful, he could fall in love with her. Maybe that wouldn't be so bad. He was scared. But he had decided to try.

John had taken the early morning flight from D.C. and had landed in Indianapolis at 11:30 Friday morning. It was crazy at the airport, apparently having a lot to do with Maddi's forum. He had arranged to stay at a hotel away from the forum, in order to have some time to himself while he was away from D.C.

Washington D.C. has a way of never leaving you alone. When you're there you're connected to everything going on. Even if you're sleeping or at home alone watching TV. D.C. is still talking to you; still pulling you into its web. All the politics, all the power. It's unending. John learned early on that whenever he left D.C. he had to make good use of the time away.

He had arranged to stay in Indianapolis through the forum and into Monday. He was perhaps hoping to spend time with Maddi after the forum—if she was interested. He hoped she'd be interested.

CHAPTER XXXI

"Ladies and Gentleman. My name is Walter Moore and I have assisted Senator Madison in the preparation of this Forum. It is my honor and my privilege to introduce to you at this time the senator from our beloved state of Indiana, Cynthia Madison."

There was a strong round of applause throughout the auditorium and Maddi proceeded slowly and deliberately to the front of the stage. She waited while the applause slowly quieted and then began to speak.

"I am very glad to see so many of you here today. Most of you are fellow physicians, and some of you are ethical lawyers." There was a collective chuckle from the crowd. Maddi continued. "I know for many of you this trip here this weekend involved canceling patients or clients, and leaving family and obligations. I very much appreciate that effort on the part of each of you. As you are all well aware, the situation that exists, which prompted this forum, is of a magnitude which I'm certain has justified your sacrifice at this time. We all know what is at stake here. At the risk of being dramatic, allow me to put it this way: unless we succeed at this time, here and now, to fix what is broken in our healthcare system, the practice of medicine in America will disappear. In its place will be something much different and far inferior I'm sure.

"As perhaps many of you know, I was a physician myself, for nearly 15 years. I loved my job, my patients and my calling. I eventually began to see, however, that the "calling" was being threatened more and more each day by a system that no longer rewarded integrity or intention, but heaped huge financial awards on those who were able to cleverly manipulate the system.

"I began to see a system where human error was called negligence and honest effort was no longer an adequate defense for failure to diagnose. I saw lawyers—and laws—gain power, while physicians and patients were losing power.

The cleverness of the attorney began to indicate the validity of a claim—not the claim itself.

"The majority of my time in Washington has been dedicated to addressing these issues. It has become my life's goal to fix this badly broken system and replace it with a system that once again relies on decency and integrity; where trueness of effort counts for something. No longer should an attorney, or an attorney group, be handsomely rewarded for altering the truth and taking advantage of another individual's suffering. No longer should our system of compensation be based on clever innuendo, at the expense of truth.

"I look for the day when practicing medicine is once again a most blessed calling. I look for the day when physicians no longer have to view their patients as potential litigants. Where we can once again be the ally of our patient instead of the adversary. This day will come—it must. Today we begin the process."

There was a dead silence. Then, suddenly, a loud applause began echoing throughout the auditorium. The clapping became louder and louder, and then individuals within the crowd began to stand up and cheer. This was definitely a speech these people had been waiting to hear, and Maddi had delivered it perfectly. The applause continued for well over 5 minutes, and then, finally died down. Maddi continued to speak.

"Thank you so much for your very generous applause. Let's face it, I am preaching to the choir here. But I know that with the energy in this room we can—and will—change the course of medicine and litigation in this country.

"This forum will be centered on various ideas and principles by which we can rewrite the way our country deals with litigation and loss. In no way do I feel we should eliminate an individual's right to receive compensation for a wrong that has been committed against him or her. I simply believe that we have lost our guiding principles and that ruthless individuals have taken advantage of that.

"Allow us here this weekend to restore those principles to a badly broken system thereby changing its face. I can only hope that then we can restore the joy in our profession that we all used to know.

"I'd like to start our first day of this historic forum by introducing one of the more prominent members of our profession. Wilson Jackson III is one of the most published Gynecologists in American history. He has done considerable work on fetal development and has spoken numerous times on the issue of stem cell research. Dr. Jackson has been written about not only in medical journals, but in the mainstream press for his repeated recognition as one of the top Gynecologists in America. Patients and peers alike have awarded him this title on numerous occasions for his overwhelming compassion and competency in his field of expertise.

"Dr. Jackson has also been sued over 9 times in his illustrious career." This comment provoked low moans throughout the auditorium. "He has now accepted this situation as the cost of doing what he loves, but, as someone who knows him well I can tell you this—Dr. Wilson Jackson III will soon grow weary of this system of blame and will choose to leave the profession, taking with him his brilliance and his wonderful and irreplaceable years of experience. This, my friends, will be an incredible tragedy. He is here today to speak to us of his experiences, and to remind us all why we chose to become physicians in the first place. Ladies and Gentlemen, I present to you Dr. Wilson Jackson III."

Wilson got up slowly and headed toward the podium. He had not been quite sure what Maddi had wanted him to speak about at this forum, but as he began preparing for this lecture he gradually stumbled onto those words he needed to share with this audience. He grabbed the podium by its sides, stood up straight, cleared his throat and began to speak.

"Thank you all so very much for having me here today to speak to you. I am aware that there are many doctors who might speak to you with far more eloquence than I am able to provide, but none will share with you what I am about to say. I have practiced medicine for a long time now, about 20 years, and I have had many more good times than bad. I have truly loved what I have done, and I have loved those patients that have given me the opportunity to care for them."

Wilson went on for the next 35 minutes extolling his regard for various aspects of physician life. He mentioned the often appreciative patient. And the opportunity to help when it's clear help is needed and no one else can provide what the highly trained physician can provide. Finally, when it seemed that perhaps he would quickly summarize the joys of medicine and conclude his speech, he said the following.

"But now, I am going to do something I never thought I would do. I am going to drop my malpractice coverage completely. I am going to sell my large home and all I own of substance. Anything that might someday be taken from me for payment, as a consequence of litigation." The crowd began to whisper and move around uncomfortably. "I will have very little so that they can 'win' very little in a malpractice lawsuit. I will no longer deliver babies—because no hospital will allow me privileges without malpractice coverage—and any surgeries I perform will have to be done in my office. My research efforts will continue untouched and my office practice should survive just fine. I will post my lack of coverage on the front door of my office. This will give a "heads up" to any enterprising patient who felt I was going to be a good mark.

"I will need to move away from my current office location—I'm sure my partners will not be prepared to do what I am doing, and thus, will not want any associated liability that might come about because of my actions. If this seems extreme, and if I sound bitter, it is and I am. I've had it. I can't seem to make myself quit—that seems like such an admission of failure—so this is the only action I can take which makes sense to me at this time. Thank you for your time, and let's all hope and pray that this forum and this effort are successful."

With that Wilson turned away from the podium and walked toward the edge of the stage. Maddi was standing just off stage and as he approached her she smiled. She then reached out and hugged him.

"Wilson, that was perfect. I could not have asked for a better opener to this event. Thank you."

Wilson looked her in the eyes. His own eyes were filled with tears.

"Maddi. I hate this. But I'm serious. I really can't play this game anymore. I'm done. I've had it." He continued walking off stage and into the back of the auditorium.

Maddi watched him walk away. The crowd had given him very generous applause, although one could sense that they were shocked by his statements. As the applause began dying down Maddi once again walked toward the podium. She looked out into the audience and was delighted to see a full media presence among the crowd. She knew that Wilson's comments would now generate throughout the nation, and she hoped and prayed people would understand what was going on here. She knew that, until the people of America understood this problem, there was very little chance that it would be fixed. And it had to be fixed.

Maddi began to introduce the next speaker. Lori Conners was an attorney friend of hers from her days at Miami University, and she had asked her to come and speak to this group about how lawyers—and the Law—had gotten to where it was today. She was a District Attorney for a small community in Illinois and thus had very little experience with malpractice cases. But she had a lot of experience with lawyers.

Maddi introduced her and she walked up to the podium. She was tall and very thin, but had an amazingly commanding voice. One could appreciate that she may just dominate a courtroom if given the opportunity.

Lori Conners began. "Thank you all so much for allowing me—an attorney—to address you here today. I know that lawyers are not a favorite among physicians, but if it makes you feel any better, lawyers don't like physicians either." There was a soft chuckle from the crowd. "You would think, however, that lawyers would love physicians, considering how much money they make off of them every year." The crowd began to laugh and clap to express their acknowledgement of her very true statement. She continued.

"There is 1 lawyer for every 250 Americans, but only 1 doctor for every 400 Americans. I don't know about you, but I'd much rather have a doctor there when I have chest pain at three in the morning than I would an attorney." The crowd was laughing comfortably now.

"In spite of how much we regard human life and wellness in this country, it is appalling how little appreciation physicians currently receive from the public in general. Doctors are blamed for everything from inappropriate estrogen usage to deaths from an FDA-approved medication."

At this the crowd exchanged knowing glances with one another as they recognized the reference to Diacam.

"If any of you were to take a moment in your free time, and peruse the web site for the American Trial Lawyers Association, you would see something quite interesting. How many of you in this room see Nursing Home patients—even if it is just the few from your practice?" There was a significant number of hands up in the air. "Did you know that the ATLA has a separate section on its website just for Nursing Home Law?" The crowd reacted with a collective groan. "And, not only that, but on that website there are numerous links to various organizations that can assist the hungry lawyer in finding and trying the case that suits him or her best. Almost a cook book approach to suing a nursing home, its staff, and its physicians." Now the crowd began to boo. The District Attorney continued. "I am not kidding. The ATLA—one of the largest contributors to political campaigns in America—has a website that promotes the suing of individuals, small companies, and corporations. Why am I so alarmed at this? Well, I'll tell you.

The attorney paused and took a sip of her water. She cleared her throat and looked out into the crowd for just a few moments. She then continued.

"There was once a day when the law was used to make things right and fair. If someone was acting in a way that hurt an individual or several individuals, and he was unwilling to alter his behavior, the law served a useful purpose. One could file a lawsuit with the hopes of reigning in this "bad actor" if you will. Lawsuits were reserved for affecting needed change from individuals or groups of individuals. If a company was polluting an area stream and refused to stop or to clean it up, a lawsuit could be filed. If successful, the suit could make the individual or company do what it should be doing in the first place. This use of a lawsuit served the greater good. It held individuals and companies responsible for their behaviors.

"Another example of a usefulness for lawsuits is the case of civil rights. People will sometimes choose to practice racism or preference in this country. Because of laws now on the books, and because of the power of lawsuits in this country, the protection of an individual's civil rights is now somewhat guaranteed. Periodically we still see the need for this type of litigation.

"But then, along came a middle-aged woman who decided to put a very hot cup of coffee between her legs and then drive away. How stupid is that!" This comment provoked cheers from the audience. "Who on earth puts a cup of hot coffee between her legs in a soon-to-be-moving vehicle? More to the point however, is what slimy low-rent attorney thinks this is an appropriate use of a lawsuit? What a travesty.

"We can all think of similar, ridiculous uses of lawsuits. Stories that—when we hear them—piss us off immediately." The crowd was smiling and laughing quietly, eagerly nodding their collective head. "We've all heard about the criminal who repeatedly tried to break into a farmer's home. Finally, when the farmer had had enough, and the local sheriff's office was unable to help him, he decided to rig a system whereby when the burglar tried to enter through a window, a shot gun would go off injuring him and stopping his attempt to burglarize this farmer. The thief came to rob the farmer again. He began to step through the window. He was shot and injured. He sued the farmer—successfully." The crowd began to boo once again. "Now tell me folks. What true purpose in society was served by the execution of that particular lawsuit?

"As I say, I could go on and on. The point I am trying to make is this. Lawsuits, once useful tools to bring about needed protections or changes, have now become the tool of clever attorneys who alter the truth in an effort to gain financially. More often than not, the attorney gains just as much cash as the plaintiff, and nothing at all is improved as far as society is concerned."

The attorney once again reached for her water and the crowd began to applaud. The attorney paused for a moment and then resumed her discourse.

"I have known Maddi since our college days and—even then—she was always trying to be a force for good. I like what Maddi is doing here today—and I like what each and every one of you stands for—one more chance to see if we can do things right in America, where we have the greatest healthcare system in the world.

"I am convinced, as are all of you here, that if we could reign in the behavior behind the majority of lawsuits in America we could allow our healthcare system to once again be affordable. Defensive medicine would go by the way side and we could allocate our precious resources much more fairly.

"It would also be very refreshing to be able to assume responsibility for our actions without a fear of litigation. This would not only benefit the Practitioners of medicine, but would benefit the nation as a whole. Innovation would take a mighty step forward as—once again—the exploration of an idea would not be met with litigation on the other side.

"How many of you are aware of why we continually have a shortage of flu vaccine in this country?" Several hands went up. "Yes, we all know about the tainted batch of vaccine, but how many of you are aware of why there are so few manufacturers of vaccine. Two major companies are responsible for the manufacturing of vaccine for much of the world. It would seem—if nothing else—like a lucrative business because of such need. Well, at one point in our recent history the Government decided to 'negotiate' with the manufacturers of vaccine to obtain a 'cut-rate' for vaccine to administer through the public health system. 'Great!' you say. Except that the price negotiated provided little in the way of profit for these companies. They would have been okay with this considering they were profiting at least a little while serving the greater good, but then began the lawsuits. Over things like reactions. Totally unpredictable and totally unavoidable. Not any that made national news, just all those pesky little suits that tie up a corporation's finances and their human resources as well. Although the suits were settled for relatively small amounts, they tied up a large amount of the corporation's finances. The companies were forced to make a decision. Continue to provide their product at very little profit with huge exposure to litigation, or quit the manufacturing of flu vaccine and avoid the headaches and the lawsuits. Guess what. The majority of manufacturers got out of the business of making flu vaccine. And who can blame them?"

The crowd was very intrigued by this bright attorney's comments and were listening intently to her every word. She continued.

"Although you might hear this story told a different way this is in essence what has happened. Interestingly, when I watch doctors walk away from their practices in record numbers I can't help but think that they too were forced to make a decision. Sadly their decision impacts us all. Even now in Ohio most pregnant women must travel over 2 hours to find an Obstetrician who is able to fit them into their practice. Most family practitioners have elected to take very few new patients and they do their best to screen for cases or patients who may present more of a litigation challenge than they are willing to bear. We are witnessing the "shrugging" of American doctors. The physicians are saying to all who will listen that they have had enough of the current system and are willing to give up all that they have worked for to avoid participating any further in the perversion which passes for practicing medicine in this country. They are tired of being referred to as 'providers' and tired of being treated as employees of the insurance companies. Most importantly, they are tired of giving everything they have day in and day out—often at the expense of their loved ones—only to be sued days later for a human mistake or tragedy. Ladies and Gentlemen, doctors are done."

There was a loud outburst of applause and cheers as the collective audience identified with every word the attorney had spoken. Many in the audience turned to the person next to them as both engaged in aggressive nods of acknowledgement. The attorney concluded.

"So, what are you going to do about this? Must you allow your system of medicine to fail completely and reach a crisis state—which is nearly where you are—or can you perhaps make choices and changes here today which will forever impact and hopefully save your profession?

"Our next speaker—your host, Senator Madison—will outline for you something she refers to as 'Maddi's Laws.' These laws are written not for the purpose of benefiting or shielding physicians but for the purpose of improving not only medicine but all commerce in America. I have read through the laws myself and I find them to be remarkably simple and perfect. They address the inherent conflict of interest which exists in much of American Law today and yet allow the preservation of the important contribution that the Law was meant to offer. I present to you once again, Senator Cynthia Madison."

The crowd was again clapping enthusiastically for Maddi and for the affirmation of the message that was being so eloquently delivered. Maddi had been back stage assisting some of the other speakers and was taken by surprise that her time to speak had come. She quickly gathered her materials and headed for the podium.

Hank was backstage helping Maddi handle some of the details and assisting in making things go smoothly. He and Maddi had very little time to talk since he arrived in Indianapolis but they had embraced and kissed, both knowing that they were starting a very important relationship. Maddi had smiled up at Hank and both had known right then where they wanted things to go. But, the forum was waiting and they put their thoughts and desires on hold.

Amanda, who wasn't scheduled to speak until the following morning, was sitting in the audience with John McCargish and Andrew Madison. The three of them were enjoying the forum immensely. John had managed to slip backstage to hand Maddi some case law information he had managed to put together in his free time, which gave some further credence and support to Maddi's legislative proposals. This delighted Maddi immensely and she knew this would give her additional ammo as she fought her battle to change the way law was practiced in America.

She and John had had very little opportunity to speak since the night John had pursued her attacker, and she hesitated to say much because of her developing relationship with Hank. John seemed to sense this and did not push her to connect with him in any way. But when he walked back out into the audience Maddi felt a pang of hurt in her heart. She really liked John. She felt so confused. She wasn't sure she was ready to give up all thoughts of a relationship with him, but she didn't want to stop what was happening with Hank either. Oh well, certainly no time to think of that while the forum was going on. She set it aside for later.

Kevin Clayborne had helped Maddi originally with "Maddi's Laws." At first Maddi had felt his help was valuable and his intentions genuine. But, just before Maddi was ready to send her final draft to John McCargish to review, she decided to show it to Clarence Morrow and see what he thought. He called her the day before the forum and asked her to wait to send the information to John and to try to find thirty minutes to talk to him sometime that afternoon.

They had met at 4:30 over coffee while Maddi was working on last-minute items for the forum. Clarence came into the conference hall and pulled Maddi aside. He'd bought the coffee for them both and found a secluded corner in order to talk to Maddi with no one else listening.

"Hey Clarence, what's up" Maddi asked, knowing that the precautions Clarence was taking suggested that all was not right.

"Listen Maddi, I don't want to throw suspicion on anyone, but how much do you know about this Kevin Clayborne?"

Maddi thought for a moment and realized she actually knew very little about Kevin. He had more or less pushed his way into this effort and she had simply felt him to be sincere. "Not much, Clarence. Why?"

"Well. Like I said, I don't want to implicate anyone in anything suspicious, but I don't like where Kevin went with some of this."

He pointed to the manuscript containing Maddi's Laws. He then proceeded to tell Maddi about some very irregular conclusions and findings that Kevin had come up with.

Apparently, at least from what Clarence could determine, Kevin Clayborne was either very inept at the practice of law, or he had an alternative agenda involving the sabotaging of Maddi's Laws.

Kevin had written up Maddi's requests in such a way that they would never pass the "constitutional test" and would thus be thrown out before they could even be voted on. Maddi would also wind up looking naive and poorly prepared—to say the least.

As Clarence investigated Kevin more closely he began to hear about possible connections with one of the administrators of the ATLA—a Roger Clairy—and Clarence began to think that the organization was not staying out of this whole process like they had thought. Perhaps Kevin was somehow working with the ATLA to completely derail Maddi's efforts. That certainly wouldn't be a surprise, but would suggest a level of deceit that neither he nor Maddi was prepared for.

He shared all of this with Maddi, who quickly concluded that what Clarence was telling her was more than likely true. She asked if he—Clarence—could look over the legal premises set forth in her laws and rewrite them if necessary. Although he was very limited in time, Clarence was able to find and change some major flaws in the writings which Kevin had clearly orchestrated in an effort to sabotage the entire effort. Clarence then sent the revised documents on to John for his thoughts on their ability to withstand constitutional scrutiny. Maddi and Clarence both knew that they would need to keep a close eye on Kevin and they decided it would be easier to do that if he were not aware of their findings and conclusions concerning his honesty.

Maddi immediately wrote him out of the forum, deciding to tell him that there were simply too many speakers. She was incredibly thankful that Clarence had discovered the deceit before it had gone too far. Once again, Maddi's friends were saving her.

Peter Smith had been watching the forum activities with a keen inter-est—not in the content, but in the Stars of the Show. He recognized a few of them from following the senator all this time.

He had come to the forum under the name of Doctor Brandt—from Tuc-son, Arizona. He had secured a room in the Adams Mark hotel and had every intention of killing Senator Madison while he was here. He had been unsure of exactly when he would make his move and was observing the forum in an effort to plot his opportunity. He had outlined all the exits, as well as how to get backstage without being noticed. He observed that many from the audi-ence were going backstage periodically and he knew he would be able to do the same with very little difficulty.

Peter had finally spoken with Frances Buckholtz that morning. Apparently Frances had been trying to locate him for weeks. Peter had decided to call him in an effort to secure funds for the hotel and all amenities relevant to his stay in Indianapolis. He also had assured Buckholtz that the Senator would be dead by that evening and he wanted to know how to pick up his payment. They had agreed that—the minute Frances saw the senator's death splattered across the TV set he would wire the remaining 25,000 dollars to a bank account specified by Peter. They would then part company and that would be the end of things between them.

Peter was amazed at how utterly stupid Buckholtz was, and he couldn't wait to part company with the man. Buckholtz had paid for the room at the hotel with his credit card and had left it open for Peter to purchase what he needed. Peter didn't care—he knew he wouldn't be caught, but he was astounded at how easily Buckholtz had made it for himself to be caught. "Oh well," he thought, "not my problem."

He'd had a great breakfast that morning—on Buckholtz—and had made it to the forum soon after it had begun. They were doing visual security checks for weapons. Peter had anticipated this and had acquired a plastic pistol that was separated into several parts. He carried it in in his camera case and was amazed at how easily he walked through the security checkpoint. Now here he was, watching, anxiously waiting for the "star speaker," Senator Cynthia Madi-son to approach the podium.

Maybe he should shoot her now, as she was approaching the podium. That would certainly make things interesting. He had already reassembled his pistol and—because of his location in the 5th row from the front—he had the perfect opportunity to shoot her from where he sat.

He thought for a few seconds more, and finally decided that, with all the chaos created by the shooting, he would be able to run out the side door into an alley behind the hotel. He knew all attention would be on Senator Madison and that he could slip away unnoticed. Peter smiled to himself. All he had to do now was wait for that perfect opportunity.

Maddi slowly walked up to the podium. She had prepared for this speech for the last several days, knowing that what she was about to say here today would be splashed across every newspaper across the land. She had been heartened and amazed over the last several days at the number of media present at the forum. Every major news organization, as well as many smaller ones, were there to cover events as they unfolded at this historic gathering.

Across the country more and more doctors were exiting their practices, and more and more patients were having trouble finding another doctor to take their place. Every state was affected, and—more importantly—every Representative and Senator had someone prominent in their districts who were affected as well.

The Country was ripe for changes and Maddi's forum was the vehicle that might offer what was needed. The media was aware of this and thus were seen throughout the auditorium. Maddi hoped to take advantage of her very large audience, and she knew the speech she was about to give was her greatest chance to do so.

She reached the podium and sat her papers down in front of her. She quickly reached down toward a glass and a carafe sitting on a small tray on a table beside the podium. She poured herself a small amount of water and took a sip to steady her nerves. She stood back up and put her hands on each side of the podium. She then cleared her throat and began to speak.

"Once again, I'd like to welcome all of you to this very important gathering. Your presence here is what will enable this forum to be the vehicle for change that it must be. As many of you know, I am Senator Cynthia Madison, and I am from this great state of Indiana. I am proud to represent Indiana, as well as the nation, at this historic event. I am also a physician and therefore have the unique opportunity of understanding more than most legislators what problems physicians are facing as they currently try to practice medicine in the United States of America. It has become somewhat of a nightmare in many instances to pursue the vocation of medicine in this country. I will try to outline in the next several minutes some ideas I have that may perhaps make the practice of medicine a noble and gratifying experience once again."

The crowd had become completely silent as they listened intently to what Maddi had to say. They all knew that it was she who had put this entire thing together, and they looked at her as their last hope to recover what had been lost from their profession. Maddi continued.

"Many of you I'm sure are familiar with a set of provisions known as 'Stark Laws.' These provisions were formulated through the efforts of a Representative from California named Peter Stark. He felt that physicians were all too often in a position to reward themselves financially by referring their patients to entities within which they—the physicians—had some form of ownership. Mr. Stark felt that this was an obvious conflict of interest and should therefore be stopped.

"He succeeded in his efforts and came up with several laws which prohibited doctors from referring any patients to entities in which the doctor had any ownership whatsoever. This was a difficult adjustment for many physicians, because they typically were the very ones who initiated such entities based on community need and the specialized knowledge one might need to have to create such facilities.

"Nonetheless, once Medicare saw the validity of Representative Stark's proposals, they adopted them and changed forever the relationship between the doctor and the facilities which provided those special items or functions the doctor needed.

"We could probably debate for hours the usefulness of the Stark Laws. It wouldn't change a thing however, because those are now the Laws that govern us in terms of our business relationships.

"One thing I will say however is that you can't disagree with the notion of conflict of interest. Mr. Stark was correct that—even the appearance of this conflict is counterproductive and harmful to the goals that are trying to be achieved by practitioners in the United States of America. Appearances can sometimes be just as harmful as reality.

"Well, I submit to you here today that those same appearances are hurting the practice of Law and all who stand to benefit from the Law. I would like to propose at this time what may perhaps be referred to as 'Maddi's Laws.'"

At this the crowd began to applaud and chuckle a bit. They seemed to appreciate the turning of the tables, but also seemed to see the true relevance of what Maddi was saying. She continued.

"As I have watched the acceleration of litigation in this country I have observed one constant truth. Regardless of the outcome of any legal matter, those typically benefiting are the lawyers themselves. Rarely does the litigant gain as much as the lawyer—on either side of the issue.

"I also observed this—the longer it takes for a case to go to trial the more money each side's attorneys stand to gain from the process. The plaintiff's attorneys win by creating a sense of inevitability that causes the defendant to settle often just to end the process. The defendant's attorneys win by racking up 'billable hours' which must be paid regardless of the outcome. Who loses here? Anybody that isn't an attorney. The plaintiff may win his case, but by the time he pays court costs and his attorney's 40 percent fee, he is left with a much smaller amount of compensation than was intended. Meanwhile his attorney has profited handily for nothing more than manipulating the laws in his or her favor.

"If the defendant wins, he walks away with nothing more than the pain and suffering of the process, while his attorney profits by the fees the defendant is obligated to pay.

"In no way does this form of compensation create the needed impetus for speedy and honest trials. On the other hand, this form of compensation creates nothing more than a prolongation of a very unpleasant and hurtful process. The lawyers have nothing to lose and everything to gain, while the plaintiff stands to maybe gain 50% of some arbitrary amount. The defendant meanwhile gains absolutely nothing. To be dragged through the muddy court system and come out innocent is certainly not a 'win' for that defendant by anyone's standards. To be sued in our current system immediately is a loss on the part of a defendant regardless of his or her innocence. Whether one is found innocent or guilty they wind up losers from the perspective of emotions and lost time. This system must be changed."

Now the crowd was clapping and cheering at the thought of possibly changing the remarkably broken legal system. They began to chant in unison "Maddi's Laws. Maddi's Laws." Maddi put up her hands to silence them so she could continue.

"Maddi's Laws, or whatever they may wind up being called, will now be outlined for all of you. I am aware that there will need to be some adjustments and alterations made to make these laws stand the constitutional tests they will face, but they basically consist of the following.

"First, with reference to plaintiff attorneys. Their maximum payment must be capped at 20% of the award after all expenses and court costs have been paid. This would reduce the 'instant millionaire' mentality that some attorneys seem to harbor.

"Second, with reference to defense attorneys. They should no longer be paid by the hour but by the case. This would assist in their efforts to make things go as quickly as possible. They should also receive incentive bonuses for successful and speedy adjudication of a case. They should receive a 20% bonus if the case is disposed of within 60 days, a 15% bonus if the case is disposed of within 90 days, and a 10% bonus if the case is disposed of within 120 days. The current average for a case—even one in which the physician is withdrawn from the suit—is 6 months, or 180 days. That is a ridiculous amount of time for one's life to be turned upside down.

"If the case is settled, the defense attorney should deduct 25% of his fee. This will create an incentive to not settle a case but to bring it to trial. I think in most instances a defendant benefits from this.

"If the case is taken to trial, but is lost—the defense attorney will deduct 10% of his fee. This creates an incentive to win the day for the client.

"If the case is withdrawn—and the defendant is cleared of any wrongdoing—the defense attorney retains his full fee. This fee will then be paid by the plaintiff. In other words, the loser pays the fees. This will make attorneys think twice before suing. No longer will there be the sense that there is little to lose so why not sue.

"I am sure that many of you who are sitting here today are capitalists in the sense that what I am advocating seems a bit too heavy handed. Perhaps too many rules governing payment. But all one has to do is look at how physicians are reimbursed to know that what I am advocating here is mild compared with the restraints imposed upon physician payment. Look at Medicare to see an example of the heavy-handedness of government and then look at Maddi's Laws and realize that they are not only fair but they pale in comparison with the oversight that Medicare subjects physicians to.

"All I am advocating is that somehow, some way we need to reign in a system of law that is wrecking the very fiber of America. Lawyers are taking advantage of every legal situation to line their pockets with no one else benefiting in any true or meaningful way. The Law has become the tool by which clever lawyers become wealthy. There is no other gain and there is no other outcome. Nothing in society is improved by their methods and as a society we are becoming more and more stifled by our collective fears of litigation.

"One very clearcut example of what I am saying can be seen by looking at school systems and the things that can no longer occur because of liability concerns. Things like teacher discipline. Or academic accuracy. In other words, there is concern now that if you give a child a poor grade you may somehow be held liable.

"Or in an organization such as Little League. Lawsuits abound, and they affect decisions concerning what can be offered based on prior litigation experience. For example, your organization sponsers a tournament and someone gets hurt and sues your organization. Next time an opportunity for a tournament comes up—well, it's voted down by the Little League Board due to prior experience with litigation.

"Another example that affects physicians and non-physicians alike is the Good Samaritan laws. Although there is some protection, we all know of individuals who did their best at the scene only to wind up with a certified letter months later. I will confess to thinking twice about helping in such a situation myself. I know that I will however, because I can and should. But, I will then potentially face the consequences of that kindness in a court of law.

"I recently spoke with a friend of mine from a small community outside Evansville. She has practiced medicine there for over 20 years and had forever assisted with the sports physicals done for her community. The school offered the gymnasium one night a year, and many of the local physicians would offer their services to provide low-cost physicals for the kids in the community. The monies taken in—10 dollars per physical—were then donated to the school sports programs. This was a win-win situation for everybody involved. She informed me two weeks ago that this will be the first year that her community—and all the docs—will not offer the pre-participation physical due to the incredible liability which now exists for such a physical. The rare—but fatal—heart pathology that might exist undetected in children, has placed an overwhelming burden on all physicians who are liable for such a problem. It is agreed that echocardiograms cannot be done on all athletes, but yet the echo often is the only true diagnostic tool which could uncover such a problem. Rarely can the problem be detected by using a stethoscope, but doctors are nonetheless routinely found to be liable in these cases. I've done some exploring across the country and I find many communities doing the same thing that my friend and her community have done. Many people lose because of this—and nothing at all is gained.

"I can site numerous examples that repeatedly substantiate what I am trying to say. Unless we act now our country and all of its wonderful freedoms will be gone, and all that will be left is a protected shell where noone takes chances. Pharmaceutical companies will no longer be willing to shoulder the potential class action lawsuit over one of their medications which survived the rigorous FDA process only to be removed from the market down the line. They will stop research, they will stop the production of medications which might be useful for diseases that otherwise have no cure.

"Flu vaccine, which used to be manufactured by many different companies, is now made by a few, with so much government oversight that innovation cannot and will not occur. There will be no discoveries made to assist in our management of the flu, except for that which can be undertaken by our already-strapped government.

"One thing that made America great was its pioneer spirit. I am sorry to say that, as of now, the pioneers are gone, replaced by lawyers in fancy suits who stand waiting—like predators—for their opportunity to twist the facts and emphasize innuendo for the mere purpose of striking it rich through the system of litigation in America today. It has to stop and it has to stop here and now—there will be no other chance for us to take back America if we don't act quickly. I submit to every one of you here—this must be done. This must be done."

There was a brief silence throughout the convention hall. Then, quietly from the back of the room began a soft but steady chanting. "This must be done! This must be done!" Gradually the chant became louder as more and more of the audience joined in. "This must be done! This must be done!" Louder and louder the chanting went on.

No one seemed to notice the quick movements of a short, stocky man in the fifth row as he reached under his jacket and pulled out his gun. He aimed up at Maddi as she stood up at the podium with her head held high listening to the affirmation of her message, knowing that—at least here in this room—her point had been made. The gentleman steadied his arm with his opposite hand and began to pull back the trigger.

John McCargish, who was chanting along with everyone else, was also standing in the fifth row, only a few seats away from the short, stocky man. He suddenly saw something out of the corner of his eye. He looked to his left catching a glimpse of the man aiming a gun at Maddi up on the stage. He immediately jumped up and headed toward him. He reached him in a matter of seconds, just as Peter was pulling back on the trigger.

Suddenly a shot rang out through the auditorium and those standing near to Peter started screaming. Chaos quickly ensued as people were looking toward where the shot had come from.

Maddi was startled and did not seem to grasp what was happening. She heard something hit the podium and she quickly crouched down behind it. She looked into the crowd and saw John McCargish struggling with someone who was holding an object which by now he was trying to point toward John. "Oh my God," she thought. "It's a gun!" She immediately ran toward the steps to the side of the podium. She couldn't let this man shoot John.

Andrew, who saw the man seconds after John, was making his way toward where the fighting had begun. He was only a few feet away when he heard the shot. He quickened his pace to try to get to the man before he could fire another shot.

A second shot rang out, and then a third. Both the gunman and John fell to the ground. People were running every which way. Maddi ran toward John, who was lying on the ground. He wasn't moving. "John, John! Wake up, John!" But he continued to lay still. She glanced over and saw a small man with sandy blonde hair lying on the floor, also not moving. He had a plastic gun in his hand.

Andrew was heading over to him. He reached him and put out his foot and kicked the gun from his hand. He checked to see if the shooter was breathing. He glanced up at Maddi and motioned to her that the man was barely breathing. Maddi was kneeling where John was laying and reached toward his neck to check for a pulse. She felt a very faint pulse and started screaming for someone to call an ambulance. She was frantically trying to assess where John had been shot and was fighting back tears as she screamed for some help.

Hank had appeared from the back of the stage when the commotion had begun. He ran up to Maddi and Andrew. "Maddi, what can I do?"

Maddi looked up at him with tears in her eyes. "Has anyone called for the ambulance?"

Hank grabbed his cell phone and began dialing 911, never taking his eyes from Maddi's tear-stricken face. He then knelt down beside her and began to apply pressure to a rapidly expanding spot of blood beneath John's left arm, where Hank was sure a bullet had entered. There was a significant amount of blood spurting out, likely from an artery ruptured by the gun shot.

Maddi was continuing to try to get John to respond, and was looking around—while fighting back tears—to make sure nothing else was happening in the auditorium. People were running every which way. A few doctors had come up and were offering their services. Maddi let them work with John while she stood up and headed for the door where she anticipated the ambulances would likely arrive.

Amanda was sitting by John's side, along with Hank, and Andrew continued to stand guard over the gunman. Maddi stood at the doorway and looked back to where John lay completely still toward the front of the convention hall. "He saved my life," she thought. "Now, can I save his?"

After what seemed like hours the ambulances arrived and Maddi directed them toward where John lay motionless. She helped them get him onto the stretcher and then insisted on going with him to the hospital. She gave Hank a long, hard look. The other ambulance—the one responsible for the gunman—was just pulling away heading for the same hospital where they were taking John McCargish. Maddi reached for Hank and looked directly into his eyes.

"Hank, here's what I need you to do. This forum is too important to be disrupted in this way. I need you to attempt to restore order and get the forum back on track. Amanda is scheduled to speak after the break. How 'bout announcing that there will be a break while things are attended to here, and then the forum will resume this afternoon in the other hall. Make sure that will work with the Hotel Manager, and then see if you can make that happen. It will be up to you to run the forum until I can get back. I know that Andrew will help you. I have the entire program written up in the back behind the stage, and I have numbers and rooms and everything on how to contact everyone involved." Hank gave her a blank look, which suggested he felt inadequate to handle the task. "Do it Hank. Please." She looked at Hank with pleading eyes. He looked back at her and shook his head. "I'll do it, Maddi. Don't worry about a thing."

Maddi headed into the back of the ambulance and it quickly sped off toward the hospital. Hank turned around and headed back inside to undertake the task of restoring order and resuming the forum.

The press was everywhere. There was no way to avoid them, and soon both Hank and Andrew were smothered with questions. Hank looked to his left and noticed a small hallway, with a door which said "Employees Only." He caught Andrew's eyes and motioned toward the hallway. Andrew acknowledged his glance, and they both quickly spun around and headed for the hallway and the door, through which they quickly escaped. Hank reached over and turned on the light. They were in a small laundry room, and Hank immediately fell back into a pile of folded sheets. Andrew went to the other side of the small room and sat on a pile of towels waiting to be folded.

Hank looked at Andrew. "Can you believe this shit?"

Andrew looked back at Hank, and they both just shook their heads.

"Unbelievable," muttered Andrew. They then began to make their plans on how to take back the forum, so they could once again try to take back America.

CHAPTER XXXII

Frances Buckholtz had been watching the news all day. He knew that whatever happened today would determine his future for many years to come. He not only wanted Senator Cynthia Madison to fail at her efforts at tort reform, but he wanted her dead. He wanted to be done with the problem of Senator Madison, and he wanted to send a signal to her brother not to mess with the mighty Frances Buckholtz.

He hated listening to all this bullshit. All Maddi's fancy talk about reform and "saving America." What a bunch of crap! He was trying to stay focused on what was going on, but he found himself drifting through many of the speeches.

He was suffering through "Maddi's Laws," while shaving. His mind was drifting to the many ways he would like to stick it to that bitch when, all at once, he heard an announcer say "Oh my God! Someone's shooting."

He saw the camera start going sideways—still filming—and he could tell there was chaos in the Convention Hall. "Finally!" he thought. "Finally it's happening. That Shit Smith is finally earning his money. Cost me enough, too."

He watched for the next several minutes, anxiously waiting to hear that Senator Madison had been shot, and the shooter had escaped. He was half-shaven, with shaving cream all over his face, riveted to his TV set in his small Washington, D.C. apartment. Gradually they started revealing details.

"There was apparently a single gunman, who fired 3 shots. It would appear that his target was most likely the senator, but she remains uninjured as far as we can tell."

"Damn!" Frances said aloud. "No way! That bitch escaped unharmed again!" He continued listening.

"It appears that the gunman himself was injured, as well as a Mr. John McCargish—a jurist from the Supreme Court. Both men are said to be in critical condition, having been taken to Methodist Hospital near the Convention Center. We will continue to provide updates on their condition."

Frances couldn't believe what he was hearing. Not only had the senator not gotten the least bit hurt, but his hit man was now in the custody of the law. Peter Smith had no reason to keep quiet about Frances' involvement. He knew this. He also knew he had to shut him up before he could speak. Who did he know in Indianapolis? Didn't that goof ball Roger have a friend he was dealing with in Indy? He'd better find out right away.

He called the office to see if they could get Roger Clairy on the phone immediately. After several seconds Roger got on the phone.

"Hello?"

"Roger, this is Mr. Buckholtz. Things are going crazy at that stupid forum that Senator Madison is conducting out in Indianapolis. I need some eyes and ears out there. Don't you have a friend there who could maybe help us get the inside scoop on what's going on? Oh yeah, and, Roger, our friend Mr. Smith is there, too."

There was silence on the other end of the line. Buckholtz continued.

"You know, the guy I hooked you up with a few weeks ago? Yeah, get this—the guy apparently tried to take a shot at the senator!"

Once again, only silence on the other end. Buckholtz kept on talking.

"I can't imagine why anyone would try to kill the senator, can you? Anyway, if you can get a hold of that friend of yours and tell him what we need. Oh yeah, they have Mr. Smith—in critical condition—in their custody at some hospital in downtown Indy. You might want to put him on that. I imagine that whatever possessed Mr. Smith to try to shoot the senator would be better left unknown … if you catch my drift."

Roger certainly did catch his drift. He knew exactly what Buckholtz was trying to do. He would try to pin the entire thing on Roger if he could get away with it. By introducing the two of them he had put him in a position of potential involvement in the attempted murder of a United States senator. That prick! Well, he did agree with one thing that Buckholtz had said—it would be best if Mr. Peter Smith never got the chance to communicate anything at all to the Indianapolis police. He immediately put a call in to Kevin.

Kevin Clayborne did not know what to think about all the chaos going on around him. He was giddy with the excitement of the whole thing. He also felt that the timing could not have been better—Senator Madison was really starting to connect with these asshole doctors and—whoever tried to kill her had done the Trial Attorneys a huge favor. Once the chaos had begun, Kevin had rushed out the back door of the Convention center, knowing that it would be better for him if he was nowhere near the Hall as these events were going on. He decided to head across the street to a café where he ordered a cup of coffee and sat down to watch events unfold. His cell phone began to ring.

"This is Kevin."

"Kevin, Roger here. From D.C. Things are heating up out there, I hear."

"Yeah, this place is going nuts. It's great stuff. I'm still in the loop—but I think the senator might have an idea that I'm working for the other side—those stupid 'Maddi Laws' sounded a whole lot better than I intended them to. She's got that asshole Morrow from Phily helping out as well. But, I-"

"I don't give a shit about any of that, dammit!" Roger sounded very distraught. There was a brief pause. "Listen, Kevin, there's something you need to do for me and the boss—Mr. Buckholtz."

Kevin immediately smiled to himself. "I knew they would eventually need my help," he thought. He kept quiet while Roger continued.

"Yeah, well, there's apparently a guy there who tried to take a shot at the senator. Mr. Buckholtz and I happen to know this guy. Now, don't get any crazy ideas—we had no idea he would try to kill a sitting United States Senator, but, we're thinking that he may want to try to make a deal with the authorities at our expense, if you see what I'm saying?"

Kevin couldn't believe what he was hearing. Those ruthless guys in D.C. had hired a hit on Senator Madison! He responded.

"I see where you're going with this. You're thinking he might fabricate your involvement in his insane and senseless plot and you're hoping he is not able to speak of your acquaintance?"

"Exactly! We thought just maybe you could find out what hospital he is at, go to that hospital, and look in on his condition. You know, like maybe a reporter or something?"

Kevin was thinking quickly to himself. "Does he want me to kill the guy? Or just pray he dies? Either way, I'm getting something good out of this messed up situation." He spoke aloud to Roger.

"I catch what you're saying, Roger. I think it would be harmless enough for me to simply look in on the guy who tried to kill my beloved senator. I imagine that such a deed would be greatly appreciated in D.C?"

"Absolutely Kevin. It was only a matter of time until we got you out here anyway," he lied. "Consider yourself in like Flynn if you can manage to keep that little bastard from communicating the lies I'm certain he'll communicate. Hell, I'll even give you my office—I'm about to move up closer to the top anyway."

Kevin was thrilled with the direction things were going. "Consider it done, Roger. I'll let you know. Keep an eye on the news because things are probably going to get more interesting here soon." And with that Kevin hung up the phone and quickly finished his coffee.

He walked out into a light drizzle that had begun to fall, and headed back toward the convention center. He was stopped by a large, well-armed policeman. "Can I help you sir?"

"Yeah. I need to get back into the convention. I'm close friends with the senator and I was calling to check on her friend that was shot. Do you happen to know if they got the shooter?"

The officer looked down at the little man, eying him questionably. "Yeah, but he's not doing so well either. They took him to Methodist as well."

Kevin smiled to himself. "Okay, thanks officer." He turned and headed for the corner to find a cab.

Methodist Hospital was a short cab ride from the Convention Center and Kevin was at the front door in just minutes. He jumped out, quickly paid the driver, and ran through the front doors. He knew he could not appear to be connected to the shooter in any way, so he had devised a story line during the very brief cab ride. He approached a young lady sitting at the front desk.

"Hello, Ma'am. I am a reporter with a local Indianapolis paper, and I am reporting on the situation with the two men who were shot at the Convention Center. Can you tell me anything about either shooting victim and their current status?"

The young lady slowly looked up at Kevin, as though she were trying to decide what she should do. Before she could respond, Kevin spoke again.

"If you're not allowed to tell me anything that's quite all right—I completely understand. How do you spell your name, Ma'am?"

The young lady looked at him with bewilderment. "Why do you want to know how to spell my name?"

Kevin grinned. "Well, if I'm going to mention that the lovely young lady at the front desk was careful not to reveal any information, I should at least have her name spelled correctly."

The young lady smiled. This made no sense, but, as long as she wasn't getting into any trouble what harm could it do? "All right, she said. My name is Belinda Myers. M, Y, E, R, S. Myers."

"Great! Now, the only thing remaining is to tell me when the two gentlemen arrived, just so I have that information correct."

Once again, the young lady paused. "What could it hurt?" she thought. She picked up the phone and called down to the Emergency Room.

"Hey Joanie. What time did those ambulances bring in the two guys from the convention center? Are they both still alive? Okay. Will they be taking them upstairs any time soon? Allright. Thanks Joanie." She looked back up at Kevin. "They arrived here at 12:46 pm, one right after another. I believe that the guy from the Supreme Court arrived first, followed by the guy they say did the shooting. They're both still alive, but the Supreme Court guy is only hanging on by a thread. The other guy is still out, but stable."

Kevin gave Ms. Belinda Myers a very big smile and thanked her again. He knew he would have to act quickly if he wanted to get to the shooter before he came to and told all he knew. He quickly headed for the elevator. He turned around one more time to see Belinda smiling from ear to ear at the thought of being mentioned so favorably in the newspaper. He laughed to himself as he got on the elevator and headed downstairs to the Emergency Room.

Maddi was holding on to John McCargish's hand as tightly as she could. He was not doing well. He was having a lot of difficulty breathing. One of the bullets had gone through his arm and into his chest, puncturing a lung. The ER doctors had placed a chest tube and were preparing to take him to surgery to remove the bullet and assess the damage. His vitals were not good at all, and Maddi knew that his chances for surviving this were not favorable.

He had tried to speak to her on the way to the hospital, but it took all he had just to keep breathing, so Maddi had insisted he stop. He just looked up into her eyes. She was crying, but she held his gaze, knowing that it might be the last time they would ever look into one another's eyes. Those beautiful green eyes.

Once they had placed the chest tube, John was able to mutter a few words. He told Maddi that he felt she had succeeded—in spite of this guy—and that he was honored to have witnessed what she had said and done. She asked him again to be quiet, as she could see the physical strain it placed on him to try to speak. He nodded, then added. "What I wouldn't have given to have known you better." Maddi's eyes filled once again with tears, and she looked down into his eyes and nodded and said "me too."

The emergency room doctors then came and rushed John into the surgical suite off to the side of the Emergency Room and left Maddi alone with her thoughts and her very great sadness. John McCargish was fighting for his life, all because of her. All because of this effort to fix a very broken system. Could the system even be fixed? After all, it was controlled by its beneficiaries. How could they be made to do the right thing? And, who could make them do it? Had anything really been gained by this forum? Was it worth a man's life? A very good man. Someone Maddi would've also loved to have gotten to know. She sat silently and waited.

She didn't even notice when Kevin Clayborne appeared in the Emergency Room. She didn't notice as he looked all around, carrying his notebook, still trying to look the part of a nosy reported. He walked quickly by her, glad she hadn't looked up to see who had gone by. He knew it was best if no one knew he was here.

He had waited for several minutes by the front desk for the receptionist to run an errand. When she finally got up to go for coffee, he glanced down at the routing slip sitting by her desk. He quickly found the name John Doe on the sheet, but saw that there were 3 John Does listed. He then looked for an arrival time of 11:46. He saw it and noted the room number. He headed for the room as quietly and unobtrusive as he could be. He walked right past Maddi, not realizing it was her until he was directly in front of her. But, she was immersed in her thoughts. She looked very sad as far as Kevin could tell. "She must know the Supreme Court guy," he thought to himself. Lucky for him that she hadn't seen him. He went around the corner and found the room of Mr. Peter Smith. He walked in.

There was no one else in the room except for the shooter himself. There were tubes and buzzers everywhere. It made Kevin a little sick, but he knew he had a job to do. He walked toward the bed to see what the situation was.

Smith was laying still with his eyes closed. He had been intubated, and appeared to be resting quietly, while the machine did his breathing for him. There was a chart sitting at the foot of the bed, which Kevin picked up. He looked inside, trying to figure out whether this guy was going to live or die. He certainly didn't want to risk killing him if he was going to die on his own! He couldn't decipher much of what was written, so he put the chart down. Just then he heard the door. He looked around and saw a middle-aged, overweight woman walk in carrying some contraption that apparently would be hung on Mr. Smith's IV pole.

"Can I help you?" she barked at Kevin. He thought quickly.

"Yeah, my name is Dr. Kevin Wilson, and I'm here from D.C. to check on the alleged shooter in this case. What can you tell me about Mr. John Doe here Ma'am?"

The nurse eyed Kevin suspiciously. "Who are you and where did you say you were from?"

Kevin gave the nurse his very best smile and repeated "My name is Dr. Kevin Wilson, and I'm from D.C. I was at the forum, so my superior—the Surgeon General of the United States of America—asked me to look in on our shooter here to see if he is in any condition to perhaps give us a little information."

At the sound of the Attorney General of the United States, the older nurse softened and decided to cooperate with the stranger.

"Well. The guy's in pretty bad shape—took a bullet through the leg here-" she pointed to his left leg, just above the knee—"and to his belly, right there, which went through the bottom of his lungs." She lifted up the cover and his gown to reveal a blood-soaked dressing covering his upper abdomen, Kevin had to fight the urge to vomit.

"Hmm. 'Looks like he took a few good shots, here. What's the prognosis?" He knew he had to sit down quickly, or was going to faint.

The nurse didn't seem to notice. "Oh, he'll be all right. We put him on this vent to protect his airway while we figured out what was up with him. We're hoping to pull the vent within the hour if his lungs can take it. Then he might be able to tell you a little something. So if you want to stick around …"

Kevin had bolted out the door and had turned the corner toward the stairwell—out of sight—just as he began retching up his morning's breakfast and his last cup of coffee.

CHAPTER XXXIII

Hank and Andrew, with help from Amanda, quickly tried to get the forum back on track. They had rounded up the remaining speakers for the afternoon, and discussed with them their plans for the revised convention. It was decided that Hank would finish up the speaking for this day, and that he would quickly review Maddi's Laws and then proceed with his intended topic. The revised agenda had been released to the media, in an effort to get the word out to everyone that—in no way—would the horrible events which had occurred earlier that day interfere with the Forum and its objectives. Because of the crime scene nature of their current convention space, they had arranged with another group to share use of their convention hall and they were now prepared to resume activities starting at 3:00 that afternoon.

Hank had tried for the last several hours to get a hold of Maddi, but she wasn't answering her cell phone. He decided not to try to run her down through the ER staff—she knew how to reach him if she wanted to talk to him.

He also knew that she had been confused. It was quite apparent that John McCargish was interested in Maddi, and that—were it not for Hank—Maddi was also quite interested in John McCargish. It was also clear that John had helped Maddi quite a bit with some of the details concerning Maddi's Laws. He knew that whatever relationship the two had, they were very fond of one another and that this was very painful for Maddi. He tried to put it out of his mind and focus on his speech for the convention.

By 2:30 that afternoon things had calmed down just a bit—although there was now definitely a media circus surrounding the forum events—and Hank was standing behind the stage reviewing Maddi's Laws so as to present them to the forum participants once again—in abbreviated form—so that they would not lose their impact.

He couldn't believe how much work Maddi had put into these laws, and he wanted to make sure that they had gotten a proper amount of recognition. He decided to try Maddi's cell phone once more before he walked out on stage. Her message came on—again—and he left her a message. "Maddi, it's Hank. Listen, I know this whole situation is terrible for you—but, I just want you to know that Andrew and Amanda and I have got things in order here, so you just do whatever you need to do there. I don't want to make things any more difficult for you than they already are. I love you." He flipped his phone closed and began to prepare for the forum to once again get underway.

A local Indianapolis paper had managed to get through to Andrew during the chaos. They quickly asked him about the alleged wrongdoings put forth by Frances Buckholtz, President of the American Trial Lawyers Association. This was the first Andrew had heard about the claims and his anger was palpable the minute they reviewed for him what had been said.

"Mr. Madison, do you have a comment?"

Andrew looked directly at the reporter, his jaw set and his eyes narrowed. He then began to speak.

"The truth, sir, is exactly the opposite of what that man has told you. It was he who provided the alcohol, and it was he who insisted we not tell, threatening to spout the same lies he told your paper if I ever breathed a word of any of it. I have stayed quiet—like a coward—for 30 years, but now the truth is out there and I will allow your readers and all who are interested to seek that truth wherever they may find it. I, for one, am an open book. I fear, however, that Mr. Buckholtz has much to hide."

He then turned and walked away.

At exactly 3:00 pm, Andrew Madison stepped onto the stage of a very crowded convention room, and proceeded to resume the Forum. He walked toward the podium and stepped up to the microphone. He slowly adjusted the mike and then cleared his throat once or twice. He began to speak.

"Welcome back everyone. My name is Andrew Madison and I am Maddi's brother." There was a loud and immediate applause throughout the small auditorium. Clearly these people had not allowed the article in the Star, and the accusations made by Buckholtz, to affect their opinion of Andrew. He smiled at the thought and then continued.

"I hate the circumstances that have brought me to this role of speaker but I am most honored to be speaking to all of you this afternoon. I would like to reassure you that Senator Madison is doing fine—she was not injured—and we are still awaiting some word on the status of her very good friend, John McCargish, who apparently saved Maddi's life." Andrew appeared to choke up at this, and he reached over and grabbed a quick drink of water.

"What Senator Madison and her colleagues have done here today, with the help of all of you in this room, is truly amazing. I am not prone to optimism, but I do have to think that if anything can change the sad state of medicine in this country it is this forum and all the ideas and ideals emanating from within this forum. I believe in the goals that are being set forth today, and I believe in Maddi's Laws and their ability to improve our country. Our next speaker is going to reiterate those laws, and then add some ideas of his own. Hopefully, by the time he is finished speaking we will have the blueprint by which we can take back America."

There was loud applause for these statements, and nods of acknowledgement throughout the crowd. Andrew cleared his throat and continued.

"It is my great privilege to introduce to you all here this afternoon a very dear friend of Maddi's. Apparently they met at Med School, and have rekindled their friendship over the last several months. I know Maddi and our next speaker have the same hopes and dreams for the future of medicine as well as for the future of our country. I now present to you all, a fellow physician, Dr. Hank Clarkson."

The crowd gave an appropriate welcoming applause as Hank headed out to the podium. He did not recall ever feeling so nervous. He reached the podium and immediately grabbed a glass and poured water from the carafe sitting beside the podium. He quickly took a drink of water and grabbed the podium on each side, and let out a very large sigh. He grinned, and those sitting closest to the front of the stage grinned back, in welcome understanding of the anxiety Hank was feeling. He cleared his throat and began.

"Thank you for your very nice welcome. As Andrew stated, my name is Hank Clarkson, and I'm a family physician from Strongsville, Ohio. I have been practicing medicine for the last 20 years or so, and I have—for the most part—loved every minute of it. Until I got sued."

Hank looked out in the crowd, he had their complete attention. He continued.

"Getting sued is so much more than simply receiving a certified letter. It is so much more than feeling nauseous as you read through the accusations being set forth. It is so much more than talking to 'your' lawyer about how slimy 'their' lawyer is and how this whole process is really nothing to worry about. It is so much more than all of that. It is shameful. Whether it should be or not, it is. Like getting punished in grade school. Or lying to your parents. Shameful.

"Once I got sued, everything changed for me. My approach to medicine was no longer joyful. It was guarded. I felt paranoid and resentful. I had a friend tell me once that lawsuits steal you away from your family and all that you love. This is the most accurate statement I have found for what happens. And it has little to do with whether you are found guilty or not. It is all about betrayal. Someone you had faith in, that you thought had faith in you, decided to go elsewhere to convey their dissatisfaction with your care. They decided to seek money to answer their concerns about an unfortunate event or outcome. They took the investment of trust you gave them—which is what a doctor does in fact give each one of his patients—and they betrayed that trust for the sake of a dollar. I can think of no greater betrayal, and I know that I will never be the same because of what has happened to me."

Hank paused and reached over for another sip of water. He looked out into the crowd and saw their very receptive faces. He was reaching them. He continued on.

"I used to think that only 'bad' doctors got sued; or maybe 'mean' doctors—doctors who didn't take time with their patients, or who allowed their concerns with financial gain to trump their concerns of caring for their patients. I now know that often very nice, decent, respectable physicians get sued, for no other reason than that they can be sued. A bad outcome is now the equivalent of malpractice, and any good attorney can make that case.

"Percentages suggest that nearly 60% of the physicians sitting in this convention hall have been sued, and that the other 40% most likely will be sued—at least once—before they retire from the practice of medicine. All of these doctors are not bad. The system has gone crazy and we must put a stop to it."

There was loud applause at this last comment. Hank looked out among the faces sitting in the audience and he felt so comfortable—and so comforted—by the recognition and understanding he saw in those faces. He continued.

"It has recently occurred to me that—as I see my 30 or so patients per day—I am at risk at least 30 times a day to be the victim of a malpractice lawsuit. Thirty times a day! And, because it is so easy and so common to sue doctors, the reality is that I am exposing myself to considerable risk every patient I see. A typical physician works 4.5 days per week in his or her office. This trans-

lates to 135 patients per week—creating the potential for at least 135 malpractice opportunities every single week that I practice medicine. Someone please
tell me of any other industry that puts an individual in such a position. Is there
any other avocation that creates for their practitioner a risk of getting sued 135
times per week? It sounds crazy, but it is in fact the truth in our current situation.

"Now, the lawyers are fond of pointing out that most cases never go to trial,
and those that do are often won by the doctors. I myself find no comfort in
this. As I said before, the process of getting sued is ruinous in and of
itself—regardless of the outcome. We therefore must change this system if we
expect our brightest and our best to continue wanting to pursue such a profession. We must change things now, or our beloved practice of medicine will
soon exist no more. You can see what I am saying, as thousands of doctors
across this country are walking away from their practices. You see it as thousands of doctors across the land are advising their children to NOT go into this
profession. You see it as thousands of doctors are gathered here today for the
very purpose of taking back our profession."

Hank paused, and the crowd gave a big round of applause for what they
knew was the truth about the plight of the American Doctor. Hank took
another sip of water and continued on with his speech.

"I would like to briefly summarize Maddi's Laws, so that they can have their
proper place in this forum. I fear their impact may have been diminished by
the horrible events which occurred earlier today. So, allow me now to state
Maddi's Laws as they will be presented in an upcoming Legislative initiative
put forth by Senator Cynthia Madison."

Hank then laid out once again the laws that Maddi had shared with the
audience, and, when he was done there was thunderous applause and nods of
approval throughout the auditorium. Hank was able to observe the many
media types in the auditorium who were taking down his every word so as to
be able to explain to their readers and their viewers what exactly "Maddi's
Laws" were. This thrilled Hank to no end. It was the purpose of the forum,
afterall, and it was clearly being achieved. He smiled to himself. He then proceeded to the heart of his speech.

"I am so pleased with your reception of the Laws that will hopefully have
some role in cleaning up the mess that passes for Litigation in this country. I
would now like to share with you another idea that I have come up with that I
think may go a long way in assisting with that goal. I would like to introduce
the concept of Medical Board Tribunals.

"We need a full scale change in the way we handle malpractice cases in America. We need to remove these cases from the courtroom and adjudicate them among doctors—and lawyers—in a separate forum. A forum that recognizes that what we do daily is not easily understood in a two-week trial. It not only takes years of training and some innate intelligence to do what we do, but it also relies on the continual acquisition of experience through the practice setting.

"No one can represent that accurately in front of a jury that doesn't understand. For them to try to understand what we experience and how we proceed with decision-making, would be the equivalent of me trying to understand what goes through a soldier's mind when he faces the enemy.

"This is why the military uses a tribunal system to judge their own. This is why we too must use the same approach if we want our profession—and the greatness of our occupation—to survive.

"The purpose of the Tribunals will be to keep medicine—and any controversy involving medicine—out of the legal system. Grievances would be filed through the Medical Boards, which would have a separate branch designated specifically for the oversight of malpractice issues.

"A patient who felt that they or a loved one had been the victim of malpractice would hire an attorney who would then file the case through the Medical Board Tribunal instead of a court of law. The board would consist of ten doctors and lawyers, who would serve staggered terms of 2, 3, or 4 years. Six of them would be selected by the Medical Board members, and the other 4 would be elected for their positions. They would receive compensation equivalent to their time spent in Tribunal pursuits. The ten Tribunal Board members would then be responsible for determining the validity of any given case. If the case is deemed meritorious they would then hear arguments by each side's attorneys and they would then make their determination.

"Malpractice insurance would also be handled through this Tribunal. All doctors would pay 5% of their net earnings annually, and this would afford them full and complete coverage. No longer would their property be at risk. Once they retired, only in the most egregious circumstances could they be 'sued' anymore.

"Pain and suffering payments would be gone. All that could be awarded would be medical costs incurred and income losses incurred. No longer could a medical malpractice suit create instant millionaires for either plaintiffs or for their attorneys."

This last comment seemed to play quite well with the audience as they clapped loudly, while also hollering out various descriptive terms for the profession of law in general. Hank went on, grinning to himself.

"For the first time ever, a physician would truly be judged by a jury of his peers. No longer would there be an attempt to allow a convoluted explanation of a medical complexity be the determining factor in a practitioner's guilt or innocence.

"If this system that I am advocating seems more favorable to doctors than the current system, well, it is. Perhaps this is what is needed to prevent doctors from leaving the practice of medicine, while their patients are left wondering 'Where did my doctor go?'

"Join me now in recommending to the powers in Washington that we have a new approach to litigation in this country. Join me in pressuring those in D.C. to adopt 'Maddi's Laws,' as well as the 'Medical Board Tribunals,' which we are advocating here and now. Not for the purpose of protecting physicians when we do wrong, but to protect us when we do right!"

This comment provoked thunderous applause throughout the convention hall.

"When we go to work each day, with the noble intent of doing good and doing right, we should expect a reasonable amount of protection for that purpose. We became physicians with good intentions—allow us to have those intentions, and act upon them once again.

Loud shouts of approval and louder applause stopped Hank at that moment. He once again took a quick drink of water and then simply stood and looked out among the crowd of physicians sitting in the loud Convention Hall. His speech was reaching them all, and he felt gratified beyond his wildest expectations. The message was getting out there. The message was being heard. He had only a bit more to say, and so he continued.

"Don't let someone sue me because I wasn't perfect today. Raise the standard—raise the bar. Doctors should be able to go to work each day without the fear of litigation for a mistake they—or their employees—may make. It is imperative that I know as I take care of that particularly complicated case that—if I truly do my best, with all good intentions—there will be no opportunist coming along to try to take advantage of the complexity of the case I so valiantly tried to handle.

"I can tell you right now—unequivocally—that if our current system doesn't change—and change quickly—the best students in America will no longer pursue medicine, they will look elsewhere to have their talents and their efforts appreciated. As a friend of mine so eloquently put it: 'What self-respecting individual would put themselves through this day in and day out?' Look around at this crowd, and look around at the exodus of doctors across this great nation, and I will tell you this—we've had it. We're on the edge. We've taken all we can take. I do not want to leave this profession; I do not want to leave my patients or their families. To be able to help these people has been the single most gratifying thing in my life. Please, help me now to restore sanity back to the practice of medicine. Help me make medicine the enjoyable, noble calling it once was. Help me now to take back the practice of medicine and to take back America!"

The members of the audience were clapping enthusiastically, with smiles on their faces. Dr. Hank Clarkson had voiced their feelings—and their pain—better than anyone else had been able to do. They were talking and grinning among themselves. Hank looked out at all those doctors—on the same page—and he too grinned. This forum would in fact change things. He wasn't quite sure how, but he knew that it definitely would. It is why he came here, and he felt incredibly gratified and relieved at the thought. He held up his hand as a gesture of appreciation and then turned and walked off the stage, still listening to the echoing applause.

CHAPTER XXXIV

Maddi did not know how long she had been sitting outside the surgery suite. She couldn't remember when she had last eaten, nor did she care. She did know she was tired, but she refused to leave the waiting area to find a place to catch a nap. She just sat and waited, knowing that John McCargish was fighting for his life.

She had quite a lot of time to think. And think she did. So much had happened over the last several months. So many major events and so many new relationships. She really hadn't had any time to reflect. It kind of felt good to just sit and think. Security had once again been assigned to Maddi here in Indianapolis. Two nondescript men in brown suits with the obvious bulge of their weapons showing through their jackets were sitting across the hall from Maddi. Keeping her safe. She didn't even seem to notice them. She was lost in her thoughts.

She was running. Running away from something. Some other kids chasing her after school. She remembered being so frightened. They had chased her before, but never for such a long distance. And they were getting closer. She remembered feeling such fear. Knowing that at any moment they would be close enough to grab her. She wasn't sure why they chased her or what they would do if and when they did catch her, but she knew that whatever it was, it wasn't good.

She heard several sets of footsteps close behind her. She kept running. Faster, faster. But they were catching her. She felt one of them put his hand on the hood of her jacket. He was pulling her backward, down to the ground. The other one ran up and threw a punch to her cheek. As hard as he could. She tried to scream but nothing came out. She kept trying to scream but she couldn't make a sound.

Suddenly she heard a low, forceful voice from the distance. "Hey, let her go! Now!" She felt the grip on her hood loosen, and the beating stopped. One kid said to the other "We gotta' get outa' here. He'll kill us!" The two boys stood and ran quickly into the woods. Maddi just lay there, crying and feeling so very frightened. She was shaking inside and out.

"Hey sis, what's up?" It was Andrew! Andrew had come to save her. She immediately felt better. She felt safe and she quit shaking. Andrew had come to save her. Once again....

"Senator. Senator. Please wake up."

Maddi looked up as she shook herself awake. It was the surgeon. She immediately sat upright and put her hand to her hair and tried to straighten herself up. She needed to prepare herself for whatever he might have to say. She stood up and looked directly into the surgeon's eyes.

"How's John?" she asked, with a trembling in her voice.

The surgeon paused and looked down at Maddi with sorrowful eyes. "I'm sorry, senator." Maddi tried to brace herself. She grabbed the back of her chair and held on. "We couldn't save him. The bullet had grazed his heart and the damage was more extensive than we originally thought."

The surgeon went on to describe what had occurred, but Maddi was no longer listening. John was dead. And he died saving her life. She had never gotten to know him, but she knew enough to know that she would miss him greatly. She felt so lonely, and so empty inside. She sat down in the chair as the surgeon continued talking about the surgery and how sorry he was.

Finally, Maddi looked up at him and asked, "Did he say anything more?"

"No ma'am, he didn't. We put him under and he never woke up. It was peaceful, I'm sure."

Maddi nodded, as though to tell him it was okay and not to blame himself. He reached out and squeezed her shoulder in understanding and turned and walked away.

Maddi sat there, in the middle of the busy hallway, with two security guys sitting across from her, and people everywhere, and felt all alone. She felt lonelier than she had ever remembered feeling in her life. She quietly began to cry.

Kevin had finally recovered from his experience with seeing Peter Smith on the ventilator. He didn't feel well, but he was no longer vomiting. He knew he had to act quickly. He headed back toward the room, secretly maneuvering so as to avoid being seen, and he quietly slipped into Peter's room. He had decided to pull the plug of the ventilator, hoping to make it look like an accident. He walked into the room, unable to look at Mr. Smith, and he headed directly for the ventilator. He saw it sitting to the side of Mr. Smith's bed. He looked for the plug. He inadvertently glanced up and saw Mr. Smith' eyes opening and looking directly at him. This nearly stopped him in his tracks. But, he knew he couldn't fail. He had to do this to achieve his goals. Besides, this guy was just some jerk-off hit man—who would really miss him?

He reached back down toward the plug and gently yanked it out of the wall. The machine immediately began beeping loudly, and Kevin knew he had to get out of there fast, without being seen. He stood up and turned toward the door. Something possessed him to look back at Mr. Smith and when he did he saw panic and fear—and anger—in Mr. Smith's eyes. He felt suddenly afraid and immediately turned and ran out the door.

He snuck down the hallway toward the same door by which he had vomited just moments before, and quickly went through the door and down the hall. After exiting out the service door to the side of the hospital he ran as fast as he could through the alley at the side of the building. Kevin felt confident no one had seen him, but he knew he would never forget the look in Peter Smith's eyes. He continued running as fast as he could, to nowhere in particular.

CHAPTER XXXV

The Forum to Take Back America was getting quite a bit of press. There were some live 'break-in' newscasts on local television broadcasts, as well as continual coverage on some of the 24-hour news channels. Many of the players in the forum had been interviewed, including Andrew Madison and Hank Clarkson. Maddi was noticeably absent, only mentioned in the context of maintaining a vigil outside the room of John McCargish, the man who had clearly saved her life.

Periodic updates on John McCargish's condition were given, as well as updates on the shooter himself. An attempt had been made to get more information concerning the shooter, but so far all that had been made available to the press was his name, Peter Smith, or so his driver's license found at the scene stated. There was some question whether this was in fact his name.

The current focus of the 24-hour news circuit was on Hank's speech, and his call for medical tribunals. Each news network had their experts analyzing the details of Hank's proposals, some speaking favorably and some being quite critical. There were concerns about constitutionality, so the news networks had their "judicial specialist" address this issue, most agreeing that it would pass a constitutional challenge. They used the precedent of the military to justify how and why it could work.

They were in the process of interviewing one of the doctors attending the forum when all at once the newscaster stopped the interview.

"Excuse me sir, I have just received word that John McCargish has died. There are no further details, and we will update you as we hear more."

Hank was watching the interview from backstage. He heard the announcer state that John had died and he felt incredibly sad. Both for the loss of John and for Maddi's loss. He wanted to go to her, but did not feel he should. He sat there backstage for several minutes thinking about what to do, knowing he had to do something.

Andrew approached him and saw the sadness in his eyes.

"Well, it looks like you've heard the news."

"Yeah, just now." Both men exchanged glances and Andrew spoke.

"Don't you think we should get over there? I mean Maddi is all alone and all." He smiled at Hank, and Hank smiled back. He stood up, slowly, and headed for the back entrance. "Yep, let's go."

The alarms had sounded immediately when Peter Smith's ventilator was no longer working. Two nurses nearby immediately rushed toward his room. They did not see the gentleman who had snuck out only seconds before.

They immediately ran to Peter Smith's side to assess the situation. His eyes were closed and his chest was not moving. One of the nurses quickly felt for a carotid pulse, while the other one tried to figure out why the ventilator had stopped.

"He's got a faint pulse!" screamed the first nurse. "Quick, get over here and let's start bagging him."

Just then the second nurse discovered the plug pulled from the outlet. "Oh my god," she screamed. "Someone has pulled the plug!"

The two nurses quickly exchanged horrified glances, and the second nurse reached down and plugged in the vent. As it began to once again take over the act of breathing, Peter Smith opened his eyes and began to grab at the tube in his chest. He was trying to pull out the tube and breathe on his own. The two nurses were trying to hold down his hands, but he eventually was able to pull the tube and started coughing and gasping for air. At that point an emergency room physician ran through the doors and took a glance at the situation in front of him.

"What the hell is going on in here?" he shouted. The two nurses quickly tried to explain, while at the same time trying to make sure that Peter Smith was breathing without difficulty. It was soon evident that he was in fact breathing okay, and the doctor told the nurses to remove the tube and the vent from the bed, and to obtain an O2 saturation level on Mr. Smith. He began asking Smith how he was doing, and if he needed anything.

"Fuck, I'm doing just great doc! Considering somebody just tried to kill me, I'm doing swell."

The doctor was somewhat taken back by this and proceeded to check his patient for adequate breathing and appropriate heart rate. "I can assure you,

Mr. Smith that we will notify the authorities immediately and look into this situation."

Just then a police officer ran into the room and threw a quick glance toward the doctor. "Can he talk?"

"Yes, but-"

"Then I'm talking to him, NOW. There's no 'but' about it." And he proceeded over to Peter Smith's bed and began to interrogate him. After several questions concerning his intentions to kill Senator Madison—all which Peter denied, he then asked if Peter knew of anyone who would try to kill him.

"You know something, copper? I think I want my lawyer." He chuckled softly to himself, as though he had just told a joke. "As a matter of fact, I think I want a whole bunch of lawyers."

The police officer looked at him curiously, and then replied. "I'll tell you what. I'm willing to get you that lawyer, but, things might just go a little better for you if you talk to me first."

Mr. Smith looked at the officer with curiosity. "Hey copper, what would it be worth to you if I could give you some information on some pretty 'high-up' individuals that had something to do with all of this?"

The police officer eyed him curiously.

"Well, it depends on what you've got."

"You won't believe what I know—and who I know it about. But I need some 'conditions' before I'll be willing to tell you guys anything."

Just then another officer ran through the door. The first policeman motioned him over to where he was standing.

"Hey Stanley, this guy says he's got some info and he wants to make a deal. What d'ya think?"

"Is it good info, ya' think?"

"Well, I don't know. Maybe Mr. Smith here could give us a hint of what he's got." Both officers looked directly at Mr. Smith with expectation.

Mr. Smith eyed them both, his dark little eyes glaring at each man, a slight grin forming on his face. After several seconds of looking back and forth at each officer, he finally spoke.

"What if I were to tell you that the lawyer I might call may have to call a lawyer himself?"

Each officer looked at the other. The first officer spoke.

"So you're telling me a lawyer might be involved in a crime? So, what's new about that?" The other officer started laughing quietly.

Smith was getting a little agitated. "What if I were to tell you that this lawyer is a pretty big deal? Not just any lawyer but one of the more powerful lawyers in the country?"

The two officers exchanged glances, curiosity now apparent in their eyes. The second officer spoke up.

"Okay, I'll bite. You tell us who put you up to this, and, if we check it out and it looks like the real deal we'll ask the D.A. to go easy on you."

Peter chuckled. "No way. I want something in writing. The sooner the better."

The first officer was getting tired of this conversation.

"Look asshole. You were caught in the act of trying to kill a United States Senator! I don't think you're in any position to be making demands of any kind. If the kind officer here tells you that he will advise the D.A. to go easy on you, then he will. So, hurry up and give us what you got—or we'll just call that D.A. right now and throw you to the system. It's up to you because I'm getting bored with this garbage you're throwing at us."

Peter looked at the officer with his green eyes narrowed to slits. His jaw was set as he considered this information. Finally he spoke.

"I was hired by the head of the American Trial Lawyers Association. I believe his name is Buckholtz."

The two officers eyed Peter carefully. Peter watched as they looked at one another, likely contemplating the value of his information. The first officer looked at the second and nodded.

"All right, Smith. What else have you got?"

"That's about it—Buckholtz wanted Senator Madison 'out of the way' by whatever means it took. So, I kindly obliged—if it hadn't been for that prick who jumped in the way." Smith then proceeded to tell the officer what had transpired between he and Frances Buckholtz. When he was finished, he added "By the way, whoever it was that just tried to kill me—something tells me Buckholtz put him up to it."

The first officer spoke. "Could you identify him if you saw him again?"

Smith replied, "I'll never forget what he looks like. Never. You guys find him, I'll ID him."

The two officers finished up with Mr. Smith, and contacted headquarters in order to have another officer sent to guard Mr. Smith's door. They then headed back to the station to begin hunting down Mr. Buckholtz and find out what they could about the attempted murder of Senator Cynthia Madison.

Hank and Andrew got to the hospital in under 7 minutes. They both walked quickly through the hospital entrance and immediately approached the Information desk.

Andrew spoke first. "We're looking for Mr. John McCargish's room."

The lady at the desk began to type on her computer keyboard. "How do you spell that name, sir?"

As Andrew spelled out John's last name, the lady busily looked at her screen, occasionally typing a word here or there. She stopped and a frown crossed her brow. She looked up from her screen at the two men. "I'm sorry sir, but he has been removed."

"Removed? What the hell do you mean he's been 'removed?'"

The lady at the desk was clearly uncomfortable. "It appears that he is, well, he is…. dead."

Both men glanced at one another. It was Hank who spoke up. "Ma'am, we know he is dead. But our friend was with him and we are trying to locate her. We think she is probably still near his room."

The front desk lady seemed to relax a bit after Hank spoke, and she looked back toward her computer screen.

"Here it is. Room 327E—downstairs in the Emergency Department. Take that elevator over there." She pointed to the elevator behind her and to the left, and both men ran straight at it. Hank pushed the button and the elevator came quickly to their floor and the doors proceeded to open. Both men stepped in and Andrew pushed the button for the basement floor.

The elevator went straight to the desired floor very quickly. The two men stepped off and headed to Room 327E as quickly as they could. When they turned the corner they both saw Maddi sitting outside the room, brushing the tears away from her face and starting to rise. She turned and saw both men come around the corner and her face immediately lightened just a bit.

Andrew got to her first and gave her a hug and looked straight into her eyes. "Maddi, I know how sad you must feel. I am so sorry."

Maddi looked up at him and smiled. "He was a good man, Andrew, and he died saving my life." Tears fell from her eyes as she spoke. Andrew hugged her tightly.

Hank approached and stood by quietly. Andrew stepped back and Hank walked toward Maddi. She immediately reached out for him and pulled him close to her. She began to cry much deeper. Hank just held her close.

After several minutes he pulled away just enough to look at her.

"He loved you, Maddi. And he died showing you that. I am sure that if he were given the option, he'd do it again."

Maddi stopped crying. She stared up at Hank with her tear-stained eyes and smiled. She said nothing and simply hugged him tighter.

After several more minutes, Andrew motioned to Hank that they needed to get back to the forum. The three of them then proceeded out of the hospital, without a word, arm in arm, followed closely by two secret service agents.

CHAPTER XXXVI

Frances Buckholtz was sitting at home, watching the proceedings surrounding the forum, amazed at all that had occurred. "That prick Smith can't do anything right" he thought to himself. But, Roger had reassured him that Peter Smith would not be talking to anyone, and that the whole thing would never get back to either of them. Frances was trying to believe that, but he knew he'd feel better when he actually heard Roger tell him that Smith was dead.

He'd been waiting for his call for the past several hours. He was starting his third Scotch and water, and hoped he'd hear soon—before he got himself stinking drunk.

Suddenly there was a knock on the door. "Why didn't he just call?" he wondered to himself. He walked to the door and opened it, fully expecting to see Roger Clairy staring back at him. Instead there stood two men in suits, one pulling out a badge and informing him that they were with the FBI. They asked to come in.

Frances was panicking. "This can't be good," he thought to himself. He was trying to quickly think how to get out of this situation, while opening the door and offering the gentlemen to come inside. He didn't have much time to think. The first gentleman quickly grabbed Frances' hands and pulled them behind him.

"Frances Buckholtz, you are under arrest for the attempted murder of Senator Cynthia Madison. You have the right to remain silent, but if you choose to give up that right, anything you say can and will be used against you in a court of law."

Frances was stunned. He didn't try to resist—he knew it would be useless. He asked the other gentleman to please lock up his apartment and grab the keys. The other gentleman did so, and the three of them proceeded out the door and into their car and quietly pulled away.

It didn't take Frances long at all to inform the FBI interrogators that Roger Clairy had "put him up to it." The interrogators weren't quite sure what to believe but they proceeded to round up Mr. Clairy for questioning.

They found him at home as well, seemingly in the same semi-drunken stupor that Buckholtz had been in. He also came willingly and they proceeded to place him in the interogation room right next to Buckholtz.

After several hours of the two gentlemen blaming each other they decided to arrest both of them for conspiracy to commit murder and they locked them away in separate cells while the two men waited for their attorneys to arrive. Although the cells were right next to one another, neither man knew the other was there. They each sat there, alone, in complete silence.

Kevin Clayborne meanwhile was sitting in a hotel room in Indianapolis, hoping and praying that Peter Smith didn't get a good look at him. He knew better, however. The memory of Smith's eyes looking directly at his made him shudder. And, the fact that the man may have survived made Kevin very nervous and afraid. He didn't know what to do. He didn't think Smith would know who he was, and he wasn't in any "perp book" for Smith to ID, but he felt it was only a matter of time before the police would peg him for the attempted murder of Smith. He needed to get out of town—quickly.

How the hell had he gotten into this mess? Those pricks in D.C. had dragged him down this dark path and now, here he was, running from the Law.

He wasn't sure where to go—he had never really been anywhere but Evansville, Indiana—except for vacations—and he had no real family to speak of. He knew he couldn't stay, however. So he quickly packed a few items in a bag and grabbed some cash and got in his car and drove. Past the downtown area of Indianapolis, past the suburbs, taking route 70 west until he felt like it would be safe to stop.

Several hours later he was still driving, unsure if he would ever feel like it was safe to stop.

News of Peter Smith's survival, and John McCargish's death filled the airwaves for many days. Intermittently, news from the forum would once again take center stage, but for the most part, the attempted murder of a United States senator, and the actual murder of a Jurist from the Supreme Court dominated the news.

The arrest of the President of the American Trial Lawyers Association managed to interrupt the 24-hour news cycle, as many Washington Insiders tried to analyze what this would mean for the future of that organization. The number two man had been arrested as well and it was unclear who was going to take their place. The organization was getting quite a public "black eye," just as the Forum to take back America had gained traction in efforts at Tort Reform.

Trial lawyers across the country felt under attack as more and more pressure was being applied to try to obtain meaningful tort reform. Maddi's Laws seemed to make sense, not only for their application in the world of medical malpractice, but in terms of tort reform across the spectrum.

Soon an organization had arisen known as "Citizens for Litigation Reform," and their goal was stated as an effort to change how Americans think about lawsuits and personal responsibility. They had begun to place advertisements on television and radio, stating simply that an honorable person claims responsibility for their actions and their choices. Lawsuits need to be reserved for those situations where no clear choice is evident and wrongdoing intentionally occurs.

The organization had begun releasing a monthly report—with specific names and cases, when allowable—of ridiculous lawsuits filed across America. USA Today's editorial staff had begun placing this information in a weekly column for all to read.

There was a hotline established for anyone who felt themselves, or their organization, to be victim of a baseless lawsuit. Lawyers were available to assess the legitimacy of a claim, and if the claim was deemed baseless these lawyers would counter sue. They were gaining traction in their efforts and many cases were going through with some success.

Maddi and her friends had wrapped up the forum successfully, basically expounding on the themes that had already been mentioned on that first, fateful day. There had been some talk about canceling the forum after John McCargish died, but Maddi insisted that it continue, stating simply that John would have wanted them to be successful. This was accepted by all involved, and the following day's lectures were continually dedicated to his memory.

Regrettably, no family could be located for John, which made Maddi all that much sadder. Eventually an aunt was identified in Philadelphia and arrangements were made to ship John's body to a funeral home there in the city.

The funeral was held on the Tuesday following the forum, and Maddi, Andrew, Amanda and Hank were in attendance. Wilson had wanted to go, but had to return to his practice, where he had been greatly missed. Besides, he had a lot of work ahead if he was going to make the bold changes he had suggested he'd make during his speech at the forum.

Clarence Morrow, who lived in Philadelphia, attended the funeral as well, and gave quite a eulogy during the service. Maddi was unable to keep from crying, and Andrew, Hank and Amanda fought back tears as well.

Once the funeral was over, Clarence invited the four of them to dinner. He wanted to share with them the status of the class action suit going forward against the doctors. Things were heating up in terms of depositions and inquiries, and he knew that Maddi and her friends would want to know what was going on.

The five of them had a delightful meal in a restaurant off of South Street in downtown Philadelphia, and by the end of the night they were all laughing loudly at the ridiculousness of the class action system in America. Toward the end of the evening, they had all agreed to come back to Philly for the actual trial which would probably occur in the next couple of months.

All of them had arranged to fly from Philadelphia back home and they headed for the airport early the next morning to catch their flights back home. They had spent the night at Clarence Morrow's home—a beautiful Tudor mansion nestled in downtown Philly with a gate keeping out the miscreants and the chaos of the city.

Andrew and Amanda had become rather close through all of this and they ended up spending most of the night sitting in the study in front of the fireplace, drinking cognac and talking about anything and everything. The sun came up the next morning with Amanda laying in Andrew's arms in the sofa with the fire down to embers.

Hank and Maddi had headed upstairs to two of the upstairs bedrooms, but quickly decided to share one instead. They had hardly closed the door when suddenly they were locked in an embrace that lasted pretty much until the next morning. They touched one another with tenderness and longing, each one trying harder and harder to please the other and make the moments last forever. They finally fell asleep in one another's arms.

When they woke they were both completely happy, and aware that they had begun a relationship they hoped could last forever. They began to discuss the future and how and when they would see each other again. Maddi had a great deal of work to do in Washington, and Hank had a busy practice—and a lawsuit—to get home to. They finally drug themselves out of bed and away from one another's grasp and got cleaned up and ready to head for the airport.

The five of them had breakfast together, and Clarence had his driver take them to the airport. He couldn't go as he had depositions that morning concerning the class action lawsuit. He bid them goodbye and let them all know that he would be in touch concerning the trial date for the suit.

The four then proceeded to the vehicle and jumped inside. On the ride to the airport they discussed all that had occurred in the past week. So many things had changed. Hopefully for the better. Maybe there really was a chance to change the litigation climate in America. Maybe medicine would truly be able to get back to its "glory days." They all hoped and prayed that John's death would stand for something, and they vowed to make it so.

CHAPTER XXXVII

Hank was incredibly depressed when he boarded his airplane. He hated to leave Maddi, and he hated to go home and face all that he had to face. By the time he landed at Cleveland-Hopkins airport on Wednesday afternoon he was nearly despondent.

It was always difficult to come home from a trip away, but more so now in light of what he had to face. He first headed to his house, which Jenny had been keeping an eye on for him, and he proceeded to attend to his messages and his mail. He sorted his laundry and began the process of getting unpacked.

He then proceeded to head into the office to go through his mail there and attend to any problems that had occurred in his absence. He was fortunate to be part of a large call group and so usually didn't have anything urgent waiting for him upon his return, but there was always a lot of mail and correspondence to catch up on, as well as lab work to review. It took him several hours to finally get through everything, and he had saved one letter for the very end. It was from his attorney, and he knew it was intended to let him know about his trial date for his lawsuit.

Apparently, the plaintiff had counted on him settling out of court, but Hank—with his insurance company's blessing—had refused to do so, and so they were headed to trial. Depositions had been taken and motions had been filed and responded to, and now it was time to get ready for court. Hank was quite nervous about the thought of going to trial and testifying, but he knew he would be able to do whatever he had to do when the time came. He slowly began to open the letter.

ॐ

"Dear Dr. Clarkson,

As per our earlier discussion this letter will serve to inform you of your trial date, now set for October 13th, to begin at 9:00 am. I would recommend that you clear all that week and the following week from your schedule at work so as to be available for the trial's duration.

Once again I recommend that you familiarize yourself with your chart and any recollections you may have concerning this case, so as to adequately defend yourself when questioned by opposing counsel.

I will contact you about one week prior to the trial date in an effort to assist you with preparations for the trial. If you have any questions between now and then please don't hesitate to contact me at the number listed below.

Sincerely,

Jimmy Johnson, attorney-at-law."

"Just great!" Hank said aloud to no one. Somewhere deep within him he realized that he had expected them to dismiss him from this case. He now realized that they had no intention of doing so and that he would have to actually go through the hell of a trial. His stomach was wrapped in knots just at the thought of it.

He left a note for his office staff to begin canceling out those two weeks for "an extended vacation," and he then headed home to finish his laundry and get ready to get back to work the following morning.

He needed to call Jenny to let her know he had gotten back okay, but he found himself hesitant to make the call. He was trying to understand why when suddenly it occurred to him. He had never truly loved any other woman except Jenny for all these years. He had never really loved any other woman except Jenny for his entire life. Now he was in love with Maddi. Did he feel guilty? Did he even need to tell her? He knew he would, whether he was obligated to do so or not. He had always told Jenny everything. He didn't know for sure, but he felt confident that Jenny would be more happy for him than sad. He finally got up his nerve and made the call.

"Jenny, it's Hank. I got home safely. Any problems?"

He loved the way she spoke to him—even on the phone. "Hank! It's great to hear your voice. That was some convention you all had out there. I was able to log onto foxnews.com to read a transcript of your speech. It was excellent! All the speeches were. Senator Madison seems like a remarkable lady."

Hank felt his heart skip a beat. "Oh, she is. And thanks for all of that. I hope it will change things. Listen, Jenny, there's something I've got to tell you." He paused for a moment. Jenny was silent at the other end. "Listen. I just need you to know this. Senator Madison and I, well, we-"

"Hank. You don't need to tell me anything. I could tell when they were interviewing you. I know what it is you want to tell me—and you don't need to say anything. I will always love you, and I want you to be happy. Please don't let our relationship affect your ability to be in love. You deserve it, and I wish you the very best. Do you understand?"

Hank was overwhelmed by how wonderful Jenny could be. She said everything he needed to hear, and he wanted to thank her from the bottom of his heart. He knew words would be inadequate, but they were all he had.

"Jenny, I thank you for that. I will also always love you. She does make me very happy, and I am optimistic that this is going to work out. You have always been there for me, and I can't tell you what that has meant through the past 20 years."

There was a brief pause, and then Jenny spoke. "I know Hank. And I will continue to be there for you if you should ever need me again. Welcome home, Hank."

They hung up and Hank sat back in his chair with a smile on his face. "The world can hand you some shit," he thought to himself, "but I have some amazing people in my world to help me deal with it. What more can a person ask for?" With that, he got up and headed to the fridge where he grabbed a beer and sat back down in front of his computer and began finishing his work for the next day.

Maddi and Hank had hugged when he was ready to board his flight, both holding each other for a very long time. They then looked at each other and smiled. The relationship that had started in D.C. had become so much more important to each of them now. They had arranged to see each other as often as their schedules would permit.

After Hank had boarded his plane, Maddi prepared to board her flight as well, hugging Amanda and Andrew, and letting them both know that she would be in touch. Once on board the plane she began to think about all that she needed to do when she got to D.C. She had a laundry list in her head that she was going through, one item at a time. She began to realize how incredibly tired she was and she slowly slipped off to sleep, leaning against the side of the plane, with her legs scrunched up beneath her.

She woke when the plane began its descent, and she gathered her things together, preparing to get off the plane. She sat waiting while they taxied and she thought of all that had happened this past week. So much excitement, so many good and positive changes in the air. Hank. And John. She would have loved a few days to think about things and put it all together in her mind, but she knew she had to get busy. She had legislation to write, and promote, and pass in the Halls of Congress and she was bound and determined to do so.

She stepped off the plane into a beautiful, sunny afternoon and headed into the airport to get her luggage. Once back outside she hailed a cab and headed for her townhouse. There were still two secret service guys following her, and seeing them made her sad, as it was John McCargish who had arranged the detail in the first place. She felt so mournful of the fact that she had never really gotten to know him. What she knew, however, made her smile. He was a truly great man, with a generous spirit and she knew she would never forget him.

She exited the cab and walked up the steps to her townhouse. She walked in, mail and luggage in hand, and began the process of coming home. She had several messages on her answering machine, most relating to the forum, and she had many letters also in response to the forum and its message. As she was playing back her phone messages, the last one in particular caught her attention. She stiffened when she heard the voice on the phone.

"Hey Maddi, it's me. You know, Kevin. I had something come up and had to leave the forum suddenly, but I wanted to tell you how wonderful you did. I think maybe we were successful. Anyway, I just thought I'd let you know how proud of you I was. See ya' soon!"

Maddi didn't know what to think. She had all but forgotten about Kevin. Ever since Clarence Morrow had told her his concerns she had pretty much written him off as a sneak and a loser. Him calling her now left her wondering if perhaps he was up to something. Well, she couldn't think about that now, she had too much to do. She'd deal with it later.

Amanda and Andrew were the last two to leave, and this gave them some more time to figure out if they were in fact falling for one another. Once they had gotten Maddi and Hank on their flights they decided to head for the airport bar and have a beer while they waited to board their planes.

They sat down and each ordered a Michelob Ultra, and they began to talk, more or less picking up where they had left off the night before in the study of Clarence Morrow's home. Andrew had shared a little bit about his journey through the jungle of medicine, and talked about the Tundra and how much clearer and more hopeful life seemed to him there. Amanda listened intently, falling more and more in love with Andrew with each word he spoke.

She had also told him her story, and how much she loved the work she was doing in Columbia, in spite of the lawsuit and all of the problems surrounding medicine these days. He listened, knowing that Amanda was one of those truly good people—in such short supply this day and age. He knew he could never return to the practice of medicine, and he wasn't sure he could ever successfully leave the Tundra, but he did enjoy hearing Amanda talk about her work.

Soon their flights were ready to board and they left each other with a long embrace, unsure of what might be next. They turned from one another and approached their prospective gates. Amanda was about to step into the line of passengers ready to board the plane when she heard someone shout her name.

"Amanda! Amanda, wait!" She turned to look and saw Andrew running toward her. "Amanda, I have no idea what on earth I'm doing, but ..." and then he proceeded to grab her and kiss her, long and hard. He then looked deeply into her eyes and quietly spoke. "I really want to see you again. I think that may be impossible, but I needed you to know how I felt."

Amanda didn't know what to do. She found herself smiling at Andrew as she looked directly into his beautiful blue eyes. "I feel the same way, Andrew. Maybe we could work something out. I may need to take a trip up North sometime, and I'm sure I'd need a guide. What d'ya think?"

He smiled back at her and kissed her again, this time for a very long time. Suddenly they were aware of her final boarding call and she slowly pulled away and ran to the door of her gate. She looked back at Andrew, who was grinning from ear to ear. They both waved, and then the door closed. Andrew headed back to his gate, wondering what on earth just happened to him.

CHAPTER XXXVIII

Kevin had driven west on route 70 for about 18 hours, finally arriving in Denver the following morning. He was too tired to continue, and he needed to stop and get himself back together and create a plan. He knew he would be easily identified by Peter Smith, but he also knew that—as long as Smith never saw him—he would be a free man.

He'd been listening to the news non-stop on, NPR, and was aware of the arrests made at the ATLA. This caused him great concern. He knew that—although there was nothing specific linking him to the attempted murder of senator Madison, and nothing specific linking him to the actual murder of John McCargish, there was something linking him to the attempted murder of Peter Smith. That something was Roger Clairy. And this made Kevin very nervous. He knew he would have to eliminate the possibility of Roger implicating him in any way.

He'd had many hours to think about things, and what he finally concluded was that Maddi was his only saving grace. After all, for all she knew, he was on her side. He would simply cement that idea in her head, and for all to see, and then if Roger Clairy made the claim that Kevin had tried to kill Peter Smith, it would appear to be ludicrous and unbelievable. He could then simply deny it. But, he needed to be sure that at no time could Peter Smith get a look at him. He had decided to change his appearance, just in case he was somehow in the limelight. He would grow a beard, and dye his hair, and get those contacts that change the eye color. He could even put on several pounds. Perfect! Peter would never recognize him.

He figured he had a little bit of work to do with Senator Madison; he knew she had changed much of what he had done with Maddi's Laws, and he knew she must have suspected something. He would call her. Touch base with her. Let her know he is still there for her. Then, if Roger ever did rat him out,

Maddi could speak in his defense. He knew that after he was done working his charm with her, she would be glad to do so. He was sure of it. He smiled once again at the thought of how clever he was.

CHAPTER XXXIX

Class Action lawsuits rarely are tried in the venue which makes the most sense. In other words, the actual trial is not held in the courtroom where the majority of the plaintiffs reside, or where the action occurred. Typically, what is done, is for the attorneys for the plaintiffs to align themselves with an attorney from a 'favorable' venue to try the case under his auspices. They seek out those court rooms which seem to reward class action lawsuits more generously, and that is the venue they then select.

The same occurred with the lawsuit put forth by the law firm of Wyatt, Hanson, Richards and Shultz. Philadelphia had proven itself to be one of the more favorable venues for this type of suit, and the law firm had aligned itself with one James T. Newkirk, attorney-at-law. He was a small-town lawyer in a suburb of Philly, who was never very busy, but always very eager for any case which came his way. He had been hand-picked by Wyatt, Hanson, Richards and Shultz because of that very fact. He was a nobody, who could get them the venue they needed.

The fact that Philadelphia happened to be where Clarence Morrow did the majority of his work was simply a detail they could overlook. After all, they had many victims of the diabolical drug Diacam and their case was a no-brainer. They had gathered over 300 depositions, from individuals across the country who had suffered some sort of liver problem, or from the families of those who had died. This case would be worth millions—maybe even billions, and the Law firm had devoted much of its resources to the prosecution of this case, knowing that every one of the major attorneys involved would wind up an instant millionaire.

The lead attorney for the case was Richard Shultz, one of the partners. He had been with the firm for nearly 12 years, but had made partner after 7 years at the firm. He was "one of the boys," and he had fit in perfectly with this law firm.

He had spearheaded the class-action lawsuit in the first place, and was now responsible for making sure it stayed on track. There were motions to file, and depositions to obtain, as well as mountains of paperwork to assemble and distribute.

In a law firm the size of theirs, the partners and senior trial attorneys had the assistance of scores of "assistants", who would do anything asked of them, all eyeing the opportunity to perhaps someday make partner.

The Firm had been started nearly 35 years by Richards and Wyatt, both now in their sixties, and both still quite active in the practice of law. Samuel Richards had become a United States senator nearly 5 years ago, and Randy Wyatt continued to spend his days at the Law Firm, mostly in an advisory role.

The Firm originally was known as "The Law offices of Wyatt and Richards," and they started out in a small building on a side street in downtown Phoenix. It didn't take them long to become successful—they were both pit-bull trial attorneys—and they were therefore soon able to recruit some top-notch attorneys from the more prominent law schools in Arizona and the surrounding area.

Their reputation grew as ruthless, successful lawyers, and soon the name of Hanson was added to their marquee. They had outgrown their quarters by then and, because of their success, were able to acquire some prime real estate in downtown Phoenix, near the center square. They pursued their first class action law suit about that time, successfully suing a tobacco company, receiving a huge amount of compensation for their efforts.

Through the years they continued to pursue noteworthy cases, and were successful most of the time. But they all knew, that, as big as tobacco was, this case with Diacam was bigger still. After all, the correlation between the taking of the drug and the deaths and illnesses accompanying the taking of the drug were no longer in dispute. All they would have to do here is direct the jury to a few key facts, parade a few invalids and family members of the deceased, and they would walk out of that court room as millionaires. The fact that many of them already were millionaires did not matter. It was never done for the righting of a wrong, and it was no longer done for the purpose of the income, it was now done for the size of the booty. The amount of the award had become a measure of prestige for trial lawyers across the country, and very few would stop what they were doing simply because they had earned "enough."

Several other firms around the country had "latched on" to this particular lawsuit, but the Firm still had the control and called the shots. Everybody involved was having quite a good time, and the mood was upbeat at the Law Offices of Wyatt, Hanson, Richards and Shultz.

Richards himself had even checked in with his boys. Although he had his hands full in D.C., he managed to keep a foot in the door at the Firm. He, too, would profit financially from this endeavor and he wanted to make sure things were going as they should.

And they were. Richard Shultz was an obsessive-compulsive individual, particularly when he was trying a big case. And this case was his biggest. He made sure he knew all the important players, and he made sure all of his underlings were doing their jobs. Nothing would go wrong with this case. It was his first big case of which he was in charge and he was letting nothing go out of the firm that wasn't first reviewed by him.

He also had read up on Mr. Clarence Morrow. This attorney would be representing the thousands of doctors involved in the case, and Shultz knew that this guy was good. He had gone against many a large firm, and had often come out ahead, well over expectations. Shultz wanted to make sure that didn't happen here. He had reviewed each of Morrow's bigger cases, familiarizing himself with Clarence's style and approach. He wanted to be able to anticipate every move Morrow would make well before he made it. He had no idea how Morrow would try to defend these doctors, when so much of the evidence clearly showed their connection to the injuries and deaths of their patients. He figured that most likely Clarence would try to make the doctors the innocent dupes of the aggressive, greedy drug companies. This could sell, except for the fact that so many of the cases occurred after the word had gone out that there might be a problem with Diacam. The idiot doctor who worked for the Pima Indians, for example. He was foolish enough to even tell the Indians about the drug problems. Yet, he allowed them to continue to take it. As if they were in a position to be able to decide such a thing. He loved it when doctors tried to make their patients accountable for their decisions and choices. It was so fun poking holes in that defense, considering the specialized nature of the choices these doctors were asking their ignorant patients to make. This was going to be a field day, and he could hardly wait.

Shultz was also looking quite forward to the depositions. Deposing doctors was such fun—they were just so arrogant. They always thought they knew so much—about everything—and it was so enjoyable to trip them up and get them falling all over themselves to try to explain their inconsistencies. Particularly in this case. Every time a doctor would try to blame this problem with Diacam on the drug company, Shultz or one of his minion would simply remind them the prescribing of the drug was under their control. They would typically then respond that they had done all the proper monitoring for the medication, but then Shultz would simply ask them why they hadn't known their patient was dying from their actions. This question would always make the docs lose their composure and once they did that, Shultz knew he had them. He then simply allowed them to "go emotional" on him, and he then went in for the kill, asking the docs if they had their mothers or fathers or husbands or wives on diacam. Of course they didn't—it was too risky. Once he got to this point, he knew he had won, and the doctors knew it too. He had done several of these depositions thus far, and they had all gone pretty much the same. He had gotten to the point where he really looked forward to them. Clarence Morrow had not yet been present for any of these depositions, each doctor had typically allowed their cases to continue to be handled by their malpractice insurance carrier's law firm. That made things even easier for Shultz, it was more or less a "divide and conquer" mentality and he was enjoying every minute of it.

As the trial date was approaching, more and more of the depositions needed to be conducted, and Shultz and his Firm were shifting into high gear in order to have everything exactly the way it needed to be in order to succeed at trial. The excitement was building and could be felt throughout the Firm. This case was going to be an amazing amount of fun, and they were all very confident of their success. This attitude was the one they would carry into that Philadelphia court room and they knew—without a doubt—that they would win.

Clarence Morrow had been practicing law for nearly 30 years. He loved what he did—most of the time. He also agreed with the majority of people who felt that lawyers—and the practice of law—were slimy and underhanded, at best. So, he tried his best to be on the "right" side of the matters at hand. That side, however, was not always the winning side, and Clarence had had to learn how to lose, and still win. He had gotten quite comfortable with the concept through the years and he was now very assured of himself with reference to his moral compass.

He was fortunate to be able to pick and choose his cases at this point in his career, and he made sure he picked only those cases which generated some passion within him. He had decided long ago that it was much easier to fight for a cause you truly believed in than to fight for the opportunity to win your point. As a result of this philosophy, and his highly regarded character, Clarence had been involved in some of the more noteworthy cases of the past several years.

He had defended a shop owner who had shot a man while trying to protect himself from that very man, who was attempting to rob his store. The shop owner had been sued by the family of the thief who had been shot, and they were trying to suggest that he had used unnecessary and excessive force in protecting his property. This argument, which had been used successfully many times in the past, made Clarence Morrow's blood boil. It was therefore, quite easy for Clarence to involve himself—body and soul—in the defense of this man who had every right to protect himself from a thief attempting to rob him, with whatever means he could utilize. This passion with which Clarence ran his defense of the shopkeeper ended up in a dismissal of the lawsuit, the news of which quickly spread among business owners across the city of Philadelphia.

Clarence had also had the opportunity to defend another business owner, named John Hayes, against an accusation of slander, put forth by a former employee of Mr. Hayes. The employee had been fired by the owner for stealing large amounts of cash, and the employee had moved to a different town and was attempting to find another job. He had listed his employment with Mr. Hayes, and his new boss-to-be had called Hayes to ask about this employee's work ethic. Mr. Hayes had told the employer-to-be about the theft and the new employer than contacted the ex-employee to inform him that he would not be hiring him, due to Mr. Hayes' comments. The ex-employee proceeded to sue Mr. Hayes for slander, and was actually succeeding in his case, until Clarence was consulted.

Mr. Hayes had heard about Clarence Morrow from a friend, and—after he told Clarence the story—Clarence immediately took control of his defense. Once he became involved he was able to accentuate the act of thievery that had occurred at the hand of the ex-employee, and almost had the employee arrested for the theft. The case was quickly dropped and Clarence Morrow had once again lived up to his reputation.

And now came the Diacam situation. Clarence knew that this case would be a bit more difficult than the prior cases he had defended in the past. The drug had truly done what the plaintiffs were claiming, and the doctors had truly prescribed it, fully aware that it might cause liver damage in a few individuals. But, defend it he would, because he knew deep in his heart that not a single doctor accused of this crime had ever intended to hurt anyone. Not only that,

Clarence was so tired of the Law being used in this way. It had become an opportunity for greedy lawyers to take advantage of others' misfortunes, and Clarence felt that it was time this stopped. He was anxious to have an opportunity to involve himself in that process.

He hadn't yet been to any of the depositions; they had been arranged prior to his taking over the "group defense" of the doctors. He knew that he needed to go; however, to find out what the lawyers from Wyatt, Hanson, Richards and Shultz were planning to do and say, as well as to assist the doctors in their defense. He contacted the Firm to find out their schedule for depositions. He obtained a list of doctors involved, as well as a listing of the lawyers handling the doctors' cases. Clarence knew that many of them would be malpractice attorneys from large firms, whose primary interest was to help the insurance company, not necessarily the doctors themselves. He wanted to circumvent that approach as quickly as possible and begin the process of getting doctors completely out from under the lawsuit's accusations.

The first name he saw on the list of doctors was a Jeremy Bourne, from Arizona. Apparently Dr. Bourne worked on a Pima Indian reservation and several of the Pima Indians had been affected by the drug. Clarence decided to contact Dr. Bourne himself to inquire about the case and about Dr. Bourne's willingness to allow Clarence to assist him in his defense.

He got a hold of Jeremy at the Clinic on the Reservation. While he was waiting for Jeremy to get on the phone, he thought about what he might ask him. He wanted to be sure not to make him uncomfortable—he knew that doctors had a tendency to become paranoid—especially with a strange attorney on the phone.

"Hello, this is Dr. Bourne, can I help you?"

Clarence cleared his throat. "Dr. Bourne, my name is Clarence Morrow and I am an attorney from Philadelphia. I am working on the Diacam lawsuit, and I just happen to be on the side of the doctors in this situation. I wondered if I might have a moment of your time?"

There was a pause on the other end of the phone. Finally, after what seemed like many minutes, Jeremy spoke.

"Okay. I'm listening, but I can't talk long, I'm already behind this morning."

Clarence smiled. "Doctors are always behind," he thought to himself. He spoke up quickly. "I was actually wondering if I might arrange some time to fly out there and speak with you. I've been needing a break from the 'big city' and the Reservation might be just the break I'm looking for."

Jeremy thought about this for a minute, then thought to himself "Why not?" He responded. "I don't have a problem with that. I'm sure we could find a hotel not too far from the Reservation. Who did you say you were again?"

Clarence knew that Dr. Bourne would try to find out some information on him before he arrived. He proceeded to tell him his name again, as well as several different numbers by which he could be reached. He added that he really did want to stay right on the Reservation, if that could be arranged. They hung up having arranged to meet the following Wednesday afternoon—Jeremy would pick up Clarence at the airport in Phoenix and they would come back to the Reservation and Jeremy would arrange some lodging for Clarence Morrow.

Clarence Morrow arrived at the Phoenix Sky Harbor Airport the following Wednesday at 12:35 in the afternoon. Jeremy Bourne was waiting for him as promised, and he had a very attractive young girl with him. Jeremy introduced both Katy and himself to Mr. Morrow and he graciously smiled and nodded to both of them.

Jeremy took note of Clarence's appearance immediately. He was a very tall man, with large hands and a wide face. He had jet black hair, thinning just a bit toward the back. He was clean-shaven, but for a thin mustache resting over his upper lip, and when he smiled he revealed a set of beautiful white teeth. He grabbed Jeremy's hand with firmness and a confidence that instantly made Jeremy feel somewhat more at ease.

Katy gave Clarence a big smile, and her dark eyes seemed to pierce his very soul as she shook Clarence's big hand. The two seemed to like one another immediately and Katy motioned Clarence toward the exit and the car waiting outside.

"We can't take too long. We've parked in one of those 'do not park' zones and I'd hate it if our car got towed away." This made Clarence laugh out loud, and soon the three of them were hurrying toward the exit.

Once inside Katy's small Toyota, the three of them were able to talk and get acquainted with one another a bit. The drive to the Reservation was about an hour and this gave them all time to talk just a bit.

Jeremy had done his homework, as Clarence guessed he would, and Jeremy knew that Clarence was the one who helped Senator Madison with "Maddi's Laws." Jeremy had found the forum to Take Back America incredibly rewarding, and it had given him enough hope to return to work on the Reservation and try to put the lawsuit behind him. He immediately felt better about Clarence Morrow once he realized he truly was on "their side," and so he was now quite receptive to his visit to the Reservation.

Clarence Morrow had also done some homework on Jeremy Bourne. He had familiarized himself with his history, including his stint in the Peace Corps. He now asked Jeremy about his time in the Corps.

"So, where were you during your time in the Corps?"

The question caught Jeremy a bit off guard—he hadn't imagined that Mr. Morrow would look into his past at all.

"Well, I went to South Africa, and I loved every minute of it." Jeremy paused a moment, obviously reflecting back on a very good time in his life. He continued. "There are times when I wish I were still back there, doing good work for people who appreciate it."

Clarence looked at him intently, and then asked "Why did you leave?"

Jeremy thought for a moment, and then replied. "I wanted to make things better for people here in my own country. I wanted to make a difference here."

"And, have you?"

The question surprised Jeremy. He hadn't really even asked himself that question, let alone some stranger asking him. He thought for a few moments. He thought about the Pima Indians, and their diabetes, and the softball team, and all the lives that had been touched since he arrived.

"Yeah, I think I have. The only thing, the appreciation is different here. Don't misunderstand—people are appreciative. And, I really didn't do it for that reason. But, I'm amazed at how many people there are ready to try to destroy any good efforts you make simply to gain prestige or money. That is something we have here that I did not have to deal with in South Africa. It has made it rather tough."

Clarence nodded in understanding. "No good deed goes unpunished, eh?"

Jeremy smiled. "Yeah, something like that I guess."

The three of them continued talking about problems on the Reservation and problems with 'the system' in America, and soon they were approaching the Reservation. They drove in and headed for the clinic immediately. Jeremy had put together all his records concerning Diacam and he was prepared to show them to Mr. Morrow. He had also copied them all—again—and offered them to Mr. Morrow to take with him if he should be inclined.

Mr. Morrow looked around him at 'The Clinic.' He was amazed at how small and bare it appeared. From what he could tell the entire clinic consisted of five rooms. There was a 'front desk' with an accompanying sitting area with just enough room for three people to sit comfortably. There were two treatment rooms, one room filled with medication samples, and another room where apparently everything else was stored, including a small refrigerator and a small square table. Mr. Morrow did not see an office for Dr. Bourne, but he noticed a chair at the small table with some paperwork scattered around and assumed that this must serve as Dr. Bourne's 'office.' Charts lined the walls of all the rooms, probably violating HIPPA (Health Insurance Privacy and Portability Act) laws in several different ways. The clinic appeared to be closed this afternoon. Clarence asked Jeremy if that was the case.

"Yeah, I went ahead and closed this afternoon, since you were coming to town. Doc Jones doesn't really work much any more and it is just easier to close it when I need to do something outside the office."

Clarence nodded, and—with prodding from Jeremy—took one of the small seats in the waiting area. Jeremy handed him a few exemplary charts and he began to go through each one of them rather briefly. Periodically his expression would change and his brow would crease. Jeremy and Katy watched closely, hoping to glean some hope from his interpretation of events involved in the case.

Finally Clarence looked up from the last file and smiled directly at Jeremy. "I think you're gonna' do fine, son."

Jeremy was ecstatic. His current malpractice attorney had told him nothing at all like that, suggesting instead that they would probably have to settle. The thought that maybe there was a way out without 'settling' made Jeremy feel better than he had felt in months. He couldn't believe it. He said as much to Mr. Morrow.

"How can you say that? Some of those people are dead because of that drug, and others of them are terminally ill. I prescribed the drug, knowing it may cause problems."

Clarence Morrow sat back, with a big grin crossing his face. "Yes, but didn't you also tell them to stop drinking alcohol? And didn't you follow them closely with routine liver function testing? Just like the prescribing information required you to?

Jeremy frowned. "Well, yes, but many of those people were never going to quit drinking, and—even though I did the requisite testing—their livers failed anyway."

"Yes, but, you have written it right here, and here, and here," Mr. Morrow was pointing to various entries in a patient's chart, "and even here you mentioned that you gave them a stern warning to either stop drinking or stop the drug. Tell me something, Jeremy, would the consumption of alcohol with the taking of Diacam make its risk much greater?"

Jeremy knew that it would. He nodded.

"Well, did these people tell you they had stopped drinking?"

Jeremy thought for a moment. "The way I handled it was like this—if they refused to stop drinking, I withdrew the drug from them. So, I would ask them at each visit if they were drinking. The ones who continued on the drug had clearly told me they weren't drinking and thus I continued giving it."

Clarence stood up slowly and walked around the small outer office area. He was clearly deep in thought. Finally, he spoke.

"Jeremy, I wonder. Do you think anybody died or is ill in this group of patients that wasn't a drinker?"

Jeremy sat back and thought about this for several minutes. He went through each 'bad outcome' in his mind, trying to think if they were drinkers. Each time he was about to come up with a patient who he thought had not been drinking he would review the chart and see it documented that the patient had been a drinker prior to starting the medication. He would then see a notation where the patient had told him he or she had stopped drinking once they were on the medication. He began to grasp what Mr. Morrow was getting at. Perhaps a case could be made that these people acted irresponsibly on their own, and he had been duped by their deception. They had then suffered the consequences, not because Jeremy was negligent, but because they were negligent themselves. Personal responsibility! What a concept!

Jeremy started smiling at Clarence, who smiled back knowingly. Katy looked on, not quite sure what was making the two men smile, but she smiled nonetheless, simply because she knew something good was happening—finally.

The three of them continued talking for several minutes more there at the clinic, then Jeremy offered to treat them all to a magnificent dinner at the local eating establishment, which also served as the local bar. They walked out the door and Clarence began walking toward the car. Jeremy and Katy started grinning to one another. Jeremy called out.

"Hey! Where ya' goin'? The Coyote Tavern is about 2 blocks from here. It's easier to walk."

Clarence grinned back at them and caught up to them as they all three walked to the Coyote Tavern. Once there they ordered beer and nachos and sat there for the next several hours enjoying one another's company and not mentioning the case at all.

Clarence couldn't remember when he had had a better time. Except for the night he took Maddi and her friends to dinner. This night was much like that night. Clarence thought quickly to himself that he so much more enjoyed the company of people like this than he did that of the other attorneys he was often forced to spend his time with. Sometimes he hated his profession. But, he also knew that he was one of the 'good guys.' He smiled at the thought and then got back to the business of having a delightful evening.

Jeremy had arranged lodging off the Reservation, because there really was nowhere to stay on the Reservation. But as the night grew longer, and the hour later, it soon became evident that Clarence Morrow would simply stay with Jeremy at Doc Jones' place, and sleep on a well-worn sofa in the living room. As they prepared to go to sleep, Clarence thought once again about how delightful this evening had been. He smiled as he quickly drifted off to sleep; glad to think he could help people like Jeremy Bourne.

CHAPTER XL

Wilson Jackson III had returned to Boston a changed man. He had made some important decisions while at the Forum, and he was ready to make some monumental changes in the way he practiced medicine.

He walked into his office the morning after he returned home ready to take on the world. He was expecting some resistance from his staff and his colleagues, but he had no idea how much there would be. He looked around at the staff as he entered their suite, and suddenly no one would meet his glance. He headed back to the office he shared with one of the other physicians in the group and sat down ready to review what had gone on in his absence. His partner was not there, and Wilson began going through reports and mail that had been sorted for him during his absence.

There was continued correspondence regarding his lawsuit—nothing new—he was a pro at this by now. There were routine letters from other specialists, and many labs to review.

Wilson approached his work diligently, finally finishing in time to see his first patient. He had decided to keep his current arrangement until the end of the year, and then would simply not renew his malpractice premium, his hospital staff privileges, or his rent agreement with his other partners. He would write them all a letter offering his resignation from the group, thinking that just maybe they would want to join him in his effort. He doubted this very much, but knew what an impact it would have on much of the area if his entire group quit delivering babies in the hospital and quit all of their high-risk procedures. He wanted that impact to be felt across New England and knew that his gesture alone would not make nearly the impact.

He had drafted his letter the night before and hoped his partners would receive it in the way it was intended. He brought them each a copy this morning and left it for them to read when they next came into the office. Wilson had never "gone solo" before, but he knew he could do it if he had to. He would have to wait to see how everyone reacted to his proposed changes, but, from the way the staff was behaving, it sure didn't seem like it was going over well.

Wilson continued to do his regular schedule and his routine surgeries and deliveries, anxiously waiting to hear what his partners wanted him to do. Several days went by, and finally, when Wilson couldn't stand it anymore, he contacted one of his partners to inquire about his status.

The partner informed him that they were having a meeting the following morning at 6:30am, and if he could be there they would let him know then what it was they wanted to do.

Wilson had already begun to take steps to reduce any significant wealth accumulation. He had a beautiful home in the suburbs of Boston, and a perfect BMW to drive to and from work each day. He had all the appropriate savings vehicles and was actually quite a wealthy man. It saddened him to think that all this would have to go, but he knew that if he was going to "go bare," and he absolutely was, then his only true protection from liability would be to have nothing for the lawyers to take. He would dissolve all of his wealth, find a comfortable place nearer to downtown to work, and get a reasonable car—maybe a VW, and try to put some funds away in a retirement fund that no-one could touch—not even him—for many years to come.

This process was quite difficult at first, but Wilson was amazed at how easy it became once he got started. His family was appalled, but tried to understand and did their best to support his efforts. Quickly, as each expensive item was sold or given away, Wilson could feel a burden being lifted from his shoulders. He began to realize how great it felt to eliminate the trappings of life. He thought to himself, "this is what it is to have nothing to lose," and he was fulfilled like he hadn't been in years.

When all his property had been reduced to cash value he was left with a sizeable amount of money. He decided to make a large donation to an inner city Clinic, and then took the remainder and locked it away in an IRA which he was reassured would not be available to a greedy lawyer who might come looking. He hoped that was the case, for it would be all that he would have when he was done with this profession. From here on out he would charge for his services the minimum that he could charge and still run his office, and accept what his patients could pay. He would try to work with the less fortunate, who were willing to accept him without a hospital or the fancy offices that some patients would expect. This was a very big experiment, but Wilson was ready to try it—he knew he couldn't continue practicing medicine like he had been. This would either work for him, or he was finished completely.

Wilson was up well before the 6:30 meeting, doing some hospital rounds, and finishing up some paper work in the office. He had had trouble sleeping and, although it isn't unusual for him to round about 5:00am, this 4:00am rounding took the staff by surprise.

Several of the hospital personnel were aware of Wilson's plan to "go bare," and most knew that the hospital would not allow an uninsured physician on staff. So, they knew that Dr. Jackson—and his 5:00am rounding—would soon be a thing of the past. This seemed to make them take a little more time to help him that morning, in any way they could. They all liked Dr. Jackson very much, and they all had an incredible amount of respect for him as a doctor and as a person. They would miss him greatly.

As the 6:30am meeting time drew near, Wilson made his way back to the office for the meeting that would determine his fate. He had already accepted that his partners could not join him in "going bare," and also could not assume any associated risk they might have if a case against him were to go badly, so he pretty much knew he was about to go it alone. This thought made him frightened—and excited. To open a small office all by himself would be scary, but the thought of creating the kind of practice he wanted, without the worries of million-dollar lawsuits, brought a smile to his face. He would miss much of the world he was leaving behind, but he would welcome the opportunity to define his future. He was ready for the meeting.

He walked through the door of the conference room at exactly 6:30, and—not surprisingly—saw all of his colleagues already there. Every one of them was an early riser, and he knew they had all been discussing things prior to his arrival. He sat down at his traditional seat.

One of his partners, Dr. Steven Stewart, opened the meeting.

"Welcome Wilson. As you might imagine, we have all been sitting here discussing your situation. We were all watching the Forum to Take Back America, anxiously awaiting your comments. Needless to say, we were shocked by your announcement, and began pretty quickly to prepare ourselves for what we may need to do in order to handle such a thing."

Steven paused, and cleared his throat. Wilson thought that Steven looked a bit uncomfortable. No surprise there. Steven continued.

"We have spent many pain-staking hours reviewing our contracts here in the office and at the hospital. Your decision to 'go bare' is in direct violation of both contracts. I have spoken with the hospital administrators and they, like us, have received the appropriate paper work from you explaining your decision and removing you from your obligations after 90 days."

Steven paused again, and Wilson found himself actually feeling sorry for him. He began to speak again, but this time a bit softer and slower.

"Even though we agree with your position on this current situation we all find ourselves in, we cannot allow ourselves to sacrifice all that we have achieved for the sake of this decision and this principle to which you have aligned yourself. We have therefore, regrettably, elected—as a unanimous group—to let you go."

At this comment Steven looked around the room for support, but the other five doctors were bowing their heads. Wilson understood what was about to happen, and he was thankful he had prepared himself. Steven concluded his speech.

"We will certainly allow you to stay as long as your coverage is in place. Once your policy has lapsed however, you must be gone from this practice. The hospital holds the same position and I'm sure will be in touch with you soon. I know I speak for everyone when I tell you that we all admire you so very much and will miss your affiliation with this group. We wish you only the best. Please keep us posted on your success."

Wilson looked around the room. All of the doctors' heads were still bowed, and he smiled to himself. He thanked them all and wished them continued success, and he reassured them that he would indeed keep them posted on his success. He stood, grabbed his briefcase and walked out of the conference room, out of the office, and into the beautiful early fall air of Boston, feeling invigorated and utterly excited about the future. He realized he was still smiling and he continued walking with quite a bounce in his step. He would practice medicine his way, and to Hell with the lawyers and their bullshit. Wilson felt free and joyful for the first time in years.

Maddi had come home to a whirlwind of activity in the Senate and around the nation. Her Forum, and all that had gone on during her forum, had created quite a stir. She knew that now was the time to act. This was the one time where she would have the attention of the entire nation and if she missed this chance there would not likely be another. She couldn't stand to think about the consequences if these efforts failed, so she hit the floor running and got to work trying to pass Maddi's Laws.

Her biggest opposition within the Senate was Senator Sam Richards from Arizona. Maddi made sure, however, whenever he spoke against her laws, that everyone knew that he was the 'Richards' in Wyatt, Hanson, Richards and Shultz. This pretty much shut his effectiveness down, as everyone saw his motives for what they were.

Maddi had succeeded in having her Laws voted on in conference, and then having them reach the full Senate for a vote. The vote was scheduled to take place in early September, and Maddi was aggressively courting Senators to guarantee a 'yes' vote for her laws.

She had also written legislation proposing Hank's idea of creating an entirely different venue to evaluate medical malpractice. She knew that this idea was going to be much more difficult to acquire acceptance and approval for, but she was prepared to spend whatever time and effort were required to get this idea turned into practice. She knew that if medical malpractice could be removed from the court system, and instead be pursued through a specified body dedicated to nothing but the arbitration of malpractice, all would benefit. Physicians should not have to fear the court system on a daily basis. She would do all she could to change the system to accommodate this idea.

She talked with Hank several times a day, and they tried to get together on weekends. Both of them were quite busy with their lives and their obligations and therefore did not see each other as much as they would have liked. Their relationship managed to grow in spite of this and it sustained each one of them through their sometimes oppressive days.

Hank's trial was scheduled for October, and Maddi did her best to clear her schedule to be available for him. She knew this would be a horrible ordeal, and she needed to help him through it.

She would periodically hear from Kevin Clayborne, but she had chosen to not reply to his phone messages. She wasn't sure what his game plan was, but she knew he wanted something from her, and she also knew she needed nothing from him.

She kept up as well as she could with the investigation into the attempt on her life and the murder of John McCargish. The authorities kept her informed, which she greatly appreciated. They had the shooter, and they had the guys behind the whole thing. They still had no idea who had tried to kill Peter Smith, and this would occasionally haunt Maddi, when she was alone with time to think about it, which thankfully wasn't very often. The FBI had elected to keep the attempt on Peter Smith's life out of the papers, but Maddi knew it had happened.

There was still a secret service detail following her—because they felt that the controversial nature of her proposed laws, combined with the prior attempt on her life, made her a potential target. It had been mentioned recently however, that they may not feel it necessary to continue, as the attempt on Maddi's life had been thwarted. Maddi was comfortable with that decision—for the most part. She knew she would feel much better, however, when they had captured the individual who had tried to kill Peter Smith.

The ATLA, meanwhile, had had quite a shakeup, as well as a whole lot of bad press. This thrilled Maddi and she tried to take advantage of that as much as she could. She would promote her legislative initiatives during the same news cycle when analysis of the ATLA's tactics, and its attempt on her life, were in the media spotlight.

She and Andrew would often talk about how amazed they were that little Frances Buckholtz had been behind the whole thing. They had known he was creepy, but they had never really realized just how low he had sunk. Although, Andrew wasn't nearly as surprised as Maddi.

Maddi thought occasionally about how Buckholtz had twisted the truth about the drowning in the lake so long ago. Surprisingly, the story never got much traction, once Andrew gave his response while at the forum. It seemed that—once Buckholtz was arrested for what he had done, the story lost all credibility.

But Maddi knew it had affected Andrew greatly. When they had finally found some time to discuss it, Maddi could see the hurt and pain in Andrew's eyes, and she knew that—sooner or later—he would have to deal with it all.

Andrew and Amanda had been keeping in touch, and this thrilled Maddi to no end. She loved both of these people dearly and she couldn't think of a better match. Andrew had returned to the Tundra, and Amanda had returned to her beloved Clinic in Columbia. They both felt at home where they were, and Maddi knew that it would be difficult for either one to leave. That would be something between the two of them, however, and Maddi was just happy to see each of them involving themselves with the other.

Clarence Morrow had called Maddi once or twice to update her on the Dia-cam case. He anticipated a November trial date, and reassured her that she, Hank, Amanda, Andrew, and Wilson would be informed of the specific date. He hoped they all might come to town to watch the trial and support him as he attempted to shut down the massive legal machine so eagerly devouring the profession they all loved. He knew they were all quite busy, but reassured them that they would all stay with him in his 'oversized house,' as he put it and that he would take care of any needs they might have. Maddi found herself looking forward to the event as though it were a concert or a play, rather than a ridiculous class action lawsuit. She and Hank would have to get him through his trial first and she hoped that would end favorably. Juries could be very unpredictable and Maddi knew that, even if Hank had done nothing wrong, a jury may sympathize with a 'bereaved' family and find in their favor. It was anybody's guess—which was just one more reason why the current system was so distasteful. Maddi would do anything she could to change it.

She kept herself quite busy in her efforts, and was actually beginning to think that things might truly be changing for the better. Across the country people had felt the impact of the exit of physicians from their practices, as access to care was becoming continually more difficult. The media continued to keep this in the spotlight and they would conjointly mention some legislation that Maddi was trying to get through. This would prompt a flurry of calls to various Senators with constituents who had been effected by the situation and slowly but surely these Senators were coming on board with the notion of meaningful reform. Maddi's efforts—and all the sacrifices—were finally paying off.

CHAPTER XLI

Kevin Clayborne was having trouble sleeping. He knew they were after him, and it pissed him off. Especially that asshole senator. She refused to take his calls, or call him back, and he had had all he could take of that arrogant bitch.

He found it difficult to eat, and had lost considerable weight since the afternoon he had tried to kill Peter Smith. Why the hell had he done it anyway? Just for those pricks Buckholtz and Rogers. He knew it was only a matter of time before they would give him up—if they hadn't already. He had to somehow get out of this mess. First, he had to get some sleep. It seemed like months since he had truly slept.

Kevin got in his car and headed to the nearest pharmacy. He grabbed some Tylenol PM and some Nyquil and headed up to the front to pay. On the way he saw a newspaper sitting in a rack with a headline about "Maddi's Laws" being voted on the following week. That fucking bitch. He had written those laws—mostly. And she was getting all the credit. It pissed him off.

Once he had paid for his items he headed to the liquor store and bought himself a fifth of whiskey. He then went back to his room and prepared to 'get some sleep.' He started with two quick shots of the whiskey. He then decided to call Senator Madison again, to give her one last chance to acknowledge him. He dialed the number. While he was waiting, he poured himself two more shots and drank them both down. He was feeling brave. The message clicked on and he began.

"Hey Bitch. It's Kevin. You know, the guy who wrote your fuckin' Laws for you. I just thought I'd let you know that I am alive and well. They're all looking for the guy who pulled the plug on that murderer—seems to me they should be givin' him an award or something. But no, they want to hang the poor guy. Anyway, you can call me back—or not. I don't really give a shit."

He then poured out two more shots. He grabbed the Tylenol pm, and quickly threw eight of the pills into the back of his throat and 'chased' them with the whiskey. He took several swigs from the Nyquil bottle and then poured two more shots from the whiskey. He was just so tired. He took a handful more of the Tylenol and once again chased them down with the whiskey. He started to feel shaky. "Maybe now I'll get some fuckin' sleep." He fell to the floor and quickly passed out, the whiskey in one hand and the bottle of Tylenol in the other.

Maddi came home late and had her hands full with her briefcase and a bag of groceries. She pushed through the door and immediately set the groceries on her table, and the briefcase on the floor. She walked over to the answering machine and began to play back the messages. She was glancing at her mail while listening. Suddenly she dropped her mail and looked directly at her machine. She heard a very drunk and upset Kevin Clayborne on the message. What disturbed her the most however were his comments about the attempt on Peter Smith's life. The press had not shared that with the public. How did Kevin know? Then Maddi panicked as it fell into place.

She immediately contacted the Investigator from the FBI who had kept her informed. She was nearly panicked as she got him on the line.

"Rick. It's Cynthia Madison. You won't believe the message that I just got on my machine." Maddi proceeded to tell him all that Kevin had said.

"Don't worry, Senator. If you can tell me about what time the call was made, I'll contact the phone company to determine from where the call originated."

Maddi listened to the message again and noted the time, according to her answering machine. "8:47 pm!" she yelled into the phone. She then heard Rick relaying this information to someone nearby. After several minutes Rick got back on the line.

"We've got 'im!" he shouted."Don't worry Senator; two agents are heading to his location as we speak."

Maddi thanked the man and then sat down to wait to hear from the lead investigator.

It was about an hour before Maddi's phone rang. It was the investigator.

"Senator. Listen, I just got word from my two agents who were dispatched to Kevin Clayborne's location. He's dead, ma'am."

There was silence as the investigator allowed this to sink in. Finally Maddi spoke.

"How did he die?"

"Well, it appears he had himself quite a party with some whiskey and some Tylenol pm. The two don't mix well at all and—according to my agents—Mr. Claybourne looked as though he hadn't eaten for days, and I'm guessing the combination was too much."

Maddi couldn't believe what she was hearing. Another person dead. She was visibly shaking so she grabbed the arm of her chair with her one hand and held the phone tighter with the other.

"Is he the one? You know, the one who tried to kill Smith?" Maddi was praying that he was, knowing that then she could put an end to the entire affair.

"We can't be sure. We're going to clean him up a bit, and then take a picture of him to Mr. Smith. I'll be sure to call you and let you know."

"Yes, please do. Oh, and thank you so much … for everything."

"No problem ma'am, just doin' my job."

Maddi breathed an sigh of relief. She prayed it was in fact him. That would end the whole thing. What started with Buckholtz, would end with Clayborne, or so she hoped.

CHAPTER XLII

September 4th—the day of the vote on Maddi's Laws—finally arrived. There had been quite a lot of attention paid to the process involved in the vote, as well as the vote itself. Maddi found herself up earlier than usual that morning, ready to take on anyone who would try to stop the passage of her signature legislation.

To date, Maddi's calculations had determined that there were in fact enough votes to pass her legislation in the Senate. It had already passed through the House without too much difficulty, but Maddi had been concerned that Senator Richards might try to sway some of his comrades in an effort to sink the legislation. From what her sources had told her, he had not made any effort in that direction. Maddi found that puzzling, but she was thankful that there didn't appear to be looming a huge senate floor fight over her laws.

Media from around the country were camped outside the Capitol building, as "Legal Analysts" on every major news station were reviewing and dissecting Maddi's Laws. They were all speaking pretty much as one in reference to the significance of the vote. It would be a huge blow to the Trial Lawyers if Senator Madison successfully passed her legislation.

Maddi was sitting in her office preparing to enter the Senate chambers. She had her TV tuned in to one of the 24-hour news stations, and a comentator was talking excitedly about the upcoming vote.

"News Organizations across the country are here outside the Capitol building, anxiously awaiting the results of the vote on Senator Cynthia Madison's "Maddi's Laws." These laws are the final result of years of research and planning by the Senator and her staff. They were presented publicly at the Forum to Take Back America, where, as many of you know, a friend of the Senator's was shot and killed in an apparent attempt on the Senator's life. The shooter was apprehended at the scene and is currently awaiting trial."

Maddi shuddered at the memory of all that had taken place at the Forum. Although much was gained, so very much had been lost. It made her sad to remember. Her thoughts were interrupted by the News Anchor once more.

"There is much talk concerning the huge impact this vote might have on the trial lawyer industry. Many of us are wondering how on earth all the lawyers that sit in the senate would ever be compelled to pass legislation that directly affects such a major voting bloc. Many feel that public opinion is so strong in favor of reform that the lawyers won't have any other choice but to vote in favor of the legislation.

The vote is to take place very soon and we will inform you—our listeners—immediately when we have word on the outcome."

Maddi looked in her mirror one last time before heading for the chamber to cast her vote on the historic laws that she had written with pain-staking detail. She hoped that what the newscaster had said was true. She felt that public opinion was on her side, but she was still very uncertain how Richards and his fellow attorneys might vote. She was, nonetheless filled with hopeful optimism, as she proceeded down the hallway and into the noisy chamber hall.

Most of the senators were present for this vote, and there was quite a lot of noise in the hall, compared to the often quiet chamber. There was a huge amount of attention being paid to this vote, and each and every senator knew they were being watched by all those who mattered.

Maddi saw Senator Richards across the room toward the back of the hall and she gave him a slight nod. He smiled showing a mouthful of coffee-and-tobacco-stained teeth and he too nodded. This unnerved Maddi a bit. Why was he so congenial? Why had he allowed this vote to proceed with so little opposition? Maddi allowed herself to think that just maybe he saw the value of the Laws for the common good, but in the back of her mind she knew better. Something was up and her stomach began to tie itself in knots as Maddi prepared for the worst.

She didn't have long to wait. The Senate Leader gaveled the group to silence and proceeded to begin the session of Congress. Some niceties and traditions were acted upon, and several minutes later it was time for discussion concerning the legislation put forth by Senator Madison from Indiana to begin.

The Senate Leader nodded to Maddi, and she stood and began to summarize the legislation and its ultimate purpose. She quickly reviewed the laws and their intended goals and then sat down.

The Senate Leader was about to call upon the senator from Illinois, when suddenly Senator Richards stood up and requested some time to speak. He was granted this time, and he then began to read from a tome by Thomas Jefferson. Maddi looked around the room, perplexed. She looked at several faces, and finally, when she looked over at the fellow senator from Arizona she realized what was happening. The other senator from Arizona was grinning from ear to ear, as were several of the senators seated nearby. Richards was initiating a filibuster!

Maddi was so angry. She looked around for some support and was pleased to see that several of the other senators were angry as well. She now knew why Richards had been so complacent. He was going to make sure that Maddi's Laws would never even be voted on. She knew he was counting on everything being so confusing that the Laws would never even make it to a vote.

"Fine," she thought. "Two can play at this game." She immediately stood up and walked off the senate floor to the hallway where the press was anxiously awaiting the outcome.

"Senator Madison! Senator Madison!" Several commentators were hollering at once for Maddi. She walked over to a gentleman from CNN.

"I can't really talk now, I'm sorry." She knew that he would be all the more eager if she pretended to walk away.

"Senator, please, just a moment of your time. Why hasn't there been a vote in there?"

Maddi looked directly into the camera perched on an overweight, poorly-dressed guy standing off to the side and she spoke.

"It would appear that the Senator from Arizona has proceeded to embark on a good old-fashioned filibuster." Maddi paused to see if the commentator jumped on this. He did not. She continued.

"I'm not sure if many of your viewers are aware, but Senator Richards is actually part of the Law Firm of Wyatt, Hanson, Richards and Shultz. He has a vested interest in the legal system continuing as it has for the last 30 years, and he is obviously not shy in staking his position." Maddi looked at the commentator who was clearly taking all of this in. He spoke.

"But Senator, surely you don't think he is going to filibuster this vote simply because of his affiliation with his old law firm?"

This was the question Maddi had been waiting for.

"Perhaps you don't realize this, but that Law Firm is the same law firm currently pursuing a class-action law suit against over 3000 physicians involving the medication Diacam, which was recently taken off the market. It would appear that Senator Richards does not want anything—including this legislation—to muddy the waters as they attempt to extort millions of dollars from medical malpractice insurance companies."

The commentator's eyes widened. "You are suggesting his filibuster is somehow related to an ongoing trial?"

Maddi paused. "All I am saying is that there is no reason on earth that the legislation which I have put forth should not be voted on here in this senate chamber today. An up or down vote is all I am asking. I think the senator from Arizona is quite aware that the votes would go in my favor, and he couldn't risk a reform to his beloved tort system. He has too much to gain from the system staying as it is."

Maddi excused herself, allowing her comments to sink in, and she quickly slid into her office and tried to call Hank. She got his cell-phone and left a quick message letting him know what was happening. She glanced over at her TV set just in time to see her interview with the CNN newsman on the air. She smiled to herself. "We'll see how successful you are, Mr. Richards."

Senator Richards continued his filibuster for the next 23 hours. Finally, when all the other senators had left the room he stopped, aware that he had in fact succeeded. He grinned to himself, thinking how easy that had been. He was exhausted, but very gratified, nonetheless. He reached down and grabbed his briefcase slowly, and then headed for the chamber door, anxious for a cup of coffee and a cigarette.

When he walked into the hallway he was immediately bombarded by the press. The same newsman from CNN had returned and immediately shoved his microphone into Senator Richards' face.

"Tell me Senator, is it true what Senator Madison is saying about you?"

Richards eyed the man carefully. He paused for a moment trying to think what Madison might have said.

"And what might that be, sir?" he finally asked.

"She says that you're only concerned with profit and that your filibuster is simply an effort to line your own pockets, as well as those of your partners in the Law Firm of Wyatt, Hanson, Richards, and Shultz?"

The newsman had emphasized Richards when he stated the name of the Law Firm, and the Senator from Arizona began to glare down at the newsman. He responded after nearly a minute.

"Let me tell you something about Senator Madison from Indiana."

The media surrounding Richards all leaned in just a little closer. This is exactly what they were hoping for—some good old-fashioned mudslinging. Senator Richards continued.

"Cynthia Madison used to be a doctor herself. Now, I don't know for sure what happened but I have it on good authority that she didn't quit medicine simply because of some new-found love for public service here in the Capitol. I'll leave it to you, sir to figure out just what made Cynthia Madison leave medicine." Richards was grinning now. "And, while you're at it, you might want to look into activities by that brother of hers, Andrew Madison. My sources have told me—though I have resisted spreading this information around—that Andrew Madison was somehow directly involved in the drowning of a 17-year-old boy back in Evansville, Indiana back in the 70's. I don't know the details—I pride myself in not digging up such dirt on folks—but you might want to find out what that is all about before you allow the Senator from Indiana to besmirch my good name."

The media went wild. This suggestion about Maddi was better than anything they had had in a long while. Several of the newscasters standing around started shouting to their cameramen to contact their sources to look into the pasts of Senator Madison and her brother. They were running every direction, trying to be the first to get the coveted dirt on the two of them. Richards silently slid away, no one interested in him any longer. He was fully satisfied with his efforts. God, he loved this town.

Maddi was tuned in to the 24-hour news pretty much non-stop since the filibuster had begun. She would sleep off and on, waiting to hear when Richards would finally give it up. She knew he had been successful in thwarting her legislation, she only hoped she too had been successful in exposing his motives.

She was getting ready to step into the shower when she heard the media start bustling toward the Senate chamber door. She then listened to the entire interview with Senator Richards.

Her hands began to shake as she listened. She couldn't believe her ears. All her time in Washington, nothing like this had ever happened to her. She felt so angry and so abused. She began shouting to no one in the room.

"Who the hell does that guy think he is? I'll show him that he can't just spout lies and walk away unscathed. That creep is in for it." But she had no idea how she would respond. She sat on the edge of the bed and tried to think what she needed to do next. Senator Richards was spreading lies—not only about her, but about Andrew. Obviously the revelations about that event at the lake—mentioned in a local Indianapolis paper—had not gained recognition in the nation's capitol. Andrew would have to go through it all again. That was even worse. She knew the drowning had haunted him for years, even though his role was innocent. She had to talk to him immediately.

Reaching a back-packing guide in the middle of the Canadian Tundra was not going to be easy. Maddi wasn't even sure how to get a hold of him. Although Andrew had a cell phone, he never took it with him when he led the trips into the Tundra. ("That's the point of being in the Remote Tundra, Maddi, I don't want to be found").

Amanda! Maddi knew Amanda would know how to reach him.

She quickly picked up the phone and began dialing.

"C'mon, c'mon, Amanda, pick up." she said to herself. After several rings an answering machine came on. After the message Maddi started screaming into the receiver.

"Amanda! Pick up, Amanda! It's me, Maddi." Just when Maddi was ready to hang up, she heard a click.

"Maddi? Is that you? What on earth is the matter?"

Maddi began to tell Amanda about the Richards interview, and she explained how she needed to prepare Andrew for what was coming. Amanda gave Maddi the number of the Canadian outpost where Andrew spent his time inbetween excursions. Maddi quickly thanked her and began dialing the number.

The call was answered almost immediately and Maddi introduced herself as Senator Madison from the United States of America, and was quickly patched through to someone in some remote location. After a brief and confusing conversation with them, Andrew was finally put on the line.

"Maddi, what's up?"

"Andrew, do you remember me talking about Senator Richards—you know—of Wyatt, Hanson, Richards and Shultz?"

Andrew remembered quite well, knowing that Maddi was probably going to have trouble getting her legislation past that man.

"Yeah, I remember."

Maddi then proceeded to tell Andrew all that had happened. When she was done, she waited for a reply. After several seconds, Andrew spoke with a calm and quiet voice.

"Maddi, I have made my peace with that whole thing. When Buckholtz got arrested for his involvement in the attempt on your life, I did a lot of soul-searching about the entire thing. It had had a hold on my life for the last 30 years. I know exactly what happened and why, and I know that—even though I wasn't at my best through that whole thing—I certainly had nothing to do with that boy's dying. I actually intend on going to see the Duggan's next time I get back to the States."

Maddi was pleased to hear this, but she knew that Richards and his cronies would nonetheless try to make this something it wasn't.

"Andrew, you might want to make that visit soon. I think Richards is just mad enough, and just creepy enough to turn this into a scandal beyond what it truly was."

"Maddi, I just may do that, but I want you to remember one thing that our uncle Mark used to tell us. Do you remember when you were practicing medicine and a patient started spreading a rumor that you were involved in a narcotics ring?"

Maddi nodded. She remembered it well. She was so angry, and there was absolutely no way to fight back. Andrew continued.

"Remember how you called me and we both wanted to put something in the paper, or have the local authorities arrest the liars? Remember what uncle Mark said to both of us?"

Maddi was trying to remember. "I can't think of it, Andrew."

"Well, what he said was 'You can't fight their lies with words—only with actions. If you try to claim they are lying you have simply created a He-said, She-said battle. But, if you simply sit back and live life well, with decency and honor—like the two of you do, the rumor will die. There will be nothing to give it life, and it will die.'

Maddi now remembered. She remembered how true those words turned out to be, and how she admired her uncle so much for having said them. "I remember."

"Good. Because he was right. And, the same words apply now. Richards has such an apparent agenda, it won't take long for that to become clear to everyone. In the meantime, all we can do is sit back and live life well, with decency and honor—like the two of us do."

Maddi smiled. Andrew was right. She loved her big brother so very much.

The filibuster, and the resultant failure of "Maddi's Laws" to pass the Senate was front-page news and continuous fodder for the 24-hour news stations for the next several days. Some instant polls had been conducted, and most people felt angry and frustrated at the outcome. This was certainly good news for Maddi, but the polls also revealed that most people were confused by the process and were therefore not sure if what Senator Richards had done was 'wrong' or 'right.' This made Maddi crazy. Her interview—exposing his agenda—had hit the mark and many were leery of his motives, but his response had also hit the mark and many of those same people were waiting to hear what horrible mishap caused Maddi to leave medicine and begin her 'crusade' to punish lawyers.

Maddi tried to think back to what Richards might be referring. She couldn't think of anything in her past that would fit with what he was suggesting. Maybe he was bluffing? Maddi doubted that—the senator from Arizona rarely said anything he couldn't somehow back up with facts. Well, Maddi couldn't worry about that now. She had too much to think about and too much to do.

Maddi tried to not listen to the news for the most part. It only made her angry. She had decided to try to bring the Laws up for another vote after the October recess, which gave her nearly a month to get public opinion behind her—and against Richards and his fellow trial attorneys. Although she had been somewhat despondent immediately after the vote, she was now ready for the fight.

She had spoken with Hank, Amanda, and Wilson, as well as Andrew several times, and they all agreed that a full effort needed to be made to show what the Trial Attorneys were about to lose, thereby revealing for all to see their very transparent agenda. They offered to help Maddi any way they could. Maddi was greatly appreciative and knew she would in fact need their help.

Hank was busy trying not to think about his upcoming trial, and Maddi knew she would need to be there with him. He was so depressed at the thought of what he was going to have to endure, and no amount of consoling on Maddi's part could change his feelings. As he had said, getting sued is a process, regardless of the outcome, and Hank was slowly being beaten down by the process. Maddi began to make arrangements to join him in Strongsville.

CHAPTER XLIII

Andrew had hung up with Maddi full of thoughts—and memories—about that day so long ago when Bobby Duggan had died. Had he truly put it behind him? Had he truly let himself off the hook and placed the blame appropriately at the feet of Frances Buckholtz—where it belonged? He wasn't sure. Maybe seeing the image of Frances Buckholtz being escorted through a courthouse in handcuffs simply allowed him to place the blame more squarely on Buckholtz' shoulders. Andrew wasn't quite sure, but one thing he was sure of was that he had to go and speak with Bobby's parents. He had no idea what it was he wanted to say to them, or what he hoped to gain from talking with them, but he knew he had to do it.

He had also found himself thinking of Amanda far more than he would have liked. Andrew had grown very comfortable in his isolation in the Tundra and a relationship would threaten that greatly. But, no matter how hard he tried he could not escape the notion that he was falling for Amanda in a big way.

He had given her a number where she could reach him—with a little effort—but so far she had only called once. That was soon after they had left one another at the airport. The connection was not a very good one, but they had managed to talk to one another for nearly a half hour, and Andrew had not wanted the conversation to end. He sensed that Amanda felt the same way.

She had talked for several minutes about how great it was to get back to work at the clinic. Her lawsuit was hanging over her head, but she was doing better at shoving it into the back of her mind and getting back to what she enjoyed at the clinic. Andrew had listened carefully, hearing in her voice a deep love for the work she was doing there. He was glad to hear her satisfied and happy, but he was saddened to think he could not be part of that world that was so important to her.

Maybe he would take Maddi up on that notion of heading to Evansville to make things right with the Duggans family, and then maybe he could just take a few extra days and visit Amanda at her Clinic in downtown Columbia. Just the thought of seeing her again made him smile. He called the airline and booked a flight from Yellowknife to Edmonton, then to Minneapolis-St. Paul. From there he would head to Indianapolis, and then home to Evansville. He decided to call ahead and let his mother know he was coming. This call was difficult for Andrew to make, but he knew he had to go home and not only resolve the issues with the Duggan's, but also maybe resolve a few things with his own mother.

She was overjoyed at the thought of seeing him and she let him know that she could pick him up in Indianapolis at any time. Arrangements were made and he took care of covering his responsibilities in the Tundra. He packed and prepared to head home to finish some very unfinished business.

Amanda was surprised at how good it was to get back to work at the Clinic. Having been away for several days she'd had a chance to reflect on all that had occurred since she started working at the Clinic. Although the lawsuit had taken its toll on her, she realized it had not extinguished her desire to take care of people and help them in any way she could. This pleased her and she decided when she got back to do her best to shove the lawsuit out of her mind and get back to doing what she loved.

She was successful with this for the most part, but there was always so much correspondence and paperwork to deal with. Depositions were in the process of being scheduled, and Amanda did her best to try to prepare for the ordeal.

The first deposition scheduled would be with the plaintiff's attorneys, and Amanda knew this would be unpleasant, to say the least. But she knew she was on the side of right and she would do her best to get that out there.

She poured herself into her work and found herself connecting with several of the newer patients that had begun to come to the Clinic for their medical needs. She was once again feeling happy both inside and out, and she felt like she had gotten back to who she used to be.

The only thing she was missing was Andrew. And this surprised her. She had never had any very serious relationships in the past, and had planned on keeping it that way for a long time. But there he was, in her thoughts throughout the day, and—no matter how hard she tried—she couldn't quit thinking about him. And when she thought of him she smiled.

She had spoken to him only once since they had all gone back home and she had enjoyed the conversation immensely. She couldn't imagine what it would be like to be so isolated, but she knew that Andrew loved his time in the Tundra, and certainly wouldn't be leaving it anytime soon. This made her sad, as she wanted to be with him so very much. She would think of this and then simply pour herself into her work even more. There were so many people that needed her help, and she and Andrew would just have to wait.

Andrew's first part of his journey had been quite pleasant, and he had found some time to get caught up on his reading. Andrew still received the medical journal JAMA, and he would read specific articles in it from time to time, just to stay current with what was going on in the medical field. This particular edition had an interesting article about a new drug being developed which was somewhat related to Diacam, but supposedly without the side effect of liver failure or death.

Andrew was reading carefully, and would only occasionally look up from his article when there was turbulence or an unexpected announcement. When he had finished the article he thumbed through the remainder of the journal just to see if there were any other articles of interest.

He was looking through various opportunities listed in the back of the journal, when one listing caught his eye.

"Looking for someone with a medical background to assist in the day to day oversight of a Clinic in downtown Columbia. Position requires a medical degree, and some experience with management. Clinical opportunity exists."

The ad went on to list a contact person. Andrew looked at the ad in amazement. There was no way this could be Amanda's Clinic. And, what if it was? He wouldn't be qualified to do that, nor would he want to. Or would he? He sat back in his seat and thought about it for several minutes.

Wouldn't that be great? He could see Amanda and be with Amanda every single day! Just the thought of it made him smile. But what about the challenges of practicing medicine in America? Could he even stand to put himself through all that again? And, why on earth would they hire an ex-physician who has spent the last several years buried in the Tundra of the Northwest Territory?

Well, there was only one way to find out. He would call them and arrange an interview. He would not tell Amanda until after the interview and he would take the opportunity to see her and be with her once again. If he got the job—a long shot—they could discuss the ramifications of the whole thing. If he didn't get the job—likely—they could enjoy several days together before going back to their very different lives once again.

When Andrew got off the plane in St. Paul, he had an hour and a half lay-over. He immediately found a phone and dialed the number listed on the ad.

"This is Julie Jones, with the Columbia Clinic. How may I help you?"

"My name is Andrew Madison, and I am calling to inquire about the position listed in the latest edition of JAMA. Is it still available?"

There was a pause on the other end of the line. "Well, we've had a few interested individuals, and I think they had decided on someone, but please hold while I look into this."

Julie Jones was gone for what seemed like hours. She finally got back on the line.

"I understand we are still interviewing for this position, but not for much longer. Are you in this area, sir?"

Andrew thought for a moment. "Well, no, but I could be really soon if that is what is needed."

"Well, I think they would like to interview you as soon as possible. How about tomorrow afternoon at about 4:00?"

Andrew knew this would not give him much time to do what he needed to do in Evansville, but he didn't want to lose the opportunity in Columbia.

"Great! I'll be there tomorrow afternoon at 4:00." He then proceeded to get directions from Julie Jones to the clinic from the airport. He then went to the ticket counter to arrange a flight tomorrow morning for Columbia.

Amanda had come back to the clinic ready to work hard, but in her absence the Clinic administrator had suddenly taken a leave of absence. Amanda had only heard bits and pieces but from what she could gather there was some question of illegal allocation of donated funds.

She had been approached about taking the position, but she knew from what she had seen that her clinical options would then be limited. She would not have nearly the connection with the patients that made her feel so fulfilled, and running a clinic was something that she had no experience whatsoever with. She did agree to be on the selection committee, however, and had already sat in on three interviews.

The first two applicants were highly qualified for the position, and the others on the committee raved about them both. Amanda did not think either one was very well suited to the job however, because neither one seemed to have any interest at all in the mission of the clinic. Neither one inquired as to funding or purpose and Amanda felt that both of them were simply trying to get some 'public service' credentials for their resumes.

The third candidate was far more promising. She was a Nurse Practitioner from Charlotte, and she seemed to be truly interested in the Community Outreach aspect of the Clinic. Amanda liked her much more than the other two, but the rest of the committee was split due to her more limited educational experience. They had not yet decided on any candidate, but they needed to do so soon as the clinic was currently being run by the secretary, who had no medical background whatsoever.

Amanda just wanted to make sure that whoever took the job would allow the Clinic to stay the way it was and not try to turn it in to a "financial success story." She would use her position on that committee to make sure that didn't happen.

Andrew got into Indianapolis at 4:30 that afternoon. His mother was waiting for him, as promised, and he was so delighted to see her. They had had their differences in the past, but time and distance had allowed them both to develop a greater fondness for one another.

They spent the trip to Evansville catching up on all that was going on 'back home.' Andrew also shared what had happened since the forum concerning Maddi's Laws and the attempt to try to create medical tribunals for malpractice cases. Mrs. Madison didn't fully understand the details of the litigation concerns in America but she listened politely as Andrew filled her in on what was up with Maddi and the legislation.

He then let her know that he would need to be leaving the next morning, and he could tell this made her sad. He assured her that, even though he had to go over to see a family about a personal matter, he would come home after and spend the rest of the evening with her. He offered to take her out to dinner, but she informed him that she had prepared his favorite meal for him—Sloppy Joes and macaroni salad—and that she would have it ready for him when he came home.

She didn't inquire as to the nature of the 'personal matter,' and Andrew was convinced that his mother was truly better off not knowing. He hoped that Senator Richards didn't try to make the whole Bobby Duggan thing too public, mostly for his mother's sake.

Once they pulled in to the driveway of their home, Andrew jumped out with his bag and headed inside to clean up and get ready to go to the Duggan's home.

He finished a quick shower and then phoned over to their house to make sure they were home. They were somewhat taken aback by his phone call, but seemed willing to see him.

He borrowed the car from his mother-just like in the 'old days-' and headed for the Duggan's home about 2 miles away. He spent the time in the car thinking about what he might say, and about what they might say in response. He tried to prepare himself for their years of pent-up anger, but he hoped and prayed they would not feel that way.

He turned into their drive and stopped the car. He turned off the ignition and sat there for several minutes collecting his thoughts. Finally he got out of the car and headed to the door. Before he could ring the bell, Mrs. Duggan opened the door.

"Hello Andrew. It's been a long time."

Andrew noted how much older she looked. It had after all been nearly 30 years, but she just looked so old and tired. It made him sad.

"Hello, Mrs. Duggan. Yes, it has been a long time. Too long."

Mrs. Duggan proceeded to invite Andrew in and she had him sit in the living room. She offered him lemonade, which he declined, and she sat down across from him. Mr. Duggan came down the stairs and took the seat next to her. He spoke first.

"Well, Andrew, what can we do for you?" He too, looked much older, and seemed like he had a perpetual frown on his face. "We saw the article in the Star a couple of months ago."

Andrew's heart sank. He cleared his throat and slowly began to speak.

"I have come to try to make my peace with the past. I am hoping that as I do that, I will allow for you to make some peace with the past as well."

The Duggans sat in silence, just staring back at Andrew. His foot started tapping, and he continued.

"I'm not sure if anyone has ever told you what really happened that night that Bobby … died." Andrew could barely utter the last word. The Duggans continued listening, their eyes now narrowed to slits beneath the frowns in their foreheads.

"I know that you were aware that I was somehow present at the lake that night, and that Frances Buckholtz was there as well. I also know that he told you that neither of us knew anything about Bobby's death." Andrew paused, licked his lips, and continued.

"Both Frances and I were there. We both know exactly what happened that night. Although neither one of us were responsible for Bobby's death, neither one of us was totally innocent either."

Mrs. Duggan took in a deep breath and held it. Mr. Duggan just continued staring at Andrew, his eyes still slits.

Andrew continued. "I'm not sure if you knew, but several of us boys used to drink beer out there once in awhile. One of Frances' friends was older and he would buy us the beer and we would sit out there and drink and have fun.

"Well, we were all risking getting into a lot of trouble for that behavior, and my mom had finally become aware of it. She let me know that if it continued I would lose all my privileges and the use of the car. More importantly, she said, I would put at risk my dream of becoming a doctor.

"This somehow finally registered with me, and on the night of your son's death, although I was there, I was not drinking. Frances—and Bobby—were."

The Duggans straightened at this information. Apparently they did not know that their son did anything like that, or perhaps they—like many parents—had chosen not to see what was in front of their faces. Andrew went on.

"Anyway, they were drinking, and I was finishing up with some things in the locker room. Suddenly I heard screaming and ran out to see Frances heading toward the lake, clearly having had way too much to drink. I ran to try to stop him, and that is when he pointed to Bobby out in the lake."

Andrew put his head down and took a big breath. He continued.

"He was waving his arms and trying to scream for help. He was going under the water and it was clear he was not doing well. Frances and I jumped into the lake and swam toward where his body had gone down. But it was too late. He was underneath the water, and—although we tried repeatedly—we couldn't find him. I had to pull Frances back to the shore—he was drunk and exhausted from the effort. We made an agreement that night to never tell anyone, and we had pretty much kept that agreement until now."

The room was completely silent. Mr. Duggan rose to his feet, while Mrs. Duggan began to sob softly to herself. Mr. Duggan quietly spoke.

"Why tell us all this now, Andrew?"

Andrew knew that question was coming and he was prepared.

"Because Frances Buckholtz and Senator Richards are going to try to use this story to discredit me—and Maddi—so as to thwart her efforts in Congress for Tort Reform. But, they are trying to make the story something it isn't and I needed you to know exactly what happened before the Senator from Arizona continued with his story. I am certainly not proud of any role I played in Bobby's death, and I am ashamed of the fact that it has taken me thirty years to come and talk to you about that night, but one thing I know for sure—I did my best to help your son that night, and I was completely sober at the time. I want you to know that, I think it's important."

There was silence once again. Andrew once again put his head down. Mrs. Duggan continued sobbing softly, and soon stood and left the room. Andrew's heart sank. All he had accomplished was to bring them more pain. Or awaken the pain they had buried. He felt absolutely awful. He began to stand to leave.

"Just one moment, Andrew." Mr. Duggan was looking straight into Andrew's eyes—a piercing, questioning look on his face.

"You are here, making us relive this incident, simply to alleviate your own role and your own silence in the whole thing?"

Andrew's heart sank. This was a mistake. And, Mr. Duggan was right. It was self-serving and—now that Andrew thought about it—quite heartless.

"You're right, Mr. Duggan. I'm sorry. I'll go now."

"Well, I'll say this for you, Andrew, you've got guts." This comment surprised Andrew. He sat back down and looked up at Mr. Duggan, who continued talking, slowly and softly.

"I always knew that Bobby didn't die alone. We were never sure quite what happened, but I knew he wasn't alone. He never was a good swimmer you know. Always a little afraid of the water. But he really thought the world of you boys. You were older, and so much more popular than he was, but you especially were always kind to him."

Andrew did not know what to say, so he simply sat back and let Mr. Duggan keep talking.

"I can remember him telling me about one time when you helped him shoot baskets at the YMCA. He wasn't really much of an athlete, but you were kind enough to stop what you were doing to teach him how to shoot. He and I were always very grateful to you for that, and I'm sure we never took the opportunity to thank you."

Andrew thought back for a moment. He remembered that day, and how he felt so sorry for Bobby because he didn't know how to shoot the basketball and had no one to show him. And Mr. Duggan was right, they never had thanked him for that, but he didn't require a thank you. It was just what you did. Mr. Duggan continued.

"I have a feeling you have beaten yourself up several times over for what happened that night, and for not telling us all these years. It wasn't right, you know. Not telling us and all. But, I think what you're doing now is what you should've done then. So, Andrew, I'll accept it as such. I certainly can't say 'don't worry about it and thanks for coming,' but I can say that I appreciate your concerns and your kindness to Bobby in the past. If anyone tries to make this story anything other than what I know in my heart to be true, about you or about Bobby, I will do my best to set the record straight. Good luck, Andrew. The world can be much like that lake—it'll swallow you up before you can find your bearings, if you're not careful. So, please, be careful."

With that, Mr. Duggan walked out of the room. Andrew sat there for several minutes, unsure of what had just occurred, or if anything good had come of the visit. He finally stood and walked himself to the door. He didn't turn or say a word, but just let himself out and got into the car and pulled away.

He took a long way home, thinking about what had just happened. As he drove he seemed to feel a huge, heavy weight come off of his shoulders. Whatever had just happened, it had been the right thing. Andrew had finally told the truth that night to the two people who needed to hear it. And, although they didn't really let him off the hook for his involvement, they seemed to appreciate the truth a great deal and Andrew felt like that would somehow help them with it all. He hoped so. It had certainly helped him.

Amanda had been informed of the 4th and final interview scheduled for the next day when she came into work that morning. She was glad to get the entire thing over with. By now she had more or less made up her mind to push hard for the Nurse Practitioner, in spite of her lack of experience. She felt her heart to be in the right place, and that was the most important thing.

She worked hard throughout the morning, trying to clear her schedule for the interview in the afternoon. She was soon consumed by the medical problems of her patients—and their social problems as well—and she lost herself inside her day.

Andrew headed for the airport bright and early the next morning. He had arranged for a cab to take him, not wanting to make his mother drive during the busy morning rush hour.

The two of them had had a delightful evening, and Andrew felt good that he was able to spend that kind of time with his mother. He hadn't slept well, as he rehashed the conversation with the Duggans over and over again in his mind.

He recognized, however, that he felt like a burden had been lifted, and suddenly he was aware of a strong desire to change many things in his life.

While on the airplane he thought about all the decisions he had made through the last 20 or 30 years. So many of them involved giving up and moving away. He wondered if so much of that had to do with the guilt he felt over Bobby Duggan's death? And now, just maybe, he could reconnect with the world again. He wasn't sure he could, but he just might be willing to try.

His flight landed at 1:00 in the afternoon and he headed for a hotel in downtown Columbia that he had booked earlier in the day. He needed a place to stay, and a place to get ready for his interview.

He had decided to not contact Amanda until after the interview, and he was anxiously awaiting the opportunity to see her again. He couldn't believe how excited he felt inside. He hadn't felt this excited about anything for years. Decades, as it were, and he still wasn't even sure it was "her" clinic.

He checked into the hotel, went to his room and began to prepare for his interview. He had put together a curriculum vitae and was wanting to spend some time going over it. He had wanted it to sound like he was fully qualified not only from a medical standpoint but from a managerial standpoint as well. He was surprised how much he wanted this interview to go well. He tried to tell himself it was simply because of his need to succeed, but he knew deep down in his heart that he wanted more than anything to be near Amanda.

At 3:30, he caught a cab and headed to the Clinic and the address that had been given him by Julie Jones. He arrived, wondering if this was in fact Amanda's beloved clinic, knowing that was probably a long shot. At least if he did end up here he would be close to her. He smiled at that thought.

He walked through the doors of the Clinic and introduced himself to the lady sitting at the front desk. She gave him a puzzled look, and glanced down toward his nice shoes and back up at his well-groomed appearance. Andrew understood, and immediately informed her that he was here for the interview for the Director's position. This appeared to make much more sense to her and she asked him to wait a moment.

She stepped through a door behind her, then quickly emerged.

"This way, sir," she drawled.

Andrew followed and was led into a small room with an over-sized table which nearly filled the entire room. There were three men and one lady sitting waiting to conduct the interview. Andrew looked around at each of them, his eyes stopping when he saw the beautiful brown hair, and adorable bright face of Amanda sitting in one of the chairs. She was looking down, working on a chart and did not see him enter the room.

He felt nervous and excited, and was astounded that a 50-plus year old man could feel this way. One of the gentlemen stood and began to introduce him.

Just then, Amanda raised her head and looked straight at Andrew. Her eyes opened wide, and her jaw dropped. She gave him an expression which more or less said "What the hell are you doing here?" and he simply grinned from ear to ear.

After his introduction he sat down and gave her a look which suggested that she not mention their connection. She subtly nodded, and the interview began.

The gentleman who had introduced him asked the first question.

"Tell us, Dr. Madison, why it is you are interested in becoming the Director of our poor clinic here in downtown Columbia."

Andrew responded with his well-rehearsed responses, and they seemed to play well with all the interviewees. He indicated his dissatisfaction with "suburbia medicine," and how he was anxious to truly help and make a difference. He also mentioned his experience as the overseer of his own practice, and his capabilities in that area.

When it seemed they had satisfied this area of questioning they then asked about his time in the Tundra. Andrew had expected this to be difficult to justify, but as he began talking about it, all at once it seemed as though his time there had prepared him for this very job. His responses were once again well received, and, when he was done he felt he'd had a very good interview.

Just as the interview was about to end, and just as Andrew was ready to leave, Amanda spoke up.

"Excuse me sir, but I have one more very important question for you."

Andrew looked straight at her, with a very puzzled expression, and he smiled and nodded. She continued.

"In this line of work, specifically, helping the needy in an inner-city community clinic, one thing becomes quite important. Our patients not only benefit from our medical knowledge, but they also benefit from our relationship to them. It is often the only solid relationship they have. So, tell me sir, how long do you intend to stay in this area? I'm not asking for a commitment, so much as just a general idea of what your intentions are?" She looked long and hard at Andrew with a solemn and intense expression on her face, her eyes seeming to look down into Andrew's very soul.

Andrew looked back at her, with the same very serious and very intense expression. He knew this was an important question on many different levels, and he was quite prepared to give a justified and appropriate response. The question had taken him by surprise, but he began to speak, knowing the answer immediately.

"God willing, I hope to stay here forever." And with that the interview was ended.

CHAPTER XLIV

Hank had done his best to put his lawsuit—and the upcoming trial—out of his mind, but he was only minimally successful. Finally, as the day of the trial approached he was almost relieved at the prospect of finally getting the damn thing over with.

There had been some attempts to settle the case out of court, but Hank was insistent they not do that, as he felt completely and totally innocent of the charges against him. His lawyer, who was an advocate for his insurance company more so than for him, finally agreed, thinking that Hank would be a very compelling witness and they therefore had a reasonable chance to win.

Maddi had flown in the day before the trial was to get underway, and Hank was overjoyed to see her. The world was so much more tolerable when she was there.

They picked up some Chinese for supper and immediately headed to Hank's house to get reacquainted. They placed the Chinese food on the table, and were heading for the couch to get comfortable, when suddenly Hank reached out and grabbed Maddi by the arm, turning her toward him. He pulled her close to him, kissing her passionately at the same time. Maddi kissed him back, folding herself into his arms. They moved to the couch, and fell onto it—neither one letting go. They couldn't get close enough to one another, and they couldn't be with one another fast enough. They clung together in an expression of their newfound love for one another. They stayed like this for many minutes, embracing each other with a contentment neither one had known for a very long time.

Maddi kept looking straight into Hank's big green eyes, and then would smile. Hank finally asked her what she was grinning about and she responded by hugging him closer to her. He hugged her back and they both knew that this feeling would sustain them through anything they might encounter.

They finally decided to get to that Chinese food they had ordered, and they caught up on the trial as well as Maddi's legislative nightmares while they were eating.

After several hours, and a delightful dinner, Hank needed to prepare for the following day's—and weeks'—events. Meanwhile, Maddi made herself at home and found a place to put her things and get acclimated to her new home for the next two weeks.

She wandered around the house, looking at pictures and other momentos. She saw numerous photos of Hank with a woman, whom she presumed to be Jenny, and a younger man, whom she presumed to be Jack. The pictures showed very happy people and Maddi knew that both Jack and Jenny were still very important people in Hank's life. She could live with that. She loved Hank, and anything and everything that went with him.

Hank meanwhile was buried over charts and papers and various documents, making sure he was ready for any question that may come up. His attorney had spent some time preparing him as well and he did think he was about as ready as he was ever going to be.

Finally, at 10:00, Hank announced that he was done, and that the two of them were going to watch some mindless TV and just enjoy one another's company. This they did, but very little TV got watched.

The two enjoyed several hours of intimacy, and Hank couldn't believe how right it felt to hold Maddi in his arms. He loved her like he had never loved anyone before—except for Jenny.

Maddi in turn felt the same way. Whenever Hank would touch her she would feel so many incredible, wonderful things, and she lost herself inside him whenever they were together. She felt like the two had been made for one another and she desperately hoped the feelings between them would survive the many challenges that lay before them.

They finally both drifted off to sleep, holding one another in their arms. They woke the next morning to the sound of a bird pecking at the bedroom window. Hank got up first, reached over, and kissed Maddi good morning. She smiled and then turned over to get a bit more sleep.

Hank prepared himself for the day, and started a pot of coffee and got the morning newspaper for Maddi to read. He had suggested that he head to court without her, and simply call her if something came up, but she insisted on accompanying him to the courthouse.

They left for court at 8:30, and arrived at the Strongsville courthouse at 10 minutes before 9.00. Hank's attorney was already present, and Hank joined him at the defendant's table. Maddi took a seat toward the back of the court-room, hoping that no one would recognize her.

Soon the judge was announced and they all stood while she walked into the courtroom. They then sat, and she struck her gavel, starting the trial of The Family of Irene Morrison vs. Dr. Henry Clarkson.

Opening statements were made, and both were rather predictable and unin-formative, or so thought Maddi. The plaintiff then called their first witness, a young nurse's aide who worked for the nursing home where Irene Morrison had died.

She nervously stated her name and her occupation for the court and was then seated. The attorney for Irene's family then slowly stood and walked over to where the aide was seated in the witness stand. He calmly asked her to describe the events that took place on the day Irene Morrison sustained the injuries that would ultimately cause her death.

Hank's attorney immediately objected, and the plaintiff attorney restated his question. Once satisfied, Hank's attorney sat down and the jury listened while the aide told her version of what had happened that day.

With direction given by the plaintiff attorney, the aide told of Irene's numerous falls, and the many times that Dr. Clarkson had been called. She then told about the last fall, and how terrible it was, and then talked about the ambulance coming and taking dear Irene to the hospital, and then them bring-ing her back simply to die in their facility.

The young aide was clearly emotional and upset by the recollection of events, as well as her role in the trial. The nurses and the aides hated it when any of the Residents died, and they also hated this process that tried to make it someone's fault. It was particularly upsetting to them all that Dr. Clarkson was being accused of negligence—they all saw him as a very fine doctor and an even finer human being.

When it appeared the plaintiff attorney was finished with the aide, she began to stand and step down.

Hank's attorney immediately asked her to please sit down, as he had just a few questions for her. This she did, visibly shaking by this point.

Hank's attorney was a boyish-looking young man, with a wonderful sense of humor. There had been many times throughout this ordeal when the attor-ney—Jimmy Johnson—had made Hank laugh in spite of how terrible he felt. There were also times, however, when Jimmy was totally inappropriate and Hank would have to remind him that a lot was at stake here.

Jimmy Johnson headed toward the witness stand and smiled genuinely at the young aide. She attempted a weak smile back. He then proceeded to ask her questions.

"Tell me ma'am, did you ever see Dr.Clarkson behave unkindly toward Mrs. Morrison? For that matter, did you ever see Dr. Clarkson behave unkindly toward any of the residents?"

The aide gave an emphatic "no sir!" and Jimmy continued on.

"Now, after Dr. Clarkson would be made aware of one of Mrs. Morrison's falls, what would he typically do?"

The aide thought for a moment and then answered.

"Well, he would always ask us if she seemed frightened, and then he would ask us to put her in a chair right beside the nurses sitting in the nursing station so they could make sure she stayed safe. Then we would have to review her meds—her medications—for him on the phone, to be sure nothing had been changed or gotten confused, and then he would recommend restraints in order to keep her from falling again."

Jimmy feigned a concerned look. "Restraints, you say? As in 'strapping her down?'"

"Yessir. Only, we aren't allowed to do that. It's against the law, and so we would have to tell him that one more time."

"Then what would happen?"

"Dr. Clarkson would ask if we had notified the family, and when we told him that we had, he asked us to remind them that we can't do restraints because of government regulations."

Jimmy smiled. "Thank you, ma'am. No further questions, your honor."

The plaintiff attorney indicated that he had no further questions, and the judge had the young aide step down.

The plaintiff's attorney called several more witnesses, all more or less attesting to the same things that the aide had said, but from a different point of view. And, with each witness, Jimmy would ask more or less the same questions and arrive at the same conclusions as he had done with the aide.

At one point, the plaintiff attorney had the Medical Director on the stand, who happened to be a fairly good friend of Hank's, and asked him to state in detail the laws governing restraints in the nursing home setting.

Maddi was watching closely as this was going on, looking at the faces of the jurors. She was delighted to see their surprise when they discovered how ridiculous and impossible the laws were. She knew this could only help Hank.

The trial went on for several days this way, with very few surprises. After the fifth day, a Friday, the judge adjourned court early and trial was scheduled to resume the following Monday.

Maddi and Hank went with Jimmy to a restaurant in downtown Cleveland to review how things were going. Hank was fighting a depression, as he felt judgment coming closer and closer. He felt like a criminal being judged for sentencing and he felt ashamed and alone.

Maddi was aware of this and did her best to reassure him, but was only minimally successful.

It was Jimmy, and his delightful sense of humor, which probably did the most to keep Hank from despairing.

"What a dumb shit that attorney is," Jimmy would say. They all three would simply burst out laughing. "I mean, what idiot allows every witness to glorify the guy they are trying to beat up?" This was funny, and true, and it helped Hank immensely.

The three of them had a few drinks and a lovely meal, and Hank insisted on paying for it, knowing he would do so either way. They all laughed at this as well, and Maddi and Hank soon left for home.

They spent the weekend catching up and enjoying one another's company. It was amazing to them both how comfortable they felt with one another, and, although Hank was tempted to talk about making the relationship something more than it was, he couldn't seem to think about anything involving the future as long as he was under the oppressive weight of this trial. So they shopped, went to a movie, went out to dinner and simply enjoyed the weekend as best they could.

Monday morning, and the resumption of the trial was almost a blessing to Hank. One step closer to ending the horrible ordeal.

The day began with the plaintiff's attorney calling his "expert witness" to the stand. A very short, somewhat chubby man began to approach the bench. He was asked to state his name and occupation.

"I am Dr. Steven Prickle, and I am a Gerontologist for the city of Cleveland."

"Please explain to the court what a gerontologist is and does."

Dr. Prickle cleared his throat and began. "Well, I specialize in medicine in the elderly. I only see the elderly and I am uniquely qualified to deal with the problems that effect them uniquely." He subtley smiled at his brilliant answer.

He was then asked to comment on the care given to Mrs. Irene Morrison during her time in Noble Manor Nursing Home.

He once again cleared his throat and tried to sit up straight so as to appear taller than he was.

"Well, although for the most part I feel Dr. Clarkson did an adequate job, I do question some of the medications that he had Mrs. Morrison on, as they can sometimes contribute to falls."

"Would it be accurate to say, Dr. Prickle, that these medications may have actually played a role in causing Mrs. Morrison's falls, and ultimately her death?"

Jimmy immediately popped up out of his seat. "I object! This attorney is trying to draw conclusions with inadequate evidence."

"I'll allow it, but watch yourself, sir. The objection in overruled."

"Once again, Dr. Prickle, would it be accurate to say that these medications may have played a role in Mrs. Morrison's death?"

Dr. Prickle looked around the room, his self-importance evident to all, and he replied "absolutely. The meds probably contributed to poor Mrs. Morrison's death."

There was a sudden hum throughout the courtroom and Maddi glanced over at Hank. He had his head down, and was subtley shaking it. The judge banged her gavel. "Quiet! Quiet! Continue."

The plaintiff attorney looked at the judge and said "that is all I have, Judge. And, the plaintiff rests."

The judge looked over at Jimmy. "Have you any questions for this witness, Mr. Johnson?"

Jimmy stood up and looked back at the judge. "I certainly do."

He walked over to the witness stand. "Hello, Dr. Prickle, although we've met before, I'll reintroduce myself to you, as you may have become confused from all the other trials you have participated in."

"Objection!"

The judge looked sternly at Jimmy. "Sustained. Stick to the point, Mr. Johnson."

Jimmy walked over to his table, where Hank was seated, and grabbed a piece of paper. "Tell me, Dr. Prickle, what is on this paper?"

Dr. Prickle looked closely at the paper in front of him. "It appears to be a medication list. According to the name at the top it is the medication list for Irene Morrison."

"Thank you, sir. Now, if you will, can you elaborate on those medications that you found inappropriate?"

Dr. Prickle took another look at the paper. "Well, yes, here is a medication called Diovan. One of the side effects for Diovan is dizziness. It is likely that Mrs. Morrison was dizzy, and therefore fell more easily."

"Thank you. Please continue."

"Well, this is a medication called Coumadin. It will often cause light-headedness. Also, if not properly monitored, it can cause excessive bleeding, as its purpose is to thin the blood. It certainly could be implicated in Mrs. Morrison's death."

"Thank you again, sir. Are there any others?"

Dr. Prickle looked at the list one more time, and then shook his head. "I think those are the two big ones that jumped out at me."

Jimmy nodded his head and then walked over to his table again and grabbed another piece of paper. He then proceeded to hand it to Dr. Prickle.

"Please tell me, Doctor, what is this piece of paper?"

Doctor Prickle once again glanced down at the paper before him, looking through his glasses perched on his nose.

"This is a diagnosis list, with Irene Morrison's name on the top."

Jimmy shook it as though he were trying to make the diagnoses jump off the page.

"Will you please read the diagnoses, Doctor?"

Doctor Prickle cleared his throat. "Certainly." He paused for a moment, and then began reading through the list.

"Well, I see hypertension—that is high blood pressure." He smiled condescendingly at the jurors sitting to his left. He then continued.

"I also see a diagnosis of renal insufficiency. And here I see Atrial Fibrillation."

Jimmy walked toward the jurors, but spoke to Dr. Prickle.

"Will you please explain to this courtroom what renal insufficiency and atrial fibrillation are?"

Once again, Dr. Prickle smiled condescendingly.

"Certainly. Renal insufficiency is when the kidneys aren't working quite like they are supposed to, and atrial fibrillation is when the top part of the heart is beating very very fast."

"Thank you, Doctor. Now, can you explain to the courtroom how these three conditions might affect a patient?"

The plaintiff attorney immediately stood up and objected. "Relevance, your honor."

Jimmy responded quickly. "If you please, your honor, I think the relevance of my question will be quite apparent soon."

The judge looked first at the plaintiff attorney and then at Jimmy. "Overruled. You may proceed counselor, but get to the point."

Jimmy nodded and looked back at Dr. Prickle. "Again, sir, can you explain the effect these diagnoses may have on a patient?"

Dr. Prickle cleared his throat and proceeded. "Well, with high blood pressure sometimes you can get headaches. It is also hard on the poorly-functioning kidneys. The function of the kidneys is important for the elimination of impurities in the blood and if they don't function properly all kinds of things can go wrong. As for the atrial fib, the rapidly beating atrium can cause the ventricles—the lower part of the heart—to beat rapidly and potentially create a deadly arrhythmia. Also, with the rapid heart beat sometimes a blood clot can be let loose which can cause a multitude of problems."

Jimmy walked back toward the witness and stood directly in front of him. "Tell me, doctor, what medications might be used to stave off some of these problems?"

The doctor thought for a moment and then softly replied. "Well, to treat the hypertension you would use one of the many hypertensives available. You would be wise to use one that protects the kidneys at the same time that it lowers the blood pressure.

"As for the atrial fib it would be a good idea to try to keep the ventricles from responding as fast as the atria is beating, so as to try to avoid the critical dysrhythmias or the blood clots, and you can do this by slowing the ventricular response, and by thinning the blood."

Jimmy frowned as though deep in thought. "Tell me, Doctor, what medications might do these things that you've just mentioned."

The doctor looked up at Jimmy, finally understanding where he was going with his questions. He cleared his throat, and then began to speak even more softly.

"Well, I suppose you might use an ACE inhibitor or an ARB for the renal insufficiency and the hypertension, and I suppose you might use warfarin for the thinning of the blood."

Jimmy kept the frown going on his face. He once again walked over to the jurors. Looking directly at them, he asked Dr. Prickle one further question. "Doctor, are Diovan and coumadin—the two drugs you've named as problems—in those classes of drugs you've just mentioned as being required for the management of Irene Morrison's illnesses?"

Doctor Prickle shifted in his seat, and cleared his throat for a third time. He looked over at Jimmy, and, with his eyes narrowed he responded.

"I suppose that the two medications would be useful for those medical conditions listed on Irene Morrison's chart, but-"

"That will be all, Doctor, thank you."

"But, but-"

"I said, that will be all."

Jimmy then went and sat down, a very satisfied look on his face for all to see. The plaintiff attorney stood and approached the witness.

"Redirect, if I may?" he said to the judge. She nodded.

"Doctor, even though these drugs may have been helpful in the management of Mrs. Morrison's illnesses, is it still likely that they contributed to her falls and her ultimate death?"

Doctor Prickle responded a little too quickly. "Absolutely!" he nearly shouted. The plaintiff attorney thanked him and sat down. The judge dismissed the witness from the stand, then asked Jimmy if he had any witnesses.

"Only one, your honor. I'd like to call Dr. Henry Clarkson to the stand."

There was once again a hum throughout the courtroom, as everyone exchanged surprised glances. Hank took a deep breath and slowly stood up. He walked to the witness stand, and raised his hand and took the oath. He sat down and took another deep breath, preparing himself to say all that he had been thinking about for nearly a year now.

Jimmy slowly approached the stand and asked Hank to introduce himself, state his profession, his credentials, and where and when he obtained his degrees. Once this was done, Jimmy looked straight at Hank and began his questioning.

"The family of Irene Morrison is here today claiming that you were negligent in the care of their mother. They've stated in their lawsuit that, because you were Mrs. Morrison's nursing home physician, that you were responsible for her safety and wellbeing twenty four hours a day. Is this the case? And, if so, do you feel you fulfilled this obligation appropriately?"

Maddi was shocked at the question. This was Hank's own attorney setting him up with a very difficult question. Why would he do this? Perhaps he was trying to eliminate and triangulate the plaintiff's case? Maddi started shivering inside as she looked at Hank trying to get a sense of where he was with this question and with the entire proceedings. She was pleased to see an almost calm appearance to his rugged features. She sat back in her chair, waiting for his reply.

Hank shifted his weight in his chair, took a deep breath, and began his response.

"While it was certainly my desire to keep Irene safe 'twenty four hours a day,' it was NOT my responsibility to do so. I'm curious where and when such expectations occurred. We as physicians have been given the incredible opportunity to care for individuals who need us. As we prepare for such a noble calling we receive countless hours of education, as well as firm guidance from those who've gone before us. One thing, however, that we don't receive are the God-like qualities some seem to be expecting. I can't be responsible for Irene Morrison—or anyone else for that matter—for 24 hours a day. I do not live in her home or in the nursing facility. All I can be responsible for is her medical care, which I believe was quite adequate.

"It occurs to me that what is happening here—and across this nation—is a gradual increase in the expectations placed on doctors by individuals, while at the same time, the doctor has lost a large amount of control over the care he or she is able to provide for a patient. Third-party payers have taken the place of individual patients when it comes to who calls the shots. Lawyers have taken the place of individual patients when it comes to addressing any dissatisfactions. No one seems to be responsible for their own situations any longer."

Hank paused, and took a quick drink of water. He then cleared his throat and continued.

"This change is occurring across the country, in every facet of life, and it is gradually unraveling the very fabric of our nation. This country was founded on a belief in self-reliance and self-determination. What we are becoming is a nation full of people who rely on others for their livelihoods and their lives.

"Why has this happened? Why have we let it?? I'm not sure I can anwswer these questions, but one thing I do know for sure—if we continue to go down this path, I promise you this—it will not be long until we no longer assume any responsibility for our choices or our lives.

"If we are not careful, we will soon cede our rights and responsibilities to a government of overseers and a corp of lawyers whose sole purpose is to ensure the rights of that government as opposed to ensuring the rights of the people who are being governed.

"Don't you all see this?" By now Hank was very animated. The sincerity he felt for the words he was saying was evident, and the jury was focused on every single word. Maddi looked at Hank, and then at the jury, and felt a bit more comfortable, knowing that at least Hank was being heard.

"As we allow lawyers to mutilate the law to serve their needs, and we allow the government to oversee our behaviour and our lives, we give up everything our forefathers fought and died for.

"To be an American is to be in charge of our own destiny. To make our own choices and to be responsible for our own decisions and the lives we ultimately live. If we continue down this current path, the eventual destination will be the diminution of our control and our self-reliance, as well as a resurgence of government control and a denial of our autonomy.

"One only has to look at recent decisions concerning eminent domain to understand the threat we are facing. The fact that—in America—the Government can simply acquire our land because they WANT it is an abomination of everything this country represents.

"How, you ask, does this lawsuit relate to the disintegration of individual rights? I'll tell you how. Right now—in this courtroom—a lawyer is trying to convince you that Irene Morrison's family had no obligation to Irene. That her outcome was purely and completely the responsibility of a nameless, faceless nursing home and a doctor the family had never bothered to meet."

Hank had raised his voice with this last comment, and his face was somewhat flushed. It was clear he felt strongly about what was occurring. The jury seemed completely absorbed by his comments.

The plaintiff attorney—and his clients—had scowls on their faces as this last statement was made. They felt indignant that this corrupt physician would try to hold them responsible for his mistakes. They glared at Hank as he continued, almost reading their thoughts

"Although I don't hold that family responsible for Irene's death, I do hold them responsible for Irene's life—at least at the end. They were the ones who had some choices here. They were the ones who elected to keep her in a facility where the Law prohibited interventions which might have protected her. The choice was completely theirs. And, if Irene had not become the victim of Alzheimer's disease, I would hold her personally responsible for her decisions and her choices. Interestingly, I think she would want and expect that. And I know one thing for sure—she would not have chosen her life to end the way it did—alone, in a nursing home. More importantly, she would not have chosen to act on the events that led to her falls and her death the way this family has chosen to act on those same events.

"Irene Morrison was a grand lady who lived a grand life. Her Alzheimer's and her death were utter tragedies that in no way reflect the glories of her life. But, they were no one's fault.

"Much like a hurricane with unpredictable and unprecedented force can level an entire city, Alzheimer's disease can level a human being. And, as the consequences of a hurricane are felt far beyond the storm's fury, so too are the consequences of Alzheimer's felt far beyond the impact of the disease on the individual.

"Irene fell. She fell because she was unpredictable and incoherent. She did not fall because of any actions on the part of the nursing home or myself. The only way to have prevented Irene's falls, including the one which seems to have caused her death, would have been to tie her down. To take restraints and hook them on her arms or legs or abdomen, and TIE THIS WOMAN DOWN."

Hank spoke with such intensity and force that several in the audience actually jumped in their seats. Several in the jury also jumped a bit, and Maddi felt like standing up and cheering. Hank was getting through to these people. They were getting it. And, just maybe, they were seeing the "big picture" of litigation in America. Maddi was excited at the thought that there truly might be a way to change how people think about this issue.

Hank took a handkerchief and wiped it across his brow. He was feeling somewhat shaky inside, but he also felt he was on solid ground. He took another drink of water and then continued.

"There you have it. At the end of a glorious and noble life, Irene's 'choice' comes down to this: be fully restrained for most of the day, or risk a fall that may ultimately kill you.

"As dreadful as either choice may be, I can tell you this—any one of us would choose the latter. Any one of us in such a position would want the choice of moving and living as opposed to being tied down and not moving and not living.

"Interestingly, as it turns out, we don't even have the right to make the first choice. It is illegal to restrain someone like Irene in any way. We could not have tied her down or caged her in like an animal, even if we had wanted to. Thankfully, we are not allowed to do so. It would be inhumane to chain someone in such a way. I think we are all in agreement.

"The fact that Irene then became "free" to fall should not surprise anyone. She was protected as well as anyone with freedom can be. Any one of us can metaphorically "fall" at any time. That is the price we pay for freedom and free will.

"When we drive a vehicle we may crash. When we walk across a busy street, we may be hit by a car. When we walk down a flight of stairs, we may trip and fall. The stairs aren't responsible for that, nor is the owner of those stairs. Falling down those stairs is a risk we take when we choose to descend those stairs.

"Please don't diminish our freedoms by making others responsible for our acting on those freedoms. Please don't diminish all that we stand for as a nation, by blaming others for the consequences of our own choices. It is a wonderful thing to have the freedom to make mistakes, to suffer consequences, to risk failures. It is how we learn and grow and become who we are. If such choices or such freedoms wind up with outcomes we didn't predict, for God's sake don't try to cast blame. Accept that the very act of pursuing our freedoms carries with it the risk of failure or defeat. Even, unfortunately, death at times.

"I do not mean to suggest that we have no responsibility toward one another. All I am trying to say, is that any time you attempt to cede responsibility from yourself to another human being you are also ceding your freedom to another. We mustn't allow this to happen!

"The lottery of lawsuits must stop. The financial gain predicated on the corrupt notion of misplaced responsibility will ultimately bankrupt this nation and its freedoms."

"Objection!" The plaintiff's attorney jumped to his feet and shouted the word at the judge. "This soliloquy is impertinent, at best!"

The judge slowly looked across her large bench at the attorney who had made the objection. She then looked over at Hank, who was sitting there, amazingly calm. After what seemed like an eternity, the judge finally spoke, turning her attention to the courtroom. "I'll allow it, as I think it is useful to gain this perspective." She then looked toward Hank. "However, Dr. Clarkson, you must hurry up and finish this rather lengthy response."

Hank looked over at the judge and nodded his head in appreciation. He then continued. "The idea that all bad outcomes must be paid for by someone else is an idea equivalent to the notion that we are no longer the stewards of our ships. It implies that we must allow others to determine our path and our choices. It allows others to be responsible for our lives.

"That is the ultimate outcome of a lawsuit such as this. If I, and Noble Manor Nursing Home, are responsible for the death of Irene Morrison, then the sad conclusion is that I, and Noble Manor Nursing Home, were responsible for her life as well. I know deep in my heart that Irene Morrison would not have wanted that. And I believe with all my being that Irene would not want what is occurring here right now.

"Our freedoms bring risks. To ascribe those risks to another is to ascribe those freedoms to another. It is to eliminate our individuality and to subjugate our free will.

"Please don't diminish Irene Morrison's proud and wonderful life by denigrating her choices and her dignity in this courtroom today. I know Irene would have chosen to walk down that hallway, and I know she would've been fully prepared to deal with the outcome of that choice. Allow her that final respect. Recognize her incredible individuality. Let her die as she lived—noble, and free."

Jimmy Johnson had stood out of the way while Hank delivered this eloquent response. He now continued standing off to the side, to allow the brilliant words spoken by Hank so beautifully to find their mark in the hearts and the minds of the men and women sitting in the jury box.

After several minutes, he thanked Hank and sat down. The judge asked the Plaintiff's attorney if he had any questions. He looked sheepishly up at the judge and quietly said "nothing further, your honor."

The judge then looked over at Jimmy. "Do you have any other witnesses, Counselor?"

"No your honor, the defense rests."

Closing arguments were given that afternoon, and the jury was sent to deliberate overnight. The next morning they indicated they had reached a verdict. Hank sat nervously with Jimmy at the defendant's table, while the family of Irene Morrison sat with their plaintiff's attorney on the other side of the room.

The jury slowly made their way to their seats and sat down. The judge asked if they had reached a verdict, they indicated that they had. The jury foreman stood and read from a piece of paper he held in both hands.

"We, the jury, find the defendant, Not Guilty."

There was a loud hum throughout the courtroom. The judge loudly banged her gavel. "Quiet! Quiet in the courtroom. Ladies and Gentlemen of the jury, we thank you for your service. Dr. Clarkson, the case against you has been dismissed."

Hank and Maddi immediately looked for one another in the very crowded courtroom. They found each other quickly, and began the process of leaving the courtroom. Once outside, they raced to Hank's car and jumped inside.

Hank turned on the ignition, and they headed into the busy traffic in down-town Strongsville.

Hank was holding Maddi's hand, and he began smiling to himself. Maddi leaned her head up against him. The trial was over. It had caused considerable change and life-altering decisions, and now it was over. Hank could go back to his life and what he did so well. Or could he? So much had changed. He knew suddenly that he could never go back. He could only go forward. He smiled and pulled Maddi closer as they headed for home.

CHAPTER XLV

After the trial, Maddi immediately headed back to D.C., where the vote for her legislation was moving ever closer. She knew she had quite a bit of work to do in order to secure the needed votes for passage so she headed back and immediately got to work.

She contacted different senators who had voted against the legislation but who she thought might be persuaded with careful pressure applied to change their vote. Doctors had continued to quit their practices, and more and more of their constituents were clamoring for something to be done. Maddi was able to put her legislation in the limelight as the "something" that would improve the system and allow doctors to return to their practices.

Hank had decided to join her. He wasn't sure what his future held, but he had hired a locum tenens—a doctor who would take over the operations of the practice in his absence—for an indefinite amount of time while he weighed his options. He wasn't sure what he would do if he didn't practice medicine, but the practice of medicine had changed so dramatically for him. He wasn't sure he could do it anymore.

He kept himself busy while Maddi was trying to collect votes, by visiting the Smithsonian Museum, as well as the Holocaust Museum. He had never taken much time for vacations, and when he did travel it was almost always to a destination where a medical conference was being held. It felt so good just to meander around town and see the sights.

He and Maddi would then meet for a late dinner either out or at her townhouse apartment—where he was staying. Sometimes he would prepare a rather elaborate meal for the two of them, and sometimes they would simply grab some Chinese. Either way they had delightful evenings together talking about anything and everything. Hank couldn't remember when he had been this happy. Even when he was married to Jenny, and Jack was young, he was always so busy. This was like a dream come true. He'd had no idea what he was missing in his crazy life as an overworked physician.

The vote for Maddi's Laws was set to happen just before the Thanksgiving break. It was two days away and Maddi was in overdrive trying to secure the votes needed to pass her legislation. As the time for the vote was nearing, Maddi became more and more unsettled. Finally, she and Hank talked about the entire situation, and why it was bothering Maddi so greatly.

"What if they pass the laws and nothing changes?" she asked.

Hank furrowed his brow and angled his head in thought. "Maddi, things will change. The Laws are good and this country is ready for them. Trust me, anything that even loosens a little bit the hold the trial lawyers have on this country will be a good thing."

They talked for a while longer and Maddi began to relax. Hank was right. Things had to change. The country couldn't go on this way.

The morning of the vote, Maddi left the house before Hank awoke. She had not slept well and needed to get out of the house and feel like she was doing something.

She grabbed her running clothes and headed for the work-out facility in the Capitol. She knew there would probably be no one in there at that early hour and she welcomed the chance to work out hard in solitude.

When she walked in there was no one there and she quickly changed her clothes and began her workout. She lost herself in her thoughts and in her music. Without her even noticing someone quietly crept into the gym.

He started running on a treadmill close to Maddi and suddenly she looked up and saw Senator Richards. She was startled, and then started chuckling as she nearly fell off her treadmill.

He grinned back at her. "You ready for that vote, Maddi?"

Her smile immediately left her face as she remembered how close it was to the time for the vote. "Yes, I certainly am. I don't suppose I have your support? And the support of that law firm of yours?"

Senator Richards started laughing, a little more than was called for. "Child, you won't ever have my vote for laws that violate the rights of my constituents. I don't think you'll have enough to pass those laws of yours." He paused for a moment, as though trying to decide if he should continue. After several seconds he went on. "It would sure be a shame if everybody in America had to find out the details of what that brother of yours got himself into so long ago, now wouldn't it?"

Maddi was surprised by the comment, although she made sure to hide her shock at Richards' blatant attempt to intimidate her. "Oh yeah, I wanted to thank you for bringing that up a while back. It seems my brother had burdened himself with that for the last thirty years, and he decided after hearing your bullshit to go talk to the family of the boy involved. They now know exactly what went on way back then and so I doubt that fabricated story of yours will have much traction."

Maddi was breathing much heavier now, and not because of her workout. She continued on the treadmill as though they were discussing the weather and looked straight ahead, determined not to meet the eyes of this lecherous man.

Richards started chuckling once again. "It's always amazing to me how some people can be so naïve. They actually think that the truth matters. Besides, you've got your own history, now don't you, Senator?"

Just then Richards shut off the treadmill and headed for the locker room. Maddi continued staring straight ahead, but she couldn't get Richards' comment out of her mind. She tried to imagine what he might be referring to. Everyone has secrets in their past. Things they aren't particularly proud of, but Maddi could think of nothing that Richards would actually be able to use against her.

She continued working out, allowing her thoughts to wander into the domain of her past, searching for a forgotten act that might be used to injure her efforts.

She was about to give up on thinking about it, and simply dismiss Richards as a bluffing old fool, when suddenly—from somewhere deep in her past—she remembered an incident to which Richards might be referring. Her thoughts returned to that time and she suddenly felt pain and grief as she recalled events from long ago. Without realizing it, she slowed her efforts on the treadmill, gradually making her way to a bench in the gym, alone with a memory that had kindly been hidden away—until now.

Maddi had just gotten started in practice. She was young and hopeful, and full of good intentions and joy at the thought of helping others with their suffering. In spite of her youthful optimism, she was painfully learning how to navigate through the insane world of HMO's and third-party payers, trying desperately to keep focused on the important task of taking care of patients' needs. Maddi had done fairly well with all of this, until Carla. Beautiful Carla Stanze. A simple birth control pill prescription and an eventual death.

But, hadn't that been resolved? Wasn't Mr. Stanze okay or at least under-standing of what had occurred? Maddi still wasn't—she probably never would be—but she no longer felt vulnerable to any legal pursuit.

Perhaps Richards was going to expose and exploit the details of that event. Not for legal purposes, but simply to try to destroy Maddi's credibility. She knew that if Richards decided to go down that road, she wouldn't be presented in a favorable light whatsoever. Her legs felt weak. She knew she had to find out what Richards was up to—if he did in fact have this information—but she wasn't quite sure how to proceed. The vote was fast-approaching and Maddi forced herself to go into the locker room and get ready to head back into the Senate chamber. Richards would have to wait.

Amanda and her committee had deliberated for only a few minutes when they unanimously agreed that Andrew Madison was the man for the job. They had asked him to wait, and he elected to walk down the street and grab some coffee. Soon he ambled back toward the Clinic.

Amanda was walking very quickly toward him with a big smile on her face.

"Allow me to be the first to congratulate you, Dr. Madison. You've gotten the job!"

Andrew smiled and rushed toward Amanda, grabbing her and kissing her, like he'd wanted to do from the minute he saw her sitting there in that meeting.

She kissed him back and they embraced there for several minutes. Suddenly, Amanda pulled away.

"Andrew, I'm not sure it's a good idea to let on that we know one another. I mean, maybe it will seem like I should have excused myself from the vote, or that I was being deceptive, or-"

Andrew put a finger over her mouth to quiet her.

"Don't worry Dr. McKinney—our secret is safe." And he laughed and hugged her. "I'll let you walk back to the Clinic, and I will follow in about 10 minutes. Sound okay with you?"

Amanda gave him a big grin and nodded. She turned and headed back to the Clinic. Andrew knew right then and there that he had made the right deci-sion. He felt alive for the first time in many, many years.

Jeremy was anxiously awaiting the trial in Philadelphia. "One thing," he thought to himself, "about a class-action suit, you aren't in it alone." And he grinned. He wanted to see the great Clarence Morrow stick it to those pricks from Wyatt, Hanson, Richards and Shultz. ("It spells WHoReS, you know," he once told Katy).

He and Clarence had kept in touch since his visit and Clarence offered to have him come to the trial and stay with him at his house in Philly.

Jeremy discussed it with Doc Jones, who agreed to step back in and run things for awhile, and he decided to go ahead and take Clarence up on his offer. He and Katy talked for a long time about whether she should go, and they finally both agreed that it would be better for her to stay and help Doc Jones manage things in Jeremy's absence.

He and Katy spent the last night before the trial together, like they were spending many nights these last few months, and then Jeremy woke early the next morning to catch a flight straight through to Philadelphia. He drove himself to the airport, checked through security, and then stepped onto the plane, sat in his seat, and took a big sigh. "Here I come, you losers, to watch you fail in your efforts to screw me." And with that, he laid back in his seat and gradually fell asleep as his plane headed for Philadelphia, and the trial of the century.

Wilson had been so incredibly busy since he made his big change. He was actually quite surprised. He thought he would have very few patients initially, but, once he let it be known that he would accept payment based on need, he quickly was overwhelmed with patients. The beauty of it was, that he didn't really care if he got paid—as long as he could pay the bills—which were few. He had only one office staff person, and he was living in an inexpensive flat that he paid a relatively small amount of money for each month. The building he was practicing out of belonged to one of his family members, and, although they hated what he had chosen to do, they allowed him to use the space rent-free.

He felt so much better about everything. He couldn't remember when practicing medicine had been so much fun. He had absolutely nothing to lose, and his patients were so appreciative of everything that he did.

Maddi had kept him up to date on things going on in Washington, as well as the outcome of Hank's trial, and he was grateful for that. He had also been contacted by Clarence Morrow, and invited to Philadelphia to watch the class-action suit as it wound its way through the courtroom, but Wilson was simply too busy, and having too much fun, to leave Boston at that time. Clarence agreed to keep him posted as to how things were going. Wilson promised to get down there for a visit sometime in the future.

Wilson knew how important that trial was. He knew that very few doctors would be willing to do what he had done, and if things didn't change, the doctors would continue leaving their practices and America would have itself quite a problem.

He hoped the trial went well, and he hoped Maddi would successfully pass her "Laws." In the meantime he would wake up early, walk to work with a smile on his face, and thank God that he had made the changes that he had.

Maddi walked into the Senate chambers at ten minutes before 9:00. She was surprised by how many Senators had elected to stay in town for this vote, but she knew that for many of them it was a significant vote., being watched closely by several different factions. There were trial lawyers on one side and constituents on the other, and it would be interesting to see who would hold the most sway over some of these congressmen.

Maddi sat at her desk and waited. She made attempts to look busy, and found a pen and paper to write down anything that came to her head. Soon the gavel sounded and the Senate was called to order. Once again, there was discussion, only this time no one ceded their time, and Maddi felt confident she had the votes in place to overcome anything Richards might throw her way.

Discussion proceeded for several minutes, which turned into about one hour, with very little that was new coming to light. They rehashed the points and purpose of the Laws, and reviewed some possible drawbacks with reference to constitutionality, all areas that had been covered before. Finally, it was time for a vote.

Maddi unconsciously began holding her breath. Senators from across the nation were voting for—or against—the legislation referred to as "Maddi's Laws," and Maddi was so nervous she thought she might have to leave the chamber.

As the senators voted, Maddi noticed Richards off to the side in a heated conversation with several of his staff personnel. He was clearly angry, and Maddi couldn't help but wonder what he was up to. Was this when he was going to reveal the "secret" he had on Maddi? Was now the time for him to attempt to ruin her reputation, as well as her efforts at litigation reform?

She waited several more minutes, watching the voting continue and watching Richards pace up and down in the aisle, still discussing something passionately with his staff personnel. Suddenly, she saw Richards turn from his staff with a scowl painted across his broad face. He waved his hand toward them, and they headed out of the chamber, as he took his seat in the third row. Maddi was unsure what this meant, but she was quite fearful that at any moment he would rise and begin speaking, discussing events from so long ago in Maddi's life. But he continued to simply sit and stare down at his briefcase in front of him.

The results of the vote were being televised, and the senators were watching the tallies as well. She was looking around the room, watching as senator after senator cast their votes. After several minutes, Maddi let out a slow breath. The legislation had passed! She couldn't believe it. She was grinning from ear to ear, so amazed that her quixotic effort had actually made it through this Senate chamber.

Suddenly she saw Richards out of the corner of her eye. He was staring at her from across the room, and Maddi could feel his dark eyes burning as he glared directly at her. He then turned away and stomped out of the chamber. His words from earlier that morning started playing over in her head. "You're naïve enough to think the truth matters." Why he hadn't spoken up now Maddi wasn't sure, but she knew she had not heard the last of Senator Richards from Arizona.

Hank had watched the proceedings from Maddi's living room. He jumped up and shouted out loudly when it became apparent that Maddi's legislation had passed the Senate. Commentators were excitedly talking about the ramifications of the success of "Maddi's Laws," and policy wonks and spin meisters from both sides of the aisle were commenting on the benefits—or tragedies—that lay ahead as a result of their passage.

Hank couldn't wait to see Maddi. They had arranged the night before to meet for lunch, but Hank knew he couldn't wait that long. He quickly jumped in the shower and got ready to go intercept Maddi before she left the Senate chamber. They had quite a bit to celebrate and he wanted to do something special. Before he left he made a quick phone call.

He sped down to where Maddi would be coming out of the Capitol building just as she was walking through the door to her car. The media were everywhere and they all wanted to interview Maddi. She answered a few quick questions and then informed all of them that she had no further comment except to say that she was delighted with the result of the vote that morning and she hoped this would be the beginning of a much better future for physicians and for everyone else in America as well. She quickly ran down the steps, trying to get to her car before anyone else cornered her. Suddenly she heard someone yelling for her. She looked out and spotted Hank between several of the parked cars. When she saw him her face lit up and she ran toward him. When she reached him she jumped into his arms and he began twirling around, both of them were laughing, and Maddi nearly crying from joy.

"Can you believe it, Hank? We did it! We really did it! I can't believe it!"

Several of the media crew standing around began filming Maddi running toward Hank and Hank and Maddi both laughed at the thought of the two of them on the nightly news with Peter Jennings, passionately embracing one another.

Hank grabbed Maddi and hugged her tight.

"Let's go somewhere—right now. Somewhere special."

Maddi was looking at him curiously. "But where?" she asked.

"I can't tell you. Just get in."

They jumped in the car and Hank proceeded to head out of the parking garage, turned down several side streets, and eventually found his way to route 395, then to route 95. They headed south for several minutes, and finally Maddi couldn't stand it any longer. "Where are you taking me, you kidnapper?"

Hank started laughing. "You'll see. Just hang on, we'll be there in a just a little bit."

As they began getting closer to Philadelphia, Maddi knew exactly where they were going. "What if he isn't there?" Maddi asked.

"Oh, he's there. I phoned him before I left your place. He's expecting us."

Maddi leaned over and hugged Hank's shoulder.

Hank continued talking. "Maddi, his trial is about to get underway and he wants us there. Your legislation has finally passed the Senate, and I think the timing couldn't be any better. What d'ya' say?"

Maddi smiled and nodded, and they both sat back looking forward to seeing their friend, Clarence, as he prepared for the trial of the century.

Andrew walked back into the Clinic, where one of the interviewers was waiting for him.

"So, Dr. Madison, did you find a place to have a nice cup of coffee?"

Andrew replied, with a smile on his face, "I certainly did. They say that it's the best cup of coffee in Columbia."

Both men grinned at the reference to the ad in the window of the local diner, and the interviewer escorted Andrew back toward where they had conducted the interview. They were all seated there, including Amanda, and Andrew proceeded to sit down.

The same interviewer then looked over at him.

"You indicated that you would like to make this area your home. Well, we are in a position to help you look at some real estate." He grinned from ear to ear, so pleased with his clever way of letting Andrew know he had been hired.

Andrew acted surprised. "So I got the job?" he asked. Amanda grinned to herself.

"You certainly did, sir. Now, how soon can you move from Canada and get started?"

Andrew thought for a few seconds. "I can start in about two or three weeks. I mean, if that's allright with you." He paused for a moment, and then added "I'm leaving nothing behind, and you're right, I'm here to stay. I just have a few small things to take care of before I make my move here."

They all nodded in agreement, and proceeded to show him to his "office-" a corner area of the large room he had walked by earlier, and they quickly introduced him to the small staff and some of the patients who were mulling around.

After several minutes, when it was nearly 5:00, Andrew decided to head for his hotel. He was anxious to find a place to stay, not sure if Amanda and he were in a position to stay together, and he decided to just stick with the hotel room for now.

As he was leaving, he caught Amanda's eye, and then walked over toward her, handing her the Hotel information when he passed by her. She grabbed the scrap of paper and quickly walked off in the other direction.

Andrew grinned to himself and headed back to his hotel room. He had forgotten his cell phone in the room and he grabbed it now and looked to see if he had any messages. Only one. He didn't recognize the number but there was a voice mail message. Just as he was retrieving the message, he heard a knock on the door. He opened the door and saw Amanda standing in front of him. He had the phone to his ear, and motioned her to come in, smiling the entire time. When he had heard the message he hung up the phone.

"Who was it?" Amanda asked.

"You want to listen?"

Amanda gave Andrew a puzzled look. "Sure," she said.

Andrew played the message back for Amanda.

"Hello Andrew! It's Clarence. I'm not sure if you will get this message all the way up in Canada, but, anyway, I thought I'd let you know that the Trial is about to get underway. I would love your presence and your support if you can. Oh yeah, and if you happen to speak to Amanda ask her to come as well. Let me know. Call me at 215-555-4875 and let me know."

Amanda grinned at Andrew. "Well, are you going?"

He reached over and hugged her. "Only if you're going with me."

They both smiled and then kissed a long, deep kiss. They embraced one another, forgetting about the trial, the Clinic or anything else for the time being. It was just Amanda and Andrew, wrapped in one another's arms, touching and caressing and connecting like both of them had been longing to do for months.

Several hours later they were still holding one another. They eventually got back to making plans to attend the trial. Amanda was due for some time off, and Andrew wasn't scheduled to begin his new job for several weeks. They made their plans and decided to leave in the morning. The rest of the night was spent with dinner in the room, the TV on, and neither one watching it, as they made love repeatedly throughout the long night. They both knew that they were ready for anything, and going to Philadelphia in the morning was a good way to start.

CHAPTER XLVI

"Ladies and Gentlemen of the Jury." Clarence Morrow's loud, booming voice reminded Maddi of what God must have sounded like when he was giving Moses the Ten Commandments.

"We are all here today to decide the fate of 3,432 doctors across this great nation. They have been accused of considerable wrong doing, not the least of which is the administration of a deadly medication, with full knowledge of its potential to kill."

The courtroom was completely quiet, as everyone listened closely to the opening arguments of a trial that had been portrayed for weeks in the media as The Trial of the Century.

All the important players were there. The Trial Lawyers Association had a representative—the new assistant to the new President—a man by the name of Billy Robertson, who was sitting immediately behind the desk of the lawyers from Wyatt, Hanson, Richards, and Shultz.

Next to him sat an aide to Senator Richards, and behind them were several families whose loved ones had been 'victimized' by the medication known as diacam.

On the other side of the aisle sat many from the media, as well as several doctors from across the nation. Directly behind Clarence Morrow's table sat Jeremy Bourne and several doctors from Arizona.

Maddi, Hank, Andrew and Amanda were all seated in the back of the courtroom on same side of the aisle as the other doctors. They had all arrived the day before and had spent a delightful evening having drinks and dinner at Clarence's home.

They had been introduced to Jeremy, and they all took a liking to him very quickly. He was ingratiating and funny and soon he felt like 'one of the gang.'

They had all turned in early, and were now anxiously awaiting what they hoped would be a turning point in litigation and medicine. They—and everyone there—knew the importance of this trial. More than Diacam and more than the physicians were on trial. The entire system of both Medicine and Law were on trial in this courtroom today. What happened here would impact the future of class-action suits across the land.

Clarence had confided in the four of them last night that, if and when, he won this trial, he planned on filing a counter suit, aimed at the lawyers of the firm Wyatt, Hanson, Richards and Shultz. In the suit he would claim that they used unjust legal maneuvering in an attempt to gain massive amounts of money, while the plaintiffs themselves were set up to gain very little. This, of course, is what always happened with class-action lawsuits—the lawyers got rich, the entity they were suing went broke, and their clients got very little in the way of compensation. Clarence was hoping to create a precedent that no longer permitted this corrupt approach to the Law. It was a long shot, but it was worth pursuing, if for no other reason than to create public awareness of one of the most sinister aspects of Law in America.

The lawyers from the firm of Wyatt, Hanson, Richards, and Shultz were all dressed in the finest suits, surrounded by many underlings from their firm, all eager to be part of this prestigious firm in such a well-publicized trial. The underlings sat by waiting, as though they might actually have something to offer in the prosecution of these villainous doctors.

Clarence preferred to work alone and to sit alone at all of his trials, and today was certainly no different. He had toyed with the idea of having Jeremy sit with him—they had become good friends over the last couple of months—but then thought better of it, knowing that he had always done his best work—and his best trials—sitting alone at the table.

He felt that it would work to his advantage, particularly today, as Shultz and his massive law firm took up nearly half the courtroom with their presence. He hoped he would achieve a bit of a "David and Goliath" appearance, and the media would jump favorably on such a contrast.

He had worked long and hard on his opening statement, knowing that whatever tone he set at that moment would likely last throughout the trial. He had rehearsed it several times, seeking just the right inflection and the appropriate nodding of his head, knowing these were the impressions that would stay with a jury.

His booming voice echoed throughout the courtroom, as he continued with his opening statement.

"You will be asked soon to decide the fate of these doctors. There will be evidence presented in this courtroom which will imply that—with full knowledge and forethought—these 3,432 doctors knowingly prescribed a deadly medication.

"You will be inundated with medical jargon and medication side effects and it will, at times, be difficult to keep all of the information straight. Sprinkled within all of this scientific information will be subtle innuendo, and it is this innuendo that I would ask you now to be particularly wary of.

"This large law firm has made it their business to cleverly manipulate the truth into obscurities and implications that result in conclusions that are inaccurate and harmful.

"Why do they do this? Is it for the purpose of bringing about change and improvements in our lives? Is it for the purpose of punishing wrong-doers so that they are unable to do wrong anymore?

"No! No, I tell you. They care nothing about these things. The reason this massive firm is sprawled out before you today is for the sole purpose of earning huge amounts of money. The wealth these trial lawyers will potentially earn from this trial means more to this firm than any revelations they might bring forth today.

"It is possible that there are lessons for all to learn here today. It is also important that we examine issues such as these about to be discussed so as to avoid potential problems and conflicts in the future.

"So, I ask you only one thing here and now. Listen closely to both what I say, and what is said by this large law firm. Don't miss a single detail. And then, when this trial is over, take all of this information and put it through your sifter of truth and see what remains. Please don't allow the cleverness and the impressiveness of this oversized law firm to muddy the waters of what is going on here today. For it is simply this: a drug manufacturer, in good faith, desiring both financial gain and improvement in the human condition, created a medication, known as Diacam. They then put this medication through extensive testing—the most extensive testing regimen existent in the world today—and the drug came out of that testing with approval and readiness. It did, as advertised, aid diabetics with the successful management of their disease like no other medication has ever done before. Unfortunately, as time went on, it became clear that there were drawbacks to this wonderful medicine. The drawbacks involved its effects on the liver. The effects were similar in nature and extent to those associated with Tylenol. These effects were then made known to physicians who acted accordingly. They—in good faith—began monitoring liver function and advising their patients to avoid liver toxins. To the extent that patients heeded this advice—and therein lies the rub—they continued healthily enjoying the benefits of Diacam. To the extent, however, that patients did not heed their physicians' admonitions to avoid liver toxins, they wound up suffering the consequences of Diacam's effects on their overly-challenged livers.

"What I am trying to say is this: the patients often have a hand in their outcomes and it must be recognized that they therefore bear some responsibility in how things turn out."

This last comment drew some frowns from many present in the courtroom. To be asked to assume responsibility for one's own wrongdoing was not a very popular notion. Clarence did not appear to be affected by their frowning in the least. He continued on, now a bit more animated.

"Are you aware, that almost no one dies of lung cancer, unless they are a smoker? And that almost no one dies of cirrhosis of the liver unless they are a drinker? And that almost no one dies of obesity-related illnesses unless they are obese? What is the common denominator in all of this? Choice. In all instances these individuals choose those behaviors and those actions that adversely affect their health and their lives. I am not condemning those choices, only suggesting that somewhere along the way we all need to be held accountable for our own choices.

"I request that you keep this in mind as you hear the evidence presented today and throughout this trial. Remember the role each one of us plays in our ultimate health, and remember that—if we want to continue to be able to choose—we must accept responsibility for the outcome of our choices.

"Listen closely to what the firm of Wyatt, Hanson, Richards and Shultz is advocating here today. I submit to you that what they want you to buy into is the concept that others are responsible for our choices. Others need to pay when a choice we've made ends up with a bad outcome. Others are to blame when things go wrong. Others, always others.

"Please don't punish these 3,432 doctors for the problems associated with the use of Diacam. Remember that no drug is perfectly safe, and that—more often than not—it is what we do to ourselves beyond the medication that ultimately determines our outcome with that medication.

"Don't let these doctors take the hit for choices others have made. Diacam was a great drug. It could still be a great drug if individuals could modify their behaviors accordingly. The fact that they couldn't—or wouldn't—should not be blamed on these physicians. They only wanted to help. They want to continue to help. Trials such as these make it more and more difficult for them to do so or to want to do so.

"Look out and see what is happening to doctors across this nation. They are tired of taking the blame for others' choices. They are tired of acting in good faith, only to find themselves at the wrong end of a lawsuit. They are tired of pushing forward one step, only to be pushed back two. These doctors are tired. They are tired. And they are leaving. One by one they are leaving their beloved profession.

"Let them know here and now that you appreciate what they do and why they do it. Let them know that their sleepless nights and their years of intense schooling are valued. Let them know that this type of lawsuit will not be honored any longer. Let them know that you, too are tired of a system that is so incredibly flawed.

"Let's start here today sending the message that personal responsibility—a principle this great country was founded on—still holds meaning for those of us sitting here now. We shall turn the corner in this courtroom at this time, thereby creating a better world for everyone of us here today."

Clarence had been standing directly in front of the jury while he said his opening statement. He now slowly turned and walked to his table, where he proceeded to sit down—all alone.

After about a minute, Mr. Richard Shultz, from the law firm of Wyatt, Hanson, Richards and Shultz stood up, calmly pressed his custom-tailored suit with both hands, and proceeded to stand where Clarence had just been standing. He cleared his throat and began speaking in a soft but forceful voice. He, too, seemed well-prepared for the magnitude of this trial.

"Ladies and gentlemen of the jury. Although I greatly respect Mr. Morrow and his well—known brilliance, I feel it is my duty to make you aware of some important inconsistencies in his opening statement."

At this comment, Maddi and her friends rolled their eyes. They all knew that they would tire of Mr. Richard Shultz very quickly.

"First, he has decided to inform you of our financial desires. Let me tell you—although I think it is obvious—this law firm is in no way in need of any financial assistance. We are a successful and wealthy law firm, and I am not ashamed of that fact.

"Like many of the physicians sitting here today, we have worked hard at our chosen profession and are not ashamed to enjoy our subsequent wealth.

"As to his admonition that we may try to color the truth for the sole purpose of monetary gain, let me say only this it is he who will try to alter the facts. It is Mr. Morrow who will try to deflect the tragedy of the medication Diacam and turn it into some kind of personal responsibility matter, when we all know—or will know after this trial—that this drug is flawed and anyone who prescribed it, knowing its flaws, did so negligently.

"No matter how hard the esteemed Mr. Morrow tries to change that reality he cannot. Diacam killed people. Doctors prescribed it, knowing it could do so. That is the very tenet of negligence and the essence of malpractice. Those are the facts. I will leave it up to you to do as Mr. Morrow has asked—sift through these facts and make the only conclusion that one could from such facts. These doctors did wrong. Knowingly. And many good people have died. Many others are damaged. These doctors cannot simply walk away from that. Please, don't let them. Thank you."

Although brief compared to Clarence's opener, Mr. Shultz' statements were powerful and convincing. Maddi and the others exchanged glances of concern. Clarence seemed unmoved by anything that Mr. Shultz had said, sitting as he had been, thoughtfully listening, giving away nothing.

The Judge—the Honorable Stephen H. Douglas—banged his gavel, initiating the Trial of the Century. He was a large, imposing presence, with a wiry mustache and only a smattering of hair on his head. His dark eyes looked out into his courtroom with depth and intensity. Clearly Judge Douglas had seen a lot in his time on the bench. He nodded toward Mr. Shultz, signifying that he should proceed.

Mr. Shultz once again stood and called his first witness.

"Mr. James Crow."

Jeremy Bourne shifted perceptively in his seat just behind Clarence, as he heard a familiar name being called. Old Jimmy Crow. The alcoholic. Jeremy knew exactly where this line of questioning was headed. And, even though he didn't feel responsible for the outcome, he knew that the questioning of Jimmy was going to be very uncomfortable.

Jimmy Crow, looking only slightly better than usual, slowly made his way to the witness stand. His hair was poorly combed, and his suit a size too big, with a somewhat wrinkled shirt underneath. He stepped up to the witness stand, and then slowly sat down.

After being sworn in he kept shifting to find a comfortable position. His anxiety was evident. Mr. Shultz approached him and smiled, trying to alleviate his nervousness.

"Hello, Mr. Crow. Would you please tell the court your name?"

Jimmy swallowed deeply, and then responded to the question.

"Jimmy Crow."

"And where do you live, Mr. Crow?"

"On the Pima Indian Reservation in Arizona."

"Are you familiar with the medication known as Diacam?"

Jimmy grinned just a bit—appearing to enjoy himself.

"Yessir. I was on that medication, until it nearly killed me."

Mr. Shultz paused nearly imperceptibly, waiting for Clarence to object, but he sat silently, with his eyes fixed on Mr. Crow.

Mr. Shultz proceeded with his questioning.

"Why do you say that, Mr. Crow?"

"'Cause that's what that letter you sent me said."

There was a unified chuckle from the right side of the courtroom, and Mr. Shultz grinned as well, trying to decrease the impact of Jimmy's last statement.

"Yes, Mr. Crow, our letter asked you about taking diacam, and it informed you of its risks. Is it fair to say then that our letter was the first indication you had of those risks?"

Jimmy thought for a moment. His brow was furrowed and his head turned to an angle as he was trying to decide how to answer the question.

Jeremy sat waiting for Jimmy to say "no," as he knew he had told him of the risks on numerous occasions.

Suddenly Jimmy spoke. "Yes."

"Yes, what, Mr. Crow?"

"Yes, that letter was the first time I had heard anything about those risks."

"Liar!" Jeremy had stood up immediately. "That is a lie, Jimmy, and you know it!"

"Order! Order in this courtroom!" Judge Douglas was clearly unhappy with the outburst, and banged his gavel loudly.

Jeremy sat down shaking his head.

Jimmy bowed his head, unable to meet Jeremy's eyes looking directly at him.

Mr. Shultz continued.

"Now tell me, Jimmy, what did we tell you those risks were?"

"You said that I shouldn't drink alcohol if I was on Diacam, and that if I was unable to stop drinking alcohol that I should never have been placed on that drug. Then you said that if I had taken that drug—and I was still drinking alcohol, that that was a problem and to call your number and you would help me with my case."

There were a few smiles in the courtroom as people recognized the tried and true methods of the class action attorney. Mr. Shultz was not fazed in the least. He continued.

"Now, Jimmy, did you suffer any consequences because you took Diacam?"

Jimmy had been well-prepared for this question. He sat up straight in his seat and answered his very well-rehearsed answer.

"Yes sir, I did. My liver is now diseased. It was not diseased before, but it is now."

"Thank you, Mr. Crow. That is all I have."

Jimmy began to stand, while the Judge asked Clarence if he had any questions of this witness.

"I do, your honor."

"Please sit back down, Mr. Crow," Judge Douglas advised.

Clarence stood up slowly and deliberately, walking toward the witness stand. He took in a long, slow breath, looked directly at Jimmy and began.

"Mr. Crow. What is your favorite drink—alcoholic, I mean?"

Mr. Shultz immediately stood up. "Objection! Relevance, your honor?"

Clarence responded. "If you please, your honor, the relevance will become quite clear soon."

Judge Douglas peered down at Clarence. "I'll allow it, but hurry up and get to the point, counselor."

Clarence nodded, and continued. "Once again, your favorite drink, Mr. Crow?"

Jimmy thought for a moment, then replied cautiously.

"Well, I guess I'd have to say that my favorite drink is beer, just good ole' beer."

"I see. Any particular kind, Mr. Crow?"

Jimmy once again had to think for a moment.

"Well, I'd have to say that Budweiser is my favorite. Yeah, Bud it is." He paused for a moment, then added, "it used to be Coor's, but that beer was just too expensive."

Clarence nodded. "I see. When was it that you used to drink Coor's, Mr. Crow?"

Jimmy frowned as he tried to recall. "Why, that's been ages ago. Like 15 years ago, before me and my first wife were married."

Clarence smiled at Jimmy. "I see. So you've been drinking beer for quite a long while?"

Mr. Shultz jumped from his chair, startling the gentleman sitting next to him. "Objection! How long Mr. Crow has been drinking has absolutely no bearing on this case, your honor."

Judge Douglas glanced over at Mr. Shultz, then back to Clarence. "Mr. Morrow, could you please move this along?"

"Certainly, your honor." Clarence walked over to the jury, and then repeated the question.

"You've been drinking beer for quite a while, correct Mr. Crow?"

Jimmy nodded.

Clarence continued, looking directly at the faces sitting in the Jury box. "Would it be fair to say, Jimmy, that you've been a heavy drinker for at least 15 years?"

Jimmy looked over at Clarence. He nodded his head, then added, "Actually, I've been puttin' away the beer pretty heavily since I was in high school—so, about 35 years."

Clarence grinned, as did many sitting in the courtroom.

"Tell me, Mr. Crow, did Dr. Jeremy Bourne place you on the medication known as Diacam?"

Jimmy looked out into the courtroom to where Jeremy was sitting. He bowed his head. He nodded. "Yessir."

"What was he treating you for, Mr. Crow?"

"My diabetes. I was what they called a la-bile diabetic, which means my sugar jumped all over the place, until Jeremy came along. He told me it didn't have to be like that and that Diacam could maybe make my diabetes easier to manage."

Clarence continued looking at the Jury. "Did Dr. Bourne perform any blood tests before he prescribed the Diacam?"

"Yessir. And he kept sticking me every 3 months. That was annoying."

Clarence nodded. "I imagine it was. Why on earth was he sticking you so often?"

"Oh, something about liver damage. But I-" then suddenly Jimmy stopped mid sentence. He looked over at Clarence, and then at the table where the big law firm was sitting. Mr. Shultz was shaking his head imperceptibly.

Clarence turned to look at Jimmy. "You were saying, Mr. Crow?"

Jimmy looked back at Clarence. "I told him that my liver was just fine, because I'd been drinkin' forever and nothing had happened to me yet."

Clarence turned back toward the jury. "And what did Dr. Bourne say to that?"

Jimmy paused and shifted several times in his seat. Finally he responded. "He told me that I had to quit drinking."

"And then what did you say?"

Jimmy bowed his head. Very quietly he muttered, "that I would."

"I'm sorry, Mr. Crow, I couldn't hear you."

Jimmy looked up, and straight at Clarence. "That I would."

Clarence turned to face the judge. "No further questions, your honor."

The judge asked Mr. Shultz if he had any questions, and he shook his head. "You may step down, Mr. Crow."

Mr. Shultz's next witness was a woman from Illinois by the name of Sandy Skallows. She introduced herself and Mr. Shultz proceeded with his questioning. Much of what he asked was along the same lines as Mr. Crow. There was the implication that Mrs. Skallows had not been adequately warned about the potential risks of Diacam, and, as a result had suffered severe and significant liver damage.

When it was time for Clarence to cross-examine the witness, he stood and approached her slowly, grabbing a piece of paper while doing so.

"Good day, Mrs. Skallows." He handed her the piece of paper. "Could you please tell this courtroom what it is that is written on that piece of paper?"

Mrs. Skallows glanced down at the paper in her hands and started reading.

"Lab Report for Sandy Skallows." Suddenly she stopped. She looked up at Clarence. He nodded, asking her to continue. Finally, hesitantly, she did so. "Hepatitis A—negative; Hepatitis B—negative; Hepatitis C—positive."

Clarence took the paper from her, showed it to Mr. Shultz, and submitted it as exhibit A. He then approached the witness stand. "When was that lab test done, Mrs. Skallows?"

Mrs. Skallows was frowning. "Ten years ago."

"Why was it done, Mrs. Skallows?"

"Because my ex-husband had been diagnosed with hepatitis C and my doctor at that time thought I should be checked."

"I see. Did you receive treatment for the hepatitis?"

"No. I hadn't gotten sick from it yet. My liver labs always came back okay."

Clarence now walked over to stand in front of the Jury. "Your current doctor, the one who placed you on Diacam. Was he the same doctor who had ordered the lab test?"

"No. I didn't want anyone to know about the hepatitis, so I changed doctors."

"I see. Did you tell your new doctor about this diagnosis?

Sandy Skallows bent her head and started fidgeting with a handkerchief in her hands. "No. Like I said, I didn't want anyone to know."

Clarence continued to look straight at the jurors. "Did your present doctor advise you about the risks of Diacam hurting your liver?"

Mrs. Skallows continued to fidget with her handkerchief. Finally, she looked up. "Yes. Yes, he warned me. He even asked me if I had any history of a liver problem. But I told him I didn't. Because the hepatitis C had never been a problem before." By now, Mrs. Skallows was starting to cry. "I still think that drug is what hurt me! I was fine until I took that medication. My liver is not okay because of Diacam!"

"That is all I have for this witness," Clarence calmly said.

Mr. Shultz had no further questions and a tearful Mrs. Skallows stepped down from the witness stand. The trial continued.

Mr. Shultz called several more witnesses, some who had damage to their livers, and some whose family members had died after having taken the Diacam. With each witness, Clarence would find either a preexisting liver problem, or a liver-damaging behavior that he would bring to light.

Maddi and her friends had watched each witness as they were paraded in front of the jury, trying to decide how the jury was interpreting all the evidence being presented. They felt that overall, Clarence had done quite well, but they knew that it was all so confusing, and that the jury may not be able to make the connection Clarence was wanting them to make between the behaviors and histories of the patients and their resulting problems with Diacam.

Mr. Shultz then called Mr. Daniel Williams to the stand.

Danny Williams looked to be about 30 years old, well-dressed, with a confident stride. He stepped into the witness stand, took his oath, and proceeded to sit down.

Mr. Shultz had Danny introduce himself. Following the introduction, Mr. Shultz began his questioning.

"Mr. Williams, are you familiar with the medication known as Diacam?"

"Yes sir, I am. It is the drug responsible for killing my mother. With the help from Dr. Green, the prescribing physician."

"I see. How is it that Diacam killed your mother?"

"She had had diabetes for years. She was placed on Diacam, and died within a year of starting it. In the hospital they told her that the Diacam had ruined her liver and that she was going to die." Mr. Williams was becoming emotional by this point. "We all flew to her side, but some of us didn't get there in time. Although Mom didn't die alone, she only had some of her babies at her side."

At this point Mr. Williams bowed his head and was visibly sobbing. Mr. Shultz indicated that he was finished with the questioning of Mr. Williams.

Clarence stood and approached Mr. Williams, who was wiping his eyes, having recovered to some degree. Clarence looked straight in his eyes.

"I am very sorry to hear of your mother's death, and the fact that not everyone made it to her side when she died." Clarence seemed genuinely concerned, and Mr. Williams nodded, seemingly appreciative of the sentiment. Clarence continued.

"Tell me, Mr. Williams. Were you very familiar with your mother's medical habits?"

Danny appeared to be puzzled by the question. Clarence restated the question.

"I mean, did you keep track of how often she saw her doctor, how often she obtained the requisite labs, and how routinely she took her medications?"

Danny thought for a moment. "Well, I have no reason but to think that Mom did all she was supposed to."

Clarence walked over to his table and grabbed what appeared to be a medical chart. He walked back over and handed it to Mr. Williams.

"Could you please tell us what you are holding, Mr. Williams?"

Danny looked down at the chart in front of him. "It appears to be my Mom's medical chart."

Clarence nodded. "Yes sir, it is. Now, could you please read the entry dated March 3rd, the very last page of the chart?"

Mr. Williams leaned forward a bit and began to read from the last page of the chart. "Note. I have on this day willfully dismissed this patient from my practice due to repeated non-compliance." Danny looked up at Clarence. Clarence stared back at him. He continued reading. "After several requests for routine lab work to be done, and after repeated calls to come in for regular appointments, I feel that Mrs. Vickie Williams is no longer willing to do what I require in order to insure her safety. I will no longer fill her medications, although I have given her refills to last until such time she can find another doctor. I have sent her this information by certified mail on this date, and I have included in that letter that I will be available for her on an emergency basis only while she finds another physician. Dr. William Green."

Danny looked up from the chart, his eyes narrowed to slits, and handed the chart back to Clarence.

Clarence turned, looked at the judge, and informed him that he had no further questions for Mr. Williams.

Mr. Shultz then had several experts take the stand, all testifying to the dangers inherent in Diacam, and how only careful monitoring and selectivity of patients could ensure safety.

The trial continued for days along this same line. Clarence continued to reveal weaknesses in testimony, based either on non-compliance or pre-existing circumstances, making sure to illustrate that any damage to the liver was never from the Diacam itself but always from a behavior or a condition that was the patient's own doing.

Finally, half way through the second week of the trial, Mr. Shultz called his final witness.

"I'd like to call Dr. Richard Prickle to the stand."

Maddi and Hank looked at one another with their mouths wide open in amazement. Maddi leaned over and whispered to Hank, "he certainly gets around." Hank smiled and nodded.

Dr. Prickle slowly made his way to the stand. His short little body seemed out of proportion to his very large, balding head. Were it not for the serious nature of this trial, he would appear quite comical.

He stepped up to the witness stand and was sworn in. He sat down, rearranging his legs several times, apparently having difficulty getting comfortable.

Mr. Shultz stood and approached him. "Dr. Prickle, could you please state your name and your qualifications for the court?"

"Certainly. I am Dr. Richard Prickle. I am a certified gerontologist, as well as a certified family practitioner, earning my undergraduate degree from Penn State University, and my Medical Degree from Johns Hopkins." He sat there beaming with pride at his accomplishments.

Mr. Shultz continued. "You appear to be well-qualified, doctor. Now, tell me if you would, your expert opinion on the medication known as Diacam, its usefulness in practice and its safety profile."

Dr. Prickle sat up straight, smoothed his hands over his pants and began. "I will state here today—unequivocally—that in no way should doctors have prescribed Diacam once there were any questions concerning its safety. The evidence had come pouring in rather rapidly and quite clearly that Diacam was not safe. This information was available to all physicians, and I strongly believe that any doctor willing to continue to prescribe Diacam once this information was available was negligent at the least, and possibly even criminal."

This statement provoked quite a hum throughout the courtroom and Judge Douglas was forced to use his gavel, and his intimidating voice to silence the crowd. Once silence in the courtroom was restored, Dr. Prickle continued.

"I believe the doctors that were willing to do this were simply choosing the path of least resistance, willing to risk their patient's health simply for the sake of good blood sugar values. I feel this behavior led directly and indirectly to the deaths and injury of many innocent patients."

The hum resumed and, once again, Judge Douglas gaveled the courtroom to order.

Mr. Shultz then turned to the jury and stated that he had no further questions for Dr. Prickle.

Clarence had allowed all of these comments and the disruption in the courtroom to proceed without his acknowledgement. He had showed no emotion whatsoever when Dr. Prickle made his statements, and he remained expressionless throughout his testimony.

He now stood slowly, remaining at his table a bit longer than was necessary, as though gathering his thoughts in preparation for battle. He walked deliberately toward the witness stand, keeping his eyes on Dr. Prickle the entire time. When he had reached the stand, he placed one hand on it and began.

"Hello, Dr. Prickle. Tell me, have you ever testified as an expert witness prior to this case?"

Mr. Shultz immediately rose to his feet. "Objection! Whether or not Dr. Prickle has testified before today is totally irrelevant!"

Clarence turned to face the judge, speaking with his unchanging calmness. "I respectfully disagree, your honor. If, in fact, Dr. Prickle has testified before now as an expert witness—especially if it has been numerous times—will be useful information for the jury to have. They will then appreciate the fact that perhaps Dr. Prickle is motivated by something other than a desire for the truth."

"Your honor!" screamed Mr. Shultz.

"My chambers now!" bellowed Judge Douglas.

The three gentlemen proceeded to Judge Douglas' chambers. They discussed their different points of view, and Judge Douglas finally came down on the side of Mr. Shultz, stating that he felt it would be prejudicial to have the jurors consider Dr. Prickle's prior expert-witness experiences.

The three of them then proceeded back out to the courtroom, and Judge Douglas requested that the Jury disregard Mr. Morrow's last question. Once said, Clarence was signaled by the judge to continue his cross examination of Dr. Prickle.

Clarence didn't miss a beat, once again, hiding any disappointment he may have felt over the judge's ruling.

"Dr. Prickle. You have stated here today that these doctors acted carelessly in exposing their patients to the risks associated with the medication Diacam."

Dr. Prickle nodded, beads of sweat now evident on his forehead, the concerns over his prior expert witness experiences apparently unnerving him to some degree. "Yes," he said.

Clarence paused and then turned to face the jury, while still talking to Dr. Prickle.

"Are you aware of a medication known as amiodarone?"

Dr. Prickle angled his head a bit as he contemplated the question. "Yes, I am. It is used for certain arrhythmias."

Clarence continued. "Yes, it is. As a matter of fact, it can be a life-saving medication. Isn't that correct, Dr. Prickle?"

Dr. Prickle nodded again, uttering a quiet "yes."

Clarence then walked over to his desk and grabbed a piece of paper, which he handed to Dr. Prickle.

"Please, doctor, if you will, tell me what you have there in front of you?"

Dr. Prickle perched his reading glasses onto his nose and glanced at the paper in front of him.

"It is a drug information sheet on amiodarone."

The many lawyers representing Wyatt, Hanson, Richards, and Shultz were looking intently at Clarence while this questioning was underway. Mr. Shultz was frowning, almost imperceptibly.

Clarence turned to the jury once again, addressing his question to Dr. Prickle. "Would you please read the portion highlighted in yellow, sir?"

Dr. Prickle looked down over his nose through his reading glasses and read from the highlighted information in front of him.

"Adverse reactions: Fatigue, dizziness, bradycardia, new or exacerbated arrhythmias-"

Dr. Prickle looked up from where he was reading, a look of puzzlement on his face.

Clarence turned toward Dr. Prickle and looked directly into his eyes. "Could you please tell the court what bradycardia, and new or exacerbated arrhythmias means?"

Dr. Prickle cleared his throat and sat up a bit straighter in his chair, clearly beaming at his vast knowledge of the medical field.

"Bradycardia is when the heart slows down a bit too much, and new or exacerbated arrhythmias means that a new irregular heartbeat or a worsening of the one you're already treating may occur."

Clarence now turned again to face the jury. He pulled himself up, standing tall and impressive in front of them.

"So, in other words, this drug might be fatal to its user?"

Dr. Prickle suddenly changed his expression. He now understood where Mr. Morrow was heading with his questioning. He nodded.

"Doctor, you're nodding your head. Do you mean to answer 'yes' to my question?"

"Yes," he spat.

"To your knowledge, doctor, has amiodarone been removed from the market? Is it unavailable to a prescribing physician?"

Dr. Prickle shifted in his chair. "Well, no, but-"

"So, we have here a medication which has been known to cause harm, yet it is still available and still being used?"

"Yes, but-"

"Why do you think that is, sir?"

Dr. Prickle paused and cleared his throat. He shifted his position once again. "I imagine it is because of its potential benefits."

"Exactly!" shouted Clarence, causing many of the jurors and the observers in the courtroom to jump a bit in their seats. Maddi grinned to herself, pleased to see the usually-reserved Clarence Morrow injecting some emotion into his case. Clarence continued.

"Exactly. The drug has potential benefits great enough to justify the potential risk of taking it. Now, tell me Dr. Prickle, are you familiar with a medication known as Lipitor?"

Many heads nodded in the courtroom, as the familiarity of this medication immediately made them feel a bit more knowledgeable and connected with the proceedings than they had up to this point.

Dr. Prickle sat up straight, adjusting his glasses once again, thankful they were heading a different direction.

"Certainly. It is used for cholesterol management."

"Correct." Clarence headed back over to his table and produced another piece of paper. He handed it to Dr. Prickle.

"Would you please state what you are looking at here, and then please read what is highlighted in yellow?"

Dr. Prickle once again looked down over his nose, through his glasses, and responded.

"This is a drug sheet on Lipitor. The highlighted area reads as follows: Precautions: Monitor liver function (before therapy, at 12 weeks after starting, or after a dose increase, then periodically); reduce dose or discontinue if serum transaminase levels reach three times normal, and if they persist. History of liver disease. Avoid significant alcohol ingestion."

"Thank you, doctor. Will you now, once again, summarize for us lay people what all of that means?"

Dr. Prickle once again adjusted himself in his seat and began.

"Well, it is recommended that you do blood tests faithfully to keep an eye on the functioning of the liver and that you stop the medication if the liver enzymes are elevated."

Clarence nodded. "Correct. If they are elevated how high, doctor?"

"Three times normal."

Clarence walked over to face the jury once again. "Three times normal. Not just a bit above normal, but three times normal. Is that correct, doctor?"

Dr. Prickle nodded. Clarence continued.

"What else does the highlighted portion state, doctor?"

Dr. Prickle glanced down at the sheet in front of him once again. He then looked up and replied in a much quieter voice. "Avoid significant alcohol ingestion while using this medication."

Clarence stood looking down, standing in front of the jury, allowing what Dr. Prickle had just said to sink in. He then walked over to the doctor, moved closer to him and quietly spoke.

"Tell me, doctor. If you were to prescribe Lipitor, and you were to advise your patient to avoid alcohol, and they assured you that they would, would you believe them?"

"I'd be obligated to believe them—at least initially."

"Then, when you did lab work, and it showed very mild liver function elevations—much less than the three times normal elevations cautioned about in the advisement—would you necessarily stop the Lipitor?"

Dr. Prickle thought for a moment.

"No, not if the patient was benefiting greatly from the drug."

"Very good, doctor." Clarence walked for a third time over to his table and once again grabbed a piece of paper. He brought it over to Dr. Prickle, who was wiping his brow with a handkerchief.

"One last time, doctor. Please tell the court what you have before you, and then read the portion that is highlighted."

Dr. Prickle—for a third time—did what was asked of him.

"This is the drug information sheet for Diacam. The highlighted portion is as follows: Precautions: Monitor liver function (before therapy, at 12 weeks after starting, or with a dose increase, then periodically); reduce dose or discontinue if serum transaminass levels reach three times normal and if they persist. History of liver disease. Avoid significant alcohol ingestion."

"Thank you, doctor. Are you familiar with Diacam, doctor?

Dr. Prickle chuckled at what he felt was the obvious nature of the question. "Of course I am. It is—was—used to treat diabetes. But, it killed people and now it has been removed from the market."

There was a hum throughout the courtroom, and Judge Douglas banged his gavel. Dr. Prickle smiled to himself, pleased with his cleverness and his brilliance in regaining the offensive.

Clarence grinned as well, and nodded.

"Well, that is exactly what we are here to decide, now isn't it Dr. Prickle?" drawing out the first part of his name just a bit longer than necessary.

Maddi and her friends smiled in the back of the courtroom.

Dr. Prickle glared up at Clarence and had no response.

Clarence continued, barely missing a beat.

"Now, doctor, I ask you this. If you were to prescribe Diacam, and you were to advise your patient to avoid alcohol and they assured you that they would, would you believe them?"

"Yes—initially, at least."

"Now, let's assume the Diacam was working well on your patient's diabetes. If you were to then do blood work on the patient, and it showed only mild liver function elevations—nothing near the three times normal elevations that the literature had cautioned—would you stop the Diacam?"

There was a long pause in the courtroom, as everyone present contemplated the significance of this question.

The lawyers of Wyatt, Hanson, Richards, and Shultz sat with their heads nearly imperceptibly bowed; Clarence stood tall and impressive, not taking his eyes off of Dr. Prickle for even an instant; and Maddi and her friends sat grinning in anticipation of the doctor's answer.

Dr. Prickle himself was shifting around in his seat, seeming to be waiting for an appropriate answer to come to him. He finally looked up at Clarence and—very softly—said "no."

"I'm sorry, doctor, what did you say?"

"I said no. I wouldn't stop the Diacam."

"Thank you, Dr. Prickle." Clarence slowly headed back to his seat. The judge asked Mr. Shultz if he wanted to redirect any further questions to Dr. Prickle. Shultz and his associates whispered quickly back and forth. The judge repeated his question, this time with some degree of irritation. Finally, Mr. Shultz spoke.

"No further questions, your honor. The plaintiffs rest."

Chapter XLVII

The trial was now in its third week. The media were following events closely, many commentators creating a horse race type of presentation, as each day brought new revelations and new allegations. Experts on both sides of the issue were doing interviews for the network news, as well as for the 24-hour news programs.

Maddi and her friends had watched the proceedings with reserved satisfaction. Things appeared to be going well for the doctors—and for The Cause, in general—but one never could predict how a jury might interpret what they heard throughout a trial.

Maddi, Hank, Andrew, Amanda, and Jeremy had enjoyed staying with Clarence throughout the duration of the trial and they were having a memorable time.

Each afternoon, after court had ended for the day, they would proceed to the same local tavern where they were actually becoming well-known and familiar to the bartender and one of the waitresses. By the end of the second week they were all treated like royalty, and they found themselves looking forward to their daily trip to the tavern.

They would typically head from there to one of the local restaurants to have dinner. They had so much to talk about each night, and were all becoming incredibly close friends.

Clarence had treated them all quite special. They wanted for nothing while they were in Philadelphia. Maddi knew she would always remember this time as one of those very good times in her life, regardless of how the trial turned out.

She was also delighted to see Andrew so happy. He was somehow different—lighter, it seemed, and she was happy to have some time to discuss all of his changes and his decisions. She had been astounded by his sudden move from the Tundra to the city, but she could see that whatever was causing all of this to happen with him was a good thing.

Maddi occasionally thought about John McCargish, and the thought would make her quite sad. She had never really gotten to know him and she would forever regret that. What she had known, however, she liked very much and she felt grateful for having known him at all.

Jeremy Bourne was also staying with Clarence, and they were all enjoying getting to know him as well. He kept to himself a bit more than they did, but gradually they began to learn a bit about his background and his life.

His time in the Peace Corps interested them all very much, particularly Amanda, who was more or less doing that type of work here in America. By the end of the two weeks, they all felt like Jeremy was becoming part of the group and he seemed to be warming up to them as well.

The days in the courtroom, and the nights out on the town flew by. They were all acutely aware of the importance of what was at stake, and they were all praying for the outcome that could truly fix the very broken legal system in America.

It was now time for the defense attorney—the renowned Clarence Morrow—to present his case. The bulk of the case consisted of having various doctors testify as to the amazing efficacy and usefulness of Diacam. They all admitted its potential harms, but concluded—in unison—that its benefits far outweighed its risks.

Mr. Shultz and The Firm were very effective in combating these claims by illustrating that—unlike amiodarone or Lipitor and the statins—there are many other effective ways to treat diabetes.

This argument seemed to hit its mark with the jury.

Clarence then presented numerous experts who validated the claims made by the Diacam manufacturers that Diacam helped with the treatment of diabetes in a way no other medication was able to, and it delayed the need for using insulin for many years.

This fact seemed to impress the jury, and by the time the trial was nearly concluded it was anyone's guess as to who had won the day.

Closing arguments were set for Friday morning of the third week, and on Thursday night Clarence practiced his statements in front of Maddi and the others.

They had all had several beers, except for Clarence, who wanted to be his sharpest for the next day's events. They were sitting comfortably in Clarence's large study, and had a delightful time pretending first to be Mr. Shultz and his crew, and then to all be jurors listening intently to Clarence's every word.

By 11:00 that night they were all exhausted, assisted by the effects of the alcohol. They headed to bed ready to be Clarence's "support group" the next day.

Clarence had difficulty sleeping that night. His dreams were vivid, and they woke him repeatedly. He was always standing in front of a jury with faceless people staring out at him. He sensed the entire court room laughing at him. He couldn't be heard over the laughter, no matter how loud he screamed. It was at that point in his dream that he would awaken, and it would then take several minutes for him to get back to sleep. He couldn't seem to find a comfortable sleeping position, but finally drifted into a good, hard sleep around 3:00am.

He awoke at 6:30am to the sound of his alarm, and the smell of eggs cooking in the kitchen.

He dragged himself out of bed and headed for the shower, hoping it would wake him up and prepare him for one of the most important closing arguments he would ever give.

Nearly two hours later, the six of them headed to the courtroom, much more subdued than usual. As it turned out, none of them had slept well the night before and all of them were nervous for Clarence and for the importance of what he was about to say in front of that Jury.

They arrived at the courthouse at 8:45, and Maddi and her friends headed for the back of the courtroom, while Jeremy took his seat directly behind Clarence.

The various lawyers from the firm of Wyatt, Hanson, Richards and Shultz were looking dapper and polished, ready and waiting at their table. They were talking quietly among themselves, and it was not lost on either side that Clarence was sitting at his table all alone.

At 9:00 sharp, Judge Douglas was once again introduced, and everyone stood. He then sat down, they sat down, and the gavel was pounded, opening the final day of the class action lawsuit against 3,432 doctors.

Mr. Shultz was scheduled to present his closing statement first and, with the Judge's nod, he slowly stood to his feet. His finely tailored suit hung perfectly from his broad shoulders, as he walked with careful deliberation toward where the jurors were seated in their box. The twelve of them sat there, expressionless, awaiting the day's events, much like blank sheets of paper waiting to be written on.

He began his closing statement with a very slow, methodical summary of the trial thus far, allowing the words to roll off of his tongue with eloquence and power, a testament to his vast experience and his profound gift when it came to this portion of a courtroom trial.

"Ladies and Gentlemen of the Jury, I am so very grateful for the time and attention you have given to this most important trial. In spite of all the complicated discussion concerning medications, side effects, indications, et cetera, the case basically comes down to one question that you all sitting here today must ask yourselves. Is it okay for a physician, to whom one entrusts his life, to knowingly inflict risk of potential harm on an individual under his care?

"Will we as a nation stand by and watch as those to whom we entrust our health and our safety carelessly allow us—no, encourage us—to take a medication which might easily kill us?

"Diacam's introduction to the armor of diabetic treatments at first seemed like a wonder drug. It improved blood sugars, resulting in overall health improvement, like no other medication had done up to that point.

"What is important to note, however, is that there are many medications available to treat diabetes. Perhaps they don't work quite as well as Diacam, but they also don't kill while they are working."

At this point, Mr. Shultz paused, allowing the impact of what he had just said to sink in.

Maddi was listening to every word very carefully. She noted to herself how beautifully this man delivered his point. Regardless of what he said, this jury was going to be very tempted to believe him.

Mr. Shultz began walking very slowly up and down in front of the jurors, being sure to meet the gaze of each and every one of them. He continued on, his voice a bit quieter.

"Information on Diacam's dangers had been presented to the medical community for months prior to its removal from the market. Every physician had ample opportunity to recognize its dangers and remove it from a patient's treatment regimen before it was able to harm or kill them.

"These doctors on trial today chose to ignore these clear warnings, choosing instead to continue prescribing this deadly drug.

"Why would they do this, you might ask? Aren't these doctors decent men and women? For the most part, I imagine they certainly are. Was it arrogance? Laziness? Ignorance? Or was it something more sinister still? Perhaps they simply didn't care about what it might do. Perhaps they had other things on their minds, and they simply couldn't be bothered by having to change things, when the medication appeared to be working so well."

At this point, Mr. Shultz stopped his stroll, looked directly at the jurors sitting before him, and spoke with an increased volume, and a convincing passion.

"After all, that would require time and effort on their part, and they were already feeling like they didn't have any more time or effort to give.

"I don't mean to imply that something such as a golf game or a trip to the beach house was getting in the way of their decision-making, but perhaps something more subtle—such as their desire to get home to dinner on time, or their longing to sit and have some time for lunch."

"These are honest desires. We can all understand how someone might want a little more time than they seem to have. We have all felt that way. However, these doctors have taken an oath to do no harm, regardless of what else they may want. Do no harm.

"It is not right for a physician, who is obligated to take care of us, to take that obligation lightly. It is not right for a physician to put anything in front of his promise—his oath, if you will. We are all at the mercy of our doctor, and we count on his judgment to be sound when it comes to our health and our lives.

"We rely on these doctors to do all they can to protect us. We rely on these doctors to know when a medication does more harm than good. We need these doctors to simply do their job and keep us safe from dangerous, deadly medications."

"I can understand how, in the beginning, they were not aware of the risks and dangers of Diacam. But once it became clear—crystal clear, I might add—that Diacam could kill, these doctors were obligated to do something to save those individuals already on the medication from near-certain injury or even death!"

Mr. Shultz had made this last statement with a crescendo to his voice. Maddi looked around and noted that all eyes were on him, as everyone seemed quite caught up in his statements, as well as his mannerisms. He had everyone listening—and believing—his every, well-delivered word, and Maddi started shifting around in her seat, knowing that she and her cause, and the cause of so many, may be lost here in this courtroom today. Her hope and her faith were fading as the eloquent Mr. Shultz continued his soliloquy.

"You twelve jurors sitting here today can change this thinking, and this behavior, by these physicians. You can send a message loud and clear to every physician out there that the patient must come first. Regardless of any relationship a doctor may have with a drug manufacturer, or, regardless of any time commitment involved in changing a patient's medication, the patient must always come first. We, the patients, need the doctors to hear this from you now. These doctors need to hear this from you here today. The doctors are the only ones who can keep us safe, and, as we put our complete and total trust in them, they must keep us safe at all costs. That trust is not to be taken lightly.

"Let these physicians here, and those across this great nation, hear the message loudly and clearly from you folks today. I can only tell you this, that if you do not do this I fear for the safety of all of us in this country. As I said earlier, these doctors must be reminded of their sacred oath to every one of us, put forth by the great Hippocrates so many years ago: First, do no harm.

"Once again, I thank you all for your service here today. And I thank each one of you in advance for the life-saving message I know you will send to physicians across the nation from this courtroom here today. First, do no harm."

Mr. Shultz slowly turned away from the jury, allowing his brilliant speech to sink fully into the psyche of each and every juror. He was smiling to himself, fully aware that he had done a miraculous job of convincing the twelve individuals sitting in the jurors' box that the normally decent physicians had behaved badly in this instance, and must be punished in order to protect us all in the future.

Maddi glanced over at Hank, who was shaking his head, he too knowing that Mr. Shultz, of Wyatt, Hanson, Richards, and Shultz had done a very good, and very clever job of convincing this jury of things that were not true. Hank squeezed Maddi's hand and whispered in her ear "don't worry. I think Clarence will undo any damage Shultz may have done."

Maddi nodded her head, hoping and praying Hank was right.

Clarence had sat through the entire opening statement, looking directly at the jury, never changing his expression, or giving away the slightest emotion.

He continued to sit quietly for another minute or two, slowly collecting his thoughts and preparing himself for this moment in history in which he found himself.

When he was, at last, ready to deliver his statement, he slowly stood up, adjusted his suit just a bit, cleared his throat, and walked with determination toward where the twelve jurors were sitting. Once again the twelve faces were looking up, awaiting the comments of the gentleman about to speak, but, they were no longer blank faces looking out from that jury box. They were now twelve individuals who had clearly been swayed by the brilliant and eloquent speech they had just heard. He had his job to do, and he prayed to God that he could do it. He cleared his throat, stood directly in front of the jury box, and began.

"It occurs to me as I stand here before you now that I am in the unique and wonderful position of possibly impacting public opinion. This trial, and its outcome, will have ramifications for years to come. What you twelve jurors choose to do here today will determine the path of this nation for years to come, especially with regard to the concept of personal responsibility.

"How, you ask, does personal responsibility come into play in a trial such as this? I will illustrate to you now how important this concept is, particularly in a trial such as this.

"Every one of you I'm sure was told at one time or another "you made the mess, now you clean it up." This is the concept of personal responsibility. You as a child, were taught that if you made a mistake, it was up to you to fix that mistake. It was one of the more important concepts we needed to learn as children. We were able to learn about consequences, and it was in this way that we basically learned about life.

"As we grew up and entered the adult world, that sense of self-responsibility became even more important. We were starting to make life choices that would impact us for many years to come. In other words, we had to live with the consequences of our choices, good or bad.

"However, as a nation, we have veered away from that concept. Now, if a mistake is made by an individual, there is an expectation for someone else to fix it. Consequences appear to be non-existent. There is a sense that bad outcomes are always someone else's fault.

"This change in our thinking did not occur overnight. As a matter of fact, it has been a rather insidious change over the last several decades. What started with a lawsuit stemming from burns caused by a cup of coffee—coffee which is meant to be served quite hot—has now progressed to a situation where food vendors are responsible for obesity."

Clarence could see out of the corner of his eye several nods in the courtroom audience. The jury, however, sat stone-faced, listening carefully to his every word. He had not yet changed their minds, but they were at least listening.

"I can still recall the day long ago when I was in 6th grade and received an "F" on a paper in math. I was typically an "A" student, especially in math, so this was quite a big shock for me and for my parents. I remember my mother asking me what happened—once I actually got the nerve up to tell her."

There were subtle chuckles throughout the courtroom, as everyone remembered what it was like to be 11 and receive a bad grade on a paper.

Clarence continued.

"I informed my mother that—although I had gotten every single math problem correct, I had failed to show my work and the teacher counted each problem wrong, in spite of the right answer! Once I informed her of this huge injustice, I sat back waiting for the sparks to fly.

"I just knew that my mother would then march into the principle's office and let him—and that teacher—have it for the horrible injustice I had just received.

"Imagine my surprise when, not only did my mother not march into the principle's office, but she instead looked me straight in the eye and asked me if I had been instructed to show my work prior to the beginning of the exam.

"I hem-hawed around, finally admitting that I had been instructed to show my work, but that I couldn't really do that because it would slow me down. My mother simply smiled and told me that I had gotten exactly what was promised, and that I had better find a way to show my work next time.

Once again there were a few chuckles in the courtroom, but mostly everyone was contemplating the lesson that Clarence's mother had taught him. Clarence resumed his statements.

"This was an important lesson for me about being responsible for my own actions. I am not sure, however, that every mother would have responded the way my mother did. As a matter of fact, I'm sure that not every mother would—or did—respond in that same fashion.

"I happen to know that a few angry calls were made to the teacher and the principle because of the perceived injustice of marking incorrect problems that were correct. Perhaps many in this courtroom would have been tempted to do the same. What a lost opportunity, however, in teaching personal responsibility.

"Not only did those kids miss an important and valuable lesson, but the teacher was then under fire for her actions and thereby began to change her approach, thus depriving many future students from learning the lessons I so aptly learned.

"That is what happens when we allow responsibility to be assigned to others instead of ourselves. The lessons learned by all involved are the wrong lessons. The student learns that a bad grade is likely the teacher's fault, the principle learns that an angry parent is easily dealt with by punishing the teacher, and the teacher learns that he or she should not try to teach these children concepts important to their future lives, but should only teach math or science or music—whatever their specialty may be.

"In short, we all lose. And the abdication of responsibility flourishes. No life lessons are taught, and if they are attempted, they fail in this culture where it is always 'someone else's fault.'

"Perhaps a clearer way to illustrate the significance of this is to look at what has happened with the manufacturing of flu vaccine. Influenza vaccines, not too long ago, were produced by many different pharmaceutical companies. Initially there was healthy competition for these vaccines to be produced. The industry thrived, and innovations and improvements in flu vaccines—and other vaccines—flourished.

"Then the Federal Government decided to step in and arrange a purchase agreement for much of the production of the flu vaccine. This agreement allowed for minimal increases in the purchase price of the vaccine, even though the costs to manufacture the vaccine continued to rise.

"Although this certainly wasn't ideal in our market-based economy, the pharmaceutical companies were willing to continue this arrangement, fully aware that they were doing a much-needed community service, albeit at a much lower profit year after year. This, by the way, is what doctors across the board now do. They accept a specified payment, which rarely increases, at the discretion of the payer, in spite of increasing costs to produce the same product. The pharmaceutical companies survived this process for many years, aware, as I said, of the needs of the community for their product.

"Then came the lawsuits. A bad reaction to the vaccine would cause a flurry of legal activity, ultimately accusing the manufacturer of some form of negligence. And the awards were huge. Always bigger and better than the ones before. The size of the awards were growing at an astronomical rate, while the financial benefits of producing the vaccine were shrinking at an astronomical rate. It didn't take long for those in charge of the manufacturing of the flu vaccine to finally say to themselves "what self-respecting organization would put themselves in this position? Decreased reimbursement with increased exposure and risk is not sound business policy, and we won't survive if we continue with such a policy." They then decided to get out of the business of flu vaccine manufacturing. We now only have four major producers of flu vaccine, and we have all seen the result of this with limited flu vaccine available year after year.

"Attempts to create a fund to handle all of the lawsuits was essentially too little, too late. And, as many of you are aware, there is always a way to get around such a limitation and such a fund, in order to go after the large corporation in the end.

"Now I ask you—what was gained? We now have annual vaccine shortages and the only ones who have truly gained, from what I can tell, are the law firms such as the one sitting over here today."

Clarence made a sweeping gesture toward the table where Wyatt, Hanson, Richards and Shultz were sitting. They glared in unison toward him, and he grinned subtly to himself, knowing he had hit an important nerve with everyone sitting in the courtroom.

"Once again, there was a shifting of responsibility from the individual to the large, faceless organization; all facilitated by attorneys looking only for a big score. The message had become this: if you suffer a bad reaction to a vaccine, let's go after the manufacturer for large dollar amounts, in order to 'make things right.'

"Can anyone sitting in this room today blame the pharmaceutical companies for their decision in this matter? I know these companies are currently the companies we all love to hate, but I think you will agree that, as far as the flu vaccine scenario goes, they made the only reasonable choice. And now, here we sit, dealing with the consequences.

"Perhaps some of you think the companies should manufacture the vaccine for the greater good, in spite of the decreased profits. After all, they can afford it, right?

"Well, guess what. That is exactly what they were willing to do initially, before the lawsuits. Lawsuits in America are so incredibly costly, and so incredibly ubiquitous, that no company can survive if they put themselves in a position of repeatedly having to deal with the threat of a lawsuit, every time someone reacts badly to their product.

"And, the lawsuits were never for small amounts of money, but always for millions of dollars. Millions! Why so much? Because the companies were large and successful and therefore worth millions of dollars in assets. In other words, the lawyers were suing for the amount they could get instead of the amount that was appropriate to send the message they were trying to send to keep a company responsive to its obligations.

"Please understand this: I do believe that there is such a thing as a good lawsuit. There is, at times, a need to keep companies or individuals in line, if you will, by whatever method will get their attention. For example, if a company or an individual denies another person's civil rights, they should and will be sued. Or, if a company elects to pollute a community with little regard for the consequences, they should be sued. It is a useful tool to bring about needed change when a corporation, or a person, behave irresponsibly.

"But these types of lawsuits are now rare. They are few and far between as we become more and more inundated with the lawsuits of the day. The majority of lawsuits now are pursued simply for financial gain, propulgated by shifting responsibility from the user of a product to the producer or deliverer of a product. And what drives this process? It is being driven by the hugh amounts of money acquired, not by the individuals involved, but by the lawyers who make millions with nearly every class action suit that is brought before the courts. The attorneys are getting richer and richer, while we, as a nation, are getting poorer and poorer. This cannot continue, or we will all pay the price for a process which successfully transfers responsibilities, and, at the same time, lines the pockets of trial lawyers across America!"

At this point Clarence banged his hand on the front rail of the jurors' box, at the same time raising his voice and reaching a crescendo that echoed throughout the courtroom.

Maddi and her friends sat up straight as they welcomed the words that resonated so clearly with physicians and others who have grown weary of the system as it currently stands.

Mr. Shultz and his associates continued their glare toward Clarence, shifting in their seats, aware that many eyes were upon them. They were now the ones under indictment, and their anger was almost palpable. Clarence looked over at the group of attorneys, keeping his eyes directly fixed on Mr. Shultz, who stared back at him with disdain. Clarence continued speaking.

"If we as a people don't somehow put a stop to this thinking, to this method of extortion, if you will, then more and more good, hardworking individuals, and more and more mostly decent, productive companies will quickly cease their responsible activities for the greater good. People such as doctors, or even teachers, will leave their professions and do other things, thereby reducing the contributions they would've made to our nation and our people within this nation.

"Don't let this happen. Already, as we are sitting here today, we see doctors leaving the practice of medicine, tired of fighting the thinking that now consumes America. They have grown weary of trial lawyers, who sue because of an opportunity, not because of wrong-doing on the part of the doctors themselves. They are tired of individuals who have not learned these lessons of personal responsibility, and, with the eager assistance of the attorneys, are willing to take any bad outcome and turn it into a lawsuit with the hope of gaining a fortune in money they did not have to earn.

"The doctors are leaving, ladies and gentlemen. Soon there will be too few doctors available, and every one in this room will feel the affects of their unavoidable choice. Many of you already have. The doctors are leaving, and if we don't act soon, if we don't act now, they will be gone.

"And who can blame them? Perhaps some of you feel it is their oath and obligation to continue to practice in spite of the realities of medicine today. In spite of their decreased reimbursements and their increased headaches, they should continue to honor their oath.

"Well, guess what. Doctors have been doing so for decades. Much like the flu vaccine manufacturers, the government involved themselves in the lives and choices of the physicians many years ago, as have third party payers, increasingly stealing the autonomy of the doctors, increasingly stealing their ability to do what they used to do and enjoy so much.

"Doctors have spent years practicing medicine somewhat disgruntled, but they chose to carry on nonetheless; it was their Hippocratic oath to do so. And they took their oath seriously.

"But then came the million-dollar lawsuits. And the explosion of lawsuits across the land. The country, at the same time was shifting its thinking and its sense of responsibilities, and this created the perfect storm, if you will. Lawyers were aggressively pursuing doctors, while patients—certainly not all of them, but many of them—were electing to give up their sense of responsibility, and reassign it to others.

"Lawyers began succeeding in changing realities, if you will, to the point where any bad outcome is an opportunity for a successful lawsuit, regardless of the doctor's ability to prevent the bad outcome from happening. Why have they been so successful?

"It is because we have abdicated our obligation to personal responsibility, allowing that notion to be abandoned. No longer does it matter if a patient makes self-destructive choices. If they are then harmed or die as a result of such choices—and a doctor was involved in any way with their care—there is a good chance that the doctor can and will be sued successfully.

"As I pointed out earlier in this trial, every single one of the victims of dia-cam chose to continue a behavior or a life style which would harm them in some way. As I have shown in this courtroom, every single one of these individuals was made aware of the risks if they continued their destructive behaviors. Every single one of the 'victims' of Diacam was also a 'victim' of his or her own self-destructive choices.

"How on earth can we hold these 3000-plus physicians responsible for what these individuals so irresponsibly did to themselves?

"Please don't misunderstand. My compassion for these individuals is strong, and I defend every one of them their right to act self-destructively. What I denounce, however, is their ability to then successfully blame someone else for the outcomes of their choices.

"There is a huge outcry in this country over the cost of healthcare. This case—and all that is wrong with this case—is the reason for these huge costs.

"Doctors perform more and more tests so they don't miss the dreaded "bad outcome." Drug manufacturers increase the cost of their medications in order to afford the lawsuits they will inevitably have to face, when one of their medications is not perfect and actually causes some harm in an isolated number of cases.

"At every point in the health care continuum there is a potential legal consequence which causes behaviors to change and costs to rise. The astronomical increases in health care spending can be directly related to the explosion in litigation in this country."

"But, the more significant outcome of out-of-control litigation is the loss of ideas. Efforts to seek better medications are thwarted for risk of a lawsuit should something go wrong. The pursuits for new technology are halted for fear of litigation if something should inadvertently malfunction. We are killing our initiative and extinguishing our innovation. The lawyers are profiting but no one else benefits from these actions in any way whatsoever."

At this point Clarence paused, and walked over to his table to take a drink of water from a pitcher sitting toward the corner of his desk. He glanced back at Maddi and the others, and was greeted with a nod and a smile from each one of them. He then looked over at Jeremy, who was grinning from ear to ear, essentially letting Clarence know that he was hitting the mark perfectly. He subtly nodded to Jeremy, as well as to Maddi and her friends. He turned back around to approach the Jury once again as he slowly continued his closing argument.

"This behavior must stop now. It must change here, today, or I promise you this—the goodness and the creativity that exists in every one of us will be crushed and eliminated by this process which seeks to gain only by another's failed—but often good—intentions.

"Save the lawsuits for their original, good purposes. Don't allow them to be abused as they are now. And don't expect these lawyers, who profit so greatly from this current system, to change a damn thing. Trust me, they won't.

"It is the lawyers, for the most part, who make the laws. A significant majority of our congress men and women have a background as an attorney. They are in charge and they are propulgating a system which lines their pockets, keeps them in control, and survives by the very fact that nearly everything we do requires some degree of legal oversight.

"The simple act of shoveling the walk is fraught with legal consequences. Allowing your child to participate in an after-school activity requires a "legal waiver." Saying the pledge of allegiance now has legal ramifications. We have become a nation of lawyers and litigants, and we cannot survive if this continues.

"The trial lawyers will tell you that they are protecting rights of the consumer, or the rights of the citizens from abuses. I am all for that. As I said earlier, I truly believe there is such a thing as a good lawsuit.

"But this process has now been tainted beyond recognition. Because of a desire for wealth and power the lawyers are now in charge and they are not about to let go of this power they have worked so hard to obtain.

"It must come from you. From the citizens of this great country. We must join forces and stand together and declare an end to this process. We must once again accept and respect personal responsibility.

"Ladies and Gentlemen of the Jury. You have an opportunity here today to become reformers. You have an opportunity here today to say "no" to the greedy trial attorneys sitting at that table over there."

Clarence once again gestured to the table where Mr. Shultz and his associates were sitting. They were nearly jumping out of their seats, with piercing glances cutting through Clarence much like knives. Clarence ignored their glares and continued on.

"Let the attorneys know that we as a nation are done with the idea of profit in the face of another's pain. We are done squeezing those who are responsible for innovation. We are done squeezing those who are responsible for caring for the sick or the less fortunate. We are done squeezing the good guys, if you will.

"What has happened to some of those individuals who used Diacam is tragic. Their suffering and loss is a terrible thing. But that is all it is. It is the result of an innovative drug, put through the rigors of the FDA clearing process, ultimately the most rigorous process in the world, I might add, which—combined with poor life style choices—caused harm to some who used it. This is a risk we take whenever we put anything—a drug or something else—in our bodies. Whenever we take any medication, or use any drug medicinally or recreationally, we are assuming risk. Diacam is no different. And now the drug has been pulled from the market, the lessons have been learned, and the losses have been tragic. Who needs to pay for that? Can anyone pay for that in a meaningful way?

"I submit to you the answer is NO! We grieve and we learn. That is what we do in this situation. We don't punish these doctors who—with all good intentions—were using an FDA-approved drug, successfully I might add. And, although this case is not specifically indicting the drug company who made Diacam, I submit to you now, we don't punish the drug company either. If they unknowingly created a drug with dangerous side effects, which withstood the rigorous FDA review, how on earth can they be responsible for what they could not anticipate? The drug helped millions with their diabetes, in a way no other drug had done before. This kind of innovation is what we need from our pharmaceutical companies. Don't hinder their desire for new and improved treatments by punishing them for unintended side effects.

"No one prescribed Diacam suspecting it would do more harm than good. And there are many, many people who used Diacam successfully. Those who encountered difficulty were already, unfortunately, putting their health at risk, long before they filled their first Diacam prescription. They had already made choices that were harmful. That is their right. But, it is also their responsibility to accept their role in the outcome. They must accept the consequences of their choices. It is what we must all do—as individuals, and as a nation.

"Starting here and starting now let's get back to the notion of responsibility for our actions and our choices. It is the fabric of this great nation, and it is what has made us such a successful, and remarkable country.

"As the great Mr. Henry David Thoreau so eloquently said, 'Thus men will lie on their backs, talking about the fall of man, and never make an effort to get up.' I say now, get up! Get up and stop this procession. Let us no longer cede responsibility to others. Change our current course now, or it will soon be too late!"

Clarence paused, hoping desperately that his words had hit their mark. He looked down at the twelve jurors sitting in front of him.

"I thank you all for your time, your patience, and your service here today."

Clarence took one last look into the faces of the jurors, gave them each a very subtle, appreciative smile, and turned toward his table, currently unoccupied.

Once he reached his table, he looked at Jeremy, who nodded his head and grinned, indicating his very favorable impression of what Clarence had said, then he looked back at Maddi and the others. They were all sitting there, as Jeremy had been, nodding and grinning. Maddi was giving Clarence a very subtle 'thumbs up,' and her smile was ear to ear. He had done it! Clarence had delivered the Closing Argument that said all the things so many of them had been thinking. Now, it was up to a jury of twelve men and women to decide nothing less than the future of medicine, and the future of America.

Clarence turned back toward the front of the courtroom and stood looking at the judge, who was busying himself with some papers on the desk in front of him. Clarence took a deep breath in, smoothed the front of his suit with his hands, and paused for just a moment. Yes, now it was up to this jury to decide the fate of the 3,432 doctors on trial, the fate of their profession, and the fate of litigation in the United States of America. Clarence had done all he could. He proceeded to sit down.

CHAPTER XLVIII

The sky was bluer than Hank had ever remembered it being. Although there was a strong wind blowing in from the north, the Erie waters were relatively calm.

Everywhere he looked he saw the beautiful lake waters meeting the horizon seamlessly, uniting with the bright blue skies surrounding him.

Every breath he took in made him feel more and more alive, as he remembered so many good things from days gone by. Memories had come back slowly at first, then had rapidly started rushing in, one right after the other. So much had happened on the lake. So many wonderful, important times. So much good that had given Hank a foundation, a place to go when the world was unsteady, a place that had centered Hank more than he had ever realized.

Finally, here he was, steering the ferry across the lake. His dream since he was a young boy had at last become a reality. Once Hank had decided his time as a physician was over, it took him only seconds to decide to run a ferry boat back and forth to Kelly's and the other Islands. The minute he had decided he felt a peace like he hadn't experienced in such a long time—except when he was with Maddi. She—and this time on the lake—had made his life whole once again.

He would rise each morning—without an alarm clock—to coffee with Maddi. He would jog to where he met up with the ferry boat so that he could prepare for the first run of the boat in the early morning. He would stay on the boat until the last run of the afternoon, and, although the days were long, they were delightful. Hank would look out across the large expanse of Lake Erie and feel a peace like he'd never known before.

Each and every day was just as wonderful as the day before it, and Hank found himself—for the first time in a long time—wanting time to stand still. He wanted these days—and nights—to last forever.

When he finished his last run of the afternoon, he would make his way back home to his small but delightful cabin on Kelly's Island. Always, without fail, as he walked toward the cabin, Maddi would be standing at the doorway with a smile on her face that warmed him down to the very depths of his soul. She would wave and he would know right then that he was truly the luckiest man in the world. He would wave back and then jog the distance between them, and, when he reached Maddi, he would hug her as though he hadn't seen her for days. He was truly home.

Maddi had settled into Island life with very little difficulty, and had quickly turned the neglected cabin into a magnificent Island bungalow. Although it was small, Maddi had been able to allocate space in such a way that she and Hank had more than enough room.

She had created a small alcove off of the kitchen, where a large picture window looked out on the lake. This is where she wrote each day. Maddi had always wanted to write a novel, and now, with so much life experience behind her, she had started the long-awaited book.

She would wake with Hank each morning, and send him off to the ferry, then she would lull away the mornings shopping for groceries, straightening up the cabin, or just strolling the Island.

Her afternoons would be spent writing, and the hours of each day flew by quicker than Maddi had ever known. She loved her life here with Hank on the Island, and couldn't remember a time when she had been happier and more content.

Her evenings were completely devoted to Hank, and as she greeted him at the end of the day, the remaining hours were spent together, doing anything that came to them. Their time was their own, and it was truly some of the best times in either one of their lives.

Their decision to make Kelly's their home had come about soon after the Diacam trial had ended. Neither one was prepared to return to their "old lives," having each accomplished so much, and experienced so many changes. Although Hank felt certain he was not returning to his medical profession, Maddi knew that—at some point—she would need to return to D.C. Although she had done so much, there remained so many other challenges for her to tackle. But this time away from Washington, spent with Hank on their beautiful Island, was incredibly precious and she would stay as long as she could. She knew that Kelly's was now her home, and she was certain that coming back to this Island would sustain her through any challenges she may yet face.

Maddi would often think back on all that had happened in the past year. So many things had changed. And she and her friends were such a big part of that. Her Laws were making their way into the books, the Medical Tribunals were getting a trial run in several states, and the 3,432 doctors who were on trial in the class action suit, well, most of them had returned to their medical practices. But there had been such a price to pay. John McCargish' death would find its way back into Maddi's thoughts whenever she was alone. It would come like a bolt out of the blue and Maddi would feel an incredible sadness over his loss. But she knew—and she hoped that somewhere he knew as well—that his sacrifice had changed America for the better.

Maddi smiled to herself when she thought back to that final day of the trial. All of them sitting in the courtroom, shifting back and forth, anxiously awaiting a verdict that was nothing less than the measure of medicine's future.

In contrast, Clarence was sitting very still, and appeared to be remarkably calm. Maddi remembered wondering how anyone could be so relaxed in such a situation. Perhaps he, too, was fidgeting and shifting around, but only on the inside.

The jury had been led back into the courtroom, and Maddi recalled the incredible quietness that engulfed the chamber. It was as though everyone in there—and across the country—knew what was at stake in that courtroom on that day.

The jury foreman stood, exchanged appropriate words with the Judge, and then proceeded to weigh in on the future of 3,432 doctors.

Maddi was suddenly aware that she had stopped breathing. She looked at Hank sitting next to her, his head bowed and his eyes closed. He reached his hand across to hers and grasped it with an intensity that was just short of painful. Amanda and Andrew were exchanging glances that suggested both fear and anticipation. They all knew what was at stake.

Jeremy was only visible from the back, and—although Maddi couldn't see his face—she was very aware of his anxiety. His shoulders were actually shaking, his head leaning backwards, and his hands clasped together in a way that suggested to Maddi that he was very likely praying.

The jury foreman began to speak. He was a very tall African American, with a deep, sonorous voice. He reminded Maddi of a preacher she had seen recently at a fund-raiser for a senator friend of hers. As his words left his lips, Maddi felt calmed just by the low-pitched song of his voice.

"We, the Jury, find the defendants not guilty."

Maddi knew she would never forget the beautiful sound of those words as they echoed through the large courtroom chamber. She paused, looked over at Hank—who was still bowing his head—and grabbed him and hugged him.

"Hank! We've done it! They've finally listened!" Hank lifted his head and looked straight into Maddi's large blue eyes.

"Yes, Maddi, we have. You have. Clarence Morrow has. We all have." He tipped her chin up toward him and kissed her long and hard as they sat in the back of the courtroom, embraced in one another's arms.

Andrew and Amanda hugged as well, and Maddi saw a smile on Andrew's face like she hadn't seen in years. It was as if he was saying "Finally. Finally the good guys have won."

Jeremy was still shaking, and Maddi thought that he might actually be crying. He had put his hand on the back of Clarence's shoulder while the verdict was being read, and now he was shaking Clarence's shoulder in acknowledgement and appreciation.

Clarence turned toward him, and Maddi was able to see his large face with a smile stretched across it and tears in his large, dark eyes. She knew she would never forget the degree of emotion that was etched into his every feature at that moment. So much effort and so much heartfelt emotion had gone into the trial and all it represented.

Slowly, some in the courtroom began to clap. Softly at first, but then progressively louder as more and more individuals in the chamber began to join in. The Judge stood immediately and banged his gavel with an intensity that would have normally quieted the most unruly crowd, but the clapping continued. After several more attempts the Judge finally laid down his gavel, sat back in his chair, and gave Clarence a shrug of his shoulders and a nod.

At that moment, Maddi felt all was right with the world. She felt hopeful at the prospect of restoring sanity and decency to a litigation process that had become so destructive and useless. Maybe things could now get better for physicians, and others across the country. Maybe doctors could get back to practicing medicine instead of practicing legal defense. Perhaps, finally, innovation could move forward once again, and Americans could pursue their lives without the overriding fear that at any moment someone could destroy everything they had accomplished for the simple purpose of financial gain. Maddi hoped and prayed that this was in fact they way it now would be.

Her Laws—and their passage in both houses of Congress—had brought the same sense of hopefulness to Maddi. The challenges they would face by the Legal Apparatus would be formidable, but Maddi felt the Laws would withstand scrutiny and challenge. After all, they had Clarence Morrow's steady hand guiding them through each step.

Maddi knew eventually the Supreme Court would be asked to weigh in on the constitutional validity of the Laws, and Maddi felt this would be another opportunity to voice the principles and the purpose behind their creation. She was struck with the irony of the Supreme Court—John's "home-" being the final say in the success or failure of her beloved Laws.

Clarence immediately began the process of a counter suit against the law firm of Wyatt, Hanson, Richards, and Shultz. Although that trial was just getting underway, the public had reacted favorably to the changes that Clarence had put forth in his eloquent closing argument.

Maddi followed closely the proceedings concerning Peter Smith, Roger Clairy, and Frances Buckholtz. These men had changed her world so dramatically, and killed a dear and wonderful man in the process.

Peter Smith was being tried on three counts of murder, not only for John McCargish, but for the two Secret Service men as well, and was biding his time in a federal penitentiary outside Washington D.C.

Roger Clairy had made a deal with the federal investigators, and was cooperating fully in exchange for a reduced sentence. He had told them everything he knew about Frances Buckholtz, and that information—combined with what Peter Smith had already given them—allowed them to go after Buckholtz with everything they had.

There is a sense of Justice within most of us—particularly within Prosecutors—that cries for attention when someone betrays that justice as clearly as Frances Buckholtz attempted to do. The president of the American Trial Lawyers Association had done horrible things—simply to secure power for himself, and that was offensive to all those involved in prosecuting his case.

His attempt to have Maddi "silenced," had resulted in the deaths of three government employees and the federal investigators were hoping to put him away for the remainder of his natural life. Because of the prominence of the case and the significant public support for Maddi, his case was fast-tracked and his trial was ready to begin.

Maddi knew she would be needed to testify, and—although she wasn't looking forward to it—she knew she would gain some much-needed satisfaction in putting that wicked man away.

Occasionally, the words of Senator Richards would haunt Maddi.

"You've got your own history, now don't you?"

There were things in Maddi's life that had not gone well—as in all lives—but she couldn't imagine what exactly the Senator had in mind, or what his intentions were for revealing Maddi's "history."

Maddi would quickly put it out of her mind, deciding it was just a bluff. But was it?

There had been a huge influx of public sentiment directed against those lawmakers who were attorneys at any point in their history. A demand for change was taking hold, and there was optimism throughout the medical community, as well as throughout the National community that litigation in America was finally returning to what the founders had intended. The expression of legitimate grievances was something all people supported, but the need for that process to be joined with the renewed appreciation of personal responsibility had become evident to all.

Many of the physicians who had left their practices were returning, anxious to once again experience the joy of practicing medicine without the overriding fear of litigation with each and every decision they made. The litigation climate in America had changed. As the incentives for the lawyers were changing—a direct result of Maddi's Laws—so, too, were behaviors. The innovations that had been suppressed by fear were once again being awakened in various industries and individuals across the nation. New ideas and new solutions, that at one time were not being pursued because of fears of litigation, were now being pursued with enthusiasm throughout the country. Things truly did seem to be changing for the better.

Maddi had also kept up with all that was going on with her brother and with her friends. Andrew kept in touch through e-mail and an occasional phone call. He absolutely loved his new position with the Clinic, and, under his oversight, the Clinic had expanded its site and capabilities to assist a greater number of patients, and a greater number of problems.

He and Amanda spent nearly all of their time there, and, apparently were delighted to be able to do so much. They appeared to be completely happy with their lives and with one another. Maddi knew that, for Andrew, this happiness had seemed all but impossible, and she was so incredibly gratified to think of him as so fulfilled.

Amanda also seemed to be doing well. She had long ago told Maddi about her parents and the times the family flew together, and often mentioned to Maddi how much she missed those days. The story of her parents' amazing life and their tragic death had saddened Maddi and she knew they had played such an important role in Amanda's life. Amanda became particularly animated when she spoke of the times they flew together, and it was clear to Maddi that Amanda truly loved to fly.

She had recently gone to a small airport near Columbia to take some refresher courses. Amanda was hoping that, soon perhaps, she could fly Andrew and herself up to the small landing field on Kelly's and spend a long weekend with Maddi and Hank. Maddi was thrilled with the idea and knew that this was such a good thing for Amanda to be doing.

She had kept up with Wilson by way of an occasional phone call, and he also seemed to be doing quite well. He continued to make sure that he had "nothing to lose," and, by doing so, continued to love his lifestyle and his practice. He hoped to be doing exactly what he was doing now for the remainder of his days, or, at least, until he could no longer physically do so.

A Boston publication had done a remarkable write-up on Wilson, illustrating his many accomplishments, as well as his amazing decision to "go bare." This allowed the issue of medical malpractice to stay in the Public's radar, giving it continued momentum for the many changes occurring throughout the United States.

Clarence had kept Maddi informed as to what Jeremy was doing. They had all become friends, and Maddi could see right away that Jeremy had such a strong desire to contribute to the "Community of Man," and she certainly hoped he had elected to continue to do so. As it turned out, he had. After the trial he headed back to the Pima Reservation with renewed interest and renewed passion. The last she had heard, the softball team was back, and the enthusiasm and the passions of the Pima Indians were being restored, as were the enthusiasm and passions of Jeremy himself.

Clarence was busy with the counter suit against the Firm, and he would also occasionally take the unusual or interesting cases that came his way. With certain cases, he would make sure to contact Maddi and the others, knowing that their input and their perspective were invaluable as he continued to try to improve the world around him. Maddi and her friends had managed to make a couple of trips to Clarence's home, and they all once again had the most wonderful of times. They would sit in the Study, drinking beer and reliving the events that had impacted their lives so greatly.

They all appeared to be very happy with where their lives had taken them—and where they had taken their lives—and this made for splendid, energizing reunions. Maddi felt quite blessed by the relationships she had made with these remarkable, interesting people, and she was certain that all that had happened to them would keep them connected for many years to come, if not for the remainder of their lives. She certainly hoped so.

The sun was setting to the west of the Island. Maddi quickly put some finishing touches on the chapter she was working on. She stood and headed to the front door to wait for Hank.

She walked out onto the small porch and took a long, deep breath. The air smelled pure and fresh. There was a chill that had crept in, and the leaves were beginning their change that would mark the approach of winter.

Maddi looked out and saw Hank approaching. She smiled and began to wave. Hank waved back and began jogging toward Maddi. When he reached her they embraced, just as the sun slipped behind the horizon.

The peace they both knew at that moment was more than either one of them had ever dreamed of. Hank put his arm around Maddi's waist and the two of them headed inside.

THE END

978-0-595-67691-0
0-595-67691-X

Printed in the United States
96482LV00008B/21/A